Questo libro
appartiene a...

....

....

Fiabe della Buonanotte

della

da un'idea di  ANDREA DAMI

Illustrazioni: Tony Wolf
Testi: Anna Casalis
Progetto grafico: Stefania Pavin

www.giunti.it

© 2002, 2017 Giunti Editore S.p.A.
Via Bolognese, 165 - 50139 Firenze - Italia
Piazza Virgilio, 4 - 20123 Milano - Italia
Prima edizione: ottobre 2002

Stampato presso Lito Terrazzi srl, stabilimento di Iolo

Fiabe della Buonanotte

TONY WOLF

DAMI EDITORE

C'erano una volta...
un brutto anatroccolo...
una casetta di zucchero filato...
un fagiolo magico... un imperatore vanitoso...
un burattino di legno... un'oca d'oro...
e uno gnomo dalla barba lunga lunga!

IL BRUTTO ANATROCCOLO

Era proprio un'estate molto calda, fatta apposta per riposarsi all'ombra delle canne della palude e covare la nuova nidiata. Mamma anatra, dopo aver deposto le sue grosse uova, aspettava con pazienza che i piccoli rompessero il guscio. Ed ecco che all'improvviso...

"Crak!... Cip, Cip!" il primo uovo si schiuse e apparve un piccolo anatroccolo.

Subito dopo si schiuse un altro uovo, e poi un altro ancora...

Ma l'ultimo uovo, più grosso di tutti, ancora non si apriva.

Mamma anatra non ricordava di aver deposto quell'uovo così grande. Come era finito lì? Si sentiva un gran battere da dentro il guscio: "TOC-TOC! TOC-TOC!"

"Possibile che mi sia sbagliata a contare le uova?" si chiese Mamma anatra. Provò a covarlo ancora un po', per vedere se finalmente si schiudeva.

Passò di lì un'altra grossa anatra, che si fermò

IL BRUTTO ANATROCCOLO

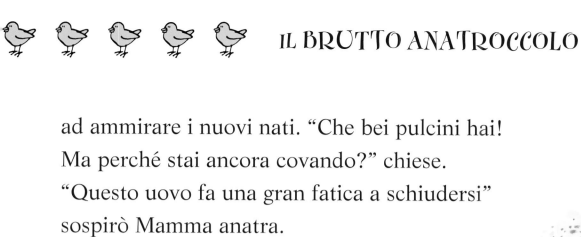

ad ammirare i nuovi nati. "Che bei pulcini hai!
Ma perché stai ancora covando?" chiese.
"Questo uovo fa una gran fatica a schiudersi"
sospirò Mamma anatra.
"Che grosso uovo! Non sarà
un uovo di tacchino? Io lo
lascerei stare. Ricordati che
i tacchini non sanno nuotare!"
Finalmente l'uovo ritardatario si aprì:
uno strano anatroccolo dal piumaggio grigio anziché giallo si affacciò
a guardare la mamma. "Com'è brutto!" pensò l'anatra. "Non riesco proprio
a capire come possa essere mio figlio!"

Gli anatroccoli crescevano rapidamente
e seguirono presto la mamma lungo
le sponde della palude. L'anatroccolo grigio
mangiava più degli altri, e in poco tempo
diventò più grosso dei suoi fratelli.

Questo però
non lo rendeva
felice: gli altri
anatroccoli non
volevano giocare

con lui perché era goffo e sgraziato, anche se nuotava meglio di tutti loro. Mamma anatra li portò alla vicina fattoria, ma anche qui tutti gli animali deridevano lo strano anatroccolo: "Che brutto, quel pulcino! Qui non lo vogliamo!" Una gallina lo prese addirittura a beccate sul collo.

La mamma lo difendeva e cercava di consolarlo:

"Povero brutto figlio mio!" gli diceva.

"Perché non sei uguale agli altri?"

Il povero anatroccolo era sempre più infelice.

Di notte piangeva di nascosto, perché si sentiva abbandonato da tutti.

"Nessuno mi vuole bene, qui! Oh, perché non sono come i miei fratelli?"

Una mattina all'alba scappò via dalla fattoria.

Svolazzò al di sopra di una siepe: un piccolo stormo di passeri, disturbato, si alzò schiamazzando dai cespugli. "Si sono spaventati perché sono brutto!" pensò il povero anatroccolo grigio.

Giunto sulle sponde di un laghetto, cominciò a chiedere a tutti quelli che incontrava:

"Conoscete degli anatroccoli che hanno le piume grigie come le mie?". Ma tutti scuotevano la testa sprezzanti: "Brutto come te, non conosciamo nessuno!".

L'anatroccolo non si rassegnava e continuava a chiedere qua e là.

Arrivò a uno stagno e due grosse oche granaiole, alla stessa domanda, diedero la stessa risposta.

Anzi, lo misero in guardia: "Scappa, scappa da questo posto! È pericoloso, ci sono in giro i cacciatori!"

L'anatroccolo adesso rimpiangeva di aver lasciato la fattoria.

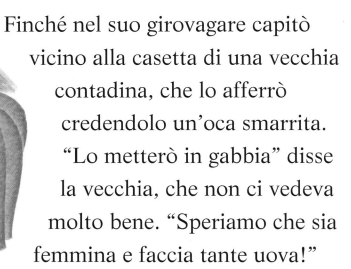

Finché nel suo girovagare capitò vicino alla casetta di una vecchia contadina, che lo afferrò credendolo un'oca smarrita.

"Lo metterò in gabbia" disse la vecchia, che non ci vedeva molto bene. "Speriamo che sia femmina e faccia tante uova!"

Ma l'anatroccolo, naturalmente, non fece neanche un uovo. La gallina della contadina lo spaventava continuamente: "Vedrai che la vecchia, se non riesci a fare uova, ti tira il collo e ti mette in pentola!". E il gatto rincarava la dose: "Speriamo che la vecchia ti cucini presto; così io rosicchierò gli ossicini!".

La contadina lo rimpinzava di cibo, brontolando: "Se non fa le uova, speriamo almeno che ingrassi in fretta!". L'anatroccolo era terrorizzato. Finché una notte, approfittando della porta della gabbia rimasta socchiusa, scappò. Arrivò a un fiume: ma anche qui non passò molto tempo prima che tutti gli animali lo prendessero in giro per il suo strano aspetto.

Venne l'autunno. Dal suo rifugio
tra le canne del fiume vide passare
un volo di magnifici uccelli bianchi
dal collo flessuoso, il becco giallo e grandi
ali, che migravano a sud. "Oh! Potessi essere anch'io bello come loro, anche
per un solo giorno!" esclamò l'anatroccolo ammirandoli da lontano.
Arrivò l'inverno e l'acqua del canneto si ghiacciò.
Il povero anatroccolo, congelato, dovette
abbandonare il suo rifugio per cercare
un po' di cibo nella neve.
Vagò a lungo per la campagna
deserta, ma poi cadde sfinito,
finché un contadino di passaggio
lo trovò e lo mise nell'ampia
tasca della sua giubba.

"Lo porterò ai miei bambini, che avranno cura di lui. Poveretto! È tutto gelato!" disse il brav'uomo accarezzando la povera bestiolina.

A casa tutti accolsero bene il nuovo venuto e fu così che l'anatroccolo si salvò da quel gelido inverno.

A primavera era diventato così grande e robusto che il contadino si decise: "Lo porterò allo stagno e lo lascerò libero!"

Fu allora che l'anatroccolo vide la sua immagine riflessa nell'acqua e...

"Possibile?! Come sono cambiato!" gridò.
"Non mi riconosco più!" Il suo lungo collo elegante era ricoperto da un fitto piumino, candido come le penne delle grandi ali.

Il volo di cigni tornò anche quella primavera dalla migrazione e planò sullo stagno.

Quando l'anatroccolo vide i nuovi venuti, si accorse che erano proprio come lui, e ben presto fece amicizia.

"Siamo cigni come te! Dove ti sei nascosto fino ad ora?" tutti gli chiedevano cordiali. "È una storia lunga!" rispose il giovane cigno, ancora stupito della sua fortuna. Ormai nuotava maestoso in mezzo ai suoi simili.

Finché un giorno sentì alcuni bambini che gridavano dalla riva: "Guardate, guardate quel giovane cigno! È il più bello di tutti!"

Si sentiva ormai tanto, tanto felice.

Nessuno lo avrebbe più chiamato brutto anatroccolo!

HANSEL E GRETEL

C'era una volta un povero taglialegna che viveva nella miseria più nera. Abitava in una piccola casa nella foresta insieme ai suoi due figli Hansel e Gretel.

Rimasto vedovo, si era risposato con una donna cattiva, che trattava sempre male i due bambini e continuava a ripetere al marito: "In questa casa il cibo non basta per tutti, ci sono troppe bocche da sfamare! Sarebbe meglio liberarci di quei due marmocchi!".

E cercava continuamente di convincerlo ad abbandonare i due bambini nella foresta.

"Devi lasciarli molto lontano, in modo che non possano ritrovare la strada di casa. Vedrai che qualcuno li raccoglierà e li sfamerà al nostro posto!"

Il taglialegna, sempre più avvilito, non sapeva che cosa fare. Era un uomo debole, incapace di opporsi alla moglie, anche se amava molto i suoi bambini.

Una notte la cattiva matrigna continuò a insistere più delle altre volte perché il taglialegna abbandonasse i figli. Hansel e Gretel, che erano ancora svegli, sentirono tutto. Gretel si mise a piangere disperata, ma Hansel la consolò:

"Non preoccuparti, riusciremo a trovare la strada di casa anche se ci lasceranno soli nella foresta!".
Uscito di casa di nascosto, si riempì le tasche di sassolini bianchi e poi tornò dentro a dormire.

All'alba, il padre e i due bambini si avviarono nella foresta a fare legna. Mentre si inoltravano nel folto del bosco, Hansel ogni tanto faceva cadere dietro di sé un sassolino bianco, che risaltava sul suolo scuro della foresta.
"Perché ti fermi, Hansel?" chiedeva il padre.
"Ascolto il canto di un uccellino" rispondeva il bambino.

Nel pomeriggio, dopo molte ore di cammino, i due bambini si fermarono a riposare vicino al tronco di un albero. Appena li vide addormentati,

il padre diede loro un bacio e poi, molto triste, si allontanò in silenzio.

Quando Hansel e Gretel si svegliarono, era ormai scesa la sera.

La bambina piangeva disperata e anche Hansel era spaventato, ma cercava di non darlo a vedere e rincuorava la sorella: "Non piangere, Gretel, e fidati

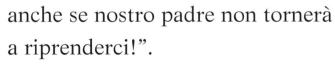

di me! Ti prometto che ti riporterò a casa, anche se nostro padre non tornerà a riprenderci!".

Fortunatamente quella notte c'era la luna piena: Hansel aspettò che salisse alta nel cielo, finché la sua luce fredda filtrò attraverso gli alberi.

"Seguimi, adesso!" disse alla sorellina.

I sassolini bianchi, illuminati dalla luna, brillavano nel buio e, seguendoli, i bimbi ritrovarono la strada fino a casa.

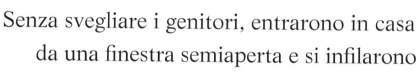

Senza svegliare i genitori, entrarono in casa da una finestra semiaperta e si infilarono a letto stanchi e infreddoliti.

Il giorno dopo la matrigna, quando si accorse del loro ritorno, scoppiò dalla rabbia e rimproverò a lungo il marito perché non aveva eseguito bene i suoi ordini.

Il padre, che era stato molto contento di rivedere i suoi bambini, era combattuto tra la vergogna per quello che aveva fatto e la paura di disubbidire alla moglie crudele.

"Non possono assolutamente stare qui!" ripeteva la matrigna. "Devi riportarli nel bosco. Questa volta farò io in modo che non ritornino più a casa!"

Hansel, che aveva sentito tutto, rincuorò la sorellina dicendole di non preoccuparsi, cr avrebbe raccolto ancora dei sassolini bianchi ma quando, nel cuore della notte, cercò di us per farne provvista, si accorse che la matrign aveva chiuso a chiave la porta di casa. Per fo la sera prima aveva tenuto da parte metà del pane secco della sua povera cena.

Quando all'alba il padre li portò nuovamente
a far legna nel bosco, Hansel non trovò
di meglio che lasciare dietro di sé
una traccia del percorso seminando
le briciole del suo pezzo di pane.
Ma non aveva fatto i conti con la fame
degli uccellini della foresta, che si misero
a seguirlo saltellando e beccando qua
e là; ben presto mangiarono tutte
le briciole cadute.

Giunti nel bosco più fitto,
il taglialegna si allontanò
con una scusa,
lasciando soli
i due ragazzi.
Hansel
allora
sussurrò
a Gretel:
"Tranquilla!
Ho lasciato una
traccia dietro di noi, come l'altra volta!"

Ma quando cercarono di ritrovare il percorso fino a casa, si accorsero con terrore che le briciole non c'erano più!

"Ho paura! Ho fame, ho freddo e voglio tornare a casa!" piangeva Gretel. Intanto scese la notte. "Non aver paura, ci sono qui io a proteggerti!" cercava di consolarla Hansel, anche se pure lui tremava nel vedere le ombre paurose della foresta.

I due bambini rimasero tutta la notte ai piedi di un grosso albero, restando abbracciati per riscaldarsi. Quando infine spuntò l'alba incominciarono a vagare nel bosco, cercando un sentiero, finché a un tratto, in mezzo a una radura, si trovarono davanti a una straordinaria casetta.

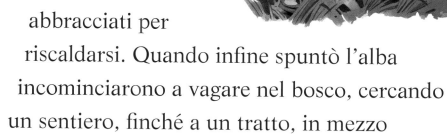

"Ma questo è cioccolato!" disse Hansel staccando un pezzo di muro della casa.

"E questo è zucchero filato!" esclamò Gretel,
assaggiandone un altro pezzetto.
I bimbi affamati si misero a mangiare i pezzi
di dolce che si staccavano dalla casetta.
"Come è buono!" diceva a bocca piena
Gretel, che non aveva mai assaggiato
in vita sua simili ghiottonerie.

"Non ci muoveremo mai più di qui!"
rispose Hansel divorando un pezzo
di torrone. Stavano per prendere un po'
di biscotto dalla porta, quando questa, senza far rumore, si aprì.
Sulla soglia apparve una vecchietta che li invitò a entrare. "Sembrate proprio
affamati, poveri bambini!" disse loro. "Venite, presto, vi darò da mangiare!"

Preparò ai bambini un'ottima cena
e poi li mise a dormire in due lettini
morbidi e caldi. I bambini, stanchi
e felici, si addormentarono subito.
Purtroppo per Hansel e Gretel,
la vecchina era una strega malvagia,

e la sua casa
di zucchero
serviva per attirare i bambini perduti nel bosco.
Erano proprio capitati in un brutto posto...
Svegliandosi il mattino dopo, Gretel vide che
la strega aveva rinchiuso Hansel in una gabbia.
"È magrolino e denutrito" spiegò a Gretel.
"Lo ingrasserò per bene e poi lo mangerò!"
Ogni giorno la strega
si avvicinava alla
gabbia di Hansel e controllava se era
ingrassato, tastandogli un dito
attraverso le sbarre.
Ma la vecchia, per fortuna, ci vedeva
poco e, in più, Gretel le aveva unto
le lenti degli occhiali con il burro...

Così non si accorse che, invece del ditino, Hansel le porgeva ogni giorno un ossicino di pollo!
"Sei ancora troppo magro" diceva la strega.
Finché un giorno si stancò di aspettare.
"Prepara il forno!" ordinò a Gretel.
"Oggi faremo un arrosto di bambino! Controlla che il forno sia caldo!"
Dopo un po', Gretel tornò frignando: "Non sono capace di sentire quando è caldo!".
Mentre la vecchia, affacciata allo sportello, controllava la temperatura del forno, Gretel con tutta la sua forza la spinse dentro e chiuse svelta la porta.

Finalmente la strega aveva avuto ciò che si meritava!

Gretel corse a liberare il fratello. Insieme si assicurarono che la porta del forno fosse ben chiusa: anzi, per essere più sicuri, aggiunsero al chiavistello un grosso lucchetto. Poi rimasero diversi giorni a mangiare altri pezzi di casetta finché, rovistando tra le cose della strega, trovarono un cofanetto pieno di monete d'oro. Prepararono quindi un bel cesto pieno di provviste e tornarono nel bosco per cercare la via di casa.

Questa volta furono più fortunati e al secondo giorno di cammino videro in lontananza la loro casa. Appena si avvicinarono, corse loro incontro il padre, che piangeva per la gioia di rivederli.

"La vostra matrigna è morta! Nessuno vi farà più del male. Tornate da me, figli miei!" disse ai bambini tra le lacrime. I due bambini lo abbracciarono. "Prometti che non ci lascerai mai più, mai più!" diceva Gretel con le braccia attorno al collo del padre. Hansel aprì il cofanetto con le monete: "Guarda, papà, siamo ricchi! Non dovrai più tagliare la legna...". E da allora vissero felici e contenti.

IL FAGIOLO MAGICO

Giacomino viveva con la sua mamma, una povera vedova, in una casetta di pietra. La loro unica ricchezza era una mucca da latte.

Quando la mucca divenne troppo vecchia, la mamma mandò Giacomino al mercato per venderla.

Per la strada, il bambino incontrò un buffo viandante. "In cambio della tua mucca ti offro cinque fagioli magici" propose lo straniero. Giacomino, incerto, esitò a lungo ma poi, allettato da una così straordinaria occasione, accettò.

Quando tornò a casa la mamma, infuriata, lo rimproverò:
"Sciagurato! Che cosa hai fatto? I soldi ci servivano per
comprare un nuovo vitello. Ora non abbiamo più niente
e siamo più poveri di prima!". Poi prese i cinque fagioli
e li gettò dalla finestra, mandando il figlio a
letto senza cena. Il mattino dopo, uscendo
di casa, Giacomino trovò un'incredibile
sorpresa: durante la notte era cresciuta
una gigantesca pianta di fagioli, così

alta da raggiungere
le nuvole! "Allora
i fagioli erano davvero magici!"
pensò Giacomino. Curioso com'era,
si arrampicò sulla pianta e, raggiunta la
cima, si ritrovò con la testa tra le nuvole.

Guardandosi intorno, vide poco lontano un grande castello di pietra grigia.

"Da chi sarà abitato?" si domandò.

Un ponte di nuvole formava un sentiero fino al

castello e Giacomino vi si avventurò.

Giunto davanti al grande portone, bussò più volte. Venne ad aprire un'enorme Orchessa, che lo fissò accigliata.

"Mi sono perso e ho fame!" disse Giacomino. L'Orchessa, che aveva otto figli e amava i bambini, lo fece entrare e gli diede una tazza di latte.

"Adesso scappa!" disse poi. "Fra poco ritorna mio marito, l'Orco, che mangia i bambini!"

Mentre stava ancora parlando,
si sentì un rumore
come di un tuono: era
l'Orco che rientrava!
"Ucci ucci, sento odor
di bambinucci!"
urlò l'Orco con
il suo vocione.

"Presto, nasconditi!" sussurrò più piano che poteva l'Orchessa spingendo
Giacomino nel forno della cucina.

"C'è un bambino, in questa stanza!" gridò l'Orco
annusando e guardandosi intorno.

"Bambini!" ripeté l'Orchessa. "Tu vedi
e senti sempre bambini dappertutto!
È proprio una fissazione, la tua! Su, siediti
a tavola che ti preparo la cena."

L'Orco si sedette e divorò una cena
abbondante e squisita. Poi,
dopo aver contato e ricontato
le monete del suo tesoro, si
addormentò profondamente.

Di lì a poco tutto il castello rimbombava
per il suo russare fragoroso. L'Orchessa
era andata a preparare il letto e
Giacomino, uscito dal forno, vedendo
le monete d'oro sul ta-
volo ne riempì un sac-
chetto e scappò senza
fare rumore. "Spe-
riamo che non
mi veda, altrimenti mi mangia!" si disse tremando
di paura. Ma l'Orco continuò a dormire e Giacomino
si lanciò con il cuore in gola sul sentiero tra le nuvole.
Arrivato alla cima del fagiolo gigante, si calò
più veloce che poté, aggrappandosi ai tralci.
Quando giunse a terra trovò ad aspettarlo
la madre, in ansia per la sua scomparsa.
"Dove sei stato? Vuoi farmi morire
di paura?" sgridò il ragazzo. Giacomino
le mostrò il suo tesoro: "Guarda!
Ho fatto bene a cambiare
la mucca con i fagioli magici!".

E le raccontò tutta la storia.

Le monete d'oro servirono per comprare
tante cose che mancavano. Quando
furono tutte spese, Giacomino pensò
di ritornare al castello sopra le nuvole.
L'Orchessa lo fece nuovamente entrare
e gli diede del latte. Poco dopo arrivò l'Orco e allora Giacomino
si nascose subito nel forno.

"Ucci, ucci, sento odor di bambinucci!" disse l'Orco.

L'Orchessa non gli diede retta
e preparò un'abbondante
cena. Dopo che ebbe
mangiato e bevuto,
l'Orco posò sul tavolo
una gallina

che faceva le uova d'oro. Giacomino, dal forno,
vide il prodigio e, quando l'Orco si addormentò,
saltò fuori e, afferrata la gallina, scappò di corsa
a casa dalla mamma.

Ogni giorno la gallina, immancabilmente, faceva
un uovo d'oro per i suoi nuovi padroni.

Ma Giacomino non era ancora soddisfatto
e tornò al castello per la terza volta.
Questa volta entrò di nascosto e si nascose
in una grossa pentola.

"Ucci, ucci!" fece l'Orco arrivando.

"Sento odor di bambinucci!"

"Sarà quel monello che ci ha rubato le monete e la gallina dalle uova d'oro"
pensò l'Orchessa e corse a controllare dentro al forno. Ma il forno era vuoto.

Dopo cena l'Orco andò a prendere un'arpa magica,
che cantava e suonava in modo meraviglioso.
Cullato da questa dolce musica, si addormentò.
Giacomino dal suo nascondiglio ascoltò rapito
la melodia e, quando sentì l'Orco russare, alzò
il coperchio della pentola e vide lo strumento

prodigioso: un'arpa
d'oro. Si arrampicò
veloce sul tavolo e... via di corsa,
con l'arpa stretta fra le mani. Ma lo strumento
svegliò l'Orco, gridando: "Padrone, padrone!
Svegliati! Un ladro mi porta via!". L'Orco si destò
di soprassalto e si mise a rincorrere Giacomino.

Il ragazzo scivolò rapido lungo il tronco del fagiolo magico, inseguito dall'Orco.

"Presto, mamma, prendi una scure!" gridò balzando a terra. "Devo abbattere la pianta prima che arrivi l'Orco!" Già si intravvedevano gli enormi stivali quando, con un tremendo tonfo, la pianta crollò trascinando l'Orco in fondo a un precipizio. Con la gallina magica che deponeva uova d'oro e l'arpa prodigiosa che suonava melodie incantate Giacomino e la sua mamma vissero da quel giorno ricchi e felici.

I VESTITI NUOVI DELL'IMPERATORE

C'era una volta un imperatore vanitoso, la cui unica preoccupazione era vestirsi con abiti eleganti.

Quasi ogni ora cambiava abito per sfoggiare la sua ricercatezza. La fama di questa sua debolezza si era estesa oltre i confini del suo impero e un giorno due imbroglioni decisero di approfittare della sua vanità. Si presentarono al Capo delle guardie del palazzo e chiesero di essere ricevuti dall'imperatore.

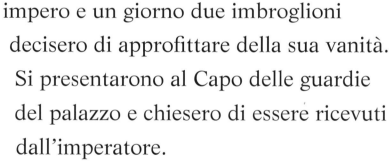

"Siamo due sarti di eccezionale bravura e abbiamo messo a punto un sistema per tessere una stoffa talmente leggera e impalpabile da sembrare invisibile. Anzi, è totalmente invisibile a chiunque sia stupido o non sia all'altezza dell'incarico che ricopre!"

L'imperatore, molto incuriosito, ricevette subito i due finti sarti, fece dare loro un sacco di monete d'oro e si lasciò prendere le misure. I due finsero di mettersi al lavoro, chiedendo grandi quantità di seta sottile e fili d'oro. Alla fine, si presentarono a corte. "Ecco, Maestà, il frutto delle nostre fatiche! Guardate che stoffa pregiata! E che disegni!"

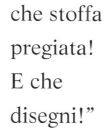

L'imperatore non vedeva proprio niente: i due avevano le mani vuote!

Ma certo non poteva dirlo: tutti avrebbero pensato che fosse uno stupido e che occupasse indegnamente il trono. Indossò l'abito e si complimentò con i sarti e così fecero anche tutti cortigiani presenti: nessuno era pronto ad ammettere di non vedere nessun vestito!

"Maestà, anche il popolo vuole vedere questo vestito straordinario!" disse il Gran Ciambellano.

L'imperatore si vergognava nel vedersi nudo davanti a tanta gente, ma poiché nessuno pareva accorgersene, acconsentì

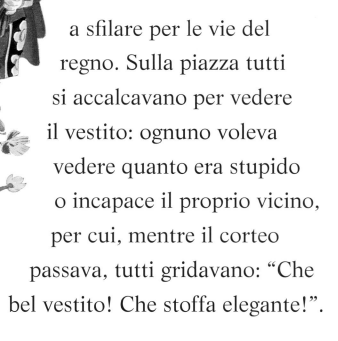

a sfilare per le vie del regno. Sulla piazza tutti si accalcavano per vedere il vestito: ognuno voleva vedere quanto era stupido o incapace il proprio vicino, per cui, mentre il corteo passava, tutti gridavano: "Che bel vestito! Che stoffa elegante!".

Ma un bambino, che usava gli occhi per vedere e la lingua per dire la verità, vedendo passare la carrozza imperiale esclamò: "Guardate! Guardate! L'imperatore è nudo!". La frase del bambino fu presto sulla bocca di tutti: "È vero! È vero! L'imperatore è nudo!". L'imperatore capì di essere stato truffato e si vergognò molto. Da quel giorno non fu mai più vanitoso.

PINOCCHIO

C'era una volta un pezzo di legno, capitato tra le mani di un vecchio artigiano, Geppetto, che voleva farne un burattino. Ma appena cominciò a intagliarlo, il pezzo di legno si mise a parlare, a ridere e a fare sberleffi. Quando intagliò le braccia e le gambe, il burattino balzò

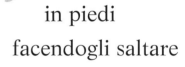

in piedi facendogli saltare gli occhiali dal naso.

"Ti chiamerò Pinocchio" disse Geppetto.
"Domani ti manderò a scuola, così diventerai un bravo burattino!"
Ma Pinocchio non voleva saperne della scuola e scappò via più veloce che poté.
Corse attraverso le strade del paese, inseguito dal povero Geppetto.

PINOCCHIO

Il burattino correva più veloce di lui
e, benché il povero vecchietto continuasse
a urlare "Fermatelo! Fermatelo!" la gente
rideva e lo lasciava passare.
Un carabiniere alla fine
lo acciuffò, ma Pinocchio
fece delle scene così pietose
che il gendarme decise
di arrestare Geppetto.
"Povero burattino!"
diceva infatti la gente.
"Chissà come lo
maltratta suo padre!"
Pinocchio, tornato a casa, si sentiva solo e affamato.

Fu perciò contento
quando Geppetto uscì di prigione e gli
promise di comportarsi bene e di andare
a scuola. Geppetto vendette la sua unica
giacca per comprargli un sillabario. Pieno
di buoni propositi, Pinocchio si avviò verso
la scuola, ma sentì la musica di una fanfara…

"Che cos'è?" chiese a un ragazzetto. "Non sai leggere?" disse questo. "È il Gran Teatro delle Marionette. Ci vogliono quattro soldi per andare allo spettacolo!"

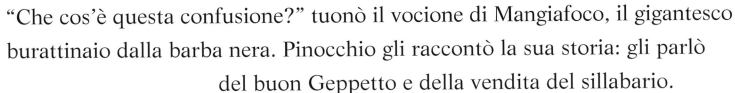

Pinocchio vendette il sillabario e si comprò un biglietto di ingresso. Le marionette lo accolsero come un fratello.

"Che cos'è questa confusione?" tuonò il vocione di Mangiafoco, il gigantesco burattinaio dalla barba nera. Pinocchio gli raccontò la sua storia: gli parlò del buon Geppetto e della vendita del sillabario.

Mangiafoco lo sgridò, ma poi, impietosito, gli regalò cinque monete d'oro da portare a suo padre.

"E ora fa' il bravo!" gli disse infine l'uomo.

Sulla via di casa, però, Pinocchio incontrò
un Gatto e una Volpe,
due vecchi imbroglioni.
"Vieni con noi, ti
porteremo al Campo
dei Miracoli, dove
potrai seminare
le tue monete
e raccoglierne mille volte tante!" proposero
quelli. Pinocchio fu entusiasta dell'idea e li seguì.
Quando venne la notte, i due imbroglioni
si nascosero nel bosco e si cammuffarono
da briganti incappucciati.

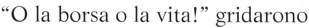

"O la borsa o la vita!" gridarono
a un tratto saltando fuori da dietro un cespuglio.
Ma Pinocchio aveva nascosto le monete sotto
la lingua.
"Ti appenderemo a questo albero finché
non ci dirai dove hai nascosto il denaro!"
lo minacciarono allora.
Tutto sembrava mettersi per il peggio…

Per fortuna una fata, la Fata turchina, lo salvò
e gli chiese di raccontarle la sua storia.
"Dove sono finite le tue monete?" chiese
al termine la Fata. Pinocchio, che le aveva
nascoste in tasca, disse di averle perse.
"E dove le hai perse?"
"Nel bosco!" rispose pronto Pinocchio.
Subito il suo naso cominciò ad allungarsi e,

più raccontava frottole,più il naso
cresceva, finché diventò così lungo
da picchiare contro le pareti
della stanza!
"Sono le bugie che dici a farti
crescere il naso!" gli spiegò la Fata.

Pinocchio si vergognò
e chiese perdono.
La Fata chiamò allora mille
picchi che beccarono il naso fino
a ridurlo a dimensioni normali.

PINOCCHIO

Il burattino si incamminò allora verso casa, ma incontrò nuovamente il Gatto e la Volpe e con loro andò al Campo dei Miracoli. Seminò il suo tesoro e il mattino dopo… le monete erano sparite, rubate dai due furfanti. "Mi sono fatto imbrogliare: sono stato uno sciocco! D'ora in poi sarò bravo e andrò a scuola" si ripromise Pinocchio. Ma a scuola diventò amico del ragazzo più disubbidiente e svogliato della classe, Lucignolo. "Vieni con me al Paese dei Balocchi, dove si gioca tutto il giorno e non si deve mai studiare!" disse un giorno Lucignolo. "No, che non vengo" rispose

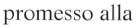

Pinocchio. "Ho

promesso alla

Fata

e al mio

babbo Geppetto

di comportarmi bene!"

Ma il burattino non riuscì

a resistere alla tentazione di

visitare un paese così meraviglioso

e alla fine partì con l'amico.

Dopo qualche mese di baldoria, un brutto mattino si accorsero che le loro orecchie erano diventate lunghe e pelose: si erano trasformati in somarelli! Lucignolo fu venduto a un contadino come bestia da fatica, mentre Pinocchio finì in un circo, dove si azzoppò cercando di saltare in un cerchio di fuoco.

Fu allora portato al mercato, dove lo comprò un uomo che voleva la sua pelle per farne un tamburo. Quando il suo padrone lo gettò in mare per annegarlo, i pesci del mare, mandati dalla Fata Turchina, lo liberarono dalla carne dell'asino. Pinocchio, felice di essere di nuovo un burattino, cominciò a nuotare, allontanandosi dalla spiaggia.

Ma le sue disavventure non erano finite: un enorme, mostruoso pescecane emerse dal mare dietro alle sue spalle.

"Aiuto!" gridò il burattino, atterrito dalla smisurata bocca che lo inseguiva. Per quanto nuotasse veloce, sentiva dietro di sé il risucchio dell'acqua che entrava nell'immensa apertura. D'un tratto si trovò inghiottito con violenza insieme a tanti altri pesci. Fu sballottato con violenza dal vortice d'acqua nella gola del pescecane, fino a rimanere stordito.

Quando rinvenne, si trovò nel buio più profondo. Cominciò a inoltrarsi carponi per quella che gli sembrava una strada in discesa, urlando: "Aiuto! Aiuto! Nessuno viene a salvarmi?".

D'un tratto intravide un fioco chiarore.
Via via che si avvicinava, si accorse
di una fiammella che brillava lontana.
Finché, cammina cammina, trovò...
... trovò il povero Geppetto, seduto
tutto solo a un tavolino, al lume
di una candela.
"Babbo mio! Com'è possibile?" chiese
Pinocchio che non credeva ai propri
occhi. Geppetto allora gli raccontò di aver percorso il mondo in lungo
e in largo in cerca del suo burattino e di essere stato anche lui inghiottito
dal mostro. "Non ti preoccupare, babbo, fuggiremo insieme!" concluse.

Approfittando della notte,
reggendo il vecchio padre
sulle spalle, Pinocchio
riuscì a uscire dalla
bocca del pescecane,
che il bestione teneva
spalancata nel sonno.
Nuotando di buona lena,
presto giunse a riva.

Da quel giorno il burattino fu sempre buono. Di giorno andava a scuola e imparava a leggere e a scrivere, mentre di notte fabbricava cesti per aiutare il suo babbo a guadagnare qualche soldo. Allora la Fata Turchina fece un ultimo prodigio: una mattina Pinocchio si svegliò e si accorse di essere diventato un bambino vero.

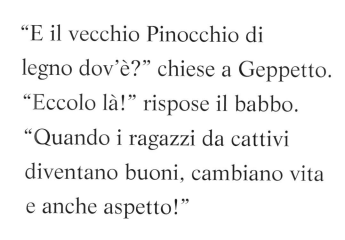

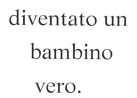

"E il vecchio Pinocchio di legno dov'è?" chiese a Geppetto. "Eccolo là!" rispose il babbo. "Quando i ragazzi da cattivi diventano buoni, cambiano vita e anche aspetto!"

L'OCA D'ORO

C'era una volta un boscaiolo che aveva tre figli.

Un giorno mandò il maggiore nel bosco a far legna.

Il giovane incontrò un ometto dalla barba bianca, che gli chiese un po' di cibo. "Va' via!" rispose sgarbatamente. "Non ho niente per te!"

Il giorno dopo fu mandato nel bosco il secondo figlio. Anche a lui apparve l'ometto dalla barba bianca.

"Puoi darmi da mangiare?" chiese. "Non mi seccare!" rispose l'altro.

Il terzo figlio, Taddeo, era un ragazzo dall'animo semplice e gentile, che molti giudicavano tonto. Anche lui andò nel bosco a far legna. Quando l'omino dalla barba bianca gli chiese un po' di cibo, Taddeo divise con

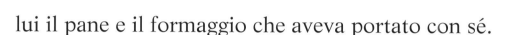

lui il pane e il formaggio che aveva portato con sé.

"Sei stato il primo a essere gentile con me! Meriti una ricompensa!" disse l'omino. "Guarda bene tra le radici di quel grosso albero, troverai un regalo per te!" e, così dicendo, sparì.

Taddeo cercò tra le radici e trovò un'oca dalle piume d'oro. Se la mise sottobraccio e si avviò verso casa. Si fermò a un'osteria e chiese da mangiare

per sé e per la sua oca, poi andò a riposare.

Una delle figlie dell'oste, vedendo quelle belle piume d'oro, cercò di rubarne una. "Nessuno si accorgerà di una piuma in meno!" pensava. Ma l'oca era magica: appena l'ebbe toccata, vi rimase appiccicata. La fanciulla chiamò in aiuto le sue sorelle, che rimasero a loro volta attaccate a lei.

Quando Taddeo si svegliò, prese la sua oca e si avviò verso casa. Le sorelle lo dovettero seguire, attaccate all'oca. L'oste le inseguì gridando, ma appena ebbe afferrato il vestito dell'ultima figlia, rimase anch'egli attaccato. Lo stesso successe a sua moglie, al curato del paese, a un contadino, a un fornaio e a una guardia che passava di lì.

Vicino al villaggio c'era il castello del Re. Era un Re molto potente e ricco, ma aveva un grosso dispiacere: la sua unica figlia aveva una misteriosa malattia che la rendeva sempre triste. Il Re aveva deciso che chiunque fosse riuscito a farla ridere, l'avrebbe sposata. Quando Taddeo con la sua buffa comitiva giunse davanti al castello, la principessa, vedendolo passare, scoppiò in un'allegra risata. Il Re non credeva ai suoi occhi e gridava: "È un miracolo!". La principessa rideva sempre di più. Mentre rideva l'incantesimo si ruppe e tutta l'allegra brigata finì a gambe all'aria. Allora nessuno riuscì più a frenare le risate della Principessa!

Il Re decise di far celebrare subito le nozze. Fu così che un'oca d'oro portò fama e ricchezza a un povero taglialegna.

RUMPELSTILTSKIN

C'era una volta un mugnaio, famoso per essere un gran fanfarone: secondo lui, la sua casa era la più bella, il suo mulino il più grande, la sua farina la più bianca. Un giorno vide passare il Re e non seppe resistere alla tentazione di vantarsi anche con lui.

"Maestà, guardate mia figlia, è la fanciulla più bella del reame!"
Poiché il Re non sembrava molto impressionato, aggiunse: "Pensate che per di più è capace di filare la paglia e trasformarla in oro!".
"Benissimo, la metterò alla prova!" rispose il Re.

RUMPELSTILTSKIN

Fece condurre la fanciulla al castello e la fece rinchiudere in una stanza con un mucchio di paglia. "Trasformala in oro!" ordinò. "Altrimenti morirai!"

La povera fanciulla, rimasta sola, scoppiò a piangere.

"Padre mio, in che guai mi hai cacciata!" disse singhiozzando, quando a un tratto le apparve davanti un piccolo gnomo con la barba bianca, che le disse: "Se ti aiuterò a tramutare in fili d'oro questa paglia, cosa mi regalerai?".

"Posso darti questo medaglione che porto al collo, è la cosa più preziosa che ho!"

Lo gnomo fu soddisfatto del regalo e si mise a filare di buona lena. La mattina seguente la fanciulla, che aveva dormito tutta la notte di un sonno agitato, vide che la promessa era stata mantenuta Quando il Re entrò nella stanza, restò sbalordito: al posto del mucchio di paglia c'erano tanti rocchetti di fili d'oro!

Il Re, che era molto avaro, non si accontentò della sua nuova ricchezza.

"Ti manderò altra paglia, perché tu la possa trasformare in oro. Se non lo farai, morirai!" disse. Di nuovo la fanciulla si disperò e di nuovo apparve lo gnomo dalla barba bianca. "Che cosa mi dai se ti aiuto ancora?" chiese.

"L'ultima che cosa che mi rimane è un anello!" rispose la ragazza.

Lo gnomo fu contento del regalo, filò tutta la paglia e il Re, la mattina dopo, poté contare felice su un mucchio di rocchetti di filo d'oro.

Ma ancora non era soddisfatto. "Filami ancora questa paglia e diventerai mia moglie" disse alla fanciulla.

Ma quella sera la fanciulla non aveva più niente da regalare allo gnomo.

"Quando sarai Regina, mi darai il primo figlio che nascerà!" disse questi.

Senza pensarci troppo, la ragazza accettò il patto e il prodigio si ripeté.

Il Re, soddisfatto e diventato ormai ricchissimo, fece celebrare le nozze.

Il Re e la Regina furono molto felici quando nacque un bel maschietto.

Ormai la Regina aveva dimenticato le passate disavventure, finché, improvvisamente, un terribile giorno, ricomparve lo gnomo.

"Sono venuto a prendere ciò che mi hai promesso!"

"Non posso mantenere quella promessa!" lo supplicò la Regina. "Ti offro in cambio tutti i miei gioielli! Chiedimi qualsiasi altra cosa ma, ti prego, non portarmi via mio figlio!"

"Ti darò un'ultima possibilità" disse lo gnomo. "Se riuscirai a indovinare il mio nome ti lascerò il bambino! Ma bada, hai solo tre giorni per scoprirlo, e tu sai di cosa sono capace!"

Detto questo, scomparve.
La Regina chiamò allora tutti i sapienti del regno, che subito consultarono i loro libri per cercare il nome dello gnomo.

Sfortunatamente però nessun manoscritto da loro esaminato parlava di gnomi dalla lunga barba bianca e capaci di fare mirabolanti magie.

Erano già trascorsi due giorni e il tempo a disposizione stava per finire, quando un messaggero del Re riferì di aver assistito, per un fortunato caso, a una strana scena. Mentre attraversava un fittissimo bosco, aveva infatti visto un vecchietto dalla lunga barba bianca che ballava intorno al fuoco cantando: "Rumpelstiltskin, Rumpelstiltskin, il mio nome è tutto qua, se nessuno lo saprà, il bambino mio sarà".

58

RUMPELSTILTSKIN

La Regina accolse questa notizia con gioia e ricompensò il messaggero con una borsa di monete d'oro.

Il terzo giorno era ormai giunto e a corte tutti aspettavano con ansia l'arrivo dello gnomo, che improvvisamente comparve dal nulla. Appena lo vide, la Regina gli puntò contro il dito dicendo:

"RUMPELSTILTSKIN!".

Lo gnomo divenne tutto rosso di rabbia, poi fu colpito da un lampo e scomparve in una nube di fumo, per non ritornare mai più.

La Regina corse felice ad abbracciare il figlioletto e gli disse stringendolo a sé: "Ormai sei salvo! Nessuno potrà più portarti via!"

INDICE

GW00729911

DASD

J. Ranade IBM Series

H. MURPHY • *Assembler for COBOL Programmers: MVS, VM,* 0-07-044129-4

H. BOOKMAN • *COBOL II,* 0-07-006533-0

J. RANADE • *DB2: Concepts, Programming, and Design,* 0-07-051265-5

J. SANCHEZ • *IBM Microcomputers Handbook,* 0-07-054594-4

M. CARATHANASSIS • *Expert MVS/XA JCL: A Complete Guide to Advanced Techniques,* 0-07-009816-6

P. DONOFRIO • *CICS: Debugging, Dump Reading and Problem Determination,* 0-07-017606-X

P. KAVANAGH • *VS COBOL II for COBOL Programmers,* 0-07-033571-0

T. MARTYN • *DB2/SQL: A Professional Programmer's Guide,* 0-07-040666-9

N. PRASAD • *IBM Mainframes: Architecture and Design,* 0-07-050686-8

J. RANADE • *Introduction to SNA Networking: A Guide to VTAM/NCP,* 0-07-051144-6

J. RANADE • *Advanced SNA Networking: A Professional's Guide for Using VTAM/NCP,* 0-07-051143-8

S. SAMSON • *MVS Performance Management,* 0-07-054528-6

B. JOHNSON • *MVS: Concepts and Facilities,* 0-07-032673-8

A. WIPFLER • *Distributed Processing in the CICS Environment,* 0-07-071136-4

J. RANADE • *VSAM: Concepts, Programming, and Design, Second Edition,* 0-07-051244-2

J. RANADE • *VSAM: Performance, Design, and Fine Tuning, Second Edition,* 0-07-051245-0

J. SANCHEZ • *Programming Solutions Handbook for IBM Microcomputers,* 0-07-054597-9

P. DONOFRIO • *CICS Programmer's Reference,* 0-07-017607-8

M. CARATHANASSIS • *Expert MVS/ESA JCL: A Guide to Advanced Techniques,* 0-07-009820-4

J. RANADE • *DOS to OS/2: Conversion, Migration, and Application Design,* 0-07-051264-7

K. BRATHWAITE • *Relational Databases: Concepts, Design and Administration,* 0-07-007252-3

M. MARX, P. DAVIS • *MVS Power Programming,* 0-07-040763-0

G. HOUTEKAMER, P. ARTIS • *MVS I/O Subsystem: Configuration Management and Performance Analysis,* 0-07-002553-3

A. KAPOOR • *SNA: Architecture, Protocols, and Implementation,* 0-07-033727-6

D. SILVERBERG • *DB2: Performance, Design, and Implementation,* 0-07-057553-3

R. CROWNHART • *IBM's Workstation CICS,* 0-07-014770-1

C. DANEY • *Programming in REXX,* 0-07-015305-1

G. GOLDBERG, P. SMITH • *The REXX Handbook,* 0-07-028682-8

A. WERMAN • *DB2 Handbook for DBAs,* 0-07-069460-5

J. KNEILING, R. LEFKON, P. SOMERS • *Understanding CICS Internals,* 0-07-037040-0

A. FRIEND • *COBOL Application Debugging under MVS: COBOL and COBOL II,* 0-07-022453-6

L. BRUMBAUGH • *VSAM: Architecture, Theory, and Applications,* 0-07-008606-0

DASD

IBM's Direct Access Storage Devices

Robert H. Johnson
R. Daniel Johnson

McGraw-Hill, Inc.

New York St. Louis San Francisco Auckland Bogotá
Caracas Lisbon London Madrid Mexico Milan
Montreal New Delhi Paris San Juan São Paulo
Singapore Sydney Tokyo Toronto

Library of Congress Cataloging-in-Publication Data

Johnson, Robert H.
   DASD : IBM's direct access storage devices / Robert H. Johnson, R.
Daniel Johnson.
       p.   cm. — (J. Ranade IBM series)
   Includes index.
   ISBN 0-07-032674-6
   1. Computer storage devices.   2. IBM computers.   I. Johnson, R.
Daniel.   II. Title.   III. Series.
TK7895.M4J64   1992
004.5′6—dc20   92-33
                                                                      CIP

1 2 3 4 5 6 7 8 9 0   DOC/DOC   9 8 7 6 5 4 3 2

ISBN   0-07-032674-6

*The sponsoring editor for this book was Jerry Papke, the editing
supervisor was Stephen M. Smith, and the production supervisor was
Pamela A. Pelton.*

Printed and bound by R. R. Donnelley & Sons Company.

Contents
(VTOC)

Preface

IBM is the second largest publisher in the world. (The United States government holds the number one position.) This book is not designed to eliminate your need to refer to the manuals that match your operating system and the hardware that you are using. We have found, however, that the sheer volume of data produced for even such a narrow subject as DASD is overwhelming for novice and expert alike. The goal of this DASD book is to give you the background and concise information you need to understand IBM and non-IBM manuals and to assist you in selecting the areas on which to concentrate your research.

The area of DASD is constantly changing. It is imperative that you test all the facts and theories given in this and any other book or paper on the DASD subsystem. Every day we learn another thing about this topic.

For Whom This Book Was Written

This text is designed for data processing people at several skill levels. Like the first book, *MVS Concepts and Facilities*, the target audience ranges from the beginning data processing professional to the most experienced. The introductory nature of the text is designed to allow anyone to pick up the book and proceed to a relatively high level of expertise in general data processing techniques.

The real value of the book is for the experienced data processing professional to understand what is covered in the book and then use it to have a dialog with all the people with whom they interface about DASD. We have many stories about how *MVS Concepts and Facilities* was used by senior technicians to begin a dialog, teach, and build a team with everyone: beginning programmers, operations and productions control personnel, other systems programmers, and management.

Operating System Environment

This book has been directed primarily to the IBM operating systems in general and the MVS operating system specifically. The techniques we discuss are universal and apply to all sizes of computers and almost all operating systems. The difference is in implementation.

A Word on the Style Used

The style of the book has been kept simple. This is an overview of DASD that permits almost anyone involved in the data processing industry to gain a better understanding of DASD. We also gathered statistics and information to make it a complete work for the practicing data processing professional.

From time to time, we will be placing information in boxes. These sometimes contain information that is very important and that we do not want you to miss. Sometimes they contain *rules of thumb*. Rules of thumb are guidelines that you can use as a measure of your situation. They are not guarantees of success. If we state, as most do in the industry, that a 30–40-millisecond response time for DASD I/O is acceptable, then it is acceptable for a large percentage of I/O operations. There are in your shop, just as in others, a number of situations where a 40-millisecond DASD response time would be fatal to the responsiveness of your application.

A good index is always a challenge. We indexed all headings of the book to make the index into an alphabetized table of contents. You can tell the indexed headings because the rules of capitalization are followed for the index entry, just as they were followed for creating the header. You may find two index entries for the same topic. If one has all capitals, it is a header and you will find most of the information there. Lowercase entries are references within paragraphs. We believe the index is one of the vital parts of a book, so if you look things up in the index and do not find them, please notify us for the next release.

What You Need to Know to Read This Book

This book is an introduction to Direct Access Storage Devices (DASD). We assume that you have some knowledge of MVS or other operating systems.

Why This Book Is Complete

Each chapter and section has been used to teach the concepts of DASD. The successes of our students sometimes overwhelm us. Minutes, hours, and yes, even days of processing were eliminated.

How Your Installation Benefits

The data center benefits if you are able to be more productive in DASD techniques. It is almost impossible for you to fail to become more productive if you use the concepts in this book—if not directly by the things you will learn, then by the ideas that it will generate in you, if you allow ideas to germinate.

What Is Included

Part 1 considers DASD from the user's perspective. The background and history are used to form pointers to the present and to the future. The components of DASD are discussed to give all the readers a solid footing to understand the DASD subsystem. Application programming requirements are described to ensure that the reader knows why DASD exists. Channel and control units are described in detail, as they are the components that access DASD and they play a vital part in understanding DASD.

Part 2 covers the control of DASD. Management concerns are presented for all to use to understand the complex interaction of data processing needs and the physical boxes of hardware. Tuning considerations give an in-depth background on channel programming and topics that affect the important aspects of tuning. DASD can be shared by multiple Processor Complexes and even different operating systems. Shared DASD considerations are more important today than ever because everyone with the latest IBM Processor Complexes has the option to run PR/SM partitions with multiple operating systems driving the same DASD farm.

Part 3 covers the various DASD generations. Pre-3380 devices are covered because there are still data centers with these devices performing data storage tasks. They also provide a window into the future. The 3380 device group is covered because that very successful generation is the most popular today. The 3390 generation is described and the reader can evaluate when to shift to the newest technology. Other DASD types are described because they provide a small but important niche in the world of data storage.

Part 4 covers systems managed storage. The focus is on the IBM implementation that they call DF/Storage Management Subsystem. First you must understand you data and how it acts. The chapter on Data in a Pooled Storage Environment introduces you to techniques you can use to study your data environment. The IBM DFSMS environment is presented to show one implementation of systems managed storage. DFSMS is presented from a user perspective. What are these constraints? What do all those new terms mean? Stay tuned!

Summary

This book is designed to assist you in the understanding, management, and control of Direct Access Storage Devices in the IBM environment.

Acknowledgments

We above all thank our wives, Marie Johnson and Kathy Johnson, for their support, love, and friendship. Without them, there would be no DASD book!

Tom Johnson did another outstanding job creating the graphics for this text. It was made more difficult by our being in two parts of the great state of Virginia, but he accomplished the task.

We would like to specifically thank Bill Fairchild for his guidance and assistance over the years, and specifically with this book. If there are any errors, they are our responsibility. If this book is a success, it is in part due to his ability to research and understand the I/O subsystem and his willingness to share that information with us and the rest of the data processing community. Bill is an international treasure. There may be others who know the world of DASD as well as Bill, but we have never found one so interested in observing, testing, and teaching what he found.

Randy Chalfant reviewed the book in its infant stage. He provided a wealth of information and ideas. Randy's knowledge added much to this volume. Randy is another of those rare individuals whose knowledge spans the entire computer industry. He has a background in hardware and he is willing to share it for the enrichment of the people in the industry.

Tom Stanley provided input for the SMS portions of the book. Tom is one of those unique individuals who is technically talented, an excelellent employee, and a great teacher. We thank him for his friendship.

We thank our employers, Landmark Systems Corporation and AAC Associates. Their support and encouragement for this project is appreciated.

The book would not be a reality if not for Jay Ranade and his vision of a few years ago. Jerry Papke, the Senior Editor for McGraw-Hill, was a joy to work with.

Stephen Smith of McGraw-Hill and his staff added real value to the book. Many writers fear the editors turn at the manuscript. We only wish they could have Stephen as their editor and then they would learn the truth: editors really make the book a polished masterpiece!

Bob:

I dedicate this book to Bob Weir, who is one of the best mentors I have ever had. Bob insisted on excellence and insisted that those who worked for him worked toward excellence in everything we did. Bob is retired now, but his influence and integrity live on in the business world through those of us lucky enough to work with him.

I also thank Ray Brow, Vice President at Landmark. Ray is one of the few technicians who successfully crossed the boundary from super techie to strategic-thinking, VP-level manager. It is no coincidence that Ray is an avid reader.

Mark Friedman, Jim Wheaton, Tom Bason, Steve Barnes, Dave Parker, and I shared an exciting journey into the world of videoconferencing to teach some of these concepts. Their professionalism surprised the professional television people who assisted us. Katie Gates was vital to our success in presenting tuning material. She did not even know how to spell MVS before she started and was asking us very technical questions about the detail at the end!

SHARE and the Computer Measurement Group (CMG) have provided me with a wealth of information. These groups provide the opportunity to learn about computer subsystems in a way that is unmatched for effectiveness.

Some of these industry experts are particularly helpful to my effort to learn. Dick Armstrong, Dieter Bahr, Tom Beretvas, Don Chesarek, Richard Clary, Jim Crane, Jim Dammeyer, Jim Doyle,

Wayne Embry, Cliff Goosman, Keith Immink, Judy Jones, Dan Kaberon, Lin Merritt, John McCann, Dale Naleway, Bernie Pierce, Bill Richardson, Keith Rush, Steve Samson, Joel Sarch, Dan Squillace, Dick Sziede, Ron Thielen, Roseanna Torretto, Cheryl Watson, Ray Wicks, and Leo Zimmerman provide me with challenging interaction. I am proud to be numbered in their company.

H. Pat Artis, Dr. Thomas Bell, Chuck Hopf, John McCann, Dr. Rich Olcott, and Dr. H. W. Barry Merrill are internationally known experts in this field. Each time I meet or see these individuals, I learn something new. It is very exciting!

My staff at Landmark also provided a professional environment at work. Their hard work enabled me to spend my nights, weekends, and days off writing this book. Thanks go to Mary Apple, Carol Crotty, Lisa Deemer, Pat Di Pierro, Kippi Fagerlund, Sarah Frey, Penny Harms Garver, Warren Helm, Debbie Hofman, Ann Lawson, Kelly Leboeuf, Russ Lilley, Doreen Mannion, Steve McVey, Jeri McDuffee, Holly McKittrick, Patty Ratliff, Anne Despeaux Reaver, Craig Stone, John Underhill, and Vanessa Williams.

Bill Mosteller, Rick Rooney, and Gordy Stauffer are true friends. Their support over the decades (yes folks, decades!) has been wonderful.

Dan:

It has been an honor helping my father write this book. He's the MVS guy, and, because of his encouragement and guidance over the years, I'm the everything-else guy. While I was growing up, he took a lot of time to patiently answer my questions and explain things about MVS (then OS). The library of manuals and books he kept at home was enough to satisfy anyone's curiosity. The ADM-3A terminal we built together from a kit, a slightly damaged 300-baud modem, the county timesharing system, and an ARPAnet not yet closed to serious students made for an enriched, fortified sandbox.

Mom got me a book on typing, and it has always been advantageous to type at nearly the speed of speech. Her insistence that we learn and properly use the language was a priceless gift, because technical ability has little worth without it. Her own attention to detail and completeness was the example that formed the basis of my professional practices.

I was fortunate to be growing up just as computing became available to kids. Marvin Koontz at Fairfax County Public Schools arranged for timeshared BASIC on HP equipment and an RJE line to the county data center long before computers in the classroom were in vogue. Ed Rice, Ricki Vick, and Charlie Fischer of Honeywell lent their souls and patience weekly so a group of 30 or so high school students could have nearly unfettered access to the most advanced equipment available.

Kids today do not have it as well, in my opinion. Fear of "hackers," justified or not, has closed off most of the avenues through which my friends and I were enriched, encouraged, and set on our course through life. Having just a PC would not have been the same. It was the time, care, and attention of many adults outside traditional schooling that made the difference to us. Now that computing technology has become commonplace in the home, I fear that kids these days have lost that essential ingredient. Teachers and schools cannot be expected to educate and guide our children unaided.

"Buy your operator a Coke," Dad advised before I went to college. I did. I married her. Kathy has put up with much agony and anguish not only through production of this book but all the time since we met ten years ago. She has been my guide, my inspiration, and my love. Our first is due in March '92, and I look forward to passing on our family tradition should Zella Josephine be interested in a Life of Perpetual Deadlines.

My specialization, if you can call it that, is writing reliable software. Whatever else I do, I do that best. The credit for organizing my professional practices goes to Dad, who sparked them, to legends like Wirth, Dijkstra, Kernighan, Plaugher, and Yourdon, who taught me through their writings, and to Dr. J.A.N. Lee of Virginia Tech, who, while attached to monitors in an ICU, realized his survival depended on programmers.

Don and Kelly Queijo shared some very rough times and survived them with us. Don showed me the payoff for meticulous quality no matter what you're doing. Both Don and Kelly have been true friends and professional associatess in every sense of the word over the years, as have Dave and Rachel Warme, Ivan and Diane Reeder, Brian Wong, and Paul Karagianis. Bless you all.

Finally, I must thank the people at AAC Associates, Inc., a most unusual professional services (communications and information systems) company for which I have had the honor of working. Tony Carlson, Warren Eder, Yvonne Adair, and Steve Fletcher have constructed the company on the firm foundation of honesty and integrity, value for the dollar, and outstanding work from outstanding people. They and the rest of the people at AAC are known for their ability to produce results where others have failed, time and again. AAC Associates graciously allowed me the time when it was necessary to concentrate on this book.

The software development team under Warren Eder has the highest concentration of raw talent with which I have ever had the pleasure of being associated. Working with Ken Bourque, Ken Chen, Dave Edgar, Elaine Harvey, Ugur Koser, Robbie Rivera, Don Slice, and Al Steele, who share a common commitment to quality, has been the most rewarding professional experience of my life. It is easy to fly in the company of eagles. And that is no exaggeration.

Trademarks and Copyrights

DASD

1

DASD from the User Perspective

From the beginning of computing until now with System/390, end users have been interested in the value that data could bring to them. End users do not really care what medium is used as long as the data is made available to them in a timely and convenient manner. Thus the evolution of storage media from cards and tapes to direct access storage was in response to end user requirements for online data.

One of the goals of this book is to make the end user, operations personnel, and systems programmer more aware that they have common goals. For data processing to add to the productivity of civilization, it is a requirement that the entire team work together. If end users ignore technology, they will suffer. If the data center ignores the end user, it will suffer.

Data seems to come in at a faster rate than we can organize it or manage it. Look at your in-mail box. If you are like most people, you are being inundated by data in the form of magazines, newspapers, technical articles, or even books like this one!

Unfortunately, the end user is not very good at knowing exactly what data he will want online in the future. We are not trying to be critical of the end user (after all, we are end users too!). We are saying that we need to study our customers and their needs, and respond to them.

This section discusses some of the concepts you are required to study. We caution you not to skip too lightly though this section. Even very experienced data processing readers can learn from these topics. Perhaps the topics we bring up can aid you in solving your DASD problems because the presentation forces you to see your situation from another perspective.

If you are an end user, knowledge of these concepts will enable you to get more value from your data. If you are the implementer of DASD maintenance (e.g., systems programmer or storage manager), these concepts will enable you to help satisfy your customers. If you are in data center management or a capacity planner, your job should include directing the long-range planning process to provide more cost-effective data management.

The penalty for not minding the data management store is being lost in a quagmire of data. The reward for understanding your data needs is efficient, cost-effective service. The choice is yours. Good luck.

1

Background and History

1.1. Introduction

If yours is like most enterprises, you do your best to protect and manage your data storage resources. You keep backups of your data, you try to keep up with the increasing need for more storage space, and you try to get the best performance out of the equipment you have. When you exhaust a resource, you try to use what you have more effectively or acquire more resources to meet present and future needs. Is this enough, or should you do more? If you and your team cannot work harder, perhaps there are ways you can work smarter.

This book is about working smarter. If you understand the technology, you can control it. If you know how your organization depends on it, you can obtain more benefit with less expense. If you understand the trends in the computer industry, you can take advantage of them without being oversold. You and your enterprise can get the job done better and become more competitive and effective. This book is direct and practical: it shows you how to do these things.

We consider IBM Direct Access Storage Devices (DASD) in this book because it is the architecture used by most large companies in the United States for data storage and retrieval. The issues we address are, however, applicable to you whether you use IBM mainframes or other vendors' mainframes, minicomputers, or microcomputers. Though details may differ, understanding one architecture makes you better able to understand another because the differences are analogous.

One reason for this is that all data storage devices share a common heritage. As we look a century back, we are surprised at how the details of the technology have changed but the issues have not. We can discuss some of the issues without becoming mired in technical detail. Computers use bits and bytes to store and manage what people see as letters, numbers, and graphics. The bits and bytes are *data*; data becomes *information* when we place an interpretation upon it. It has always been that way. Someone did not just wake up one morning, however, and decide to invent DASD. As with most of humankind's inventions, DASD was born of a series of necessities. The history of DASD begins, therefore, with a country that grew too quickly.

When the U.S. census takers come to your home at the beginning of each decade, they are counting people just as the human race has done for well over six millennia. There are many reasons for doing so, but the result is a lot of data. In fact, a census predicament gave birth to the first automatic method for collecting and processing data.

In the 1880s, the U.S. Bureau of the Census had a big problem. The population was expected to grow by over 25% and census taking and reporting required over five years to finish! It did not take Einstein to figure that a new census would begin before the one for the previous decade could be taken and processed.

That sounds funny to us today, but out there in corporation land, we have many systems reporting on the previous month well after the 15th of the following month. The worst one I saw was *six months late!* Talk about old news.

Fortunately for us all, Herman Hollerith got a job at the Bureau of the Census.

1.2. In the Beginning There Were Holes

Most of the older "introduction to data processing" books include the study of the classic Hollerith punched-card data processing system. You can get the details in those books. In short, the 1890 census was completed in less than half the time it took to do the 1880 census, even though there were over 25% more people.

Who cares, you might say? That was such a long time ago with machines found only in museums. Look at the past as an opportunity to avoid problems in your life now. Mr. Hollerith's problem was a late reporting problem. If you have the same sort of problem at your company, what would your value be to your employer (or client if you are a consultant) if you could solve that problem? What if you could do things twice as fast with less work? That thought excites us, as perhaps you. Innovation often is seeing something that others have not seen. We will see this theme often in this book.

What problem was Mr. Hollerith trying to solve? He had to get the information into a format that could be analyzed faster than contemporary manual techniques permitted. He wanted to record names, addresses, demographic data. He wanted counts of each type of data. He wanted to reap the benefits of automation.

The secret Mr. Hollerith rediscovered was the punched card system. (Punched cards were used years earlier for controlling automatic weaving looms.) People were interviewed. The collected data was taken back to a central site to be recorded, collated, and counted. Data was punched into a card that used a code system (certain punches represented certain characters). The machinery and system was Mr. Hollerith's contribution.

Figure 1.1 shows that data collected about a family was collected and transferred to punched cards. The sheer number of cards quickly became a problem. When magnetic tapes were developed, the data was stored as *card images* on tape, and the cards could then be (forgive the pun) discarded.

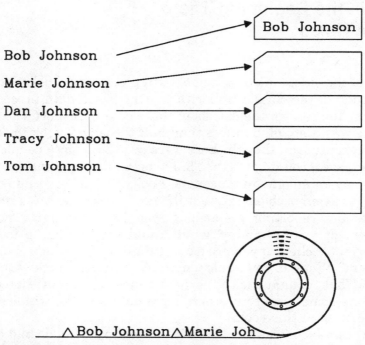

Figure 1.1 Cards and Tapes. The modern history of data storage began with the Census Bureau's needing to store the names, addresses, and other information about people they counted. The punched-card system was created to store data *and continues today* in some locations. Magnetic tapes were then used to reduce the media volume and speed up processing.

It must have worked. The 1890 census was completed quickly and efficiently. The 1990 census, even with its prodigious mass of collected data, was completed before the end of the year! What if you could complete your management reports just-in-time as the month ended? Talk about excited management!

The above is not just a history lesson. Mr. Hollerith designed his system to create and manipulate cards with 80 columns across the card. I do not know exactly why he picked 80 columns. Maybe that is how many he needed to represent census data for an individual. Maybe he picked the overall size of the card to be the same as that of the dollar bill at the time.

How many characters are displayed per row on a CRT terminal? How many data sets can you count in VM, MVS, and VSE that use 80-byte images? Now you know where that comes from! The latest versions of VM/ESA, MVS/ESA, and VSE/ESA start up with 80-byte image files. It was just a few short years ago that the MVS SYS1.PARMLIB (the start-up library) no longer required logical and physical 80-byte images.

More of this history is firmly embedded in present-day computing, however. The code Hollerith used to represent data on his cards influences the character codes we use every day.

The Hollerith card was divided into twelve rows. Each row across the card had a value. The top row was "12", the second "11", the third through the twelfth were "0" through "9" (so logic was not Mr. Hollerith's strong suit).

In Figure 1.1, the first character recorded, "B", is a "12" punch and a "2" punch. The character is mechanically read into a "computer" for processing. When the System/360 was born, the cards were read into central storage and converted to another format—Extended Binary-Coded Decimal Interchange Code (EBCDIC).

The EBCDIC code for "B" is C2 in hexadecimal. Let us see: C in hex is 12 in decimal, and 2 is...how about that? The EBCDIC used in our contemporary, high-tech equipment translates into placement of holes in cards!

1.3. Data Volume and Use

As the census takers discovered, data collection can become an enormous undertaking. The census has grown from 80 million people to over 250 million people. Think of the punched cards that would be needed to hold all our current population statistics! Clearly something faster and better than punched cards had to be developed.

For example, think about your personal phone book. All of your family and friends usually fit in one of the pocket or desk telephone directories. How do you update your book? Do you copy it completely every few years? Do you have loose-leaf pages? Do you store it in a computer? In any case, it is probably manageable. Now look at the telephone directory for any large city. How would you manage that volume of data? Probably with a different technique than you use for your family and friends.

> ¤ The amount of data you are trying to manage and how it is accessed helps determine the type of medium on which it should be stored. Small volumes of data will be treated in one homogeneous group, while large volumes of data will be treated as part of another homogeneous group. What's large? We will get to that later.

In Figure 1.2 we see how the amount of data and access patterns determine the storage medium.[1] The magnetic tape at the top of the figure contains many records. One record with a key of *AARDVARK* is separated by many records from that with a key of *JOHNSON*. If the data must be accessed sequentially, as magnetic tapes must, the program must read all the records until it reaches the one with a key of *JOHNSON*.

Choose sequential, magnetic tape media for large data volumes on which the data should be processed sequentially. Choose DASD media for relatively small volumes that will be processed directly. DASD allows the *JOHNSON* record to be accessed directly.

1.3.1. Life Cycle of Data

Data begins its existence when someone captures some information and stores it on a recording medium. We are writing this book by typing characters. The life cycle of these words begins

---

1 Medium, media, which is it? The Latin word "medium", meaning "the middle", is the singular form; "media" is the plural in Latin and English. Is a set of platters affixed to a spindle singular or plural? We consider it a medium. A reel of magnetic tape is a medium. Several of either or both are media.

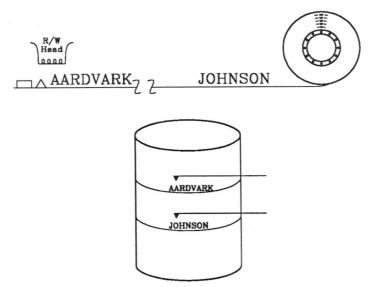

Figure 1.2 Data Volume Effects. After cards, magnetic tape volumes were used to hold data. Tape was a fast, efficient medium to read records sequentially as the records passed quickly under the read-write head. As the volume of data grew, it took longer and longer to locate the data. For a tape data set, all the data set records would have to be read and inspected to get to the JOHNSON record, assuming the file was in sorted order. If it was not sorted, then all the records in the file would be read. Once the file was placed on DASD, the device could move a read-write head directly to the record to read just the required record *directly.*

right now. As they are stored, though, they are just beginning a very long journey.

Data in the computer industry is almost always captured first to DASD. The data spends some time on one medium and is usually moved to some other. You will see as you go through this book that it is best for all concerned if a storage manager detects and moves the data from place to place to suit its access patterns. For now, let's look at the life cycle of data.

1.3.2. Allocation Time

Think of the life cycle of a data set like the time line you probably drew in school many years ago. A time line is usually used to

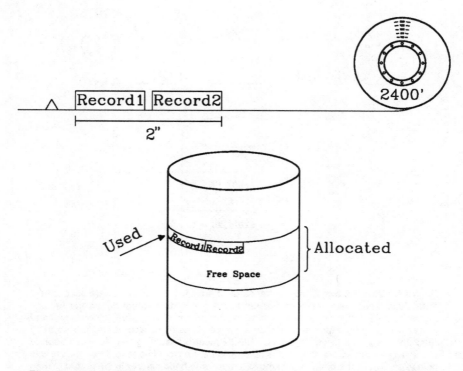

Figure 1.3 Size of Data Set at Allocation Time. With tape, the size of the data set does not have to be exactly calculated at allocation time. With one record, you get one tape reel. With DASD, the data set's expected size is explicitly or implicitly specified. Space can be specified in blocks, tracks, cylinders, or megabytes. [Megabytes are allowed only under Systems Managed Storage systems and some versions of ISPF data set allocation panels (3.2).]

graphically show a series of events over a period of years. Data sets may have a life of years. The birth of a data set is the time when space is allocated for it.

Allocation is a term most commonly used in MVS because of its roots in OS/360, where the allocation routines would find space for data and mark the volume table of contents of the data volume with the data set name and some attributes. In fact, allocation time is a valid concept for VM, DOS, IBM personal computers, Apple personal computers—every data processing system. You do not notice it so much with these other operating systems because allocation is done dynamically as data is added to files.

Figure 1.3 shows the allocation of a two-record data set on tape and on DASD. On tape, the data set uses approximately two inches for the data. Other data sets can be allocated on the tape. Once a data set is allocated on tape and another is allocated after it, however, the first data set cannot be extended or have any other records added to it without destroying the second and subsequent data sets. Adding data to the first data set destroys previously written data.

In the case of allocating the data set on DASD (under an MVS or VSE environment), the *expected size*, or *primary space*, is specified. No other data set can be assigned to the *free space* used in this allocation until the data set is freed.

Will all the allocated space be used? That is the question. If it is eventually used to contain data records, then the primary space was correctly specified. If it is never going to be used, then the primary space was not correctly specified, and that space is wasted. This might seem obvious, but few people are careful when choosing primary allocations.

> ¤ Wasted free space is the number one enemy of anyone in data processing. It is the number one enemy because it wastes more money than either you or I could imagine. You will see that one of the greatest benefits of converting to Systems Managed Storage is the benefit of using more of the DASD space for which we are paying.

The VM, PC, and minicomputer users do not get away unscathed. I can hear you now: "our free space is allocated only as there is data to write to it". PC DASD users pay the performance and space price of fragmentation, and VM users pay the space price. Each DASD organization has its advantages and disadvantages. Some are less obvious than others.

Figure 1.4 shows what happens as a file grows. In the case of tape files, the system (actually the access method) just asks for a

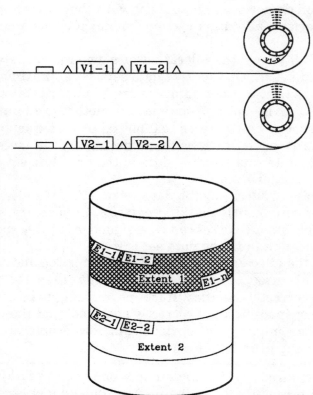

Figure 1.4 Data Set Creation. In this example a data set is being created. For tape access, as the first (or subsequent) tape volume fills up (physical records V1-1 through V1-n), another tape volume is allocated (records V2-1 through V2-n). For DASD data sets, the primary extent (extent 1) is filled with records E1-1 through E1-n. If more records are added than can fit into the first extent, another extent is added for records E2-1 through E2-n.

new tape to be mounted, and the program continues on its merry way. The program does not really know or care that volume one contains records V1-1 through V1-n (where n is the maximum number of physical blocks on the tape) and volume two contains records V2-1 through V2-n. The file could have 1, 16, 200, or hundreds of volumes.

For DASD records, the MVS operating system allocates data sets in *extents*. An extent is a contiguous region of DASD space. Each extent may be located in a different area of the DASD's magnetic data recording surfaces. Once a data set is created, it is possible to increase the space allocated to it. The operating system does so by acquiring additional extents.

However, several rules impose limitations on the number of extents that an MVS data set may occupy on DASD, unlike sequential data sets on tape. Two allocation values are supplied to MVS for a data set, its primary and secondary allocations. These may be in one of several units, but the rules are the same regardless of the units in which these parameters are specified.

The first rule is that the primary allocation must be achieved within 5 extents, and each secondary allocation must also be achieved within 5 extents. The second rule is that the total allocation for a data set, whether extended or not, must be achieved within 16 extents per volume for non-VSAM data sets and within 127 extents for VSAM data sets. If the data set is allocated across more than one volume, then a non-VSAM data set may, for example, contain more than 16 extents, but the maximum per volume remains in effect.

For example, suppose the DASD space for a non-VSAM data set were specified to be 10 tracks for the primary allocation and 6 for each secondary allocation. Suppose the primary allocation is achieved with 2 extents of 7 and 3 tracks each, and the first secondary allocation is achieved with 4 extents of 1 track each and 1 extent of 2 tracks. So far, the data set spans 7 extents.

How many additional times may the data set's allocation be extended? It depends on how many contiguous, free areas remain on the volume. If all remaining areas are single tracks, then the second secondary allocation would fail, even if 100 free tracks remain on the volume. One cannot allocate 6 tracks from a set of 1-track free areas without blowing the limitation of 5 extents per allocation.

Suppose instead that all remaining free space on the volume is in contiguous, 2-track areas. In this case, the data set may be extended using 9, or 16 − 7, more extents. At 6 tracks per secondary allocation, using 2-track extents, the data set may be extended 3 more times: 18 tracks may be added. At this point,

16 extents are allocated to the data set, so no more may be allocated on the same DASD volume.

Why is this important? It should be clear that from a fragmentation perspective, primary or secondary allocations that are too small can increase fragmentation of the volume as the operating system enforces the extent rules. (It can also artificially limit the maximum size of a data set.) On the other hand, primary or secondary allocations that are too large result in space allocated but not used. The former costs money in terms of performance, and the latter costs money in terms of DASD paid for but unusable. Almost all data management products, such as DFDSS or FDR, have the ability to defragment DASD data sets. Volume defragmentation is the process of copying data sets from one place on a volume to another place on the volume to combine extents.

1.3.3. Backed-Up Versions

Before we get too far into the discussion, I want you to start thinking about backup and recovery. *The time to consider backup and recovery is as you allocate a DASD data set.* In Figure 1.5 a data set has been allocated on volume DATA01. The data is vulnerable to loss from the time the data set is allocated and the first data is written until the time the data set is not being used by anyone (batch or online job) and a backup is taken.

After the data set is closed, it can be *backed up* to another DASD volume (e.g., DATA02) or it can be copied to a tape data set (e.g., TAP001). Backup to another DASD could be as simple as a one-for-one copy, or a DASD space manager could make a backup of the data set in some compressed format.[2]

If the data set is very important, or the data set contains highly volatile data or data that is expensive or impossible to recreate (e.g., telephone orders from a customer), "real-time"

---

2   Such as for DFHSM level 1 backups, described later.

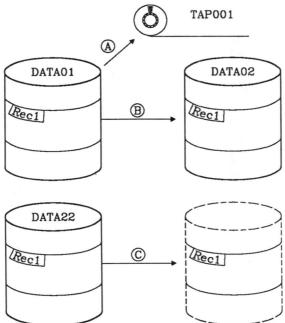

Figure 1.5 Backup Copies: Manual or Automatic. As data is collected, the end user should create another copy of the data for archival use in case the data is damaged in some manner. In case *A* above, the backup is on magnetic tape. In case *B* above, it is a second DASD copy that is created *after the data set is completed.* In case *C* above, the data is automatically copied to a second DASD by the 3990 model 3 dual copy feature. The dual-copy volume does not have a separate volume serial number. It is the same as the primary volume.

backups can be made with the IBM 3990 dual copy feature to make *shadow copies* of the data as it is being written.

Such duplexed data is not a new idea. In the early 1970s systems were written which wrote to two different DASD devices to provide instantaneous recovery. These systems issued two I/O operations to two different actuators. The software had to keep track of the two actuators. Now, software does only one I/O and hardware such as the 3990 model 3 storage controller does two. The result is less overhead (and possibility for error) inside the processor.

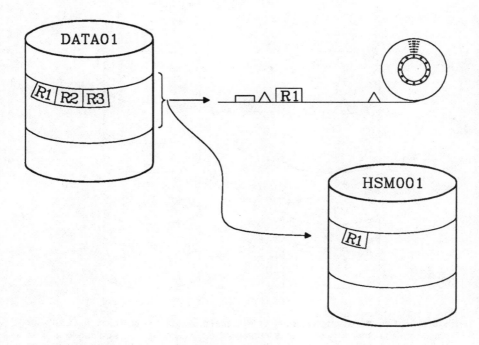

Figure 1.6 Archived Data Sets. After a period of time without use, a data set may be migrated —moved—from the DASD device it is on to either tape or another DASD device. It is almost always compressed. The space is freed and is available for use by other data sets or other data set extents. Note that three records are compressed into one record.

Other software and hardware vendors write data to two volumes at the same time to be able to recover from DASD failures. These *fault tolerant* systems can recover from media outages, even if failure occurs while the file is open and being used. Some combine this with *transaction protection* to ensure that a complex update is entirely complete or entirely backed out.

Data center management purchases DASD to provide space for its users to create and use data sets. In many cases the data set is created and not used for a while, or it may never be used again—we forget the data set exists. (Old age is cruel: the first two things to go are our memory—and I forget what the second one is. Oh yeah, hair.) To reduce the cost of old age, data set management software is designed to migrate unused data sets from DASD to another medium.

Look at Figure 1.6. The data set could be moved to another DASD volume, but in order for this to make sense, the data set management software must compress the data into a smaller DASD area. From what you have learned so far, you should be able to envision that simply doing away with allocated but unused space would yield good compression.

Data set management software can cram more data into less space by compressing the data. For example, a series of like characters (called a *run*) such as blanks can be encoded, or more sophisticated adaptive compression can be used at the cost of processing time. This is graphically shown by the data set on DATA01. Three records are compressed into one record's space on volume HSM001.

IBM's implementation is the Data Facility Product Hierarchical Storage Manager, or DFHSM. There are a number of other non-IBM software products that provide the same functions. These data management products move data sets between primary DASD and secondary *levels*. For DFHSM, a *level 1* volume is usually another DASD containing compressed data. A *level 2* volume is the final destination for migrated data, usually magnetic tape but possibly another DASD. Generally, as the level number increases, access speed and required storage space decrease.

¤ The compressed data set is not directly usable by your programs. The records no longer have the format recognized by the access methods your program would use to read and write the records.

The technology exists in PC DASD controllers to dynamically compress data as it is written to storage media and expand it as it is read. The relatively slow data transfer time of a PC allows this to be done in hardware. Likewise, compression is available with some network products. This technology has not yet

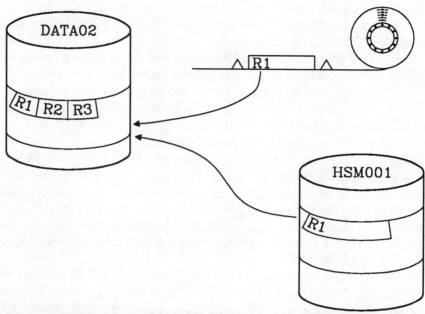

Figure 1.7 Recall of Archived Data Sets. If the data set was migrated to tape and a program issues an open for the data set, then the storage management program issues a mount for the tape it is on, finds a new DASD volume with appropriate space, allocates space, and restores the data set. If the data set was migrated to DASD, the same process is followed except, of course, that no tape mount is required. One compressed record converts to three uncompressed records.

reached mainframe DASD controllers. (Then again, why would a DASD vendor sell you something that would keep you from having to purchase more DASD?) There are software compression programs from non-IBM vendors which compress and decompress data inside central storage to save DASD storage.

Suppose the data set is removed from the original volume, DATA01, but remains on HSM001. The data is then not safe if volume HSM001 is damaged for some reason. Another concern is loss of the catalog or data set that the data set management software uses to locate and decode the compressed data set.

> ☐ If the data center loses the DFHSM catalog, it loses all
> migrated data sets on the level 1 volumes. Migrated data
> is not backed-up data.

Figure 1.6 shows that the data set could be archived to magnetic tape. This option frees up data space on DASD and gives the added benefit of having a copy that can be moved to another location. If you store migrated data sets on tapes that are *offsite*, you significantly increase the time to recover the data set if a program or user wants the data. In this case, even if you keep duplicates of migration tapes, the data is not safe: magnetic encoding will deteriorate over many years to the point where the data is no longer readable.

Figure 1.7 shows the reverse process. A request for the data set is made and the data set management software must find space on an available volume. The software then moves the data set back to the volume, and the data is available to the user program.

1.4. Management Concerns

The capital resources of a data center are purchased and accounted for by the management of the data center. This section outlines some of the areas you and your company should agree upon to ensure that the DASD investment is bringing the best return on investment that it can.

The list is not all-inclusive. It is intended to start your creative idea machine flowing. If the DASD you are using is not cost-effective, then eventually management will dispose of it. Come to think of it, the same goes for you and me.

1.4.1. Legal Considerations

We store data for many reasons. Most of them are for our immediate data processing needs. For example, we read payroll files to produce payroll checks so that people like us continue working.

The payroll file created as part of the payroll cycle has other valuable uses. The accounting department uses it to create reports for the federal and state governments. Files live on and on. The payroll file probably has to be saved for a certain number of years as a result of finite, legal requirements.

What is saved in a file can have other legal restrictions. There may be legal limitations on how and to whom personal information about individuals or information about other companies may be distributed.

In honoring legal requirements, remember that backup and archived versions of the data may exist. Just as you should keep or destroy the carbon copy of your personal charge receipts in case someone goes through stores' trash, fishing for fraud, you must protect the *carbon copy* of data backups.

1.4.2. Availability Management

Availability management is the discipline of making (in this case) DASD data sets available to the end users whenever they need the data. If you are successful all the time, then you have 100% availability. Availability is an elusive concept. 99% availability sounds pretty good. What if we guaranteed you 99% availability for each component that provides you with access to your DASD data sets?

Look at the components: actuator, HDA, drive, control unit, and channel. Suppose the channel is out 1% of today, say from 9:00 to 9:14 (1 percent of 24 hours is 14 minutes). Suppose as we are fixing the channel we kick the control unit and break it: 9:14 to 9:28—oh yes, another 14 minutes. The control unit falls over and hits the drive and pulls the plug out: 9:28 to 9:42. When we set things up again, the HDA is damaged: 9:42 to 9:56. You have lost much of the morning, and we are just getting started. But hey, *we are maintaining 99% uptime!*

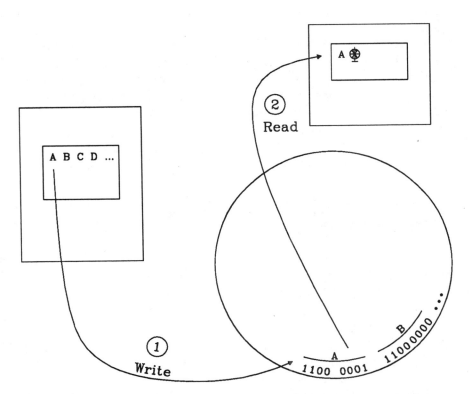

Figure 1.8 Data Checks. When a record is written to DASD, the read-write heads turn bits on and off to store the data. In this example, a record with "ABCD" is written to the DASD platter. Only this time, the letter "B" should be "11000010" and is left as "11000000". The "2" bit is lost. At some later time, a read command is executed but discovers the lost bit. The result is a data check.

That was a silly example, but you would be surprised at how many data centers still evaluate their availability by measuring components and not what the end user sees. We are sure our readers will do much better, of course.

If you are a systems programmer and find it difficult to empathize with end users about downtime, suppose your television set had 99% uptime. If the 1% downtime occurred at the end of the football game or during the climax of the movie, how might you react?

Percentages may be used both as a statement of service levels, forming a goal to be reached, and as a measurement of actual performance. Service-level goals are set from the users' perspective, measurements from the data center's, and having numbers for both allows them to be compared to gauge success. We have been conditioned as part of American culture to consider "$19.95" the same as "$20", but when it comes to mission critical applications within an enterprise, the cost of that nickel can be enormous.

1.4.3. Data Checks: The Perversity of Inanimate Objects

Data checks may or may not be detected at the time a physical record is written to the DASD surface. In Figure 1.8, a program is writing four characters—"ABCD". As the head is passing over the spot on the platter, it misses writing one of the bits in the letter *B*. (EBCDIC represents the letter "B" with the binary value 11000010, or C2 in hexadecimal.) In the figure, one of the bits (x'02') is not recorded properly.

Only when the record is read (seconds, hours, days later) is this error discovered by the error-checking circuitry (the checksum bits do not add up). The I/O operation for the block of data on this DASD is interrupted while error recovery tries to fix up the block. This interruption is called a *data check*.

In some cases the hardware can figure out what the error is and correct it automatically. This case is one of a *single bit error* and can be overcome by almost all DASD hardware. Some DASD can recover from double bit errors or even triple bit errors. When more bits are in error than can be recovered, then the surface of the medium is really damaged and the only "fix" is to restore the backup of the file (presupposing you have one) and restart processing.

If the data was written with a dual copy facility, chances are good that the correct data can be read from the intact medium. You can see how much manual intervention can be saved by dual copy.

You will see that advances in technology allow us to have multiple copies of the data available to recover from almost any error condition. This *duplexing* of DASD records will probably be done only for very valuable data sets or data that is recorded without any other possibility of recovery. Security and convenience come at a hefty price.

1.4.4. Deletion of Backup and Archive Versions

The reason we back up data sets is recovery. A copy of the data set is saved at a specific point in time. The time chosen by a data set administrator usually synchronizes the contents of the backed-up data with some business milestone (e.g., processed and printed the payroll checks for January 12). Most backups are taken, however, *just in case*—to protect the work done during the last 24 hours. However trivial the data, "we lost a day's worth" goes down a lot smoother than "we lost a month"!

Backup frequency used to be determined by the human resources that could be applied to the task: operators had to be available; backups took a certain amount of time. As you move towards systems managed storage techniques, you will need to rethink backup strategies, including the nature of the data and the frequency with which it is backed up.

Backing up data only if it has changed can reduce the time required to have full backups and allow them to be taken more frequently. (Almost all backup programs can use the *data-set-changed* bit in the VTOC or VSAM catalog to limit redundant backups of the same data.) Larger-capacity backup media can reduce operator intervention during the process. You may not ever want to back up some data sets, such as sort work, paging, and other transient data. Systems managed storage will allow

3380			
100−103	104−107	108−10B	10C−10F
AE4	BD4	BD4	

3380	3380	
200−203	220−223	224−227
AK4	AK4	

3390	3390	3390
308−313	300−307	314−31F
B24	A24	B24

Figure 1.9 Adding DASD Devices. As DASD requirements grow, and the data center adds space, more physical units are added. Either new strings are added or physical units are added to existing strings. The architectural design dictates how the devices can be added. Some [e.g., 3390 (on the bottom) and properly configured 3380 (in the middle)] can be added with the other devices on the string operational. Some (e.g., most 3380 on the top and all previous generations) must have all devices in a string powered down to add additional devices.

you to classify data not only for performance reasons but also for availability and reliability.

The reason we archive data sets is to allow more important data to use the space. When a data set has not been accessed for a long time, we are in fact using the DASD space it occupies for long-term storage. This is rarely cost-effective. Once this data is archived to *near DASD*, however, the primary DASD may be used more effectively, yet we can still access the archived data: it can be retrieved explicitly with a DFHSM command or implicitly by attempting to access the data set through JCL or TSO allocation commands.

Ironically, as more data sets are archived, automatic dearchiving works better because there is more free space to allocate when the archived data sets are needed.

1.4.5. Device Installation Management

As access requirements for DASD volumes increase, the data center will want to add volumes to satisfy the users' needs. **Configuration planning avoids outages and allows the data center to be more flexible.**

> ¤ We have chosen to use the term "device" for the box on casters and the term "actuator" for the thing with one volume serial number. IBM and others use the term "device" to represent the smallest unit of DASD (e.g., a volume with a single serial number) *and* to represent a box that can be rolled around on casters. Other terms may be used: an actuator may be called a spindle, a logical volume, or a unit (as in one *unit control block*.)

In Figure 1.9, a data center has three strings of DASD. The first contains three 3380 devices (100–10B), and the data center has planned for a fourth device (10C–10F). These are the *Extended Capability models*. Unfortunately, the entire string must be taken out of service (powered off) to add the fourth device.

The second string contains two 3380 AK4 devices (200–203 and 220–223). The devices are *Enhanced Subsystem models* and have been butted together to form two joined strings. The entire string does not have to be taken out of service to add a *B* device to either of the head-of-string devices, because two AK4 models have been placed together to form a four-path head of string. If the two heads of string were not joined, the string would have to be powered down to add devices.

The third string contains two 3390 devices (300–307 and 314–31F). Note that the addresses are not consecutive, as they were on 3380 devices. The *A* unit can have four or eight volumes, and

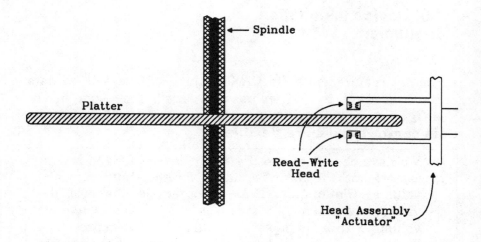

Figure 1.10 Read-Write Heads. The first read-write heads were wire-wrapped electromagnetics. Several heads were mounted on an "actuator". The actuator is moved to a "cylinder position" above the spinning platter. Technological advances made the head smaller and the actuator smaller.

of course they use addresses X'00' through X'07'. The B unit on the right is installed, so the addresses must start at X'14' and may go as high as X'1F'. Only one head of string is present or needed because the 3390 has four paths built into the head of string. Later chapters will describe these arrangements in detail for all DASD types.

When management wants to expand the string to its maximum, a second B unit is added and would be addressed as X'08' through X'13'.

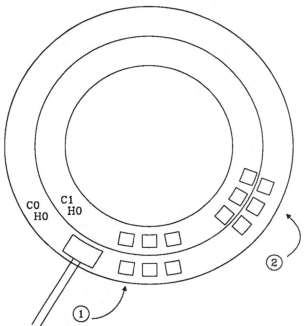

Figure 1.11 Improved Recording Density. A second way to improve recording density is to make the bits closer together. The more bits you record on a track, the more data you can store on the actuator. As manufacturers packed cylinders closer together and bits closer together, the movement of the read-write head became more critical. Sometimes the head would write data in the center of the track as in *1* above. Sometimes the head would write the data at the left-of-center or at the right-of-center (in *2* above). The read-write head would have to move slightly to read properly, and thus the concept of *head-shaking* came into being. The actuator would rock the mechanism a small percentage of the width of a track and attempt to read a block that could not be read on the first pass. Head shaking is awful; each try is a full rotation or about 16.7 ms added to the device response time.

1.5. Architectural Improvements

One of the truths about DASD is that every new device gets smaller in physical size, larger in bytes of storage space, more expensive in real dollars, less expensive in bytes per dollar, more reliable in mean time between failures, and less reliable in the amount of data lost per failure.

The industry term for this phenomenon is *architectural improvements*. As you read about the following architectural goodies, keep in mind that truth. The more things change, the more they remain the same.

1.5.1. Thin-Film Heads

The read-write head is where the bits hit the road. It seems that the engineers have improved this component more than any other. Later discussions of the individual devices will show you how smaller heads enable us to double and triple data density, but for now let us take a generic example.

In Figure 1.10, the read-write head literally flies across the platter as the platter is spinning. The head assembly, or *actuator*, moves the arm across the platter to position the read-write head at a specific cylinder position. It is easy to see that if the cylinder is 10 units in width and you reduce the size of the read-write head by 50%, then the cylinder can be only 5 units wide. *The actuator's density is instantly doubled!*

1.5.2. Improved Recording Density

A second way to make more fit into less is to improve the recording density, or the size of the bits on the platter. If you make the bits half as big, then you can squeeze more bits per square inch of platter surface, and you again multiply the number of bytes on the device.

With all this squeezing, there eventually comes a limit to what the device can reliably accommodate. The head could always write and read exactly in the middle of the track, as shown at point *1* in Figure 1.11. To put this into perspective, imagine yourself driving down a highway. You keep exactly in the middle of the lane 100% of the time, don't you? Of course not. The drive actually does a lot better than you or I at staying in one relative

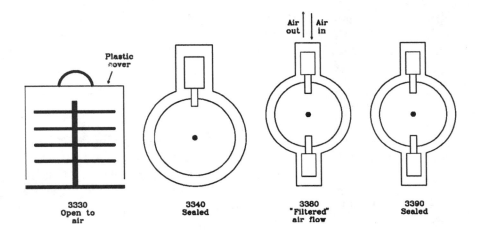

Figure 1.12 Generic DASD Types. Early (e.g., 2314 or 3330) removable media devices had platters on spindles with plastic covers. The heads were housed in the actuator housing. Different packs mounted on the device used a single set of heads to read and write the data. The result was a very wide-track architecture and lots of head-shaking going on here. Later the 3340 had read-write heads inside the removable package. The 3380 and 3390 family also have read-write heads inside the package. One major difference between the 3380 and 3390 is that the 3390 is in an air-tight container. These drawings are virtual representations. The two actuators of the 3380 and 3390 are actually on the same side.

position, but it does not always work exactly in the center of the track.

At point *2* in Figure 1.11, some records are written near the left boundary of the track and some are written near the right boundary of the track. The inverse square law of distance versus intensity applies here: if everything goes well, the head can read the weakened signal and correctly read the data. If it cannot read the data on the first pass and has to go around again, an awful thing happens—an additional rotation's worth of time (16.7 ms on some 3380 models) is added to the I/O service time. You will learn more about this in later chapters.

The result is that almost every generation of DASD has different sized platters. The size of the platter also causes some other physical laws to dictate the rest of the device. For example, in Figure 1.12 the general shape of the devices proceeded from open canisters (e.g., 3330 devices), to sealed devices (e.g., 3340 devices), to partially sealed devices (e.g., 3380 devices), to completely sealed devices (e.g., 3390 devices).

1.6. Summary

DASD devices were created and have evolved as the data processing industry responded to end user needs to have more and more data instantly available to them. The progression of data from punched cards to magnetic tape to Direct Access Storage Devices (DASD) began over 30 years ago and is proceeding at a rapid pace today. The pace will increase as we go into the 21st century. (Once programs break when two-digit years roll over from 99 to 00, however, maybe users will wish they had less data on DASD.)

Once data is created on DASD, the backup and migration to archived data storage (on either other DASD or magnetic tape) is a concern for all. End users should be aware of where copies of their data reside. Data center management should be concerned with how many copies of a certain data set exist and whether the data is on the most cost-effective medium.

Once backed up or archived, data sets lead multiple lives. A data set may be on other DASD (e.g., DFHSM migration level 1) or on magnetic tape (e.g., DFHSM migration level 2).

DASD as a component of a computing center (from your personal computer to the largest computer) rapidly becomes the most critical. If the data disappears, there is not much computing or printing to be done. Many data centers have come to a grinding halt by having one or more DASD devices out of service. A measure of availability should be maintained, but it must be reasonable.

Errors on DASD—*data checks*—should be understood and monitored. Recovery of errors may be fatal. The lost data may be unavailable, or the recovery may take time to perform. The response time of the I/O request is lengthened. In any case, DASD errors are important.

Device installation management practices should be understood by data center personnel. The end user should be concerned with outages required to install and maintain DASD. Hardware architecture does exist for *nondisruptive* installation. The architecture is expensive, though, so it may not be cost-effective for the end user's application, but the business should make those determinations. **Do not let nondisruptive and expensive DASD be forced on you. Justify them if you can with a cost-benefit analysis.** Where else would the money be better applied?

Architectural improvements are being made every year. IBM produces a new series of DASD about every 18 months to 2 years. As with nondisruptive devices, it should be a cost-justified business decision whether you use the newest devices or stay slightly behind to get the cost savings of used hardware.

If every generation has new architecture, you should be aware of what the architecture does for your business and what it means to your applications. You may not need to know every detail, but, for the money, you should expect an explanation of the device.

1.7. Questions

1. Explain Herman Hollerith's contribution to the historical perspective of DASD.

2. What effect did the size of the punched card have on DASD files and most current operating systems?

3. Explain the difference between allocating a data set on magnetic tape and allocating a data set on DASD.

4. Suppose a DASD volume contains 275 tracks of free space distributed as 3 areas with 25 contiguous tracks each and 10 areas with 20 contiguous tracks each. If a non-VSAM data set is created on this volume with a primary allocation of 100 tracks and secondary allocations of 35 tracks each, what is the maximum number of tracks that could be allocated to the data set? Would the system necessarily succeed in doing so?

5. Explain the difference between a backup version of a data set and an archived (or migrated) version of a data set.

6. Why should you be concerned with backed-up versions and migrated versions of a data set?

7. What are the primary installation differences between the 3380 architecture and the 3390 architecture?

8. What are the two major architectural improvements for DASD that affect the storage capability of DASD?

9. Describe a DASD *extent* on IBM CKD DASD.

2

DASD Components

Effective use of IBM's operating systems, unlike most others, requires that you know how their DASD is structured. If you do not, the penalties may be to buy more DASD than you really need, put up with poor response time, or suffer apparent shortages of space. Systems Managed Storage, which we will encounter in later chapters, promises to insulate you from these concerns, but you would be at a disadvantage if you did not know from what concerns you are being insulated. SMS cannot do the whole job.

In biology, one can only partially understand the behavior of an animal without knowing what it is made of and how its pieces fit and work together inside. Likewise, one cannot know why a Direct Access Storage Device behaves the way it does without knowing something of its internals.

This chapter gets the terminology straight and raises important issues addressed in the remainder of the book. We follow the progress of an I/O operation from the processor through the device and back, and identify those segments of the process most likely to cause performance problems. To begin, we need to agree upon names for the various DASD components. For the IBM and IBM-compatible industry, these electrical and mechanical components are:

1. **Platters** are used to store the data. These are circular metal plates stacked vertically or horizontally inside a drive mechanism that rotates all the platters together, as a unit. These plates are coated with a material that can be magnetized to store data. Sometimes platters are called *disks*, but we avoid this term because of its confusion with *devices* (see below). The set of stacked platters used to be called a *disk pack* but has been repackaged on contemporary DASD into the *HDA*.

2. **Read-write heads** suspended at the ends of **access arms** move in a line between the inner and outer edges of platters. This movement, called *seeking*, positions a head to read or write data from different positions on the platter.[1] To read or write data at a particular place, the heads are positioned, one is selected, and the platter rotates until the desired spot is under the head.

3. **Actuators** are the combination of the access arms and electronics that controls the movement, head selection, and data transfer. To the end user community, an actuator is known as a *volume* and identified with a *volume serial number*.[2]

4. **Head Disk Assemblies (HDAs)** contain one or more actuators. This is important, because an HDA is a field replaceable unit (FRU). If one actuator breaks, the entire HDA, possibly containing more than one volume of data, must be replaced. (You will see more of this when we discuss DASD errors.)

Some industry experts, including the people who repair the devices, occasionally forget this detail. More than one customer engineer has asked the authors to prepare a single

---

1   Some DASD are called *fixed-head* devices [e.g., IBM 2305 drum (all 72 tracks had dedicated heads) or the IBM 3350 with fixed-head feature (two cylinders had dedicated fixed heads]. The *fixed* refers to nonmovable heads positioned in one place over the platter. These are special cases and generally not in service anymore.

2   An exception is that a *dual copy volume*, in which data is written simultaneously to two actuators, appears as a single volume to the end user.

actuator for HDA replacement and forgot that two actuators were leaving the premises.

5. **Devices** contain one or more HDAs. This is the second D in DASD. In non-IBM architectures, this device is called a *disk* (or *disc*) *drive*. The box you purchase or lease may be a *3390 device* and may contain many actuators.

   Some authors, including IBM, refer to an actuator as a *device* and thus equate volume to device. The authors believe doing so is confusing. Throughout this book we will call the addressable part of a DASD an *actuator* and the box on casters that is rolled into and out of computer rooms a *device*.

6. **Strings** are one or more devices that are connected together. The devices on the string are assigned sequential device addresses. The number of devices and, therefore, the number of actuators are dependent on the DASD type.

7. **Heads of string (HOS)** can store data just like the other devices on the string. The HOS is the first device on a DASD string and has extra electronics to interact with the controllers and control which devices are active on which controller paths.

2.1. Platters, Heads, and Arms

The first D in DASD implies that data may be accessed in somewhat small quantities and at any point on the magnetic medium. The components that position, read, and write the data are collectively called an *actuator*.

Almost all reads or writes to DASD transfer one or more complete physical blocks to or from a spinning platter. An executing application program may access records, but the access method it uses actually reads and writes entire blocks. In this chapter, you may assume that accesses are in terms of blocks.

The DASD architecture does not limit access to whole blocks transferred to and from spinning platters, but this characterizes

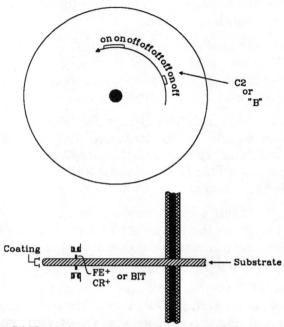

Figure 2.1 Platters. DASD that have rotating media contain one or more platters on a central spindle. The platter is usually a very light substrate material (e.g., aluminum) with a magnetic coating. Magnetic bits are energized or turned on to indicate *one* or turned off to indicate *zero*. The platter surface above shows a binary 1100 0010 (hexadecimal C2 or the letter *B*).

the vast majority of I/O accesses on a processor complex. Solid-state devices (SSD) move data to and from semiconductor memory stored outside the processor complex. No "spinning platter" exists inside an SSD.

Another type of transfer is read-by-relative byte access. If only a few bytes from a physical block are necessary, then the device can be directed to read without data transfer until a position within the block is reached, continue reading while transferring data, then ignore the rest of the block. One large full-text information retrieval system allows read-by-relative byte access to its files. Only the needed data is read from the DASD platter surface. This minimizes buffer sizes and partially reduces connect time for large blocks.

2.1.1. Platters

Data is stored on DASD on a circular platter. Some authors compare the DASD platter to phonograph records or compact discs, but the analogy is weak. A record has a single groove running in a spiral from the outer to the inner edge, whereas data is stored on a DASD platter in concentric rings called *tracks*. DASD, records, and CDs all store data, but the latter two spin at a much slower rate than the current mainframe DASD platters [3,600 to 4,260 revolutions per minute (RPM)].

Data is stored on the platter by magnetizing a minuscule region of the platter's surface coating. You can think of each bit as occupying one region that can be magnetized in one of two ways: *on* or *off*, *one* or *zero*.

This is not actually what happens, because magnetism is an analog physical phenomenon. Several recording methods are popular, with such names as Run Length Limited Code (RLLC) and Modified Frequency Modulation (MFM). These are attempts both to get around and to take advantage of the physical properties of the magnetic media and read-write heads. Thinking of the data as being stored serially (one bit at a time) is sufficient for our purposes, because once the data bits make their way into the digital electronics, they are indeed "on" or "off".

Data is recorded serially with 8 bits per byte. (Unlike in central storage, the parity bits that help ensure the integrity of the stored data are not on the track with the data bits, but are stored elsewhere on the platter.) Each track, from the outermost to the innermost, holds the same number of bytes; the number of bytes per track varies between DASD models. Data is recorded with a higher density, then, on the inner tracks (closer to the spindle) than on the outer ones.

In Figure 2.1, the letter B is recorded on the surface of the disk by turning on the first 2 bits, turning off 4 bits, then 1 bit on and

1 bit off. The result is a binary *1100 0010, C2* in hexadecimal. (EBCDIC specifies this value for the character *B*.)

The platter and shaft are shown on the bottom of Figure 2.1. A center post holds the platter (together with all the other platters, not shown). The substrate is a very thin coating on the surface made up of iron oxide (Fe^+) or chromium oxide (Cr^+) particles. The thickness of the substrate plays an important part in the engineering design of the DASD.

Platter diameter for the 3390 generation of DASD ranges from 9.5 inches to 10.5 inches, depending on the manufacturer. At this size the manufacturer can completely enclose (hermetically seal) the DASD components because the heat generated by the spinning platters can be controlled. Some personal computer platters are as small as 48 mm, or 1.8 inches.

2.1.2. Thin-Film Heads

As the platter rotates, the read-write head flies over the surface of the platter. It remains above the surface of the platter on a cushion of air created by the spinning platter. This is called the *Bernoulli effect*. The shape of the head is aerodynamic like that of an airplane wing, so it really is flying!

To put this distance into perspective, the head over the surface is like a Boeing 747 airplane flying 600 miles per hour inches above the runway. A human hair or the ridge of oil left by a fingerprint on the surface of a DASD platter is huge by comparison.

Figure 2.2 shows one of the architectural advancements to the DASD, the thin-film head. Each generation of DASD shrinks one or more components. (One can almost hear the engineers yelling, "Honey, I shrunk the heads.") Heads depend on physics to do their thing, and the physics of electromagnetic fields determines how wide a swath the head cuts.

In Figure 2.2, the head on the left is reading or writing a portion of a track that is 10 units wide. The head on the right is new and improved, requiring only 5 units to store and retrieve

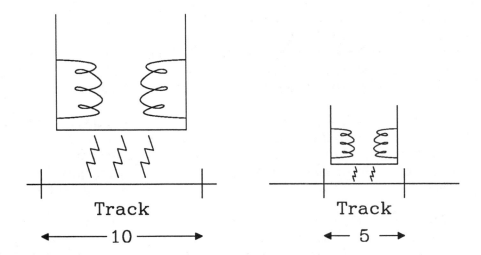

Figure 2.2 Thin-Film Heads. Improvements to a DASD head allow the head to fly closer to the surface and magnify/demagnify smaller tracks with smaller areas of interference. The above shows a 50% reduction in the area required to record data and thus doubles the capacity of the recording surface.

data on the surface of the platter. You can see that by using the heads on the right, you can double the number of tracks on the same surface of a DASD, and therefore double the amount of data stored on a single surface. The architecture on the right is referred to as *thin-film heads*.

The result is that many architectural upgrades to DASD exactly double the number of cylinders on a volume. Think of the last time you were stuck in traffic on a highway. If everyone drove cars that would fit in a 5-foot lane instead of a 10-foot lane, each of our crowded highways could handle twice as many cars because the lanes could be half the size.

2.1.3. Read-Write Arm

If a read-write head were in a fixed position over the surface of the platter, data could be accessed with the head only along a thin, circular stripe of the rotating platter, and the rest of the platter would be wasted. Fortunately, each head is mounted on an *arm* that extends and retracts, moving the head from one stripe (track) position to another. The term for this movement is *seeking*.

An *actuator* consists of a head and arm for each surface of the stacked platters and an electromechanical gizmo[3] that simultaneously moves all the heads to a spot the same distance from the center of their respective platters. Once positioned, only one read-write head at a time transfers data to or from its platter surface.

Different generations and models of DASD have different configurations of read-write heads. Figure 2.3 shows two hypothetical possibilities. On the left is an actuator with six arms; each arm holds two read-write heads, one for each side of a platter. The 10 user-accessible heads are labeled *0* through *9*.

Also shown is an extra head labeled *CE*. This is an abbreviation for *customer engineer*: special commands from the control unit use this head to perform diagnostics and surface analysis. It is not available for normal data storage, but it is essential for the use of the other heads. (We will see why shortly.) Some devices also have a separate servo head for track orientation to determine start of track.

The actuator on the right in Figure 2.3 has 15 user-accessible read-write heads and one CE read-write head. In this example, four read-write heads are on each actuator arm. One disadvantage of this architecture is that a wider platter is needed to provide two areas for the heads to operate. The advantage of two

---

3   Such as an electromagnetic voice coil closed loop servo. Glad you asked?

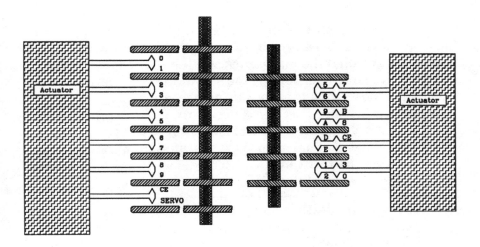

Figure 2.3 Read-Write Arms. Every DASD contains a slightly different configuration of read-write arms. This figure shows single read-write heads per arm (on the left) and double read-write heads per arm.

sets of heads (four on each arm) is that the number of platters is cut in half, a significant manufacturing advantage.

2.2. Addressing Data by Track

What are these heads doing? Data is recorded on concentric (i.e., separate), complete circles called *tracks*. The platter is spinning, and the data bits move under the read-write head. A logical *beginning of the track* is marked by an **index marker.**

2.2.1. Physical Track Geometry

The data track itself does not contain a physical index marker, but the position is sensed by the *CE* read-write head over a special track called the *servo track*. All the platters are attached at the center and thus spin at the same rate, so when the servo track says "now", this goes for all the heads.

In Figure 2.4, the first record read from the track after the index marker is assumed to be record zero, or the first record on the track. The end of one record is separated from the beginning of the next on the track by a gap. The device can sense, or read, records and gaps until it reaches the one it needs.

> ¤ The idea of waiting for the spinning platter to reach a particular record is a very important one in tuning DASD I/O operations. The wait is identified as a rotational position sensing wait. Be sure you understand this idea. Understanding and knowing how to eliminate this wait may be very valuable to you.

These gaps between records give the channel and control unit time to fetch the next CCW from central storage. For example, an efficient channel program may ask for two or more records to be read in the same operation. When the first record is finished, the channel and control unit must have time to fetch the next CCW (channel command word, or instruction) and do what is necessary to prepare for the second record.

The time (and thus the physical size of the gap) has remained relatively constant, because until the 3390s the number of rotations per minute (3,600) was constant. If the density (bits per inch) increases, the gap is the same physical size but contains many more bits because of the density increase.

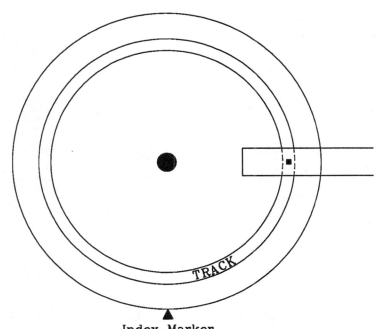

Index Marker

Figure 2.4 Tracks. Each surface of a DASD platter is logically divided into tracks. A track is a complete circle of area on the platter and is a certain width. Unlike a phonograph record, the read-write head does not follow a concentric circle, moving closer to the center as the platter spins. Instead, after the end of the track, the beginning of the track appears under the read-write head.

If the device spins faster (e.g., 3390 at 4,200 rpm), the gap is larger, and more data bits pass under the read-write head in the fixed time required for negotiation of the channel protocol.

> ¤   More data is lost to gaps as DASD becomes more dense and spins faster. The penalty for small block sizes increases.

2.2.2. Fixed-Block Architecture (FBA)

Two types of track formatting are in use. Fixed-block architecture (FBA) is used in a few IBM devices. Count-key-data (CKD)

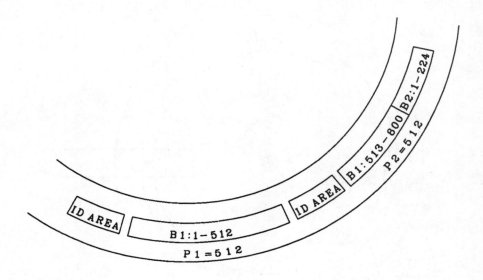

Figure 2.5 Fixed-Block Architecture. Fixed-block architecture predefines the physical block size of the records. In this example, 512 bytes are selected for the physical block size; the logical block size is selected as 800 bytes. The logical block spans multiple physical blocks. The first 512 bytes are on physical block *P1*. The other 288 bytes are in block *P2*.

architecture devices are by far the most prevalent. A DASD is built using one or the other. If the device is made to be formatted with fixed blocks, it cannot have CKD records.

Figure 2.5 shows a fixed-block architecture. Tracks are formatted at the time of manufacture. Each track contains several fixed-block records (the size of the track divided by the number of bytes in the fixed block). Each block has an *ID area* associated with it that contains the block number and the cylinder and head numbers. There is a gap between each block and ID area.

A block may become defective.[4] An indicator in the ID area shows that the block is defective. An alternate block is assigned

4   The term "defective" means that data cannot be written to or read from the spot on the platter that the block covers. Some defects cover more than one block and may even cover more than one track.

and contains data pointing to the defective block it replaces. Most FBA tracks contain extra blocks at the end of the track for these replacements. Most FBA devices also contain alternate cylinders to receive data from defective tracks.

Blocks on FBA DASD are located by using a relative block number. The DASD subsystem converts the block number to a track address and sector location on the track and begins transfer of data. An operating system can combine multiple blocks for transfer at once.

The example in Figure 2.5 shows a single 800-byte physical block being written onto a device that is formatted in 512-byte blocks. The device automatically fits the physical block written by the application into the blocks on the surface of the platter.

You should see one advantage of this architecture. The surface is formatted with the same size block. Once formatted, the surface does not need to change even though the application block size might change. In count-key-data format, if a file extends into a new track, the track must be erased to ensure that records are not used accidentally.

FBA devices were IBM's first attempt to free the end user from having to know the number of bytes each track would hold, the number of tracks per cylinder, and the number of cylinders per actuator. The dream was that the end user would only need to know the number of blocks each device could hold.

Unfortunately, the small physical block size—512 bytes—and the very large number of programs dependent on the count-key-data architecture doomed FBA devices on MVS systems. Applications on the small and midrange System/36, System/38, and AS/400 systems were rarely sensitive to DASD geometry, so FBA is successful there. The VM and VSE operating systems make good use of FBA devices because the FBA device is cost-effective for small installations. IBM eventually began to use FBA devices to hold microcode on their large processor complexes. IBM could provide the devices to their microcoders even if they could not convince the rest of the data processing industry to use the devices.

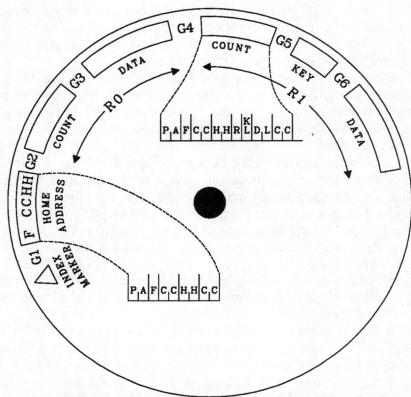

Figure 2.6 Count-Key-Data (CKD). Records on a count-key-data architecture device require three distinct areas for each physical block. An 8-byte count area describes the following block and an optional *key*. If the file structure has a key separate from the physical block, that key identifies the contents of the block. Finally, the data portion contains one physical block.

2.2.3. Count-Key-Data (CKD) Architecture

Count-key-data devices are by far the most prevalent DASD type. As in FBA devices, a data block is stored on the surface of the platter by the application or the operating system. As in the

FBA device, the beginning of the track is located by an imaginary index marker.

Home Address

The home address follows the beginning of the track. (See Figure 2.6.) It contains the following parts:

1. Physical address (PA) is a 2-byte field used by the control unit to ensure that the read-write heads are positioned correctly.

2. Flag (F) is a 1-byte field that contains bits to show whether the track is usable or defective, and whether the track is a primary track or one of the alternates available for assignment. The value 1 shows the track is usable; 2 indicates the track is unusable; and the address in the count area of R0 is the address of the alternate track.

3. The track identifier (CCHH) has:
   a. The 2-byte cylinder address (CC).
   b. The 2-byte track address (HH).

4. The cyclic check (the second CC) is a 2-byte field used for error detection and correction.

The home address is written at the factory and only by authorized programs, such as ICKDSF when one or more tracks need to be reformatted. Special channel commands are required to access the home address.

Two names are interchangeable in describing the area under a read-write head: head and track. There is a one-to-one relationship because each read-write head is positioned over a single track at any point in time. The architects of CKD could have minimized confusion by calling the address CCTT for cylinders and tracks. You, however, will not be confused!

R0 Track Descriptor Record

The first count-key-data record is identified as record zero. IBM usually starts numbering items starting with zero, because zero is a number (all bits turned off) and should not be wasted. Only mere mortals think everything starts with the number 1.

There may be a more serious reason for record zero. The protocol for formatting write operations states that the channel program must first successfully search to the count field of a previous record (n − 1). Since the IBM track format standards call for an R0 on every track, we can safely search to R0 and format-write record 1.

R0 Count Record

The first record on a track is record zero. If the device is formatted with IBM standards, R0 has fixed, special formats. Every record has a count area. Every count area is the same size. The count area is a 13-byte record, as shown in Figure 2.6:

1. Physical address (PA): a 2-byte field containing the physical address of the track. It is the same as in the home address.

2. Flag (F): a 1-byte flag field, the same as in the home address; it may also contain some data stored by the control unit.

3. The track identifier contains:
   a. A 2-byte cylinder number (CC) of this track or an assigned alternate.
   b. A 2-byte head or track number (HH).
   c. A 1-byte record number (R). Zeros here gives us a clue as to why this is called *record zero*.

4. A 1-byte key length (KL) of the external physical key. For R0, this value is zero: there is no key associated with a standard R0. The hardware will allow you to put a key on R0 if you really want to. The track may not be readable by other utility programs.

5. A 2-byte data length (DL) of the following data record. For standard R0, the data area is always 8 bytes long, so this value is X'08'.

6. A 2-byte cyclic check area used for error detection and correction.

The repetition of the track address (CCHHR) in these records is the basis for saying that CKD is a *self-describing* architecture. The electronics can always tell where the arm is positioned by reading the home address and comparing where the arm is with where it should be.

The CCHHR of the remaining records on a track can be anything, and it seems the hardware does not know or care. The CCHHR of R0 can also be anything unless the home address flag byte says the track is defective.

R0 Key Area

The physically separate key area does not exist for standard IBM record zero formats.

R0 Data Area

The data area of a standard R0 is 8 bytes of zeros.

Record 1

Now look at record 1 (R1) in Figure 2.6. Each physical block written to CKD devices can be two or three areas of data on the surface, separated by gaps.

The first area is called a *count area* because it contains the key length and data length of the following record. If standard access methods are used, the count area for all user records on a track is formatted the same as for R0, except that it contains no defective track data.

Gaps are areas where no data is stored between records. They are approximately the size needed for the electronics to complete

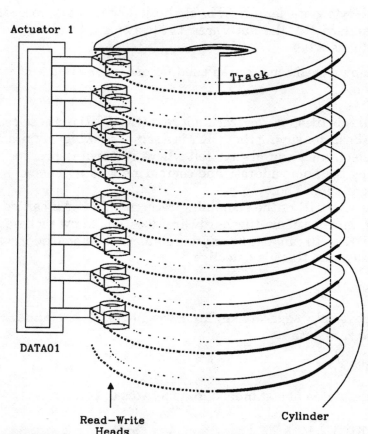

Figure 2.7 Cylinders. A cylinder is all the tracks that can be accessed by having the actuator read-write heads in one place. How did the industry decide on that name? A geometric cylinder is a thin-walled tube open at either end. If viewed from one end, a cylinder is a perfect circle. If you place all the read-write heads in one position, then each is traveling in a circle just over the platter. Now envision all the heads riding next to the surface of a cylinder.

work with one block and get ready for the next block. The size varies depending on device type, record type, and length, but is about the size that would be taken by 500 to 700 bytes, or about 150 to 200 microseconds of spin time.

The key area is an optional area that is rarely used by application programmers because it is difficult to use, but it is still in use in many system-oriented data set architectures. The most common are VTOCs on volumes (44-byte key) and partitioned data sets that have an 8-byte external key indicating the highest member name in the associated data block.

If the key area exists for a data set, the data set is said to be *formatted with keys*. Keyed data sets can be searched by creating channel commands to logically (equal, greater than, less than, etc.) search the values in this keyed area for specific values.

Do not confuse this with keys supported by access methods such as the Virtual Storage Access Method (VSAM); these keys are part of the data record, and a method other than the DASD key support is used to locate them. VSAM stores keys embedded in the data and in another part of the file, the index, which contains the key and a pointer to the physical record.

> ¤   Stop here and be sure you understand the idea of gaps. Understanding and using this information could make your job of understanding DASD very profitable. If a gap is 512 bytes long and the physical record size of your data is 512 bytes long, what does that tell you about the amount of the track that is wasted by short block sizes? It would be about 50% wasted. What if the blocks were only 80 bytes long? Each data center should look at data sets and ensure that no physical block sizes are less than some reasonable minimum (e.g., 4,096 bytes).

2.3. Addressing Data by Cylinder

The term *cylinder* denotes all the data that can be accessed with the arms extended, and thus the read-write heads positioned, at one particular spot over the platter. The application can read or write any of the data covered by the cylinder without moving the arms. Moving the arm (seeking), a physical process, requires much more time than switching heads, an electronic one.

In Figure 2.7, there are 9 platters with 16 read-write heads. The top and bottom surfaces are not used. The heads are labeled head zero through 14 (3380 or 3390 architecture). The heads are positioned over an application data set that has two consecutive cylinders allocated to the data set.

Suppose there are 10 records per track in this data set. The application could read records 1 through 10 without experiencing any delay to move the arm (the records are all on track zero).[5]

The application could read records 11 through 20 without head movement (the records are on track 1). This could continue until record 151 was needed (10 records per track times 15 tracks per cylinder). The arm would then have to move (seek) to the next cylinder.

¤ Be sure you understand the idea of seeking. The example given is the simplest one possible. What would happen if the second cylinder were in a second extent at the other end of the volume? The seek time would be considerably longer, as the arm would have to move a much longer distance. You should ensure that important, heavily accessed data sets have close *locality of reference*. The least amount of time is wasted if the cylinders are next to each other.

2.4. Alternates, Spares, and Other Back Pockets

DASD manufacturers provide alternate tracks so end users can be assured that they can access data from cylinder zero track

---

5   If the device is shared with another processor complex or if other data sets are open on the device from this processor complex, the head could be at another location when the application returns to its data set.

zero through the highest cylinder/track in the architecture. Bad tracks are mapped to alternates, and the DASD transparently accesses the alternates. The end user formats the volume by running a utility program (ICKDSF) that writes a volume table of contents (VTOC) on the volume. The VTOC describes the space available and used. The VTOC architecture does not have provision for marking certain tracks as never available for allocation.

Physically, things are a bit different. The following tables give the primary, alternate, diagnostic, and device support tracks for the most recent IBM DASD. These addresses denote the physical track positions on the platter, which are not necessarily the same as the coordinates supplied by the user.

3380 Characteristics			
Type of track	**3380 A, D, & J**	**3380 E**	**3380 K**
Primary tracks Low/high	00000000 0374000E	00000000 06E9000E	00000000 0A5E000E
Alternate tracks Low/high	03750000 0375000E	06EA0000 06EA000E	0A5F0000 0A5F000E
Diagnostic tracks Low/high	03760000 0376000E	06EB0000 06EB000E	0A620000 0A62000E
Device support Low/high	FFFD0000 FFFD000E	06F40000 06E5000E	0A6B0000 0A6D000E

3390 Characteristics			
Type of track	**3390-01**	**3390-02**	**3390-03**
Primary tracks Low/high	00000000 0458000E	00000000 08B1000E	00000000 0D0A000E
Alternate tracks Low/high	04590000 0459000E	08B20000 08B2000E	0D0B0000 0D0B000E
Diagnostic tracks Low/high	045B0000 045B000E	08B40000 08B4000E	0D0D0000 0D0D000E
Device support Low/high	04810000 0482000E	08D90000 08DA000E	0D190000 0D1A000E

Figure 2.8 shows the 3390 architecture for single-density volumes. The user cylinders (zero through 1112) can be used until

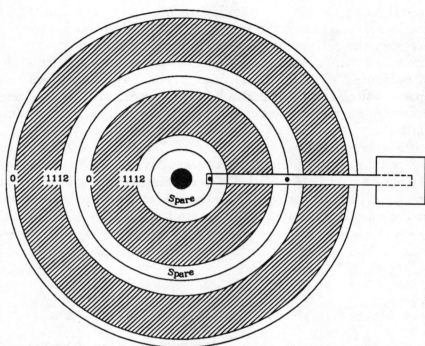

Figure 2.8 Spare Cylinders. Almost all types of DASD have one or more cylinders designated for the testing and recovery of data. These *spare* cylinders cannot be directly accessed by unauthorized programs—but are placed into use by testing programs (e.g., ICKDSF) or recovery programs (e.g., ICKDSF assigning alternate cylinders).

one of the tracks becomes unusable. If, for example, cylinder 1, head 4 becomes unusable, it is replaced by the first alternate track, CCHH 04590000, cylinder 1,113 head zero.

The following table shows the primary and alternate track contents. The home address of each points to itself. The R0 count area of the primary track points to the alternate track, and the R0 count area of the alternate track points to the bad primary track.

Type of track	Home address (FCCHH)	R0 count area	R0 data area
Primary track	02 00010004	04590000 00000008	00000000 00000000

Type of track	Home address (FCCHH)	R0 count area	R0 data area
Alternate track	01 04590000	00010004 00000008	00000000 00000000

2.5. Actuators a.k.a. Volumes

The combination of the read-write heads, the arms and their movable platform, the surface of the platter, and the electronics that glue these together is called an *actuator*. Most operating systems use the term *volume* for the DASD cylinders accessible by that electromechanical combination, so the two terms usually are synonymous.

In Figure 2.9 you see a single set of platters that contains two "actuators". Both are sealed inside the same *Head Disk Assembly (HDA)*.

> ◻ When one set of platters contains two actuators, recovery can be painful. An error on one requiring its replacement **forces your data center to dump and restore both!** Most IBM-compatible manufacturers (e.g., Hitachi and Amdahl) house only one actuator per HDA and thus can claim easier recovery than IBM.

2.6. Devices

A *device* is what you buy from IBM or one of the IBM-compatible manufacturers. A device contains two or more HDAs. Figure 2.10 shows a typical 3380 or·3390 device with two HDAs, each HDA having two actuators. Thus, there are four actuators or four volume serials associated with this device.

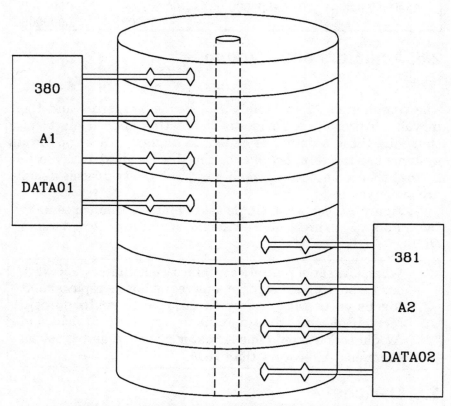

Figure 2.9 Actuators, Volumes, or Units. Each spinning set of platters can have one or more sets of read-write heads or actuators. IBM also uses the term *volume* or *unit* to describe the actuator. Most IBM architectures have two actuators per HDA that are assigned even-odd ID numbers. In this case, one set of spinning platters has two actuators identified as *380* and *381*. The most important thing to note is that the two share a common disk surface. If anything happens to the disk surface, then **both actuators are affected.** Both actuators have common electronics (e.g., drive power) and separate electronics (for actuator movement and head selection). Some electronic errors cause problems with both actuators; some cause problems with only one actuator.

Circuits

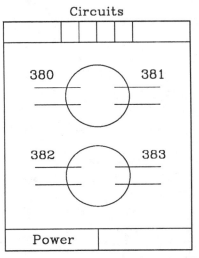

Figure 2.10 Devices. What you order from IBM or another vendor is a device. Some devices are fully *populated* (e.g., 3380-type devices—you always get two HDAs and four actuators). Some devices can be ordered with less than maximum actuators (e.g., 3390 devices).

¤ It is helpful to have a schematic drawing of your computer room and the DASD interconnections. Usually there are several views or layers you might want to draw: logical connection (what devices are connected to what control units and channels), physical connection (where they are on the floor), and one with all pertinent information about the device (volume serial, channel paths, serial number, lessor, lease end date or depreciation end date, logical control unit, and physical control unit. If you use a Computer-Aided Drawing (CAD) program, such as AutoCAD, you are more likely to keep your schematic up to date.

2.7. Timing Considerations

You will learn more about channels in a later chapter, but a basic definition of a channel is one or more CPUs that step through a list of 8-byte *channel command words* (CCW). This list is called a *channel program*. Each CCW has a command code together with other data. The CCW is passed to the specified control unit. The control unit interprets and converts the CCW to electronic commands for the devices attached to the control unit.

Most programmers and analysts (and even systems programmers) do not get to see channel programs. CCWs are usually built by the application's access method. Nevertheless, it is vital to understand this flow from application program to access method to device.

The best software monitors (e.g., Landmark's TMON/MVS) show interactively the CCWs that are being used against devices. The following discussion centers on a typical channel program that might be built for an application programmer. The basics of the channel program are a series of CCWs:

1. **SEEK**. Moves the head to a specific cylinder. The SEEK command is generally created by the operating system.

2. **SET FILE MASK**. Sets the rules of the channel program to follow. Among other things, *SET FILE MASK* restricts the range of data that can be accessed by the rest of the channel program. The *SET FILE MASK* command is generally created by the operating system.

3. **SET SECTOR**. Tells the device which sector of the platter contains the record.

4. **SEARCH ID EQUAL**. Tells the device which record to look for.

5. **TIC**. *TRANSFER IN CHANNEL*, or loop until the record is found. Unlike other CCWs, TIC is not passed from the channel to the control unit. The TIC is a conditional branch in the

channel program and forces the channel to return to the previous CCW (i.e., the channel loops) until the conditions for the previous CCW are met. For example, if a *SEARCH ID EQUAL* command was just previous to the TIC, the channel would keep returning to the *SEARCH ID EQUAL* until an equal condition or an error condition is detected. When a matching condition arises, the TIC is bypassed, and the next CCW just after the TIC is executed.

6. **READ or WRITE data**. Transfers the requested block to or from central storage.

□ *Device End* indicates the end of the channel program and is a signal to the operating system that the application that requested the I/O operation can now be dispatched for further work. The input or output should be accomplished. (The I/O could be successful or have an error, but it is finished.)

2.7.1. Decomposition of I/O Response Time

The elapsed time an I/O request requires to complete is called the I/O response time. This is measured from the time a program requests a physical block of data (usually done through the access method) until the time data is in storage and made available to the application.

This section examines an example of a regular or *nonextended count-key-data* channel program. Extended count-key-data (ECKD) channel programs are covered later.

The time a nonextended count-key-data channel command string takes to complete can be summarized in the following steps:

1. **CPU queue**. An application or system program asks for an I/O command chain to be started against an actuator. The actuator is busy with another request on the same system, so the request is placed on a queue waiting for the actuator to finish whatever it is doing. This is sometimes called *Wait for Device* or *Unit Control Block (UCB)* queuing. The operating system resource for the device is the UCB. Queued requests are awaiting their turn to control the UCB.

Most operating systems allow the I/O requests to be queued based on the priority of the requesting task. If this is done properly, online interactive subsystem I/O requests will be started ahead of batch job I/O requests.

CPU queueing is where you and your friends step on each other. Although queue wait times are a tuning topic and not necessarily a DASD one, it is important to note that I/O operations may show terrific response times from the device perspective, because the device may be servicing the queue quite well, while exhibiting unacceptable response times from the application perspective, because the queue is too long.

◻   Even with I/O queuing, a batch job can interfere with higher-priority tasks. Batch I/O requests are usually of much longer duration because properly tuned batch requests ask for large amounts of data. Once started, any batch job locks out even the highest-priority job (even MVS itself) until the I/O completes.

---

2. **Path busy**. The UCB is now free, but the channel/control unit path to the device is busy. The channel may be busy with a request from another task to another device within this processor complex, or the control unit may be likewise busy, or the control unit may be busy working on a task from another processor complex.

3. **Device busy**. The device may be busy processing a request from another processor complex.

4. **CCW fetch**. Once the equipment in the path is no longer busy, the CCWs are fetched from central storage, and channel program execution begins.

5. **SEEK**. The SEEK CCW command is executed. The device is selected, but the actuator read-write arm is positioned at the wrong cylinder. The device disconnects from the channel and the arm begins to move to the correct cylinder.

¤ All DASD I/O operations must begin with a SEEK CCW. That was not always true. You used to be able to get away without a SEEK, but the 3880 and 3990 control unit microcode has new features that will likely make your channel program fail if a SEEK is not in it.

---

6. **Select head**. Part of the seek operation is to set the electronics to select the specified head for the data transfer.

7. **Latency**. The SET SECTOR CCW is processed. The head is selected, and the channel directs the device to search for a specific sector of the platter to prepare for the data transfer. The device disconnects from the channel so others can use the channel while the platter is spinning.

8. **RPS reconnect**. The device, head of string, and control unit make connection again to the channel.

9. **RPS miss**. The device, head of string, and control unit fail to make connection (one or more were busy doing something else), and the device must wait until the platters make another complete revolution before retrying the reconnect.

10. **SEARCH**. The SEARCH CCW is processed. The device is told to search for a specific record and go on to the next command when the search is successful.

11. **Transfer data**. The READ or WRITE CCW is processed. This step is what the end user really wants—data transfer.

This step also takes the least time! For a 4,096-byte block on a 3.0 million byte per second (2.86 MB/s)[6] channel, it takes approximately 1.36 milliseconds for data transfer, yet performance tuning experts are happy when an average I/O takes 20 to 40 ms.

12. **Channel protocol.** The channel must complete processing and free up the resources used for the input/output operation. This time is often ignored in calculations, but as the times get shorter (due to caching operations), this time will become a larger percent of the service time.

The time each of the above steps requires differs by orders of magnitude. For example, the CCW fetch in Step 4 above takes far less than the 16 milliseconds it takes for an RPS miss in Step 9. We will now look at the portions that are in the DASD subsystem.

2.7.2. MBBCCHHR

MBBCCHHR[7] is an 8-byte field used to *address* a record. Back in the early 1960s, the hardware developers designed an architecture for Direct Access Storage Devices. They tried to devise a record access scheme that would work for all possible devices. Today, we know about and use the cylinders, heads, and records from their architecture, but the full design has room for a device we don't see much anymore: the data cell. The fields of MBBCCHHR are:

1. **M** is the extent number. *M* is used by the software as the relative number of the Data Extent Block (DEB) extent. *BBCCHHR* below is used by both hardware and software.

---

6   DASD vendors usually use the prefix *mega* to mean 1,000,000, but this is misleading because other data storage measures use *mega* to mean 1,048,576. Note that the data transfer time is calculated with the proper units.

7   "MBBCCHHR" may be pronounced "mumble chirr".

2. **BB** is the bin number. A long time ago in a faraway place there existed a DASD called a data cell, also called the *noodle picker*. It had 10 bins of 2-inch by 12-inch magnetic tape. Part of the SEEK command was to select this bin, so the first 2 bytes (and yes, you could reference a hypothetical data cell of 65,536 bins) identified the bin. Today, this is represented by the two hexadecimal zeros in the front of a seek address.

"DASD" does not necessarily imply spinning platters. A solid-state Device (SSD) is a DASD with no moving parts!

3. **CC** is the cylinder address for the data.

4. **HH** is the read-write head to select. This would allow a theoretical device with 32,768 (or 65,536, if one used the high-order bit) heads. That would really be a device to see!

5. **R** is the record to select. The record is not part of the seek address but is conveniently located for the SEARCH ID command that requires the record number.

2.7.3. CCW Fetch

We now turn to the portion of device response time that is not delay but hardware performing work. The first is CCW fetch.

The channel must retrieve each 8-byte channel command word to decode the command and take the appropriate action. The control unit uses a smart approach to minimize this delay. For example, some control units read both the SEEK and SET SECTOR commands, and then handle all the arm movement and delay at the control unit level without returning to the processor complex's central storage between them. Extended count-key-data commands also give the control unit advance knowledge of what the channel commands will ask for.

CCW fetch takes a very short time to accomplish, and many response time calculations omit it. The channel must be connected in order to fetch anything from central storage. The time

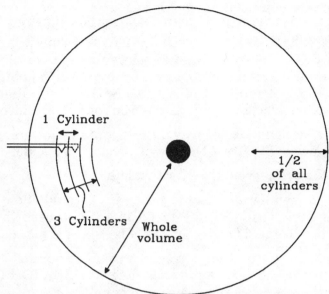

Figure 2.11 SEEK: Move the Arm. The actuator is said to be seeking when the read-write arm assembly moves from cylinder to cylinder. Seeking the whole volume means that the arm moves from the outermost (cylinder zero) to the innermost (cylinder 1,112 for 3390 single density). Most performance comparisons are for how long it takes the actuator to move a half volume, for 1-cylinder movement, and for 3-cylinder movements.

is important but usually small enough not to affect our calculations. (We tend to waste big time elsewhere.)

The first three generations of DASD connected to get the SEEK command, disconnected, connected to get the SET SECTOR CCW, and disconnected again almost immediately to wait for the sector to appear. The latest generation of IBM DASD tries to do this with one access to central storage.

2.7.4. SEEK—Move Arm

Figure 2.11 shows a sample DASD platter. The SEEK portion of an I/O could require that the arm be moved just a few cylinders or the entire radius of the platter (the whole volume). The amount of movement depends on what the operating system is doing on the volume. On a very active TSO or VM DASD, the arm could randomly move from one end of the volume to another. On a volume that contains a very large data base, it could be random during the day and tend to be sequential at night as the data base is rebuilt or backed up.

On some volumes the heads rarely move by program control. We saw a JES2 checkpoint volume that actually wore a hole in the platter because it rarely moved more than cylinder zero to 5. (Well, not quite a hole, or the edge of the platter would have dropped off.) The 5-cylinder checkpoint data set was allocated, formatted, and stayed in use for years.

Some of you may be asking, "Why does a 5-cylinder data set consume a whole 3380 volume?" The checkpoint was the only data set on the volume because the activity of I/Os from JES to the volume exceeded the number a single volume could supply. Additionally, JES2 locks the volume (with RESERVE) so other systems are locked out of the volume for long periods of time.

> ◘ BJ's Rule: If the DASD is working properly, don't try to fix it unless the return on investment makes the effort worthwhile. In this case, many would not want to disrupt the JES2 checkpoint to move the head. If it keeps your JES from crashing, it may be worth it.

The above rule did get one data center in trouble when they had a few of these never-move-much volumes, and someone came in to test all the volumes. The heads tried to move to the device support tracks and crashed with great fanfare! The heads had, you see, worn a grove in the surface. (You might say the BJ rule is groovy.)

IBM has added microcode in their hardware to move the arm randomly over the entire surface at various times. This action spreads the lubricant and moves the heads across the surface to keep everything working nicely. The result is that IBM no longer guarantees that the head will be where the last channel program left it; hence the requirement for a SEEK command in every channel program.

In Figure 2.11, you see the most common seek time considerations. Some calculations consider that on average, the arm will move one-third the cylinders. More recent data says that arms typically move only a few cylinders. IBM now quotes the time for one- and three-cylinder moves. Hitachi even adds another read-write head to make a one-cylinder move take no seek time!

Seek times are sometimes a significant portion of device response time. Seek time is really a function of how the data is being accessed on the actuator.

> ¤   A general rule is that if there are many data sets in use
> by a large number of requesters, more SEEKs result. The
> minimum seek time is in the range of 0–3 ms. Moving the
> head across half the volume takes about 9 ms, and across
> the whole volume about 16 ms.

What do you suppose the random seeking performed by the control unit to exercise the read-write heads does to seek time? The authors have not found documentation on the interval of this random seeking. It may change from release to release of the control unit microcode.

Another point should be considered concerning DASD response time. Think about a program reading a sequential file. Assume that the file has two cylinders of data on a 3390 device. As the program reads the file, it goes from cylinder 10, head 0 to cylinder 10, head 14. In this case, assume the data set was allocated a cylinder at a time and the second cylinder was not adjacent to the first. *A SEEK is required to get the next record.* If the next cylinder is adjacent to the first cylinder, then a minimum SEEK is required between records. If the next cylinder is somewhere else on the volume (or on another volume in a multi-volume data set), then the I/O access time between these two requests will be vastly different. Some non-IBM devices (e.g., Hitachi 7390 emulation of the IBM 3390 devices) have two heads for each track. Seek time for a one-cylinder seek would be zero in that case.

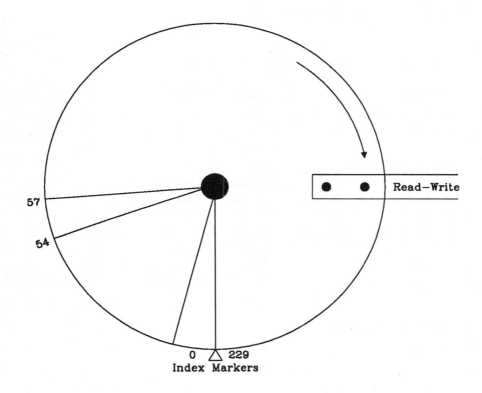

Figure 2.12 Rotate: Set Sector. The platter is logically divided into a fixed number of *sectors*. The *index marker* is a logical spot on all the platters which is the start of the track. This example shows the 229 sectors for a 3390 device.

One final controversy over seek time exists with the combination of multiple volumes onto one actuator. If you have two actuators and combine them onto one dual- or triple-capacity volume, are you increasing the time for the seek component of DASD response time? The answer is probably yes. Does it matter? Only your analysis and monitoring will tell. You will see more about this topic when we get to the tuning discussion.

2.7.5. Rotational Latency

The next time frame for an I/O operation is the wait for the head
to be positioned at the proper position for reading or writing. The
SET SECTOR channel command tells the device on which sector
of the track the requested record starts. This architecture has
been around since the second generation of DASD (first available
on the 3330 devices) and works well but can be deadly to I/O
operations.

If you think about it for a bit, you will realize that a good
estimate of latency is one-half a rotation. In Figure 2.12, the arm
is about three-quarters of the way to the last sector on a 3390
device. If the requested record started in sector 57, the device
would attempt to reconnect at about sector 54. The latency would
be one-half a track. For random I/O requests, the head would be
positioned at a random point on the track in relationship to the
location of the next record.

2.7.6. RPS Reconnect

When the read-write head reaches a few sectors before the requested sector (*Rotational Position Sensing*), the device attempts
to reconnect to the head of string and channel. This time could
be considered part of the latency because they overlap. The
difference is that the *device is busy while it is trying to reconnect*.
You might think the reconnect time is not important, but it is a
point of conflict for the electronics to overcome.

2.7.7. RPS Miss

From the performance perspective, an *RPS miss* is the deadly
event that occurs when the spinning platter reaches the position
indicated by the SET SECTOR command, but one or more of the

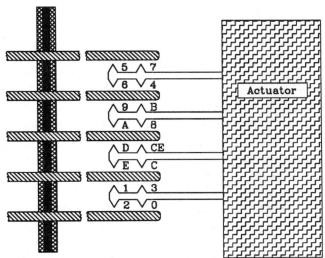

Figure 2.13 Head Selection. After the cylinder is selected and the head moved to the proper place on the platter, the electronics selects the proper head for the actual read or write. In this example, the program has read all the data on track zero and now reads the data from track 1. The device may be able to service the request in the time after the last record is read off track zero and before the first record of track 1 is encountered.

head of string, control unit, or channel are not available to reconnect and continue I/O processing. If they cannot synchronize in time, the desired sector rotates out of range, and the I/O is delayed until the sector rotates near the heads once again.

In Figure 2.12, if the RPS reconnect was started in sector 54 but didn't connect until after sector 57 was passed, the device would have to wait until sector 54 passed under the read-write head again, or almost one complete revolution later. An RPS miss always adds the length of time the platter requires to make approximately one complete rotation. The duration is 12–16 milliseconds for 3380s or 9.5 or 12.5 milliseconds for 3390s.

A single RPS miss is bad enough, but this can happen time after time. It can deteriorate to the point that a single I/O requires *several seconds* to complete. We agree this is unlikely for most of you, but what if it does happen to your data set?

2.7.8. SEARCH ID

After successful reconnection, the next group of channel commands in a standard channel program are usually "search" commands to inform the device to wait until the platter has rotated so that the needed record is at the read-write heads. The device initiates the reconnect when the platter has rotated near, not at, the desired position. The time is usually about 0.2 ms, about the time it takes three sectors to pass under the heads.

Searches may be multitrack. The device searches from track to track until a search is successfully completed or an error condition is found (e.g., no record found). These data searches are very expensive to the channel architecture not because the device is busy for the entire duration of the search but because the channel is, too. For example, the VTOC and partitioned data set (PDS) directories are searched this way. Overuse or misuse of multitrack searches can induce RPS miss for other devices that use common components in the path as the multitrack search hogs the connection.

2.7.9. Select Head

The channel transfers the *HH* part of the search ID address in the channel command. The 2-byte binary number is the head number to be selected. Recalling your binary arithmetic, 2 bytes can contain numbers from 0 through 65,535. The designers of this architecture seem to have had great hopes for the number of heads on an actuator. Most data centers do not have that many read-write heads in all the devices on the floor. Some cities do not have that many mainframe read-write heads!

In Figure 2.13, assume the device has finished reading all the records on track zero and receives a READ command for records on track 1. The actuator heads do not move. The actuator just selects head 1 to perform reads and writes. The select-head processing causes very little delay. Selection is performed inside

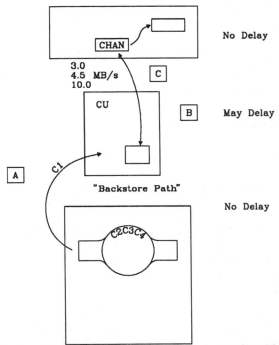

Figure 2.14 Data Transfer to the Control Unit. As data is transferred from the platter, it must be moved directly to the control unit. There can be no delay between the time data is being read off the track and the time it gets to the storage in the control unit. With cached control units (e.g., 3990 model 3), the data may stay a while in the control unit before it gets transferred to the channel and storage in the processor complex.

the head of string and device, and by definition the device is logically connected and ready to go. The duration is less than 0.1 ms and is discounted in many response time calculations, but keep it in mind.

2.7.10. Data Transfer to Control Unit

After all this work, we are finally ready to transfer data. In Figure 2.14, we see a record consisting of the letters *ABCD* (shown in its EBCDIC equivalent in hexadecimal—*C1C2C3C4*).

At *A*, in Figure 2.14, the data is moving from the device to the control unit. The control unit to device is called the *backstore path*.

The control unit may pass each byte of data to the channel (noncached) or it may store the data in the control unit until the channel can accept the data (cached).

2.7.11. Path Considerations

Cache: Store and Forward

Two types of caching exist. The first was a special type called speed matching buffers. The second type is the cache we know today in the 3990 model 3 or non-IBM control units.

Speed matching buffers were introduced with the 3380 DASD. A problem existed. The 3380 transferred data at a maximum of 3.0 million bytes per second (2.86 MB/s). IBM had introduced the 308x family of processor complexes that supported this rate, but all the rest of the IBM line was limited to 1.5 million bytes per second (1.43 MB/s). When the 3380 started to read a block of data, the device had to transfer each byte at 3.0 million bytes per second. It was like the children's game of hide and seek: Ready or not, here I come!

The control unit engineers devised a new set of rules. The channel program would say what it was going to do before it got started. The control unit would make room inside the control unit and transfer data at 1.5 million bytes per second (1.43 MB/s) to and from the processor complex. It would transfer at 3.0 million bytes per second (2.86 MB/s) to and from the 3380 DASD.

Speed matching buffer control unit operation was the first of the nonsynchronous control units. The idea caught on. IBM started building the microcode in the control unit to *automatically* do the store-and-forward data requested by channel programs even if the channel and device were transferring at the same data rate. Control unit cache became a reality.

One wonders why the microcode did not read the entire channel program from central storage, then decide the complete request boundaries to optimize the I/O process.

Path Contention

As you can see at in Figure 2.14, there remains the possibility that the control unit cannot get the data into the processor complex. All 308x processor complexes only access data at 3.0 million bytes per second (unless a special feature is added to allow 4.5 million bytes per second transfer). 309x processor complexes allow 3.0 and 4.5 million byte transfer rates. ESCON channels started with a transfer rate of 10 million bytes per second (9.54 MB/s), but the ESCON architecture allows over 100 million bytes per second, so speed matching and caching will be important for some time.

Channel Contention

Another delay is channel contention. Most 308x, 309x, and ES/9000 processor complexes, operating with MVS/XA and MVS/ESA, have the channels rather than the operating system controlling the channel delays. Channel delays still occur but are masked inside the channel.

Central Storage Contention

Central storage contention was a problem in some of the early, smaller processor complexes. In these, channel access to central storage required CPU cycles to transfer data (called *cycle stealing*). These channels are sometimes referred to as *inboard channels*.

The 308x, 309x, and ES/9000 processor complexes no longer require CPU time because they have their own processors. They are still physically located inside the Processor Complex, so they

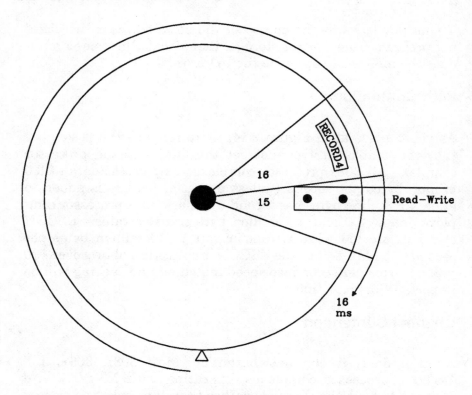

Figure 2.15 How to Lose Wait: RPS. One of the longest time delays in DASD I/O accesses is the Rotational Position Sensing wait. In this figure, the record wanted—record 4—is requested just after the read-write head passes it. The device must wait a full rotation to try to read the record again. For almost all devices, the time is 14–17 milliseconds—an eternity for I/O processing. Most of the hardware and software I/O tuning is designed to help DASD go on a diet and lose wait.

operate like the *outboard channels* of the 168 family of processors.

The overlap problems are still there, but time is no longer taken away from operating system tasks to transfer data through a channel.

2.8. How to Lose Wait: Rotational Position Sensing

Of all the parts of I/O response time, Rotational Position Sensing miss is the worst. You cannot really speed up the channel, or the rotation of the device, or the microcode. You can, however, control RPS miss. As Ed Sullivan would say, this is the "really biggg show." If the device cannot reconnect, the entire I/O operation is delayed about another 16 milliseconds while the device waits for the platter to spin around again. Put another way, **one RPS miss is twelve times the data transfer time for a 4-Kb block!**

□ Busy volumes and strings cause RPS miss to devastate I/O response times. It only takes a few RPS misses to make I/O access times top the 100-ms mark. Put another way, those I/O accesses require one-tenth of a second. Ten take one second. If your CICS subsystem requires ten I/Os per transaction, then the minimum response time is one second if the transaction does no other work! Do you have poor response time? Guess where to look first!

2.8.1. Actuator-Level Caching

Hardware can help you in *losing wait*. Cache controllers buffer up blocks to help eliminate the device as a major delay component. Some non-IBM manufacturers (e.g., Hitachi 7390 "actuator-level caching") have cache buffers in the actuator. The 7390 always has sector-ready indicated. IBM has this in their non-synchronous ESCON-capable 3990.

Hardware assists are designed to read blocks on a track even if not asked by the application code. To avoid the problem in Figure 2.15 where record 4 is missed, the hardware tries to anticipate when record 4 is wanted. For example, when record 1 on the track was read, the hardware could read all the records on the track. If record 3 was requested, the hardware could read the rest of the track in anticipation of records 4–n being requested.

2.8.2. Buffering

Software can help you in *losing wait*. The simplest is just buffering your I/O accesses. Many years ago a great UPI photographer told me any camera had a zoom lens. You just held onto the camera and zoomed in or out with your feet. You zoomed in by walking toward your subject, and you zoomed back by walking away. The same could be said for DASD I/O. Buffer up 10, 20, or 50 physical blocks and you will have very little delay or RPS miss. Cheap. Fast. It works running under System/370, System/370 extended architecture, or ES/9000, and with any of the operating systems on those platforms.

Buffering I/O data blocks may not be as good as cache devices, but it may be the most cost-effective solution. Buffering can be done today without waiting for hardware acquisition and installation.

2.8.3. I/O Elimination

Other software also can do away with RPS miss. Data in Virtual, Hiperbatch, VSAM local shared resources, and other techniques get the data blocks you need in storage and keep them there for you to use again.

These techniques are gathered under the term *I/O elimination* because they use operating system and subsystem techniques to provide the data for you in virtual storage. One example of this is CICS Local Shared Resources implementation in either above-the-line storage or expanded storage Hiperspace buffers. When a CICS application asks to read a buffer, CICS looks in one of its buffer pools for the data block.

> ▭   Almost any CICS application can benefit from Local
>   Shared Resources implemention. If you are not using it,
>   you should ask why!

2.9. Summary

Direct Access Storage Devices are constructed of electromechanical parts that provide rapid access to physical data blocks. Disks or platters provide the surface on which to record data. Read-write heads on access arms move across the surface to fixed positions on the surface called tracks to read or write data on the surface.

The combination of platters, electronics, and read-write heads is called an actuator. Most current architecture DASD have one or more actuators packaged in a Head Disk Assembly (HDA). Two or more HDAs are packaged into a device. Connecting several devices to each other forms a string of DASD. The first device on a string is a head of string (HOS) that has additional electronics to control which device is active on the two or four paths to a string.

Tracks can be formatted using fixed-block architecture (FBA) or count-key-data (CKD) architecture. FBA devices are preformatted surfaces with (usually) 512-byte blocks that are used to store the end users' data. CKD devices are only formatted with a self-defining track format consisting of a home address (HA) and record zero (R0).

A fixed number of tracks are grouped into a cylinder. A cylinder is all the tracks that can be accessed by the actuator with the read-write heads stopped at one position over the track. The number of read-write heads equals the number of tracks in a cylinder.

All DASD contain cylinders outside the reach of the non-authorized user. Alternate tracks can be assigned if there is a bad spot on the track in a primary track. Diagnostic tracks are for the hardware and software to use to perform testing procedures. Device support tracks contain information used to keep information about surface defects and dual volumes, and as a checkpoint during volume initialization using ICKDSF.

DASD response time is a function of what the end user's channel program requested. One of the largest components of response time is Rotational Position Sensing (RPS) misses. If an RPS miss occurs, it may add 50 or 100 percent more time to the I/O access time. Hardware solutions (e.g., caching at the device and control unit level) and software solutions (e.g., buffering, Data in Virtual, Hiperbatch) greatly reduce the RPS miss problem. DASD response time measurement ends when the device sings *Device End*.

2.10. Questions

1. Describe the DASD components that store and retrieve the data when a read or write input/output operation is requested.

2. Why is RPS miss so important to avoid?

3. What is MBBCCHHR?

4. Decompose DASD response time and describe each component and what effect it has on the total response time.

5. Describe the format of a fixed-block architecture track.

6. Describe the format of a just-formatted count-key-data track.

7. Describe the process for assigning alternate tracks on CKD devices.

8. Describe the process for assigning alternate blocks and tracks on FBA devices.

9. Describe Rotational Position Sensing and explain why RPS miss may be a large portion of the read-write time for a DASD device.

10. What is the significance of *Device End* from a DASD at the end of a channel program?

3

Application Requirements

The previous chapter introduced the issues of Direct Access Storage Devices themselves, from the channel programs supplied in the Processor Complex through the device operations necessary to carry them out. What is the point, though, unless these devices can do real work for people? That is the concern of this chapter.

We begin by looking at how users access data. Then, we look at how applications can organize this data to support user activity. Finally, we look at the operating system components (access methods) that support various kinds of data organization.

3.1. Data Access Considerations

Direct Access Storage Devices are used to store data for the end user community and the data center. This section covers the topics that should be agreed upon by all concerned.

3.1.1. Security

When they hear the word "security", the first thing most people think of is passwords and permissions: keeping sensitive data and system controls out of the hands of spies, extortionists, hackers, and other criminal miscreants. That is certainly one of the goals any security arrangement must meet. In our day-to-day work, however, security should play an important role in ensuring that data is accessed properly, not just legally.

Security is not just protection from the "bad guys". Most losses occur at our own hands through carelessness, stupidity, or both. Many mistakes are quite sophisticated and appear stupid only in retrospect, once we understand what happened. By using the tools in our arsenal, those supplied by the operating system and those in our own application design, we can benefit from automatic detection of mistakes and intrusions before they cause regrettable or unrecoverable damage to data or people.

Adequate protection for data assets is an achievable goal for a data center. Perfect protection from all sources is always too expensive. Too little protection is also too expensive. Many data centers make one of two mistakes with their security arrangements. Either they practice *reactive* security administration, or they dump far too many resources into one kind of security and in the process ignore other kinds that are equally important.

One data center at a university had reactive security. On their VM system, a DASD area called a *minidisk* belonging to the MAINT user ID contained unencoded user IDs and logon passwords for the entire system. (VM now encodes these passwords.) One user could access another's minidisk by specifying its read password. MAINT's minidisk password was, believe it or not, *MAINT*.

A group of students guessed this and capitalized on their find, and a rather embarrassed university felt obliged to prosecute them. The university then *reacted* by properly protecting the minidisk and urging that state law be changed to make it easier to prosecute in the future.

What those students did was wrong. What the university did in not protecting the most sensitive DASD area on the system was wrong as well as stupid, particularly in a university environment. Many vendors ship their operating systems with default passwords. These days, password expiration features help prevent this kind of mistake, but you might be surprised how many systems remain exposed in precisely this way. Don't handle security by waiting for it to be breached: you may not, after all, detect it.

As for devoting too many resources to one kind of security while ignoring others, ask yourself where the DASD is. Is it all channel-connected to your mainframe? What about all those workstations on everyone's desk tops? Physical security is possible for a workstation, but you must lock the office door. The security and integrity of data is often overlooked, however. One company's 5-year plan resided entirely in a spreadsheet stored on a PC that was never backed up. Is any of your company's critical data vulnerable in a like way?

We have heard many end users, data center management, and technical people say something like "We do not have anything to steal." Security is not just "Who would want to steal from us?" Security is who is responsible for the data. You can lose other things besides the data. Lost manpower used to recover data accidentally lost is one of the most hidden and may be the most expensive. Incorrect data that is used to make decisions causes uncountable losses. We concentrate on these issues in the following sections.

Before we go on, though, there is another aspect of data security you might like to ponder. Our computer systems often store more than impersonal data about our business. Many also store details about real people's lives. What data is stored and how is a decision made to satisfy business objectives, but we are human and so are they. We have an *ethical responsibility* to preserve the privacy of the people whose data we store, whether or not the law or company policy prescribes it.

Usually, breach of privacy lies more in the potential than in actual practice. Today's relational DBMS makes it quite easy to

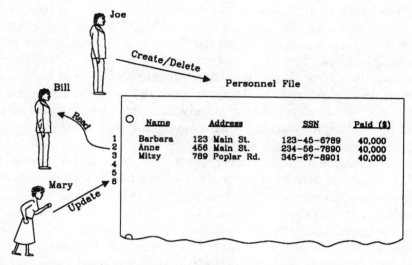

Figure 3.1 Security: Who Can Do What to the Data. When the enterprise installs a security system, each file may have security attributes associated with the file. The attributes control who has access to the data. In this example, Bill can read the data but cannot update the data. Mary can update the data—which means she can also read the data. Most security subsystems also distinguish between those who can create a data set or who can delete (scratch) existing data sets. Joe can create and delete the data set and therefore is the data administrator for this data set.

combine data from a number of sources if a key field, such as the social security number, is present in all sources. "Who would do that with our data?" you ask. One of our own country's corners of dark history should answer that satisfactorily; fortunately, Senator Joe McCarthy had no DB2. Not all countries have our Constitution, either.

People are becoming more sensitive to how their data is handled. One microcomputer software company attempted to market an inexpensive and detailed demographic database on CD ROM. They were so deluged with objections from the public that the product never made it out the door. People do care what you do with their data, and it is *their* data.

We now return to the more mundane issues of DASD security.

Who Can Create or Delete Data?

Figure 3.1 shows a typical personnel file that might be a data set on DASD. Someone or some group should be the owner of the data in that they can create and delete the entire data set. This is not so easily determined as you might think. There may be a payroll department that "owns the payroll files", but there is probably a production control department, an applications programming department, and a systems programming department that may, at times, need to create or delete production data sets.

Who Can Read the Data?

Of course people in the payroll and personnel departments should be able to read all of the data. They probably maintain the information. But whole groups of people in the organization may have a need to know at least some of the items in the file. Bill in Figure 3.1 may have a need to know the first two items in the file for an address list. He should be given access only to the names and addresses.

The operating system provides DASD security only at the file level. Data base management systems (DBMS) and transaction processing systems must control record- or field-level security. DASD security only says, "Can Bill open this file for read access?" If so, Bill gets all the records in the file.

Who Can Update the Data?

In Figure 3.1, Mary has the authorization to update the records in the personnel file. One thing most data administrators forget is that if Mary can update a file, she has the capability to destroy the file or at least make it unusable unless the programs she uses control access and edit changes.

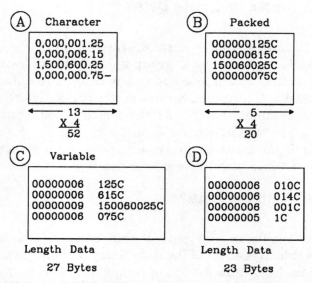

Figure 3.2 Size: Small Is Beautiful. Stored data usually contains numbers. The System/390 architecture provides the user with several formats. In *A* above, each fixed-format-character number requires 1 byte of storage. The 4 fields require 52 bytes of storage. In *B* each fixed-packed number requires a nibble (half a byte) and the 4 fields require 20 bytes. In *C* above, the format is still packed but is now variable format only using the exact number of bytes to hold a value but requiring a 4-byte length field. In this case it requires 7 bytes for storage more than in *B*. It may not be cost effective to use variable formats with small data areas. In *D* above, using the same techniques as in *C* but with smaller data areas, it requires 23 bytes to represent 7 bytes—over three times as much.

3.1.2. Size of Data

DASD contains bytes, or characters, of data. Some of the area is wasted. Sometimes the entire byte is not needed to represent data. Sometimes parts of a byte are not needed to represent the data. How much of a DASD record is not used? A good clue is that most compression techniques claim compression to *one-third* of the original size. If the tape dump, DFHSM compression techniques, and other data squeezers can get that much compression, would you think we could be more efficient in our use of DASD space?

One large accounts receivable data base (9.6 gigabytes) we observed had its data processed by the IBM 3480 IDRC simulator to see if the hardware compression would reduce the number of tapes needed to back up the data. This program reads tape versions of DASD files and projects how many tape cartridges will be saved if the installation adds the 3480 IDRC feature or purchases the 3490 tape drive.

IBM expects to see hardware compaction routines reduce the number of tapes by a factor of 3. The accounts receivable data set showed only a 1.75 reduction in tapes. The reason was an efficient data record layout that minimized wasted areas in records. *The systems analyst staff had already compressed the data* using good programming techniques and was using DASD *42% better* than the average system.

Who cares, you say? What if that 9.6 gigabytes really took 16 gigabytes to store on DASD? The cost to the data center would have been an additional 6.4 gigabytes of data for the projected life of the data base. Those application programmers saved their company many thousands of dollars.[1]

How did that application group do such a good job? Figure 3.2 shows several standard record formats. Character and packed are shown using fixed-field techniques. Each field is the same size. The last two show variable format, where a 4-byte length field is used to describe the length of the data plus 4 bytes for the length field.

In Figure 3.2 at A, four numbers are stored with 1 byte for each digit. Each number requires 13 bytes of storage, 12 for the digits and 1 for the sign. Four numbers require 52 bytes. Some of you readers are laughing at this, but this exists in a lot of places. Multiply the space savings by thousands or millions of records and divide by the space on a DASD volume. It is easy in

---

1   Thanks to Sue Courter and her staff at Beverly Enterprises for showing that good application design can make a data center run efficiently and cost-effectively. Dale Waddell of Mead Data Central also used data compression techniques to save over one-half million dollars of DASD.

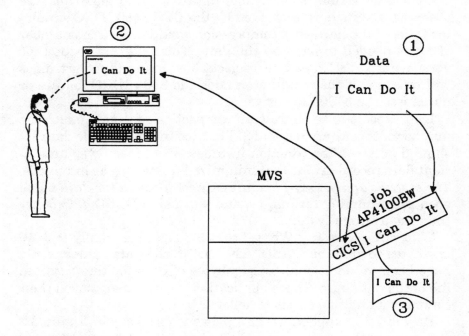

Figure 3.3 When Is Data Needed? Data at *1* above is stored until it is needed by a program such as CICS (for terminal display) or by a program running in batch mode (to write to a printer or another file). A person waiting for the data should be given access faster than a batch job. In most cases it is more cost-effective to give better response time to people than to batch jobs.

COBOL to create this situation. It is even easier in DBMS because the representation is hidden!

The first and easiest change is to pack the data. In Figure 3.2 at B, you see that the packed-format version uses only 20 bytes, over 50% less than the character version. In COBOL, only the data format need change; in assembly language, character to numeric conversion (and the validity checking, because the program's author is a good programmer) can be eliminated. The packed version uses less raw CPU power to process, but this is a DASD book: it also reduces the DASD I/O.

Now it gets complicated, because as with all tuning efforts you can make it worse! In Figure 3.2 at C, we use a variable-length data representation. This allows you to retain only the significant characters but requires the overhead of a 4-byte length field. This format looks as if it saves space but is actually 7 bytes longer than plain packed fields. For very small records (Figure 3.2 at D), plain packed is best.

What is the moral of this? Know your data. Create fields with properly defined formats and save a bundle.

3.1.3. Speed of Access

If space is money, so is time. What time goals are to be met for the data? In Figure 3.3 we see two different types of data access: batch and interactive.

At *1* in Figure 3.3, some data exists and contains the characters "I can do it". If interactive CICS users (at *2* in Figure 3.3) want the data displayed at their terminals, then the speed of access must be less than one-tenth of a second (and, more important, consistent) to keep the average end user happy.

At *3* in Figure 3.3, a batch job wants to print the data on a report. The same data is used to achieve a new service objective. The batch job could wait without harm for up to several minutes for the data to become available. The data could be located on a tape reel or other archived source. Unless the volume of data and the response time of each record made the total elapsed time of the batch job unacceptable, the data could be kept almost anywhere and take almost any length of time to be accessed.

Again, as with most generalities, you must keep in mind your loved ones. Some batch jobs are very valuable to an organization—payroll and accounts receivable, for example—and their elapsed time may become the hot topic of the day.

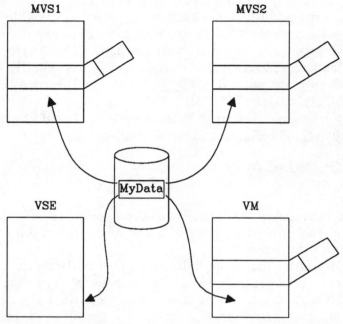

Figure 3.4 Sharing Data. Some data may be needed by applications in different processor complexes running mulitiple copies of MVS, VM, VSE, or TPF. As long as all applications are reading the data, multiple shared-spool applications can access the data. Problems arise when two or more processor complexes try to update shared data because the queueing mechanism is in the operating system. The sharing systems may even be in the same processor complex in PR/SM partitions. More of these concepts will be discussed in the section on shared DASD.

3.1.4. Sharing Data

In Figure 3.3 the data may be shared between the batch job and the CICS online transactions. If both the CICS and batch jobs are reading the data, there is no problem with data integrity. There may be a big problem with CICS response time if the transactions are trying to access a file being read by a batch program. We already have mentioned CICS Local Shared Resources (LSR) to overcome this problem.

If one or both of the systems want to update the data, then special precautions must be taken to protect the validity of data.

A more important and complicated type of data sharing is shown in Figure 3.4. There are four Processor Complexes. Two run MVS, one runs VM, and one runs VSE. Tasks running in all four could want to access the DASD data set called *MyData*. You see from the chapter on the hardware that the control unit can have eight paths to a string of data. ESCON Processor Complex architectures allow almost unlimited access to a string of data.

The chapter on shared DASD will cover these considerations in more detail. For now, just remember it is very important to define who will access the data and what platform (or operating system) will be used to access the data.

3.2. Data Components

The basic building block of a DASD file is a physical record. It is made up of logical records and fields within those records. We use the term *physical record* or *block* to describe the record as it is passed from Processor Complex to DASD. We use the term *logical record* to describe a record as it is seen from the application viewpoint. Application logic reads and writes logical records. Physical devices read and write physical blocks.

3.2.1. Fields

Figure 3.5 depicts the relationship between the fields of a record and what is written onto the DASD platter. The logical record is made up of four fields: *name, address, phone,* and *amount*.

Each field is a data item representing a piece of information. In the example, *name* could be the complete name of a person. More likely it would be just the last name of a person, and another field would contain the first name of the person. The usual reason for separating the first and last names is to allow you to sort the data by the last name.

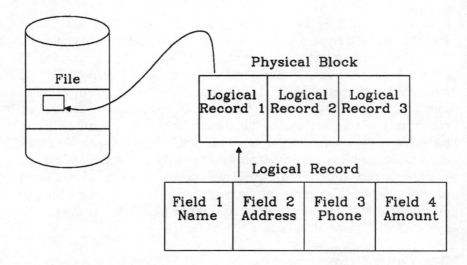

Figure 3.5 Records and Fields. A DASD file contains one or more physical blocks. Each physical block is made up of one or more logical records. Each logical record has one or more fields.

The fields could be formatted in any of the acceptable System/370 or System/390 formats (e.g., character, packed decimal, binary). Remember, though, that all the fields are just 8-bit bytes.

3.2.2. Records

The combined fields make up a logical record. A program must define the record in its work space. If the program is going to write the record, the program passes to the access method a single logical record. If the program is going to read the record, the program must provide a place for the access method to put the data.

In both cases, the program defines the displacement (starting position) and length for each field within the record.

3.2.3. Blocks

Combining logical into physical records is called *blocking*. In Figure 3.5, each physical record is blocked with three logical records. For write operations, when three logical records are created, a physical block is written to the DASD with a channel program. For read operations, when a single logical record is requested, then three logical records are brought into central storage at one time. The access method determines which blocks are needed and when to do I/O.

Records do not have to be all the same type. It is common to have an indicator in the record denoting its record type. In our example, we could add a field to show record type and keep other information about this entity. For example, we could keep the person's home address and work address without defining two address fields for every record. Several records of different types could be used to describe this entity, a person.

3.2.4. Files or Data Sets

Files are groups of physical records that store logical records. Another term used in the IBM world is *data set*, and the two names are used interchangeably. When a data set is brought in its entirety into virtual storage and accessed through the paging subsystem, it may be called a *data object*. We ignore these nuances and refer to any group of records that contain organized data and are created, read, and updated by programs as a *data set*.

Unfortunately, "data set" also means something completely different to communications hardware people. But this is a DASD book, so we will continue.

If more than one program is going to access a data set, then all programs must know the record types and have a definition of what each field (at least the fields that they share) means.

The data set may contain from a few records to the largest number of records supported by the access method and the IBM architecture. The DASD architecture allows you to create (allocate) a data set but write no records into it.

> ¤ Do not allocate data sets and leave them empty. Not only does it waste space, but also some archiving subsystems that are designed to move data sets from place to place get confused when a data set is empty.

The maximum number of records depends on the access method chosen, the logical record size, the physical record size, and the medium on which the records are stored. Once the logical size of a record is determined in the design stage, and you can estimate the number of records expected in the file, you should estimate the storage requirements to predict what kinds of management are required for the data set.

3.3. Access Methods

Access method is the generic name of the programs supplied by IBM to read and write data to and from DASD and other devices.[2] The programs are loaded into the address space of the requesting program by the *OPEN* function.

Access methods provide a number of services for the programmer. The first is to prepare virtual storage at OPEN time: buffers are allocated, control blocks are verified and initialized. DASD catalogs and volumes are searched for data. Access methods accept data stored in the application program's logical record and move it to the physical output record. Access methods control movement of physical records to and from the device asynchro-

---

2 Most of IBM's access methods for I/O are in the Data Facility Product (DFP) provided by IBM, but other vendors provide access method routines for their products.

nously with application processing to take advantage of processing and I/O overlap.

Access methods also provide exit routines. An *exit* is a documented interface in which the access method (or other operating system component) calls a user-written procedure when specified conditions arise. Two such conditions are *end-of-volume* and *end-of-file*.[3]

Through this mechanism, the access method can allow the application program to find another part of the file on another tape or DASD volume or to do special processing when the end-of-file is reached.

Access methods provide or write channel programs that I/O devices execute. It is possible to bypass access methods by writing your own channel programs.[4] This requires intricate knowledge of the device that will execute the program, and knowledge of operating system control blocks for I/O and other supervisor services.

Although some efficiencies can be had by doing so, this can make it difficult for the application to take advantage of new kinds of devices. It also adds an application maintenance burden that is difficult to manage. For these reasons, even assembly language programmers use the standard access methods most of the time.

It is time to look at the standard access methods. Access methods read and write physical blocks on DASD. (The access methods do support other device types, but this is a book on DASD, so we will limit our discussions to DASD accesses.) Some access methods manipulate the data very little or not at all, so

---

3   The specifications for exits usually require access to machine registers, so exit routines are usually written in assembly language. One routine might service the end-of-file exit: when a file is being read and the last record for this file on this volume is detected, the end-of-volume exit is taken. If the exit routine finds more volumes and so advises the access method with its return values, the application program continues as if nothing happened. If there are no more volumes, then the end-of-file exit routine is called to wrap up and transfer control to the programmer's *AT END* routine or to the EODAD part of an assembly language program.

4   Special assembly language macros (e.g., XDAP, EXCP, and STARTIO) are provided for these adventurous types.

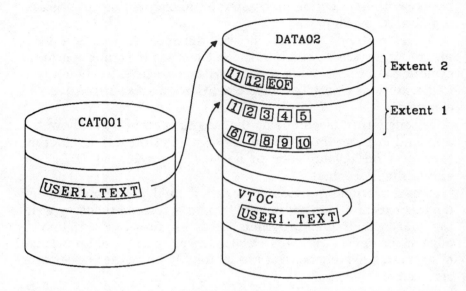

Figure 3.6 Non-VSAM: Sequential Access. Files usually are accessed through a system catalog. In this example, volume *CAT001* contains a pointer to data set *USER1.TEXT.* The Volume Table of Contents (VTOC) points to the first extent for the sequential data set. Files accessed with the sequential access method are processed from the beginning of the file to the end of the file. The access is *not dependent on the location on the disk.* In this example, the file has 12 records. Records 1 through 10 are located in the first extent—in the middle of the volume. When the file was created, the operating system chose space closer to the front of the volume to place the second extent.

the application designer knows exactly how the data is stored on DASD. Sequential and partitioned access methods are examples. For indexed types (VSAM and ISAM), the access method makes some decisions on the physical blocking and partitioning of the data set into subareas. If you are going to control your DASD, you will need to figure out what these subareas mean to your data and your DASD.

3.3.1. Sequential Organization (SAM)

The simplest and most popular organization is sequential. IBM uses the term *Sequential Access Method (SAM)* to refer to both the access method and files supported by that access method. Another term you might see is *SAM-E*, or SAM Extended, which has some additional features.

Figure 3.6 shows a SAM file and the structure that is required to access the data in an MVS or VSE environment. A DASD volume contains a *catalog* that associates data set names with names of the DASD volumes that contain them. Here, the catalog says the data set with the name *USER1.TEXT* is on DASD volume DATA02. If you look in the *Volume Table of Contents (VTOC)* on DATA02, you find data that indicates where on DATA02 the data for USER1.TEXT is stored. The data set was defined with room in the first extent to contain 10 physical blocks, and those 10 have been written to the file. Extent 2 contains room for five more records. Only two (11 and 12) records have been written into the second extent.

The end of the data set is marked by a special record (data length of the count field is all zeros) called an *End-of-File (EOF)* record. Note that the VTOC can be anywhere on the volume. The second extent can be nearer the front of the volume than the primary or first extent. Secondary extents can be larger or smaller than the primary extent.

3.3.2. Partitioned Organization (PAM)

Partitioned Access Method (PAM) data sets subdivide the allocated space into two areas. The first area, in the first extent of the data set, contains physical records 256 bytes long: this is the directory of the members contained within the remainder of the data set.

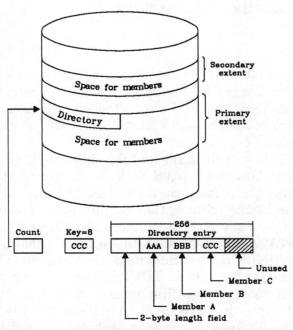

Figure 3.7 Non-VSAM: Partitioned Access. The Partitioned Access Method (PAM) file is really two files in one. The first extent usually holds two differently formatted types of data. The first is the partitioned directory. Each directory record is 256 bytes long with an 8-byte key. The directory entry can be from 12 to 74 bytes in length depending on the amount of user data. The remainder of the first extent is room for the members of the data set. Other extents are also room for members of the data set. Once the directory is created, it cannot be extended without OEM software or IBM's PDSE.

In Figure 3.7 you see the three portions of the physical block of a partitioned data set. The *count* area is there, of course. The 256-byte data area is a directory block and contains the information about members in the data set. The length of the member information depends on the contents of the data set, for example whether it contains source or load modules.[5] The directory entries are kept **sorted in ascending order by member name.**

---

5   A *load module* is generally the output of a linkage editor. It can be loaded into central storage and executed by the CPU.

The *key* area of the record is an 8-byte field that contains the name of the last member in this directory block. In this example, the last member is named *CCC*, so the key is set to *CCC*.

The very last directory entry will always be followed by an overhead-type entry with a member name of x'FFF...FF', and thus the 8-byte key will also be x'FFFFFFFFFFFFFFFF'.

The PAM organization is designed to take advantage of DASD data searching hardware. Any program looking for member *BBB* can use the hardware SEARCH ID channel command, setting the comparison to *equal or greater*. The search would end by reading in this block, and therefore finding member BBB. PAM data sets are used to store load modules, so it is advantageous to have the DASD perform the search while the CPU does other things.

There are two things to note about the extents for the partitioned data set on this DASD. Space for the directory entries is taken out of the primary extent. If, for example, you specify in ISPF that there can be 1,000 directory blocks for a partitioned data set, you have just used up 1,000 256-byte blocks of DASD space, which is many tracks. The entire directory is formatted at the time you allocate a PDS. To test this, allocate a PDS using ISPF with ten directory blocks and time your response time. Repeat the test with 1,000 directory blocks and you will see the difference.

The second thing to note is that secondary extents are obtained apart from the primary extent. As you learned from **MVS Concepts and Facilities**, with the standard partitioned access method, as you add members, you advance the end of the file and allocate additional extents until you compress the data set. (This refers to PAM compression, not generic data compression.) Partitioned data sets running under non-IBM vendor enhancement packages or IBM's PDS/E do not have this problem with the unused space.

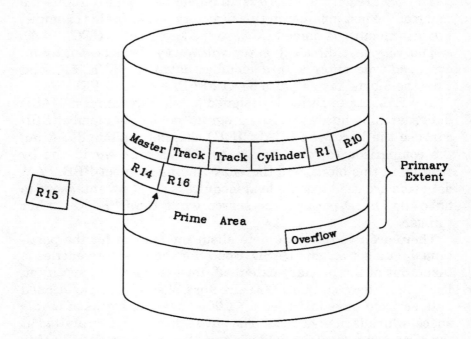

Figure 3.8 Non-VSAM: Indexed Sequential. The ISAM primary extent may contain a master index area, one or more track index areas, and possibly a cylinder index area. The prime area is for records, and the records **must be inserted in order on the track.** In this example, the second track contains record 14 and record 16. Record 15 is to be inserted. This is the simplest insertion: record 16 is moved down and record 15 is inserted.

3.3.3. Indexed Sequential Organization (ISAM)

ISAM was the first access method supplied by IBM to access data by jumping directly into the file at the location of a particular record.

Before we get too far with the ISAM discussion, we should say that we do not recommend that you use ISAM for new applications, and you should convert existing applications to some other access method. ISAM is difficult to use, hard to manage, and not very efficient. It has been superseded by better access methods.

Having said that, there are always reasons to use what you have working. Your data center may be stabilized. Your data center may not be growing, and you may not be developing many new applications.

An ISAM file is a sequential file that contains an index structure to point to records in the file and a means of inserting records.

In Figure 3.8 a simple ISAM data set has records containing keys of 1, 10, 14, and 16. A program can read the file sequentially or jump directly to the record with a key of 16. The access method determines where to jump based on a series of indexes.

The lowest level, always present, is the *track index*. One track index exists for each cylinder in the prime area. It is always written on the first track of the cylinder it is indexing. Most of the track index has pointers to data using the home address of the track.

Therein lies the primary problem with this access method. The home address, a physical attribute of the volume the data set resides on, is contained within the data portion of the data set. The result is that ISAM data sets cannot be moved on a particular volume, nor can they be archived from the volume without using the ISAM utilities. The reason is that the data portion cannot just be moved. It must be moved and portions changed to reflect the new data locations.

The next higher index level, always present, is the *cylinder index*. These entries point to the home addresses of the track indexes, and therefore to the cylinders of the prime area.

The *master index* is the highest level of index. Its entries contain pointers to the home addresses of cylinder indexes. You built a master index if the cylinder index was larger than approximately four tracks.

Look back at Figure 3.8. If record 14 was in the second cylinder, then the pointer to record 14 would point to the home address of the second cylinder of the data set.

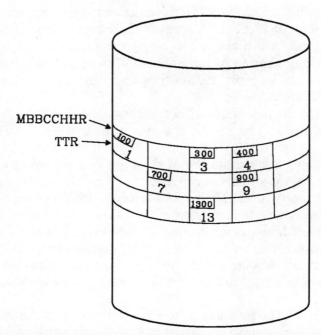

Figure 3.9 Non-VSAM: Basic Direct Access. Files created using BDAM must have some programmatically created relationship between the record key and the position of the record within the file. In this example, records with keys 1, 3, 4, 7, 9, and 13 are in the file. Direct access devices cannot have unused space between records, so the file has been preformatted with empty records. The program must provide the access method with a pointer into the file using one of two possible techniques. The first is to fully describe the location on the disk using the MBBCCHHR description. The second is to provide the relative location within the file's extents using the TTR format.

We want to insert record 15. If it will fit on the track at the front of the data set (the *prime* area), then record 16 is moved down the track and 15 is inserted. If record 15 will not fit on the track, it is inserted in place of 16, and 16 is moved to an *overflow* area.

Sounds like a great idea. The architects only made one mistake. The overflow area is searched one record at a time. If you have only a few records inserted and in the overflow area, then response time is not too bad. If you have a large volume of inserted records, then response time for ISAM data sets becomes unacceptable. What is worse is that the channel is dominated while the ISAM overflow area is searched. **Everyone else suffers!**

3.3.4. Direct Organization (BDAM)

Another great idea that never panned out really well in most installations is an access method that allows the end user to jump directly into a data set and read multiple records. This is the *Basic Direct Access Method (BDAM)*.

Again, we do not recommend that you use BDAM as an access method, with several notable exceptions. Many non-IBM data base subsystems, large information retrieval systems, and utilities such as SAS® [6] use BDAM for their files. Let them do the accesses. If you are working for one of those companies and are responsible for maintaining the common modules that do I/O, you should be digging into the IBM manuals and source code for this access method to fully understand it.

Figure 3.9 shows a simple BDAM data set on DASD. The data set must be preformatted with records (similar to fixed-block architecture DASD tracks). In the example, records 1 through 15 are formatted, and 1, 3, 4, 7, 9, and 13 have valid data. You could read the file sequentially and just skip the invalid records. To get directly to the ninth record, with a key of *900*, you would need a pointer to its location.

The first method is to give the relative block that you want. If you know that a key of 1300 maps to the 13th block, you would specify relative block 12. IBM likes to number things starting with zero, so "relative" means how many from zero.

The remaining possibilities require the program to specify hardware information about the address of the track and of the

---

6   SAS is a registered trademark of SAS Institute, Cary, NC.

record on the track. The first is its actual address (similar to ISAM's home address) in a new format.

Having read previous chapters, you are familiar with cylinders, heads, and records. This one is formatted **MBBCCHHR**. This 8-byte field fully qualifies a DASD location:

1. **MBB** is the extent and bin number in case your DASD was a 2321 data cell.

2. **CCHHR** is the cylinder, head, and record to be accessed.

If the program keeps the MBBCCHHR in a file, the BDAM access method is just as bad as ISAM. The file cannot be moved without adjusting these pointers. For this reason, most DASD data movers are reluctant to move BDAM data sets. If you wish to move BDAM data sets, you should verify that this type of data linkage is not used.

The authors strongly recommend that you not use any program that uses this method unless you absolutely must, and then you may want to segregate these data sets on a single volume.

Two other methods exist to access BDAM that are "data-mover friendly". The first method, *relative track address*, uses a 3-byte binary number, TTR, to point to the proper record:

1. **TT** is the relative track from the first track of the data set. The first is zero.

2. **R** is the record on the track.

The second method, *relative track and key*, uses the relative track (as above) to get to the proper track and then uses SEARCH ID CCWs to search for the record on the track with the provided key. To use this hardware search, the records must be formatted with the separate key area.

The reason these last two can be moved from place to place on a DASD volume or from volume to volume (but only if they are the same device type or same geometry; the target volume track size must be less than or equal to the origin volume track size) is

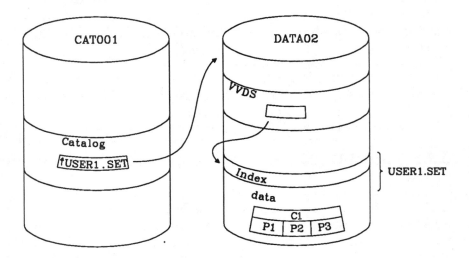

Figure 3.10 Virtual Storage Access Method. Data sets created using VSAM must be accessed through a catalog. This figure includes the catalog pointer just to emphasize that point. A VSAM data set has an index component (if it is an indexed VSAM data set) and a data component. They may or may not be adjacent to each other.

that the access method computes the correct track. It takes the actual address (CCHHR) from the start of the data set and adds the relative track to get to the correct track.

In our example, assume each track contains five records. The CCHH of the first track is 00010002, or cylinder 1 head 2. The TTR of the first record is 000001 (relative track zero, record 1). Add 0000 tracks to 0002 tracks and you get CCHH of 00010002 and record 1. The TTR of the seventh record (key = 700) would be 000102. Add 0001 to 00010002 and you get 00010003 (cylinder 1, head 3).

These examples do not cross cylinders, but when your track counter exceeds the tracks per cylinder for the device on which the data set is stored, then you start at zero for the tracks and add 1 to the cylinder. It is actually more complex than that:

remember that storage for data sets is allocated in *extents*, or contiguous areas on the DASD, but the extents themselves may be scattered all over the DASD. Your calculation must allow for the *TT* value to move into another extent of the data set that may start at a different CCHH of the volume.

◻ Note that data records begin with *1* because record zero is already required on a track as the track descriptor record. Although it may seem that IBM is not consistently counting from zero, they really are!

3.3.5. Virtual Organizations

IBM identifies several access methods as *virtual*. The first, VSAM, is just another type of access method. The others are truly virtual in that their data is stored and accessed in virtual storage (a job's address space) and mapped to DASD.

Virtual Storage Access Method (VSAM)

The *Virtual Storage Access Method (VSAM)* was designed to provide the systems analyst with an access method that would replace all other DASD access methods. IBM intended the 1973 release to provide direct access for online, interactive use and efficient sequential access for batch processing.

VSAM has not completely taken over as an access method but has become one of the most prevalent. VSAM is somewhat simple to use, but it is very easy to get into trouble with it in performance, space allocation, and access. There are a number of excellent books in the Jay Ranade series which discuss these topics (see the front of this book for a list).[7] This section will concentrate on the DASD effects.

---

7 Yet another shameless plug, but worthwhile for you, really.

All VSAM data sets must be cataloged, so the DASD volume in Figure 3.10 has a catalog. (A catalog says which volume has a data set.) A pointer in the catalog indicates that data set *USER1.SET* is located on DASD volume DATA02. When the first VSAM data set is allocated on a DASD volume, VSAM creates a *Volume Data Set (VVDS)*. VSAM manages one of these on each volume, regardless of how many VSAM data sets are created thereafter or how many users access them.

One important thing to note is that it takes three DASD accesses to open a VSAM data set. First, the catalog is read; second, the VVDS is read; third, the VSAM data set is reached. This is a simple, small VSAM data set, but the data could be spread over multiple volumes. It can get really complicated.

VSAM data sets can be formatted and accessed in several ways. The data may be indexed or accessed in a manner that does not require the index portion of Figure 3.10:

1. *Key Sequential Data Set (KSDS)* always has both an index portion and a data portion. You will see two DASD areas allocated. The index portion contains a compressed version of each key stored in data records and a pointer to the data portion where the record with that key resides. The pointer is very "data-mover friendly". It is the relative byte of the data portion, so any VSAM data set can be moved from place to place on a volume or from volume to volume without problems.

2. *Entry Sequenced Data Set (ESDS)* does not have an index portion. As a record is written to an ESDS data set, VSAM returns to the application the relative byte of the record, and it is up to the application to keep track of the location.

3. *Relative Record Data Set (RRDS)* also has no index and is similar to the preformatted BDAM data set in that it has a number of slots. The application fills and reads the slots by supplying VSAM with the slot number.

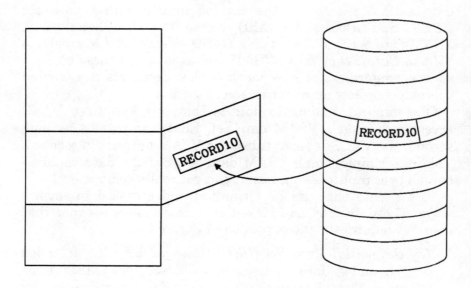

Figure 3.11 Data-In-Virtual. You can create data sets in virtual storage by using the DIV facility. DIV data sets are *LINEAR data sets*. The example above shows a DASD data set created by IDCAMS that is mapped into virtual storage so that the program can read in only the table entries that are necessary. Only the updated records are rewritten to DASD.

4. *Linear Data Set (LDS)* is a VSAM-generated data set that is the same as Data in Virtual (explained below) but is now an *official* data set.

VSAM reads and writes *control intervals*. In Figure 3.10 a single control interval in the data area contains three physical records. From what you know about the size of gaps on DASD records, you can imagine the waste if VSAM picked 512 bytes as a physical record size for your VSAM data set.

> ☐ Ensure that your VSAM data sets are properly blocked for acceptable DASD effectiveness. Use an *IDCAMS LISTCAT* or other utility to list the attributes of your VSAM data sets, and be sure block sizes are not less than 1,024 bytes.

Data-in-Virtual (DIV)

Data-in-Virtual is a programming access method introduced in MVS/XA. A program can access data on DASD as if it were in virtual storage. The access is similar to the AS/400 or System 36/38 data base accesses. The end user defines a data set as a Data-in-Virtual (DIV) object. The entire data set, or a part of it, can then be accessed by an application program as if the data set were in virtual storage. The data set is accessed using the same operations as for "working storage".

IBM introduced DIV as a way to improve application performance by reducing the amount of unnecessary I/O while processing a file. The theory is that without DIV the application program would read in unnecessary data in order to find that required for the application.

In the table below, a sample data set is created. It is a DIV data set because the *LINEAR* parameter is supplied in the *CLUSTER* IDCAMS command.

Sample JCL to Create a Data-in-Virtual Object

```
//STEPNAME EXEC PGM=IDCAMS
//SYSPRINT DD   SYSOUT=*
//DDNAME   DD   UNIT=3390,VOL=SER=VOLSER,DISP=OLD
//SYSIN    DD   *
 DEFINE   CLUSTER (NAME(FIRST.SECOND)
          FILE(DDNAME)         -
          VOLUMES(VOLSER)      -
          TRACKS(10,1)         -
          SHAREOPTIONS(1,3)    -
          LINEAR     )
```

Once the data set is created, the end user can use the DIV assembly language macro to add or retrieve records. DIV is designed for applications that must access a large amount of data in read-only mode. As there is no facility to access DIV

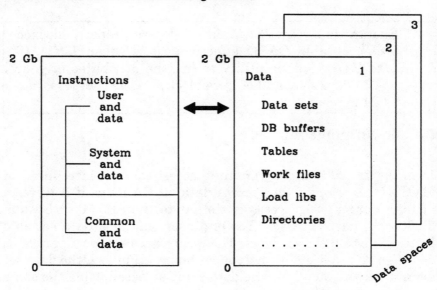

Figure 3.12 Data Spaces. MVS/ESA introduced a new type of 2-gigabyte address space. The 2-Gb space cannot contain instructions (except instructions treated as data—load modules that are moved in and out) and does not have all the common storage mapped, so the entire 2-Gb can be used. This figure shows that you can have multiple data spaces. Data spaces are byte addressable and do not require expanded storage to implement.

directly from a high-level language (e.g., COBOL), someone in the installation must write the assembly language code and provide modules that programs written in high-level languages may call to access DIV objects.

When should you select Data-in-Virtual? Performance is best when the data set is not large, it is actively referenced, and the references are proximal (i.e., within the same virtual page) to avoid straining the paging subsystem.

Data-in-Virtual services process the data set in 4,096-byte blocks, or 4-Kb units. Not surprisingly, this is the same size as a virtual storage page. The data can be mapped to virtual storage in the user's address space, a data space, or a shared or non-shared hiperspace. The latter options are only available under MVS/ESA, of course.

You will choose a *VSAM LINEAR* data set if the data is to be permanent. You may choose one of the others if the data set will only hold temporary data.

In Figure 3.11 the application program has read in record 10. It is coming from a DASD, so it is a *VSAM LINEAR* data set.

One of the reasons DIV is not yet very popular is that the access is complicated, and extensive assembly language knowledge is required to access the data.

Data Spaces

Data spaces are one of two types of special address spaces introduced in MVS/ESA. Data spaces can be accessed a byte at a time the same as the virtual storage in the user's address space. You can move, compare, or perform arithmetic operations on the data in a data space.

Unfortunately, access to data spaces requires the end user to have extensive knowledge of assembly language and write macros to create and access the data space. You even have to manage the area within the data space by creating and deleting *cell pools*. A data space is available to the task that creates it or, with additional coding, to other tasks.

The data space is a substitute for virtual storage or temporary DASD data sets for temporary work files, copies of permanent data sets, or tables or arrays.

One good example of data space use is to read an entire data set into virtual storage and access it. For example, one application had the names and addresses of all the vendors for a particular company. The data set was too large for a COBOL table. It was even too large to read into virtual storage because of the program and other data that had been loaded. A data space was created and the entire table was read into virtual storage. It was searched to match vendor names and vendor numbers to invoices. The result was that DASD I/Os to the vendor file were almost completely eliminated.

In Figure 3.12, we show the virtual storage of an application program. The program has created one or more data spaces to

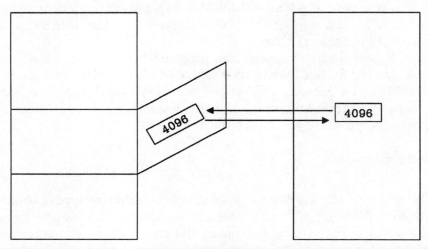

Figure 3.13 Hiperspaces. Another MVS/ESA improvement over the 2-gigabyte address space adds a dimension that improves the performance of data movement to and from these extended data spaces by limiting movement to 4,096-byte pages. Hiperspaces require expanded storage to be on the processor complex.

hold the information needed for this application run. The program must load the data space(s) itself. When the program is done, it must delete the data spaces. The payback for all this work is that the program can run without doing DASD I/O to those files (except when the data set is initially read in from DASD and, if modified while in virtual storage, written out to DASD for permanent storage). Sometimes, and for some files, this can make or break response time goals, particularly for interactive applications.

The cost is that the system may have to page the data into and out of central storage. If the paging subsystem must do a lot of work, the DIV may be more costly to the data center as a whole than regular access methods.

Hiperspaces

Hiperspaces have many of the same characteristics as data spaces. The primary difference between a hiperspace and a data

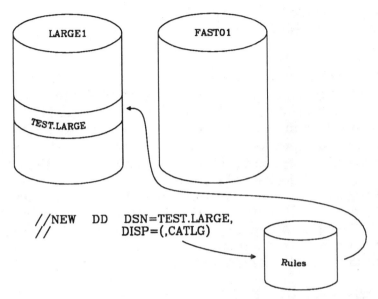

Figure 3.14 Systems Managed Storage. SMS actually is not a data set organization but an operating system implementation of a different method of allocation of all types of data sets. In this example, a user's JCL allocates a data set, but unlike the normal method of allocation, the system uses a set of rules to locate the volume and even assign attributes to the data set.

space is that the application cannot access the hiperspace a byte at a time. Regular instructions do not work with hiperspaces.

Again, intricate assembly language routines must be written to use hiperspaces. Access is only to 4,096-byte blocks (again the size of a virtual storage page). If your data set was blocked at 4,096-byte physical blocks, then you could use hiperspaces to read the entire file into virtual storage and eliminate any further I/O operations to the data set. The assembly language macro *DSPSERV* creates a hiperspace. The assembly language macro *HSPSERV* reads from or writes to a hiperspace.

In Figure 3.13, a hiperspace is shown and the movement of data from the hiperspace to the user's virtual address space is shown.

3.3.6. Storage Management Subsystem—Let MVS Do It

Storage Management Subsystem (SMS) is not really an access method but an organizational architecture that enables the data center and the end user to manage DASD volumes. Many of the issues involved in using the DASD access methods we just covered are concerned with management issues apart from data representations and linkages. Later you will learn SMS in detail, but for now let's look at where it fits in.

In Figure 3.14 you see a very brief set of JCL to allocate a DASD data set. It contains only the data set name and a disposition. There is no space specification. No block size, logical record size, or record formats are specified.

The difference is the *rules* file.

3.4. Summary

Applications require the end user to consider a number of issues when creating and using data on DASD. The first, and of prime importance, is who is going to access the data. The second is the size of the data set. Small, medium, and large data sets have vastly different requirements.

After you have identified the "who" and the "what" of data access, you must consider whether the data is to be shared. From personal computers to the largest mainframe available, data sharing considerations take on vital importance. Special things must be done to protect the integrity of the data while providing rapid access.

A DASD data set consists of physical records that contain logical records that contain fields. A group of data sets may be viewed as a single entity.

Data stored on DASD can be accessed with a number of IBM standard access methods or a wide variety of roll-your-own combinations of DASD and virtual storage. The standard access methods are Sequential (SAM), Partitioned (PAM), Indexed Sequential (ISAM), Direct (BDAM), and the Virtual Storage Access Method (VSAM).

Several Data-in-Virtual access methods are available to the assembly language programmer. Data stored on DASD can be mapped to virtual storage within the address space of the application, to an ESA data space, or to an ESA hiperspace.

The Storage Management Subsystem has been introduced to make DASD access even more complex. Later in this book we will look at SMS in detail.

3.5. Questions

1. Define the standard access methods and state when you would use each of them.

2. Define the difference between data spaces and hiperspaces for data storage.

3. What considerations should the data set designer evaluate when creating a DASD data set?

4. Invent a data set and a use for it, and identify the security considerations relevant to its use.

5. What are the data sharing considerations for a new data set?

6. Describe the components of a VSAM data set and identify what effect each has on the virtual and DASD storage used for data set access.

4

Channels and Control Units

4.1. Introduction to Channel Architecture

All I/O devices are connected to the Processor Complex through channels and control units. Channels are inside the Processor Complex and control units are external to the Processor Complex in a separate box. Today, control units have more raw processing power than most Processor Complexes of just a few years ago. Control units with cache storage have more central storage than most Processor Complexes of just a few years ago. Channel and control unit knowledge is vital to all who are interested in making their I/O operations (and therefore their applications) operate in the most effective manner.

4.1.1. Channel Concepts

There should be nothing mysterious about how channels and control units make I/O devices accessible to a program running in a CPU. For many people, it is enough to know that there are Processor Complexes and I/O devices, and data can be moved between them somehow. To be really effective, you must understand what the components are and how they function in the system when improving performance, planning a new system, adding I/O devices to an existing system, or diagnosing component malfunctions.

The principles involved are present in every commercially available computer, down to the personal computer (PC) on your desk. (The personal computer does not have separate control units.) The names may be different, the electronics are different, but the job remains the same: a general-purpose CPU must be able to send data to an I/O device and receive data from it.

Let's look at a personal computer (PC) first, because it is easy to open it and point at its components. We will compare this simple architecture to the more complex one of a mainframe Processor Complex. Although we are thinking about an IBM PC/AT in particular, you probably can find similar components in your PC regardless of brand. If you take the cover off your PC, you will see that the CPU in the PC is plugged into a large circuit board, called the *motherboard*, containing many other chips and a row of three to eight long connectors, called *slots*. (See Figure 4.1.)

One or more of these slots are occupied by *adapter cards*. Most adapter cards are designed to interface with I/O devices, such as monitors, printers, modems, or disk drives. Each adapter card is designed for a particular type of I/O device. You cannot, for example, plug a disk drive into a monitor adapter card. (Some adapter cards are designed for several different I/O devices, but that is more a matter of real estate: the different circuits required for each type of device are combined on the same card.)

The slots are usually all the same. Each slot has a number of electrical connections, and each connection carries a particular electronic control or data signal. The motherboard, including the CPU, is designed to work with adapter cards in these slots in a certain way. Likewise, an adapter card is designed to use and respond to signals in the slot in a certain way.

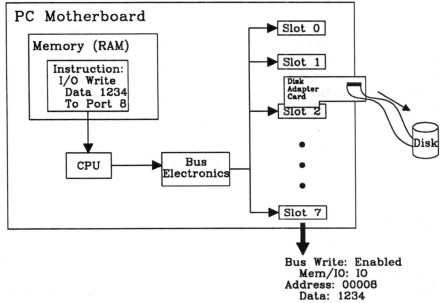

Figure 4.1 I/O In a Smaller Environment. The CPU in a personal computer executes the *I/O write* instruction. Bus electronics encode the port address, data, and control signals simultaneously on all slots. Only the disk adapter card responds to I/O address *8*.

There are characteristics of the electronics and CPU that permit software to control and respond to I/O devices using the slots and adapter cards:

- The CPU has general-purpose I/O instructions permitting software to exchange data with particular adapter cards.
- There are electronics (called Dynamic Memory Access, or DMA) on the motherboard that permit some types of adapter cards to access system memory without constant attention from the software.
- There are interrupt electronics that permit an adapter card to cause the CPU to stop what it is doing and turn control over to a particular piece of software for a time.

In a PC, I/O instructions contain a *port address* that is simultaneously available on all the slots. An adapter card is designed (or set, using switches) to respond to a single port address or a range of port addresses. That is why an adapter card may be plugged into any slot without informing the software. The most common are the COM1 and COM2 ports. Many of you have installed or configured PC cards to enable you to have two communication ports. You then have to tell your communication software which port to use by specifying COM1 or COM2. This is very similar to the mainframe Processor Complex, as you shall see. The difference is that your friendly IBM customer engineer (or non-IBM customer engineer) sets the "switches" and the extra "ports" cost a teensy bit more than your PC.

4.1.2. Mainframe Structure

Now let's leave our desk and go back into the computer room. You will find it difficult to take the lid off your Processor Complex, and you will not be able to find a motherboard with slots or adapter cards all in one place. The pieces are all there, though they look different and are a bit more complex. Instead of finding all the pieces inside one box, you find several boxes connected with cables. Compare Figures 4.1 and 4.2.[1]

A *channel* is an integral part of the System/370 architecture, like the slot and its supporting electronics in a PC. Channels and slots serve similar functions in their respective architectures. Instead of a slot into which an adapter card is inserted, a channel terminates in a connector at the bottom of the Processor Complex. Instead of an adapter card, there is a *control unit* located in another box.

The channel and control unit are connected with electrical or fiber optic cables; one end plugs into the Processor Complex, the other into the control unit. You can think of these cables as

---

1   Most computer rooms are *closed shops* to maintain security and organization, but everyone in the data processing industry should get a tour of his or her computer room. Ask for one.

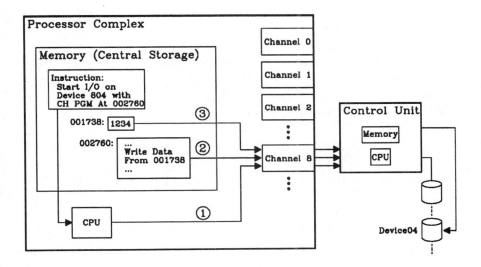

Figure 4.2 Starting an I/O. When the CPU executes a *START I/O* instruction (for System/370) or a *START SUBCHANNEL* (for Extended Architecture or Enterprise Systems Architecture), the instruction gives a device identifier and channel program address to the control unit. The control unit fetches the channel program instructions and data from central storage through the channel.

extension cords that carry control and data signals between the two. The control unit and I/O devices are connected with similar (though different) cables, much as I/O devices are connected using cables to adapter cards in a PC.

All the channels in many Processor Complexes (e.g., 308x and non-ESCON 309x) are the same. In theory, any type of control unit can be plugged into any channel. The software inside the Processor Complex must be told what type of control unit is plugged into which channel, but the electronics do not care. Each control unit, like the adapter cards in a PC, is designed to work with a particular type of I/O device.

Some Processor Complexes have optical fiber cables to control units. You cannot, of course, plug bus and tag cables into optical fiber channels or vice versa.

I/O devices are attached to control units. You cannot plug a DASD into a tape drive controller, for example.

As with the PC, there are characteristics of the electronics and CPU inside the Processor Complex that permit software to control and respond to I/O devices using the channels and control units. The CPU has general-purpose I/O instructions, controllers can access central storage without the simultaneous attention of the software, and there are facilities to interrupt what the CPU is doing and cause it to do something else.

The I/O instructions in a Processor Complex are similar to those in a PC in that they specify an address, but this address references a particular channel or subchannel (device). If you recall, the address in a PC I/O instruction does not reference a particular slot. There are many more significant differences between I/O instructions in these two computer architectures, so using one type of computer to understand another can be carried only so far.

Nevertheless, as you can see, the small, simple PC has some things in common with the much larger Processor Complex. Although the details of the electronics and software are very different and unique for each kind of computer, they share the same principles. We now abandon our poor PC and concentrate on the details of how a Processor Complex exchanges data with I/O devices.

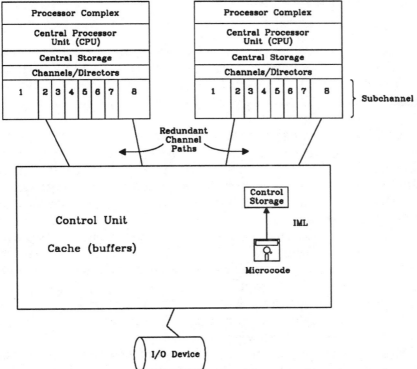

Figure 4.3 I/O in Mainframe Environments. The mainframe channel architecture performs the same basic functions as a PC channel architecture, but does so from more than one CPU inside a Processor Complex or from multiple Processor Complexes. The reason is that I/O devices are configured externally from the ability to process instructions. The above logical presentation shows two Processor Complexes accessing a storage control unit.

4.2. Processor Complex to I/O Device

This section introduces the concepts of moving data to and from the DASD devices. The concepts presented are generally available for non-DASD devices too.

4.2.1. Channel Paths

In Figure 4.3, you see a schematic representation of a system: two Processor Complexes, a control unit, and an I/O device are shown as boxes, and the cables connecting them are shown as lines. A set of I/O devices connected to a controller is called a *string*.

Note that the fourth box down inside the Processor Complex is labeled *Channels/directors*. In most modern Processor Complexes the connection electronics is called a *channel*. In the 3033 Processor Complex channels were combined into *directors*, but that name was eliminated when the 3880 control unit was developed with directors.

Channels are numbered for identification. Control units also have a unique number identification but are known to the data center personnel by the number of the channel to which they are attached. I/O devices are also numbered for identification. The combination of a channel and an I/O device number is usually called a *device address*. In the case of DASD, this address is used by the software to identify a particular actuator.

Must a control unit be connected only to a single channel? That is sometimes the case, but not always. It depends on the particular control unit model. Must a control unit be connected only to a single Processor Complex? Again, it depends on the control unit.

In Figure 4.3, a single control unit and its attached devices are connected to two Processor Complexes. The Processor Complex on the left side can access the control unit and its devices using channels 2 and 8. That Processor Complex may be running MVS, VM, VSE, or any of the System/370 or System/390 operating systems.

The Processor Complex on the right side can access the same control unit and devices using its channels 2 and 8. That Processor Complex may also be running any of the System/370 operating systems, and not necessarily the same operating system as the Processor Complex on the left.

Although the same channel addresses are used on both Processor Complexes, they need not be. The control unit could be connected to channels 2 and 8 on one Processor Complex but 3 and 7 on the other, for example. The reason we use the same channels on both is to minimize confusion, not only in the example but also in real life. This permits us to identify the box that is the control unit by its channel address or addresses without further qualification. It also helps to have the channel numbers the same on two Processor Complexes when one may be used to take over for the other in the case of a primary CPU failure.

In the following, then, when we say *channel 2*, we mean the channel inside the Processor Complex with the control unit attached to it. Also, when we say *access a device*, we mean *access a device through its control unit*.

Channel path 8 is redundant with path 2: there are two ways to access the same data on each Processor Complex. Most data centers configure this way intentionally to get **performance** and **availability** advantages:

- Performance is enhanced by taking advantage of parallel I/O operations for two or more devices. *Redundant channels do not help access to a single device.*
- Availability is enhanced by having redundant channel paths to the same control unit: if one path becomes unavailable, the data is available through the other.

The System/370 architecture allows I/O operations to proceed simultaneously if they are on different I/O devices and channels. A channel requires some time (albeit small) to initiate and service an I/O operation. If *channel busy* time becomes a bottleneck, this constraint can be relieved by splitting the load among two or more channels.

Not only is performance enhanced, but the system can tolerate some kinds of component failure. In the example, the operating system can access a device through both channels, 2 and 8. If either of those channels becomes *broken* or *unavailable* for some reason, the end users can still access their data if the control unit and device remain functional.

What is one way a channel could be unavailable but not broken? If the Processor Complex were physically partitioned (e.g., 3084 physically partitioned or PR/SM), with channel 2 in one partition and channel 8 in the other, and the operating system in one partition failed, users could access their data through the other partition.

There are two other kinds of redundancy that data centers may employ for the same reasons as channel redundancy. First, redundant controllers can be used with some DASD models. In this case, if one controller fails, the other can be used; the two controllers share the I/O load with each other. We highly recommend two control units (or two power-separated sides) for each string of DASD.

Second, redundant DASD can be used for enhanced availability. One way to do this is with *dual copy*, in which each I/O write operation is performed simultaneously on two different actuators. If one actuator fails or its data becomes corrupt, the data is available on the intact device. We recommend this feature only for very valuable data because the cost of implementing dual copy is relatively high. See the section on *dual copy*.

Now we will look at ways control units are physically attached to their Processor Complex(es).

4.2.2. Parallel: Bus and Tag Channels

The original System/360 connection from the Processor Complex to the control unit was through large (one inch in diameter) cables with plugs about the size of a person's hand. Two cables are required for each connection and are called **bus** and **tag** cables. The architecture specifies a maximum distance of 400 feet between the Processor Complex and the last control unit on the string. (Remember that a *string* is a set of devices connected to the same controller.)

The same parallel architecture moved into the 1970s, 1980s, and 1990s. Its use spans from the System/360 architecture to the

System/390 architecture. It is most often associated with the System/370 architecture.

Parallel connection means that a wire is assigned to each of the 8 bits in a data byte and others are reserved for parity and management of the data being transferred. **42 conductors are required for each parallel path**, with 84 total for a single bus and tag cable pair. The connectors usually have gold-plated connectors.

The parallel transmission is the reason for the 400-foot distance limitation. Think about it. You and eight of your friends get in eight different vehicles and try to drive from point to point in a large city and reach the same point within hundredths of seconds. The task is even harder with parallel cables.

The parallel System/370 cable length limitation causes problems for very large data centers. They may have so many I/O devices that all the control units cannot be located within a 400-foot radius of the Processor Complex. The limitation can cause problems for any size data center: sometimes the only space for growth is a room more than 400 feet away. The trend toward automated, or *lights out,* operations begs for flexibility that the old architectural limitation cannot give.

4.2.3. Non-ESCON Solutions

Using optical fiber technology, there are several ways to get around the parallel architecture limitations. The information is passed between Processor Complexes and control units as light signals. An optical fiber carries the light from one end to the other. The signals travel faster and more intelligence can be carried over time on fiber than on copper. Moreover, signal attenuation is lower with fiber, so signals may travel further without requiring amplification.

IBM sells a 3044 Fiber Optic Channel Extender that is a box with bus and tag plugs in one side (like a control unit), but the *bus does not stop here*. The 3044 converts the signal into optical fiber signals and transmits the signal up to 6,600 feet. A data center could place disk and tape drives on other floors of a building or even in other buildings. A data center may take advantage of fiber technology with the lowest expense this way.

Before you rush out and place an order with your IBM salesperson, investigate options available from other vendors. For example, Data Switch has tested products to extend DASD up to 2,000 feet, whereas IBM supports DASD at only 800 feet. Data Switch also has extension devices for tapes and printers that run 200 miles and require no host-resident software.

4.2.4. ESCON Solutions

When IBM introduced the System/390 architecture on September 5, 1990, most people agreed that a new architecture was born. New software and new hardware was included.

Optical fiber connection is *serial* data transmission. Management and data bits are transmitted one at a time to a receiver that puts them together on the other end of the cable. It may sound slower, but with faster data transfer technology the transmission can be much faster. Original transfer rates of 10 megabytes per second were increased to 17 megabytes per second. These will increase to hundreds of megabytes per second.

We view the announcements as upward compatible extensions to the System 360 architecture of 1965. Don't get us wrong. It is a giant step forward, but just another step. What does the ESCON architecture gain for us?

The IBM ES/9000 series integrates fiber directly into its systems architectures. IBM positioned its ES/9000 series, called *Summit* before its release, to take full advantage of fiber technology.

The ES/9000 channel subsystem uses independent processing units to control data movement from devices to central storage. The optical fiber cables plug directly into the Processor Complex on one end and the control unit on the other. No 3044 is needed.

IBM, of course, recognizes that a lot of hardware is installed in the data centers before optical fiber channels. They provide conversion for non-ESCON control units called **ESCON converters**. The converter does the translation from serial to parallel. The protocol remains bus and tag: think of it as bus and tag on light. IBM announced the early versions of the ES/9000 processors with either bus and tag (parallel) or fiber (serial) channels.

The 3990-3 control unit has options (field upgradable) for fiber optic channel connections, so you can switch an entire channel from bus and tag to the new serial channels. Now there are three ways to sling a channel. The first is conventional (**B/T**), using the parallel bus and tag protocol over wire. The second, called **Fx**, is a serial version of the bus and tag protocol over optical fiber. The third is *serial* (**S**), using the framing protocol over optical fiber. Serial channels are strictly point-to-point, while both bus and tag channel link implementations may be daisy chained.

Reasons for ESCON

The two main benefits of this architecture are flexibility in where to place devices and improved *availability* for your data center.

First, ESCON gives the data center flexibility to place devices at a location that is not in their data center. Some authors refer to the data center as a *glass house* because it was the rage for many years to build glass walls around the data center so visiting VIPs and executives could see where all the data processing money went. Security and common sense have prevailed, and most data centers are now enclosed.

Why might we want parts of our data center located away from the main computer room? Take the most simple reason. Daily backup tapes are created for data set backup, usually placed into boxes, and sent *offsite* to safeguard the data in case a local disaster (e.g., fire, water damage) disables the data center. Wouldn't it be better to have a few tape drives at another building and have the tapes that were designated as offsite backup tapes directed to that building?[2] It would save considerable resources.

Online DASD storage could also benefit. What if DASD located in another city were made to be dual copies of online data? Any problem in the data center could be overcome by switching to the Processor Complex in the remote city.[3]

Do not be fooled into thinking that this flexibility is useful only to very large installations.

Second, ESCON allows a *properly configured* system to change the hardware without shutting down the system. Most data centers have over 90 percent of their downtime scheduled for maintenance. Much of that is adding or moving devices. Of course, ESCON will not help much if the outage is for water cooling, electrical, or other environmental situations.

ESCON Migration and Configuration

Installation of the ESCON architecture should be viewed as a major change in the way you do business. The connections are similar to those needed for communications equipment, and proper planning and documentation at the start will make the system manageable in the future. Failure to plan and execute properly could result in the same sort of disaster that many communication experts found themselves in with coaxial and twinaxial cable—a closet full of a jumble of wires.

Optical fiber channel connections are designed to remove the limitations imposed by parallel channels so that control units and devices can be placed further from the Processor Complex. The first implementation of optical fiber channels limited the distance for all devices to approximately 9 kilometers.

---

2   The September 1991 announcements provide for tape drives to be located at 23 kilometers (14.3 miles) from the Processor Complex.

3   The September 1991 announcements introduced laser technology and 9/125 micrometer single-mode fiber optic cable which allows ESCON-attached DASD to run at 9 kilometers (5.5 miles).

The second implementation moved to 60 kilometers (37.2 miles) for channel-to-channnel connections, 43 kilometers (26.6 miles) for 3174 and 3172 communication control units, 23 kilometers (14.3 miles) for 3490 tape drives, and 9 kilometers (5.5 miles) for 3990 storage control and 9340 DASD subsystems. The architecture is theoretically limitless because it uses the same technology as our long distance phone companies use for telephone calls. In the future some data centers will have data centers in one city, DASD in another, and tape drives in still another.

Other ESCON Uses

Optical fiber cables are not just for DASD. Another implementation for optical fiber cables is combination of multiple Processor Complexes into a **Sysplex**. The first implementation of that technology is the IBM 9037 Sysplex Timer, which synchronizes the time-of-day (TOD) clocks to within 600 milliseconds for the various CPUs that are logically linked together.

Optical fiber cables can also emulate channel-to-channel (CTC) adapters. The Global Resource Serialization (GRS) component of MVS uses CTCs to control access to enqueues across Processor Complexes. The early ES/9000 processors did not have the microcode available, and many companies could not even partition their machines even though PR/SM was on the machine.

The next implementation of ESCON connectivity will probably be shared expanded storage. Central storage will probably not be shared because central storage architecture allows byte access and the management of 2 gigabytes of data a byte at a time is far more expensive and complicated than the management of 2 gigabytes of data 4 kilobytes (Kb) at a time. Expanded storage is accessed either by special instructions (e.g., move page) or operating system components.

Shared expanded storage will allow operating systems to share control blocks and internal parameters. Processors miles apart will soon be sharing storage, not just DASD! The VTOC update problems may go away. Think of the entire VTOC for a DASD volume read into shared storage for all components in the Sysplex.

As we get to Sysplexes connected miles apart, all data can be made available to all processors. This sounds farfetched today, but think of where you are today and where we were just 20 years ago!

As with adaptation to any new technology, IBM (and other non-IBM vendors) has a small problem with completely replacing a channel architecture. What do they do with all the control units in the field that have only bus and tag receptacles? There's a large demand for this *old* equipment to remain in service. Consumers can be influenced to replace old technologies when the cost of their maintenance overtakes that of their replacement.

4.2.5. Channel Operation

Channels move data from Processor Complexes to control units using well-defined channel protocol. A channel can operate in two modes: burst or byte mode. Three types of channel protocol exist: selector, byte multiplex, and block multiplex.

Burst Mode

In burst-mode channel operation, the I/O device monopolizes the channel during transmission of information. The burst can consist of a few bytes, a whole physical block of data, a sequence of blocks, or status data.

All Direct Access Storage Devices operate in burst mode. Once they get started on a block, they do not want to stop transferring data until the end of the block.

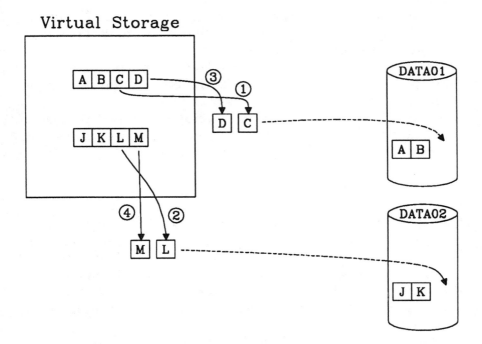

Figure 4.4 Block Multiplexor Channels. Physical data blocks on channels operating in block multiplexor channels can interleave blocks going to two different devices on the same channel. In this illustration, actuator *DATA01* is receiving four blocks, *A, B, C,* and *D.* Actuator *DATA02* is receiving four blocks, *J, K, L,* and *M.* The channel can transmit block *C* for DATA01 and then block *L* for DATA02. The interleaving allows maximum throughput for the channel architecture because the channel can minimize device delays.

Byte Mode

In byte-mode channel operation, the I/O device monopolizes the channel for one byte at a time.

Selector Channels

Channels operating in selector mode start an I/O operation with the first block to transfer. The channel stays connected to the device until all channel program words are complete or the channel program is terminated for some other reason. The channel is busy for all other devices until the entire group of blocks is transferred for that device.

Selector Channels existed in Processor Complexes only up to the 308x series of processors. In System/360 Processor Complexes, you could order selector channels. In the 303x and 308x family, you could specify the selector mode for 3400 tapes or other devices, because these devices had to operate in selector mode.

Byte Multiplexor Channels

Byte Multiplexor Channels operate in byte mode. They are used where many, relatively slow I/O devices share the same channel, and each is given a short time slice of the channel's attention.

Byte is the most efficient for very slow devices. It is mandatory for certain very old teleprocessing terminals and for slow card readers such as the 2501 (should you ever run into one in a museum).

While you cannot purchase Byte Multiplexor Channels, your data center may have byte-mode devices attached to today's channels.

Block Multiplexor Channels

All DASD should be placed on channels designated as Block Multiplexor. Block Multiplexor Channels transfer data in burst mode while a physical block of data is being transferred.

The channel can connect/disconnect dynamically any number of times to the same device for one channel program. What does this interleaving of channel commands gain for us?

In Figure 4.4, two tasks have built streams of blocks to be written to **two different DASDs**. Blocks A, B, C, and D are to be written to DASD volume DATA01. Blocks J, K, L, and M are to be written to DASD volume DATA02. Both DASD volumes are on the same channel. Volume DATA01 is ready for a block, so the channel transfers block *C*. Nothing else on the channel can happen until block *C* completes. If there is a delay by DATA01 in accepting block *D* (e.g., seeking, error recovery, set sector delay, etc.), then the channel can begin transferring block *L* to volume DATA02. The blocks are said to be *interleaved*.

> ◻ The channel can interleave as many of these I/O devices as it has channel commands awaiting service **as long as the channel is operating in block multiplexor mode**.

This note is a warning that DASD is normally configured in block multiplexor mode, but in some older hardware in use today, they can be specified as *selector*. Selector mode would wait for all blocks (*A* through *D*) to complete before *J-K-L-M* were attempted. You would be surprised how often I have heard about DASD control units being incorrectly specified, resulting in very long I/O service times.[4]

4.3. Control Units

Control units are large computers that control access to devices. In the case of DASD, the most modern control units from IBM are the 3880 and 3990 series of control units.

4.3.1. Path Considerations

Figure 4.5 shows a typical configuration. If you have 3880 model 3 control units, it is a good idea to pair them **for availability purposes**. The 3880 is divided into two *storage directors*. The

---

4   Thanks to Jim Crane for his outstanding work on identifying and correcting selector-mode problems using DASD.

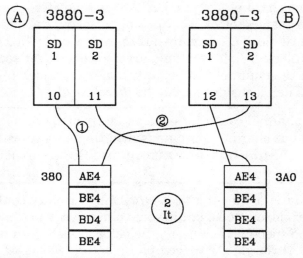

Figure 4.5 Two Channel Paths. Control units are required to access DASD devices. A feature of the DASD device head of string that allows more than one control unit to access the string is called *two channel paths*. Above, either control unit *A* (through storage director 1—path 10) or control unit *B* (through storage director 2—path 13) can access devices 380 through 384. Strings 380 and 3A0 are said to be configured for availability—failure of one control unit would not prevent access to the devices.

two storage directors of the IBM 3880 are very dependent on each other. (This is not true of the non-IBM control units or the IBM 3990.) Many problems with the 3880 require the entire box (both directors) to be powered down.

> ¤ We **have had** IBM CE's tell us that an entire 3990 box must be powered down to get a failed-side back online. They (and second level) did not know that pressing the *power on* button will bring a failed, and fixed, side back to life. You may want to note this to save a major outage with a 3990 control unit.

In the figure, the string of 3380 devices on the left side can have two channel paths connected to the AE4 head of string. The data center could connect storage director 1 (path *10*) to the first channel path and storage director 2 (path *11*) to the second channel path. All volumes on 3380 devices 380–38F would be dependent on control unit *A's* being well enough to function.

Instead, if more than one control unit were available, one path could be serviced by path *10* through control unit *A* and the second path by path *13* through control unit *B*.

The phrase *configured for availability* means that if one of the two control units became disabled, the end user could access all the data of both strings through the remaining, functional control unit.

We have found many data centers that do not have their control units so configured. Their justification is often is that the control units were ordered one at a time, and no one got around to recabling the control units. I recommend that they copy the circle in Figure 4.5, and then they will get a *round 2it*. Make the time to do important tasks.

> ¤   BJ's Rule: Some people make things happen. Some people ask why things happen. Some people ask, "What happened?" Become the person who makes things happen.

If your data center is configured with all strings going through a single 3880, then make a plan to reconfigure your DASD farm to get your control units and strings configured properly. Note, we did not say "balanced", Configuring properly will be discussed later.

We often saw that this configuration enabled us to endure hardware problems without our end user community ever knowing about the problem. In one case a control unit was disabled for a whole week! Ask yourself, *what would happen if my customers could not access their data for 7 days?*

The following figures use the IBM 3990-3 cache control unit as an example, but the concepts are valid for all versions of the IBM cache control units (e.g., 3880-21, 3880-23) and for OEM equipment (e.g., Amdahl, Hitachi, etc.).

The 3990 model 1 provides two storage paths and is designed for midrange Processor Complex installations. The 3990 model 2 provides up to four paths to DASD and is designed to be function-

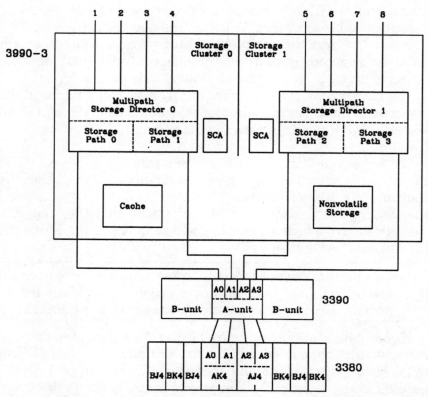

Figure 4.6 Four Channel Paths. With 3990 control units and four-pathing 3390 or 3380 devices, the same configuration for availability is achieved, but now there are performance benefits to the configuration. Above, a single 3390 with two storage clusters (same as storage directors in 3880 control units) services one string of 3390 devices (must be in four-path mode) and one string of 3380 devices (can be in four-path mode if *J*s or *K*s).

ally equal to two cross-configured 3880 model 3s. Neither the model 1 nor the model 2 has cache storage. The model 1 cannot attach 3390 DASD because it does not have the required four paths.

Figure 4.6 shows the 3990 control unit attached to a string of 3390s and a string of 3380s. Eight channel paths (1 through 8 at the top) are pictured, with four paths into each DASD unit.

One confusion with *eight paths* is that it looks like you could have eight paths to these strings of DASD from a single Processor Complex. Not true. The architecture allows only four paths from any single Processor Complex.

4.3.2. Timing: Channel End and Device End

When an application task requests an I/O operation, it is performed asynchronously for the task. Device **service time** is the elapsed wall clock time from the time the application requested the I/O until Device End is received. The task will wait for an I/O operation only if it completes all work (usually processing) before the I/O subsystem finishes with the request. Since Processor Complexes are orders of magnitude faster than the I/O components, most tasks end up waiting on I/O.

> ◻ The fastest I/O is no I/O at all. The IBM Washington Systems Center reports that 80% of all performance problems are related to I/O.

Two points in time are important to the operating system and to the tasks requesting the I/O. The first is **Channel End** (CE), when the channel has completed the requested operation and is now free to do other work.

The channel is not busy (and thus can present Channel End) when a DASD is seeking or moving the arm from one spot to another or when the DASD is executing a SET SECTOR command and waiting for the platter to spin into place. CE is not important to the requesting task; the work is not complete.

The second is **Device End** (DE), when the device has completed the requested operation (or faked by the control unit in caching operations). Device End is the signal that the actuator has performed all operations for the channel program and the task can be dispatched if it is waiting for the block to or from the device.

In the following discussion, the I/O operations will be very simple. Single blocks of data will going to single places on the DASD. If you are doing performance analysis or modeling, do not use such simple channel operations; complex is better in that case. However, the diagrams would become too complex to show multiple blocks and long channel programs.

4.4. Cache Storage

Cache storage refers to Random Access Memory (RAM) in a piece of hardware. Cache is *volatile*: when the power is turned off, the data in the RAM is also lost. Cache is used to speed up some processes. In the case of DASD, cache is used to overcome the physical motion (which is very slow compared to cache speed) required to read or write a block of data.

Cache storage in a control unit is an expensive resource outside the operating system's control. The operating system may affect how the cache responds, but cache is under the control of the microcode in the control unit. Several operating systems poll the cache control unit (e.g., every 2.5 minutes) to see how it is responding.

IBM also takes the approach that every DASD should be a cache candidate. Their implementation is therefore to turn on cache for an entire actuator and let the control unit manage the resource. Some non-IBM manufacturers allow the data center to specify which data sets are to get cache access. The latter approach is aligned better with protecting your *loved ones* than full utilization of all resources.

The following sections discuss the possibilities for cache in DASD control units.

4.4.1. Read Hit

Figure 4.7 shows the logical representation of a read hit. A read hit occurs when there is a request to read one or more blocks into

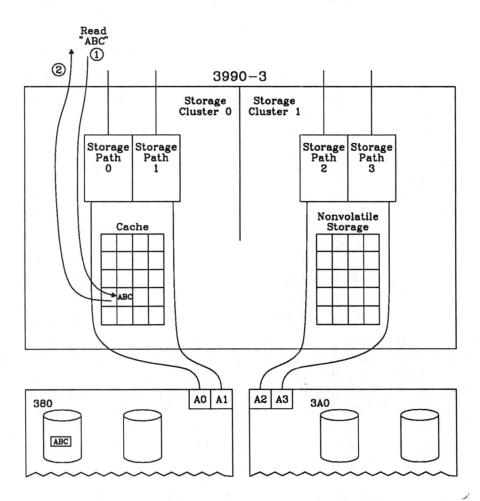

Figure 4.7 Read Hit. The first possibility for an I/O device access through a cache control unit is a *read hit*. In this example, actuator 380 is asked to read block *ABC*. The block has been read before, and the contents of the block are still in the control unit cache. This is the fastest access for any I/O and is usually completed in approximately 3 milliseconds. No device delay is encountered. No seeking. No RPS misses. In fact, the channel never disconnects.

the Processor Complex, and the read can be satisfied by data stored in the cache. Read hits are very good. Why? Speed. Blinding speed. A read hit can be satisfied [both Channel End (CE) and Device End (DE) presented] in about 3 milliseconds. A DASD I/O can take from 40 milliseconds to several seconds!

In Figure 4.7, the DASD device at 380 contains a block of data *ABC*. At some time in the past, the block had been read into cache and passed on to the virtual storage of some task. Now (at *1*), if another task (or even the same task) in the Processor Complex wants to read the same block, the block will likely be found in the cache. The block can be moved into virtual storage (at *2*) by the channel/control unit.

> ¤   For the second read of the same block, the channel and control unit never miss a beat, assuming channel program execution was not interrupted by another, interleaved access. Another assumption is that the block has not been flushed out of the cache. This I/O is as almost as fast as it can ever be performed: device service time should be approximately **3 milliseconds**.

We say "almost" because there is a slight amount of overhead, somewhere between 0.1 and 1 millisecond, for the search of the directory cache. Without cache, if the *read* hits the real DASD at just the right time, it may be possible to get the block directly from the DASD faster than a cached read hit could find it. This all assumes that the channel speed is not greater than the device rotation speed, and besides, how often do you suppose reads from DASD get that "lucky"?

You may be asking yourself, "If the block was read once, why can't both tasks share the block? After all, neither will update it." It could be shared, but the access method does not do this automatically. If the block were placed in an area of virtual storage that all tasks in the operating system could access (e.g., in common storage, PLPA, CICS Local Shared Resources in MVS, or VM shared segments), then the block could be shared. Most

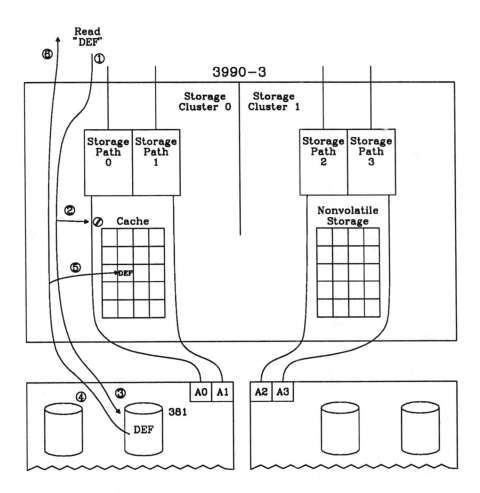

Figure 4.8 Read Miss. When an I/O request is issued and the block is not in cache storage in the control unit, the action is called a *read miss*. In *1* above, the seek, set sector, and read are issued for block *DEF*. At *2*, the block is not found, so the control unit starts a normal read (seek, set sector, and wait for rotation) and the channel disconnects from the control unit. After the device and control unit synchronize the reading of the block (at *4*), the block is placed into cache (at *5*) and transferred to the channel (at *6*). No extra time is consumed by a read miss; it just takes approximately the same time as a noncached read.

data requested is not shared. Examples are source libraries, catalogs, directories, etc.

4.4.2. Read Miss

Figure 4.8 shows what happens if the block is not in cache when some task wants to read the block. At *2*, the block is not located in cache. The control unit reads the block from the device (at *3*) and starts transferring the data to the Processor Complex (at *4*). The control unit places a copy in cache (at *5*). Depending on other parameters, the control unit also will start to read other blocks around the requested block. The reading of other blocks will tie up the backstore paths from the 3990 control unit to the DASD string.

The service time is **severely increased** for a read miss. It increases from about 3 milliseconds to 40–60 or more!) milliseconds. The time is not much greater than if cache was not involved.

One reason for the increased service time is, of course, that the block cannot be accessed from cache but instead must be accessed from spinning platters on DASD. A second possible explanation is that the 3990-3 control unit can transfer data between it and a Processor Complex at *channel speed.*

ESCON serial channels, using the framing protocol instead of bus and tag, are expected to operate at 10 million bytes per second (9.54 Mb/s).[5] Some System/370 channels can operate at 4.5 million bytes per second (4.29 Mb/s). Some System/370 channels can operate at 3.0 million bytes per second (2.86 Mb/s).

Cache data can be transferred at channel speed. The 3380 device operates at 3 million bytes per second (2.86 Mb/s) and the 3390 operates at 4.2 million bytes per second (4.01 Mb/s). In this case the data from a 3380 would have been transferred at 4.29

---

5   DASD vendors usually use the prefix *mega* to mean 1,000,000, but this is misleading because other data storage measures use *mega* to mean 1,048,576.

Mb/s had it come from the cache, but it is transferred at 2.86 Mb/s from DASD.

4.4.3. Write Hit

Figure 4.9 shows what happens if a write is requested and the block is found in cache—a *write hit*. The application program issues a *write* (at *1*).

Storage path 2 was selected by the operating system (370 mode) or by the System/370 or System/390 microcode as an alternate path to device 381.

The control unit finds the block in cache and updates the copy in the cache block (at *2*). The control unit continues writing the block to the DASD device 381 (at *3*). When the device has successfully written the block, the I/O request is marked with Device End (at *4*). This is true for the 3990 model 3 in which DASD fast write (DFW) cache fast write (CFW) were both not specified. For 3880 model 3, cache is bypassed totally on all writes (except to mark it invalid if found in cache.)

The service time for the I/O request is not significantly penalized for a write hit. The I/O operation was going to go to the DASD in any case.

The procedure may be altered if either DASD Fast Write or Cache Fast Write, described later, are enabled. For 3880 models, cache is bypassed totally on all writes, except that if the data is found in cache, the cached version is marked invalid.

4.4.4. Write Miss

Figure 4.10 illustrates a write miss. The application has requested to write block *JKL* to device 381 (at *1*). The block is not in cache. A cache slot is selected and filled (at *2*), and the block is transferred (possibly some time later) to the DASD device (at *3*).

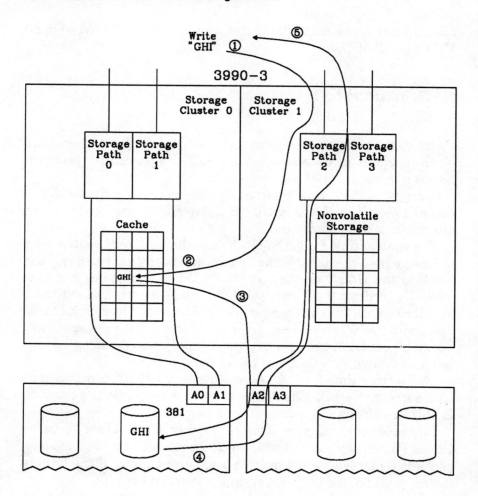

Figure 4.9 Write Hit. When a block is asked to be written and the block is in cache, the operation is a *write hit.* In this example, block *GHI* is being written (at *1* above), and it is found in cache. This makes sense, as many updated records are read into central storage, updated, and then quickly rewritten. The control unit and cache cannot just update the cache (at *2*) and continue because the record would be in volatile (no power = no updated record) storage. So the I/O request is delayed while the control unit and device write the record to DASD (at *3*), and then the channel program is terminated normally (at *4*). We show the I/O operation completing through another path because the four-path mode does not care which path was used to start the I/O operation.

The Channel End and Device End are presented to the Processor Complex to show that the process is completed.

The service time for the I/O request is not significantly penalized for a write miss because the added cache management time (0.1 ms) is small compared to the total (20–40 ms).

Again, the procedure may differ depending on Fast Write. No cache slot is selected on any cache model except for a 3990-3 with DASD Fast Write enabled, in which case there may be a delay writing the data to DASD, or with Cache Fast Write enabled, in which case the data may never be written to DASD.

4.4.5. Dual Copy, Fast Write, and Other Black Box Things

The 3990 model 3 is a major step forward in I/O architecture, because the control unit can be instructed to provide CE/DE to the application **before** the spinning DASD has received the data. IBM calls their implementation of this **Extended Functions,** and they can only be used on the 3990 model 3.

In most DASD models preceding this, IBM and other manufacturers would not present CE/DE to the application before the data was written to DASD for fear that some component failure would occur after the application was notified but before the data was really there.

For example, think about the payroll department entering a transaction to give you a $10,000 pay raise. The transaction is entered. The application requests the I/O operation. The I/O subsystem gets the data and marks the transaction complete. The terminal operator thinks the job is done. The operating system thinks the job is done. The DASD is not even spinning! In the ensuing manual recovery, there is nothing to remember your pay raise. Too bad! You lose!

Some I/O requests are so important that it is imperative for the data to be correctly recorded. One operating system, the Transaction Processing Facility (TPF) distributed by IBM, was written by the airline industry. It is also used for passenger

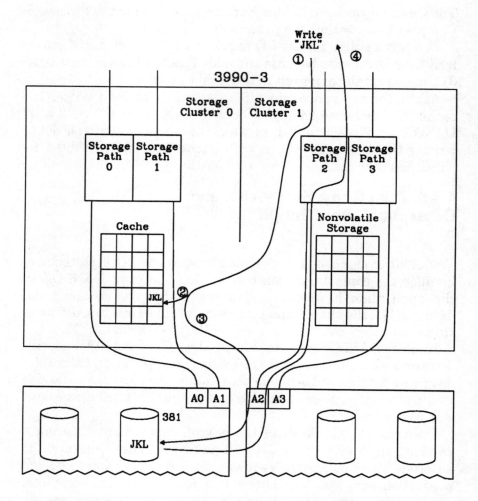

Figure 4.10 Write Miss. A block written to a cached device is a *write miss* when the block is not found in the cache at the start of the I/O operation. In this example, block *JKL* is being written (at *1* above), and it is not found in cache. The record could be a new one or an updated record that was flushed out of cache storage before it could be rewritten. Just as a write hit, the system cannot just update the cache and continue because the record would be in volatile (no power = no updated record) storage. So the I/O request is delayed while the control unit and device write the record to DASD (at *3*). After the record is safely on the disk surface (at *4*), the device signals completion. The only real difference between a write hit and a write miss is that on the write hit, the block was found in cache and updated there as well as written to the volume.

railway reservations and by some financial transaction processing firms. If you call the airline and request a reservation, the system has only one chance to record the data. (Data availability is so critical to TPF applications that transactions are also written to tape in real time as they are written to DASD.)

Some I/O requests are not important because their recovery is implicit in the restart operation initiated when a task fails to complete successfully. For example, some temporary data sets, such as sort work areas, are "recovered" by being reconstructed when the task is rerun. If the device fails, so will the task; if the task is important, its failure will be noticed, and it will be restarted. In this case, the loss of the temporary data has no lasting effect.

The solution to these problems is **nonvolatile storage**. Figure 4.11 shows a battery inside the control unit connected to the NVS. The battery may last approximately 48 hours to protect the data in NVS in case of power outage or equipment failure until the I/O subsystem can be fixed and powered up to complete the write operation to the spinning DASD.

Destaging is the process of moving data stored in cache to permanent storage on DASD. If data cannot be destaged because of a failure of either the DASD or the control unit, the data is said to be **pinned**. The data center must take some action to recover or discard pinned data before the region of cache occupied by the data can be reused for other data. See the section on pinned data.

4.4.6. DASD Fast Write

DASD Fast Write (DFW) is a feature that uses NVS and allows a physical block to be written to cache and saved in nonvolatile storage (NVS) to free up the application while guaranteeing that the data will be written to the DASD. It improves performance because write hits and full track format writes do not need to complete on the spinning DASD before the application is free to continue. It does not affect availability of the data because the

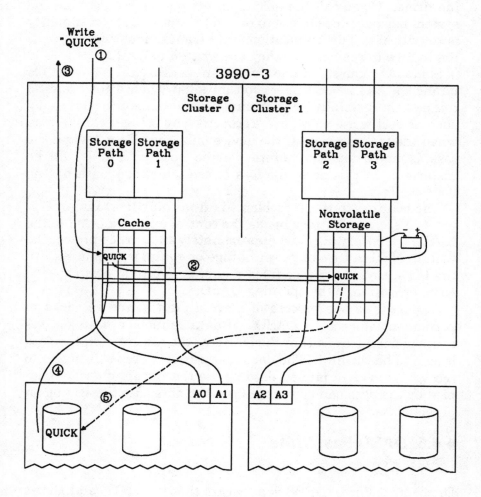

Figure 4.11 DASD Fast Write. The problem of slow write commands is overcome by the DASD Fast Write feature of the 3990 model 3. In this example, at *1* above a write command is issued to a device specified as available for DASD Fast Write. The block is written to cache and to nonvolatile storage at *2*, and the channel command is completed with Channel End and Device End at *3*. The application can continue processing. The control unit moves the block to the appropriate DASD at its next opportunity at *4*. If some component fails, the control unit can move the block to DASD by using nonvolatile storage at *5*.

data is preserved in NVS. No modifications to access methods or applications are required. Figure 4.11 shows the following flow:

1. The application requests the write of a block *QUICK*. The block is copied to cache.

2. The block is copied to nonvolatile storage (NVS).

3. Channel End and Device End are presented to the Processor Complex. The block is in cache and safely in NVS. The application program is free to go on to other instructions, even to ask to write another block.

4. The block is moved to the target volume, and the NVS slot is marked as available. This may take a very long time (30 minutes to an hour). The cache slot is not freed at this time; this keeps the data available for a future read or write hit.

5. If for some reason the subsystem fails, the copy in NVS can be moved to DASD when the subsystem is restored.

Many kinds of subsystem failures can occur, and it is not always true that data stored in NVS can be successfully written to DASD. The importance of NVS is, however, that improving performance with DASD Fast Write should not reduce data availability below that expected from the DASD itself.

4.4.7. Dual Copy

Another of these extended functions is called *dual copy*, because a shadow copy of an entire actuator is maintained by the control unit. One actuator is called the *primary device*; this is the one that appears to be functional to the host systems. The second actuator is called the *secondary device*; data written to the primary is duplicated on the secondary.

A duplex pair must be initialized with the IDCAMS utility. This takes up to 20 minutes. During this time, the control unit copies the contents of the primary actuator to the secondary actuator. The control unit does not know which tracks are part of a data set and which are not, so every track is copied.

In the event that one of the actuators fails with a permanent error, that actuator becomes the secondary, and the functional actuator becomes the primary, regardless of which was which before the failure. Data is not written to the new, failed secondary but instead is preserved in NVS until the two actuators are restored as a duplexed pair. At that point, the control unit may resynchronize the two actuators by writing the data stored in NVS.

Dual copy is for really important data. The application and operating system think they are writing to and reading from a single actuator. In actual practice, the control unit makes a complete copy of the volume on another actuator, and each write is duplicated in cache storage and nonvolatile storage, and written to the shadow volume.

Think disaster recovery. You should make dual copy volumes on a separate string from the primary copy volume. The string of course has to be on the same 3990-3 control unit.

Why would a data center design and configure such a system? Some reasons are:

- Files on the volume are very volatile. For example, CICS and IMS logs contain data required to back out transactions if the system fails. Losing any of that data, even minutes before failure, translates directly to loss of employee productivity and is highly noticeable in the enterprise.

- Files are so valuable that they warrant the added expense of two volumes for one volume of data. For example, JES checkpoints are important to system recovery, and using dual copy for these is faster than dual checkpointing because the overhead is moved out of the Processor Complex and into the control unit. Another example is customer files. Depending on their visibility, customer files can translate into real customer relations, and losing data can cause an enterprise loss of credibility.

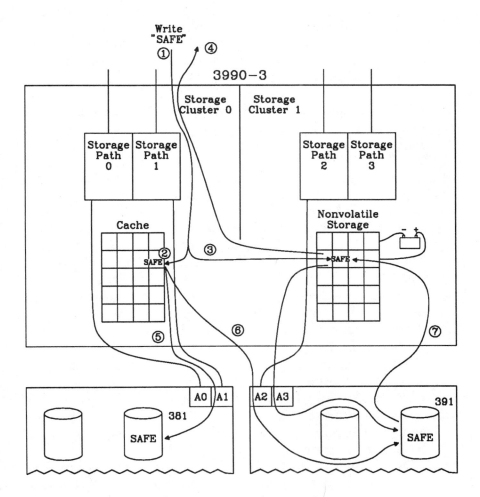

Figure 4.12 Dual Copy. The problem of absolute data availability is overcome by the dual copy feature of control units such as the 3990 model 3. In this example, at *1* above a write command is received to a volume that has a dual copy volume associated, and active. The block is copied into the cache at *2*. The physical block is copied to the nonvolatile storage at *3*, and the channel is notified that the I/O completed satisfactoraly at *4*—usually 3 milliseconds. The physical block is scheduled to and written to the DASD volume at *5* and to the dual copy volume at *6*. The nonvolatile storage block is released. If some failure occurs and the primary volume cannot be used, then the control unit uses the alternate. The control unit may have to move one or more blocks to the dual copy volume directly if write operations cannot be made to the primary volume from cache.

• The continuous availability of read-only data is important. A duplexed volume may be established for data that is not updated but for which the inability to reliably read the data without human intervention would cause ramifications that make the added expense justifiable.

Figure 4.12 illustrates the flow of a write operation to a dual copy volume. The application requests a write of block *SAFE* (at *1*). The block is not found in cache, so it is stored into cache (at *2*). The block is simultaneously written to nonvolatile storage (at *3*). Channel End and Device End are presented to free up the application (at *4*). The I/O operation is started to the primary volume (at *5*) and the secondary volume (at *6*). After the blocks are written to DASD, the NVS is freed (at *7*).

By adding DASD Fast Write to the equation, the application could be notified of Device End before either DASD was accessed (after step *4*). Both the primary volume (381) and the secondary volume (391) could be written because a *SAFE* copy is in NVS.

There are several caveats for dual copy volumes. The first is a performance penalty for data checks. If a read request cannot be satisfied from cache, the control unit attempts to read the data from the primary actuator. If a data check occurs, the control unit reads the data from the secondary actuator. Thus, I/O response time may be increased even though data is reliably read from the duplexed pair.

The second caveat involves alternate track assignments. If the secondary actuator has a track assigned as an alternate track, and the primary actuator has that same track assigned as a normal user track, user data may be overlaid. This is because alternate tracks are handled by the actuator. The control unit has no way of knowing that two data tracks at different logical track addresses may equate to the same spot on the platter.

4.4.8. Cache Fast Write

Cache Fast Write (CFW) is similar to DASD Fast Write but improves performance while possibly affecting availability of the data. CFW data is written directly to volatile cache storage (i.e., not NVS), and no attempt is made to write the data to DASD until a good reason comes along.

One good reason is if the cache management algorithms decide that the cache storage is needed for other data. Another good reason is if a channel command is executed to force the data to be written. A *Perform Subsystem Function* command is available to commit or discard data written to cache. Committing the data forces the data to be written to DASD, and discarding the data frees the cache area where the data was stored *without* writing it to DASD.

Figure 4.13 shows the logical representation of Cache Fast Write. The application asks to write a block *SORT* to device 380 (at *1*). The Processor Complex is returned CE/DE after the block is written into cache (at *2*). The block is not copied into nonvolatile storage. At some time after the channel disconnects from the control unit, the control unit may write the data to the DASD (at *3*).

What happens if the subsystem has an error after the channel is given CE/DE but before the block is written to DASD? The block is gone. The operator is notified, and the job can be rerun if the user desires.

When would you use Cache Fast Write? Sort work data areas and other temporary data sets are tempting, but you should consider the best places to apply this resource. Sort work data sets and temporary data sets are usually created and used by batch jobs. Can you afford to have your cache memory filled with batch blocks? Should you reserve your cache for your *loved ones*—CICS, IMS, TSO—where they can boost people's productivity?

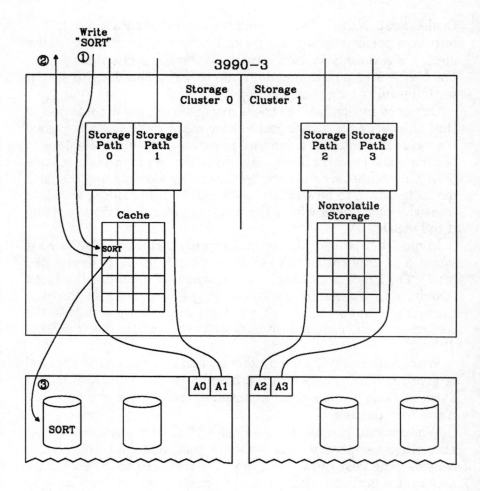

Figure 4.13 Cache Fast Write. Some blocks do not really need to go to DASD if there is a failure. One example is a sort intermediate data set. The program writes a block at *1*. The block is placed in cache and the channel program completes normally with Channel End and Device End at *2*. The requesting program can continue. The control unit moves the block to the appropriate DASD at its next opportunity at *3*.

4.5. ESCON Considerations

If your channels and control units use parallel or bus and tag technology, there is only one way to connect them. Turn the entire computer room over to the vendor(s) and hope they do not bend a pin or step on the water pipes under the floor and flood your entire machine room. Then wait for them to finish. Then hope your system will come back to life.

ESCON technology gets us closer to do-it-yourself cabling (and the trouble associated with that) for devices. You will see more on this topic in later chapters.

First let's define the environment. ESCON exists only on ESA/390 hardware that includes ES connection architecture. Some ES/9000 Processor Complexes have this architecture, some do not.

The 3990 control unit can have both ES and parallel interfaces, but either one or the other must be used to a specific image, or instance of an operating system running a Processor Complex. You cannot mix and match.   (You can, however, use different interfaces to different images running on the same Processor Complex.)

In Figure 4.14 we show two Processor Complexes connected across 6 kilometers, and they share common DASD located up to 9 kilometers away through 3990 control units. This represents a large installation, but a small data center that has outgrown its limited space could place its DASD and control units on another floor so the data center can grow without major construction efforts.

If you thought you needed a Computer-Aided Drawing (CAD) program to map out your computer room before optical fibers, you will really need one now. For those CAD programs supporting layers, or selectable overlaid views of a drawing, seeing all the possible layouts may require several layers.

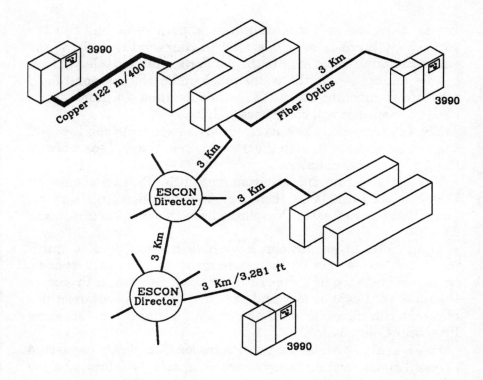

Figure 4.14 ESCON Connectivity. The topography of this architecture is switched point-to-point and point-to-point and allows multiple Processor Complexes as well as their peripheral devices to be connected over a wide range of distances. Note that a single Processor Complex can have both fiber optic and parallel or copper cabling.

4.5.1. ESCON Links

An ESCON link is a physical connection between an optical transmitter and an optical receiver. In Figure 4.15 we show the components of the optical fiber link. These are (from left to right in the figure):

1. Duplex connectors allow manual connection of optical fiber cables. They may be *physical contact connectors* (fiber ends are touching—the kind IBM recommends) or *nonphysical connectors* (fiber ends are not touching).

2. An IBM jumper cable, sometimes called an *orange cable*, is used only within a building between devices or from a device to a distribution panel. They may be ordered in standard lengths from 12 feet (approximately 4 meters) to 400 feet (approximately 122 meters) or custom lengths to 1,600 feet (approximately 488 meters).

3. Distribution panels are used to connect links to channel paths, devices, building-to-building, or floor-to-floor connections within a building.

4. Single trunk connectors carry a single signal from point to point.

5. Trunk cables are generally used between floors or buildings and are similar to telephone trunk cables. The optical fiber trunk cables carry from 12 to 144 fibers (6 to 72 pairs), with a pair required for each link.

6. Splices may be made in long runs of trunks if they must be repaired. Splices may be *fusion* or *mechanical*.

4.5.2. ESCON Trunks

Optical fiber trunks are the prevalent type of carrier in the communications industry. You cannot turn on the television without seeing the latest AT&T, MCI, or Sprint advertisement about who has the most, best, quietest, or fastest optical fiber backbone network. With ESCON your data center will be able to hear a pin drop.

Trunks are not just for building-to-building or city-to-city. Even the smallest data center could use the flexibility of trunks. Some considerations are:

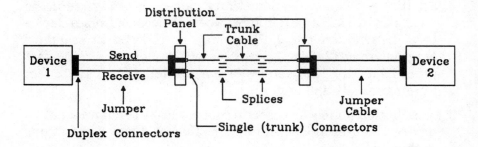

Figure 4.15 ESCON Links. The architecture is a two-conductor connection that allows sending and receiving data at the same time (i.e., full duplex to communications experts in the audience). Cables can be either jumper cables or trunk cables, the main difference being the connector type. Connectors allows maintenance personnel to disconnect and reconnect (after device isolation) device paths as easily as you plug and unplug your table lamps.

- Where are your current devices and where would you like them? Out of space? Think about moving your control units and DASD to another floor or part of the building.
- Plan for expansion. If your DASD farm is growing, where will it be in a few years?
- Think about security. If you are going to place equipment outside the normal confines of your secure computer room, what extra precautions will be needed?
- Spare optical fiber cables. When running trunks it is often easier and cheaper to run all you will need to use in several years. Additional fibers are also used to replace ones that are intermittently causing trouble.

Some additional considerations become important if your fiber cable leaves the building:[6]

- Do you have the necessary right of way required to install the cable?
- For Escon director (ESCD) redrives, will you put an ESCD on top of a telephone pole or in a parking lot? If you have these problems, you may wish to investigate different solutions to the ESCD such Data Switch.
- What happens if Mom and Pop's Backhoe Service wipes out a fiber trunk? Does your company's insurance policy cover repairs? Do you have a redundant trunk leaving the building by a different route?

While this book was being written, common carriers have been in the news for their catastrophic failures, knocking out telephone service for entire metropolitan areas and regions. Whether this is due to fiber trunk cuts, outages of redundant power sources, or human error, the result is the same: businesses that depend on communications get to take a very expensive and quite lengthy coffee break.

Contracting with more than one common carrier does not necessarily protect you against failure. Four bridges cross the river to New York City. How many carriers' fiber trunks do you suppose cross on the Brooklyn Bridge? What might happen to them if something runs into the bridge?

Check with your common carriers to determine where your signals are routed on their trunks. Ensure that you really have redundancy and not just two bills to pay.

> ◻ BJ's Duplicate Redundancy Rule: Don't route redundant fiber together. Avoid the Brooklyn Bridge Syndrome.

---

6   Thanks to Randy Chalfant who provided a wealth of ideas for this and other parts of the book. Randy is another of those rare individuals who has the ability to see what can be, and is willing to share what he knows with others.

4.6. Summary

Channels are internal computers inside a Processor Complex that control access to control units attached to the channel. Control units are computers external to the Processor Complex which convert channel commands to electrical commands that instruct devices attached to the control unit to perform actions such as read or write data.

Channels come in three flavors. The first is made of copper and is called *bus and tag*. These channels operate in parallel manner (all data bits leave the channel at the same time and arrive at the control unit at the same time, and *vice versa*). The second is made of optical fiber cable and is called *ESCON Fx* channels. They operate in serial fashion, where the parallel bus and tag control signals and data bits are communicated one bit at a time from the channel to the control unit. The receiver puts the bits together to make a control sequence and a byte (8 bits) of data. The third also uses optical fiber and is called *ESCON S* channels. These use a protocol different from bus and tag but are capable of much faster transmission rates.

Channels may operate in block multiplexor mode (where blocks may be interleaved between devices) or byte mode (where bytes of a block may be interleaved). All DASD channels operate in block multiplexor mode. Data centers with older, System/370 (pre-XA) Processor Complexes must also ensure that the block multiplexor channels are not specified as a *selector* type, which will cause great degradation of DASD I/O operations.

Channel End is presented to the Processor Complex when the channel is free to perform more channel operations. Device End is presented to the Processor Complex when the device has performed all tasks in a complete channel program.

Cache storage is special central storage in DASD control units and is designed to hold records to prevent having to go to the spinning DASD for retrieval or storage.

A read hit is the condition where a block was requested from a device and the block is found in cache. This is the fastest I/O possible, at about 3 milliseconds, for DASD with spinning media. (Solid-state DASD can be much faster, e.g., 0.5 milliseconds.)

A read miss is the condition where a block read was attempted but the block was not found in cache. The time for the I/O is approximately the same as if cache were not involved, but there may be some repercussions after the read completes, e.g., anticipatory staging.

A write hit identifies the case where a block was asked to be written to a device and the block is found in cache storage. With the 3990-3 without Extended Functions, the cache record is updated and then written to DASD. Device End is presented when the record makes it safely to DASD. If the 3990-3 is using nonvolatile storage to keep a block, Device End may be presented at the end of the cache block update.

A write miss identifies a write of a block that is not in cache. The block is transferred to cache and DASD, and then Device End is presented. If Cache Fast Write is in effect, the channel program ends when cache is updated.

Data centers can allocate a complete actuator to exactly map another actuator on the same control unit. All write commands to the primary volume will be duplicated on the dual copy alternate.

ESCON channels require the data center to understand, plan for, and install a completely new technology. It is similar to the technology used for telephone conversations carried by the long distance carriers. Optical fiber cables carry the data blocks. With the new architecture comes the ability to have devices operating much further from the Processor Complex and at much faster rates than before. At this writing, the maximum distance for 3990 DASD control units is 43 kilometers, but we can expect improvements to increase the distance and transmission rates.

4.7. Questions

1. Describe the two modes a channel can operate in (selector and block multiplexor). What type should all DASD control units operate in?

2. Describe the two topologies for channels.

3. What does *Channel End* mean to an application I/O?

4. What does *Device End* mean to an application I/O?

5. Describe a read hit and give the performance implications.

6. Describe a write hit and give the performance implications.

7. When might response time be worse when caching is enabled than when it is not?

8. When would a data center define a dual copy actuator?

9. What makes ESCON channels different from parallel channels?

10. How do ESCON Fx and S channels differ? What advantage does an Fx channel have over an S channel?

Controlling Direct Access Storage

After you understand the geometry of DASD, the next major area to understand is how to control the DASD. Data center management and end users should team up to put into practice procedures that will cost-effectively use the expensive DASD resource.

Many data centers try to do this job alone. Nothing could be more wrong. The end users must specify requirements for their data. How long will it be kept? How much are they willing to pay to keep the data? You had better know what you are doing. We have seen more than one data center and end user environment not in concert waste a lot of money trying to get data and response times and applications to work properly.

The place to start is *service-level objectives,* which fully specify who is to do what, when it will be done, and who will be accountable for the pieces of the application.

5

DASD Management

5.1. Installation

Installation of Direct Access Storage Devices (DASD) involves configuration planning, software upgrades (operating system and firmware), hardware installation, and preparation of the DASD surface for data storage. Surface preparation is required because channel commands assume that the disk and platter have been formatted. Unformatted devices would not have the areas defined for seeking (arm movement) or searching (selecting an area on one particular track). In other words, on a clear disk, you could seek forever.

This chapter discusses the initialization and maintenance of DASD devices. For IBM devices, the IBM program Data Support Facilities (ICKDSF) is used. Be sure you have the current documentation for the release you are using. We often see people in data centers trying to install and test the operating system without current manuals. A note for individuals responsible for disaster recovery: the initialization program documentation must be available offsite for use in large and small disasters. Those copies of documentation must also be kept up to date.

> ¤ **Be very careful when working with ICKDSF.**
> ICKDSF is a very powerful program, and you can destroy
> data quickly and efficiently even if you do not want to do
> so.

5.1.1. Introduction

DASD management seems very simple. You purchase DASD,
install it, allocate space on it, scratch data sets off it, and replace
it when it wears out. It's like having children: you have the child,
raise it, and it goes about its business when grown. *Ha!* Both
tasks are much more complex than that. We will leave you to
discover, if you have not already, the wonderful complexity of
raising children and concentrate instead on DASD in this chapter.

Figure 5.1 shows several DASD management facets. The first
is the *environment*—how much space and air conditioning the
device requires. IBM and other vendors love to accentuate the
environmentals because all generations have better environmentals than the previous generation. All are smaller and use
less electrical and air conditioning resources. Some people try to
cost-justify new hardware on environmentals. Mostly, the data
center leases or purchases DASD and keeps it until well after the
lease or depreciation ends.

The second is *availability*—what percentage of the time the
device is available for the end user. Availability is a tricky issue.
On the one hand, a newer device is built with better components
and therefore should be available more of the time than previous
generations. It never seems to work out that way. The new
equipment inevitably has bugs or errors in the microcode or just
early failure in the components. The previous generation usually
has been around long enough to have a solid record.

The third is *performance*—how rapidly the device processes
I/O requests. Usually the performance potential of newer devices
is better than that of previous generations. Performance is third
because configuration and management are much more important issues. We have seen configurations so bad that no tuning

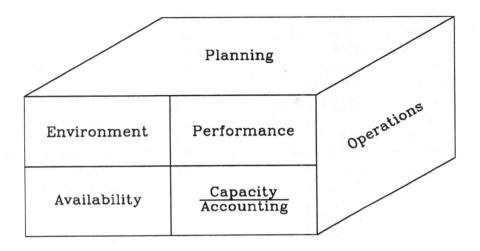

Figure 5.1 DASD Storage Management. The four facets of DASD management are environment, availability, performance, and capacity/accounting. People doing these funtions are either in planning departments (e.g., DASD management or systems programming) or in operational departments (e.g., monitoring and tuning or production control).

could overcome the problems. As you will see, performance has two aspects to it. Instantaneous performance is important because that affects response time for interactive users. Overall performance is important to track because that shows the health of the entire DASD subsystem.

The fourth facet of DASD management is *capacity/accounting*—is there enough room on the DASD to hold the data you need to store, and who is using that space? As everyone soon discovers, DASD space must be managed. Even a customer base of one (e.g., on personal computers) eventually uses all of the space on a device. Someone must clean off unused data. Some data can be archived to tape. Some data can be scratched. All of it must be managed.

> ¤ Data grows to match available storage capacity. The rate at which this occurs is a measure of how well, or poorly, the capacity is managed.

For a customer base of more than one, you should have some accounting method to charge back the resources. Therein lies a real problem. How and when do you survey the DASD to build accounting information? Most large data centers scan all DASD late at night and calculate which groups use the space.

This approach misses two important areas of DASD management: Who allocates space during the day and scratches it before the DASD space allocation programs run at night? Who runs jobs during the day that use large amounts of storage (e.g., temporary storage for SORTs) that adversely affect other end users?

One enterprising end user we knew used the data center's own space manager to migrate all the user's data at 8:00 P.M. and reloaded it at 8:00 A.M. to bypass the space accounting routines.

What, then, should be the goals of effective DASD storage management?

1. Manage the DASD storage in the most cost-effective manner to accomplish the business needs of the company. Add DASD storage *just in time* to meet business needs.

2. Improve the service provided by the DASD subsystem. I/O requests should be completed by the DASD subsystem to meet service-level goals, which in turn meet the business requirements of the company.

3. Solve storage management problems in the shortest, most cost-effective manner possible.

4. Protect the data. Have in place a backup plan that works.

5.1.2. Configuration Planning

The first step in DASD management is to install devices on the computer room floor. Configuration planning is the part of this procedure that determines where in the computer room the devices are to be placed. DASD do not need water cooling but do need electricity and ample air conditioning.

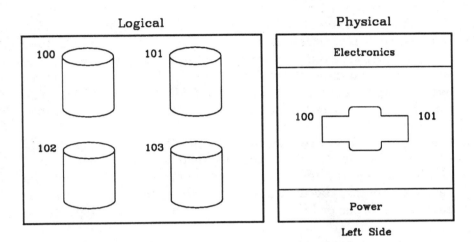

Figure 5.2 Logical and Physical Views of DASD. The diagram on the left shows a logical view of a 3380 DASD. Four actuators are pictured: 100, 101, 102, and 103. These reside in a 3380 device. The physical representation is shown on the right. The doors on a 3380 are on the sides. This view is from one of the two sides. At the top of the device are racks for electronic cards that control functions of the device. Suspended in the middle (one accessed through the left door, the other from the right door) are two Head Disk Assemblies (HDAs). The actuators are at the front and back of the HDAs. On the bottom are the power supplies and the circuit breakers for the components.

You should start with a scale drawing of the data center and plan where all equipment will be placed. IBM provides clear plastic templates representing its equipment to make a manual configuration drawing effort possible. We have used a PC-based Computer-Aided Drawing (CAD) program to make scale drawings of the floor and equipment. It allows superimposing separate drawings, or *layers*, each in a different color. For example, blue might be physical box locations, green coolant, yellow electric, and red data cables.

> ❑ Place your devices carefully in the computer room. Install them in one spot and leave them alone until you absolutely must move them.

Starting with the 3380 model K and continuing with the 3390 devices, IBM recommends that you reformat (translation: take full backups, wipe out all your data, and do a complete restore of the data) if you move these devices at all! In the San Francisco earthquake in October 1989, some DASD devices were toppled over but lived to tell about it: their data remained readable. Don't count on it, however.

Figure 5.2 shows two views of DASD. Your drawings should show the logical view, not the physical view. You will find it helpful to have the following information about the device: the device's address, the device serial number, the device type, capacity, the owner or leasing company, and the lease or purchase dates.

For each actuator you may want to show the actuator device addresses, the HDA serial numbers, the internal (the one end users see) volume serial numbers, the generic name, and the use (e.g., SMS work, paging). Printouts of this configuration are helpful to operations and maintenance staffs as they work with the hardware configuration. They are also helpful to performance analysts trying to determine why I/O response time suddenly changes in one part of the DASD farm. If you keep these drawings up to date and distribute updated copies, you may find performance problems are anticipated instead of being solved after the fact.

5.1.3. Connecting DASD

The IBM devices had only two paths for I/O activity until the 3380 model K with the optional four-path installation. The architecture of the older generation head of string (HOS) and the *B-units* do not allow additional device attachment unless the entire string is powered off.

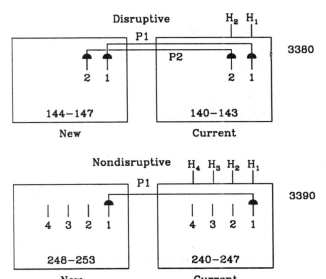

Figure 5.3 Disruptive and Nondisruptive Installation. The 3380 (standard D and E) devices have two paths for I/O accesses. Attaching any new device to the string requires the entire string to be powered down. The 3380 model K (if configured with the optional four paths) and the 3390 (four paths are standard) allow a new device to be attached while all the other devices are in use.

In Figure 5.3, the devices at the top are 3380 standard architecture. The data center wants to add the device on the left (144 through 147). All four devices (140–143) must be offline to all Processor Complexes and powered down for the customer engineer to connect *P1* and *P2* cables.

The term used for this type of installation is *disruptive* because service is interrupted for the other devices on the string. You might guess that one path at a time could be varied offline and used to connect and test the new devices. This was not to be until four-path configurations.

The 3390-type devices at the bottom can have the left device added without any interruption to devices 240–247. You can even add a new string to the control unit. Only one of the four connections is shown for clarity. The customer engineer takes one path at a time. In the figure, *P1* is varied offline and connected. After successful installation, the path is varied back online for the Processor Complexes to use. Each of the four paths can be attached in this manner.

The term *nondisruptive* does have some caveats; it should really be called *near nondisruptive*. Real nondisruptive would be to roll in a new box, connect it to some head of string, and vary it online. Installation still takes a lot of coordination.

> ¤ Remember that you may have to have all devices planned and in your system generation[1] to take advantage of nondisruptive installation. Until you install MVS/ESA 4.2, you must have the device defined in the MVS I/O device generation (IOGEN) and the Input/Output Configuration Program (IOCP) file.

5.1.4. Performance Considerations

Performance considerations will be covered later in more detail, but the things covered there will be useless if the configuration is wrong.

In Figure 5.4 we see a 3990 cache control unit and a string of 3390 devices. On several occasions we have seen a data center try to replace the old hardware with the latest hardware and assume that the *faster and newer* devices will service their requests. Their failure was a shock to them.

The figure does not give us any indication as to how many I/O operations will be started to this configuration. If this configuration replaced several control units and several strings of DASD, the result could be worse performance than before.

---

1 *System generation* is the process of constructing a usable system from components shipped by the vendor, together with parameters that you cannot modify once the generation is complete.

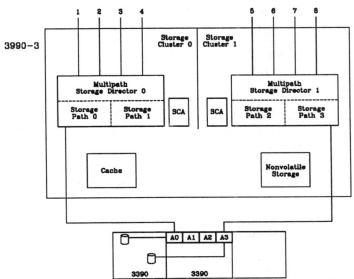

Figure 5.4 Configure for Performance. This configuration is a fast state-of-the-art DASD server. Will it perform adequately for its owner? Maybe it will and maybe it will not.

□ An I/O operation is initiated by a machine instruction. The Start/IO (SIO) is used in the MVS/370 environment. The Start Subchannel (SSCH) is used in the MVS/XA or ESA/390 environment. Do not confuse the term *EXCP* (EXecute Channel Program or application program I/O supervisor request), which is an accounting measure of input/output operations. If you add up all the EXCPs for all tasks in a time period, this will have no correlation with the number of *start subchannel*s per second as reported by the hardware.[2]

There are four paths from each of two Processor Complexes, and each can access any of the 3390 actuators. There even is a cache of some size. The question is still not answered. If 2,000

---

2 Check with user groups such as SHARE for availability of modifications to report I/O activity not normally reported by the operating system.

write operations per second were tried with this configuration, a good guess would be that the subsystem would be overloaded.

> ¤ Configure the number of paths and the number of actuators on the paths to match the I/O load that will drive the devices.

We have seen one instance where a 3081-class Processor Complex was configured with two 3380 strings with two channels shared by both strings. The I/O rate needed was approximately 300 per second, and the configuration could not sustain the load. Purchasing two control units and four short strings removed the bottleneck.

5.2. Initialization—ICKDSF

A DASD device must be *initialized* after it is installed and declared ready for use by the vendor's customer engineer. Today the data center is responsible for initialization and certification. It was not always that way. For 3350 and previous devices, the vendor was responsible for initialization.

The initialization process rewrites all tracks on the surface of the device and writes a Volume Table of Contents (VTOC) on the device. The factory performs extensive surface analysis on the platters before shipping them. IBM provides the Device Support Facilities (ICKDSF) program product for the data center to maintain DASD. You may also see ICKDSF called DF/DSF, because it came from the first separation of function: Device Facility/Device Support Facilities. IBM has since renamed all of the *Device Facility* prefixes to *Data Facility Product (DFP)* to repackage the data management software.

ICKDSF is one of the first programs that IBM supported for all of its operating systems: MVS, VM, VSE, and standalone. The reason is simple: anyone running one of these operating systems must format and maintain DASD. We again caution you to ensure you have the correct version of the ICKDSF product.

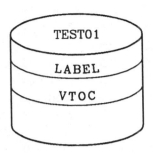

```
//step        EXEC  PGM=ICKDSF
//SYSPRINT    DD    SYSOUT=*
//SYSIN       DD    *
   INIT  UNIT(cuu) NOVERIFY VOLID(TEST01) -
         NOVALIDATE NODATA
```

Figure 5.5 DASD Initialization: Minimal. When a volume is first placed into service, it must be initialized with ICKDSF. The Home address and record zero are read, validated, and rewritten with a formatting write to erase the rest of the track. This process takes just a few minutes. The result of this operation is a DASD volume with a label and a Volume Table of Contents (VTOC).

Once inside the manual, also ensure that you are looking at the correct section!

You may want to do your own surface analysis to be sure you can read and write successfully before turning the DASD over to end users. We strongly recommend that you do your own surface analysis.

The following describes initialization for an MVS volume, or actuator, in particular. The VM operating system organizes its DASD a bit differently. We will briefly examine VM's use after the Volume Table of Contents (VTOC) is described.

5.2.1. The Label Track

Figure 5.5 shows a formatted volume. A standard IBM formatted DASD always contains three records on the first track of a volume and a group of records on some other part of the volume called a *VTOC*.

The first track is called a *label track*. The first record (cylinder zero, head zero, record 1) is an *IPL1* record. The second record (cylinder zero, head zero, record 2) is an *IPL2* record. These two records are used if the volume contains IPL text to bootstrap one of the operating systems from this device. In all other DASD devices these records contain *dummy* IPL records to place the Processor Complex in a disabled wait state if the DASD is IPLed.

The third record (cylinder zero, head zero, record 3) is the volume label record. It contains the volume serial number of the actuator and a definition for the *extent* used by the Volume Table of Contents (VTOC). The VTOC can be placed anywhere on the volume, but it must be allocated in a single extent, i.e., it must occupy contiguous storage. If you do not know where to place it, start it just after the first track. Displacement X'0F' is the VTOC pointer in the CCHHR format.[3] If you choose the second track of a DASD, the value of *0000000101* indicates that the VTOC is located on cylinder zero, track 1, record 1.

The remainder of the first track is usually reserved for IPL text in case the device is formatted or updated with IPL text for one of the IBM operating systems. See the following section for VM exceptions.

5.2.2. Volume Table of Contents (VTOC)

The second area of a newly formatted DASD actuator is the Volume Table of Contents, or *VTOC*. The VTOC indicates which contiguous areas, or extents, of the volume are allocated, and records data for each data set created on the volume. The VTOC occupies one or more tracks in size (except in VM). VTOC records are called *Data Set Control Blocks (DSCBs)*. DSCBs may be in

---

3 The notation CCHHR implies 5 bytes of data: 2 bytes for the cylinder number, 2 bytes for the head number, and 1 byte for the record number.

several numbered *formats*, depending on what data they contain.

VTOC records are divided into two parts. The first part is a 44-byte *key* which contains either the data set name (if a *Format 1 DSCB*) or other information (if any other format). The operating system can use the name in this hardware key to scan for data sets.[4] A command sequence is built to search through several tracks using a multitrack *SEARCH ID EQUAL* CCW.

A freshly built VTOC contains two nonempty records. The first is the VTOC descriptor, or *Format 4 DSCB*. The second is a free space record, or *Format 5 DSCB*, that describes all the free space on this volume. The remainder of the VTOC is preformatted with *Format 0 DSCB* records, consisting entirely of zeros. Any other DSCB can be built from a Format 0; when no more Format 0 DSCBs remain, new data sets can no longer be added or old data sets extended on the volume.

When a data set is allocated, a *Format 1 DSCB* is created for it to describe several data set attributes and its first three allocated extents. Additional *Format 2* and *Format 3 DSCBs* may be linked to the Format 1 DSCB to describe indexing data and additional allocation extents, respectively.

The following example shows the contents of a VTOC for a newly initialized, single-capacity 3380 device with one sequential data set allocated on it.

1. Format 4—VTOC Header:
   a. 44 bytes of X'04' identifier.
   b. X'F4' Eyecatcher.
   c. XL5'0000000103' Highest address of a Format 1 DSCB. The record number is 3 because there is no active VTOC index. The value would be X'35' if the volume has an active VTOC index to indicate "look through the whole VTOC".
   d. XL2'02E2' Number of Format 0 DSCBs left in VTOC. Fourteen tracks times 53 DSCB's per track less one (only 52

---

4   Unless you are using the *indexed VTOC* feature, explained later.

DSCB's on the last track) less three in use is equal to 738 decimal or X'02E2'.

e. XL4'03750000' CCHH of next available alternate track.

f. XL2'000F' Number of alternate tracks.

g. X'00' VTOC indicator.

h. X'01' Number of extents in VTOC.

i. XL2'0000' Reserved.

j. XL4'0376000F' Device size in cylinders (CC) and heads (HH)

k. XL2'BB60' Device track length (47,968, not 47,476).

l. XL4'00000020' Keyed record overhead.

m. XL2'0000' Device tolerance.

n. X'35' Number of DSCBs per track.

o. X'2E' Number of PDS directory records per track.

p. XL8'0000000000000000' VSAM time stamp.

q. XL3'000000' VSAM catalog indicator.

r. XL8'0000000000000000' VSAM catalog match time stamp.

s. XL4'0000000000' Reserved.

t. XL4'0000000000' Pointer to first Format 6 DSCB.

u. XL10'0100000000010000000E' VTOC extent pointer in the format TTSSCCHHCCHH where TT is the extent type, SS is the sequence number (relative to zero), CCHH is lower limit, and CCHH is upper limit. Here we have 14 tracks starting at cylinder zero head 1 and ending with cylinder zero head 14.

v. XL25'0' Reserved.

2. One *Format 5* that indicates that there is space on this volume.

a. XL4'05050505' DSCB indicator; this and the next 40 bytes are in the *key* area.

b. XL5'001E037300' Free extent in the format RRRRCCCCHH where RRRR is the relative track address of the first extent, CCCC is the number of cylinders available and HH is the number of tracks available. Here we have free space starting at relative track 30 (cylinder 2, head zero) and containing 883 cylinders for allocation on this single-capacity 3380. For dual- and triple-capacity 3380 and 3390 devices this would be the corresponding value of the total number of cylinders, less 2 cylinders (one for the allocated data set and one containing the label and VTOC tracks).

c. XL35'0' Seven available extents as free space gets fragmented.

d. X'F5' at location X'2C' which is the Format 5 indicator.

e. Xl90'0' 18 available extents for more fragmentation.

f. Xl5'0000000000' Pointer to the next Format 5 when one is needed for fragmentation.

3. A *Format 1 DSCB* is built for the data set allocated on the volume.

a. CL44'name' is a 44-byte data set name. This is in the hardware key area and can be scanned by channel commands.

b. X'F1' Identifier.

c. CL6'aaaaaa' Volume serial number on which this data set exists.

d. XL2'0001' Volume sequence number.

e. XL3'5C0001' Creation date. In this example January 1, 1992; the date is stored as "YY0DDD".

f. XL3'63016D' Expiration date. In this example December 31, 1999.

g. X'01' Number of extents on volume.

h. X'00' Number of bytes used in last PDS directory block.

i. X'00' Reserved

j. CL13'IBMOSVS2' System code.

k. XL3'000000' Date last referenced.

l. XL4'00000000' Reserved.

m. XL2'4000' Data set organization (sequential).

n. X'C0' Record format (undefined).

o. X'00' Option codes.

p. XL2'0FF0' Block length (4,080).

q. XL2'0000' Logical record length (0 because the record format is undefined).

r. X'00' Key length.

s. XL2'0000' Relative key position.

t. X'F0' Data set indicators.

u. XL4'00000000' Secondary allocation (none).

v. XL3'000000' Last used track and block on track.

w. XL2'BB60' Bytes remaining on last track (47,968).

x. XL2'0000' Reserved.

y. XL10'8100000100000001000E' in the format TTSSCCHHCCHH where TT is the extent type, SS is the sequence number (relative to zero), CCHH is lower limit, and CCHH is upper limit. Extent information. In this case, one cylinder is allocated, beginning at cylinder 1, head 0 and ending with cylinder 1 head 14.

z. XL25'00' The rest is zeros.

Everyone wonders how large to make a VTOC. If you make it too small, you will discover this quickly, because jobs will begin to abnormally terminate. You may never know if you make it too large unless you look. The calculation is simple: add the number of data sets to be allocated to the number of other DSCBs (e.g., Format 3 DSCB extenisons for data sets with over 3 extents) needed and divide by the number of keyed 140-byte records that a track can hold. Round up to the next track.

The hard part is to predict how many data sets will be allocated. For some volumes, this may be easy: one large data base data set may be allocated to fill the entire volume, so the answer is one data set. Usually, though, you format the volume and step back to get out of the way for data set allocations.

At the end of the chapter, we give rules of thumb for you to make an intelligent estimate. Estimates are just that. Managing your data requires that you know your data.

Fixed-block architecture (FBA) devices use 140-byte records in their VTOCs, but these are stored in VSAM relative record data set format. Three records fit into each 512-byte block.

5.2.3. VTOC under VM

The VM Control Program component, *CP*, supports both CKD and FBA devices. VM is more a *hypervisor* than a complete operating system. Its function is to create the illusion of multiple Processor Complexes, called *virtual machines*. Each virtual machine has a complement of *virtual DASD*, each of which is called a *minidisk*.

VM Minidisks

A minidisk resident on a particular DASD model acts, within a virtual machine, just like the real DASD actuator, except that the maximum number of addressable cylinders (CKD) or blocks (FBA) is smaller. VM carves up its real DASD into minidisks, maintaining records of where each minidisk begins and ends on the real actuators in the VM Directory.

The real DASD actuators, from their VTOCs, appear to be empty but fully allocated. For example, a CKD actuator does contain a VTOC beginning at cylinder 0, track 0, immmediately after the label record. This VTOC contains only a Format 4 DSCB and a Format 5 DSCB. The Format 4 DSCB indicates that the VTOC's *CCHHR* extent goes from cylinder 0, head 0, record 4 to cylinder 0, head 0, record 5. The Format 5 DSCB is constructed such that there is no free space available on the DASD. If a Processor Complex running another operating system, such as MVS, accesses the real DASD, it sees one that has no data sets allocated on it but also has no free space available.

The VM Directory entry for each minidisk identifies the actuator and the real starting and ending cylinders (CKD) or blocks (FBA) where the minidisk is allocated on the real DASD. Operating systems running in virtual machines, called *guest operating systems*, are then free to organize their minidisks in any way a real, but smaller, DASD actuator may be organized.

If the guest operating system is MVS, then it may write its own VTOC on the minidisk and allocate data sets normally.

Under VM, however, a DASD actuator need not be used to store minidisks. It can be *dedicated* to a virtual machine as a native actuator, in which case the guest operating system manages the entire contents of the real actuator.

When the guest operating system performs DASD I/O using a minidisk, CP modifies the channel program referencing the virtual minidisk so that the channel program may be executed by the real storage controller on the real actuator. A dedicated actuator may be accessed more efficiently than a minidisk because less overhead is required in channel program translation.

Shared File System (SFS)

The minidisk DASD allocation scheme is a very efficient method of carving up DASD space for VM (or more specifically, interactive CMS users). Minidisk allocation suffers from a number of limitations. One of the worst, from a management perspective, is that a fixed amount of storage is allocated to a purpose. (Some claim minidisk allocaton is a *benefit* to the data center because the end user cannot use more than the specified number of cylinders.) Early IBM claims for SMS were DASD savings in the 30% range. Multiply your DASD budget by 0.30 and carry those savings to your companies profit. If you do not want to take credit for that, call us!

Latest versions of VM support the Shared File System (SFS) which more closely emulates the MVS and VSE DASD allocation system. A common catalog contains pointers to the end-user's data space but the space is allocated in a large pool of DASD.

SFS is a requirement for VM to fully implement DFSMS/VM. Any system managed storage implementation must be able to allocate storage from a common pool. VM minidisks cannot do that.

5.2.4. Indexed VTOCs

IBM created the VTOC architecture in 1964. In the early 1980s, IBM introduced *indexed VTOCs*. The ICKDSF utility can convert a normal VTOC into an indexed VTOC.

Under MVS, when a VTOC is indexed, special data sets are created on the volume to provide faster, more efficient free space allocation and deallocation. A bit is set in the Format 4 DSCB indicating that the Format 5 DSCBs are no longer valid.

5.2.5. Minimal Initialization

A minimal initialization builds and writes cylinder zero track zero of a volume with the standard records and any IPL data supplied. An empty VTOC is created. If the volume had alternate tracks assigned, then they are reassigned in sequential order within the alternate track area.

In Figure 5.5 you see the JCL to perform a minimal installation. The two keywords *NOVALIDATE* and *NODATA* indicate a minimal installation. The IBM-supplied program, ICKDSF, is used for formatting volumes. In these examples whole DASD volumes are formatted, but the program can also work on selected tracks. Be sure you use the manual for your version of ICKDSF to get the correct parameter format.

Minimal initialization takes only a few minutes. After all, it is just writing one block for each track on the actuator.

5.2.6. Medial Initialization

A medial initialization performs all the functions of the minimal initialization and validates every track. Validation is performed when the keywords *VALIDATE* and *NOCHECK* are present in the control statements. ICKDSF then reads, validates, and rewrites every home address and record zero of every track.

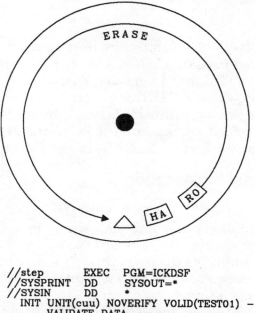

```
//step       EXEC  PGM=ICKDSF
//SYSPRINT   DD    SYSOUT=*
//SYSIN      DD      *
   INIT UNIT(cuu) NOVERIFY VOLID(TEST01) -
        VALIDATE DATA
```

Figure 5.6 DASD Initialization: Medial. ICKDSF has been commanded to initialize a track with *VALIDATE* to indicate a medial initialization. Medial installations take about 45 minutes.

Medial initialization takes approximately 45 minutes for a whole single-capacity 3380 volume. Note in Figure 5.6 that the track has an *ERASE* line after record zero. Whenever a record is written on a track, it can be written by two different types of *write* channel commands. The first is like this one, a *formatting write*, and is called *Write Count, Key, and Data*.

The second is a *nonformatting write* that leaves any data before or after the specific record untouched. Examples are *Write Key and Data* and *Write Data*. The ability to update a single record is the attribute that makes DASD so vital to data processing.

The formatting write erases the rest of the track. If any records had been there (e.g., record 1, record 2), those records are overwritten with zeros. The medial installation depends on the device to detect that the track clearing is successful. You depend on the belief that a track that can be cleared in this manner can have data written on it and later read.

> ¤ ICKDSF has been improved to checkpoint the initialization of volumes. The locations successfully formatted are kept on the diagnostic tracks. If the initialization is interrupted for any reason, ICKDSF can be instructed to take up at the next track to be formatted. This is a real time saver.

5.2.7. Maximal Initialization

When IBM transferred the responsibility for maintaining DASD to the data center, they provided the same capability that field engineers had for testing DASD. The OLTEP program was used by the field engineers to exercise DASD to ensure that the device was ready for customer use. ICKDSF contains a DASD exerciser. Parameter *CHECK(n)* indicates *maximal* initialization or exercise of this disk.

Unfortunately, the latest versions of ICKDSF support this parameter only for the older devices (e.g., 2305, 2314, 3330, 3344, and 3350). The data center can still get surface checking for fourth-generation (i.e., 3380) and fifth-generation (i.e., 3390) devices by using the *INSPECT* command with the *CHECK(n)* parameter.

IBM limited this INIT parameter in favor of the INSTALL function (see below) for newer generations. One reason given for the removal is that customers were using CHECK(3) and assigning skip displacements and alternate tracks when no serious problem existed. We interpret that statement to read, *If you stress DASD too much, it will break.*

The maximal initialization performed all the functions of a medial initialization and checked every track surface for defects, assigned alternate tracks if needed, and reclaimed alternate tracks if warranted.

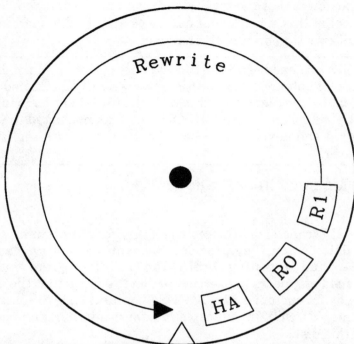

Figure 5.7 Medial Initialization: What Happens. Why does it take 45 minutes to format a DASD using medial formatting? The program writes and rewrites data on the track, using a large *record zero*, to check the surface. Special bit patterns are used to stress the hardware.

Reclaiming alternate tracks may sound a bit strange. How could a bad track suddenly get better? Where do you buy antibiotics for DASD?

> ¤ *The electrical components (boards in the device and control unit) can trick the operating system into assigning alternate tracks when the surface is not at fault!* You may want to inspect any volume involved in error recovery by the head of string, device, or control unit to be sure that alternate tracks have not been assigned in error.

A record zero is written that fills the track and is used to ensure that the entire track surface is usable. If errors are found,

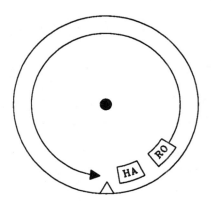

```
//step        EXEC PGM=ICKDSF
//SYSPRINT...
//SYSIN       DD *
   INSTALL UNIT(cuu)
      IF   LASTCC<8 -
         THEN DO
            INIT UNIT(cuu) NOVERIFY NOVALIDATE -
               NOCHECK VTOC(1,0,15) -
               VOLID(volser) INDEX(0,1,14)
```

Figure 5.8 DASD Initialization: INSTALL. The actuator at address *cuu* will be initialized. A VTOC will be written starting at cylinder 1 head zero and be 15 tracks long. A VTOC index will be built just after the volume label at cylinder zero, head 1 for 14 tracks (the rest of cylinder 1).

skip displacements are assigned to allow future blocks to be written successfully.

The following JCL was used with release 9.0 of ICKDSF to perform a surface analysis of 3380 devices. Some installations keep a copy of an earlier release of ICKDSF to retain the ability to really exercise 3380 volumes.

JCL to Run Maximal Formatting of 3380s
| ```
//STEP     EXEC  PGM=ICKDSF
//SYSPRINT DD    SYSOUT=A
//SYSIN    DD    *
  INIT UNITADDRESS(cuu)  CHECK(n)   -
     RECLAIM VOLID(volser) VTOC(2,0,1)
``` |
```

5.2.8. INSTALL Initialization

Figure 5.8 shows the JCL needed to initialize a DASD volume using the INSTALL parameter. The INSTALL parameter performs the same function as a medial initialization. INSTALL also sets 3390 devices to 3380 track compatibility mode if you must run that way.

INSTALL does not write the VTOC or write proper home addresses and record zeros. It is unclear why the INSTALL routines were not written to complete the job. Perhaps it is because ICKDSF was designed by electronics engineers, not programmers or end users. You must run the *minimal* function to format the volume.

Do not run the *medial* function. Some of us learned the hard way that a 45-minute *install* and a 45-minute *medial* initialization just wasted 45 minutes for us.

The example in Figure 5.8 shows establishing an indexed VTOC. This second *inventory* data set for a DASD volume keeps track of the free space in a different format than the *Format 5* DSCBs. It is also used for DF/Storage Management Subsystem.

The *indexed VTOC* can be created here, at initialization time, or later with the *BUILDIX* command.

While you are at it, you probably should allocate the other inventory data sets for a well-established volume. A VSAM Volume Data Set (VVDS) and a Basic Catalog Structure (BCS) catalog are needed if VSAM data sets are to be allocated on the volume. Allocating them at initialization time places the data sets near the VTOC for optimum performance. The jury is still out on VTOC placement, however: whether it should be at the front of the volume or at the one-third or halfway point.

In the following JCL, *volser* is the volume serial number you have created, *pp* and *ss* are primary and secondary allocation amounts in tracks, and *mastercatname* is the name of the master catalog. Note that we use the SYSALLDA generic name for the device type. SYSALLDA is available if you have generated your system using the IPO system.

```
                 JCL to Allocate Other Inventory Data Sets
//step1      EXEC PGM=IDCAMS
//SYSPRINT DD    SYSOUT=*
//SYSIN    DD    *
 DEFINE CLUSTER(NAME(SYS1.VVDS.Vvolser) VOL(volser)  -
     NONINDEXED TRACKS(pp ss )  )  CAT(mastercatname)
/*
//step2      EXEC PGM=IDCAMS
//SYSPRINT DD    SYSOUT=*
//SYSIN    DD    *
 DEFINE UCAT ( NAME(catalog) VOL(volser) ICFCAT      -
      FREESPACE (20 20) REPLICATE IMBED              -
      TRACKS (pp ss) SHR(3 4) BUFFERSPACE(12291)     -
      STRNO(3)      )                                -
  DATA ( CISZ(4096) BUFND(4) TRACKS (pp ss ) )  -
  INDEX ( CISZ(4096) BUFNI(4) TRACKS (1 1 ) )  -
   CAT (mastercatname)
//step3      EXEC PGM=IEHLIST
//SYSPRINT DD SYSOUT=*
//name1    DD UNIT=SYSALLDA,VOL=SER=volser,DISP=SHR
//SYSIN    DD *
   LISTVTOC FORMAT,INDEXDSN=SYS1.VTOCIX.volser,VOL=SYSALLDA=volser
```

The rules of thumb for how to initialize your DASD inventory data sets are given below. These are estimates, however; only you are responsible for and authorized to make these decisions. The admonition *know thyself* applies here. Decide what to do and watch it like a hawk!

Note that our recommendations allocate cylinder boundary chunks if more than a few tracks are needed. The first reason is that these data sets are very important and very volatile, and rounding up to a cylinder boundary gives a little extra room for miscalculation. The second reason is that we still believe cylinder allocation is faster and more reliable.

Number of data sets	Size of VTOC in tracks	Size of Indexed VTOC (tracks)	Size of VVDS in tracks
20	1	2	3
100	3	2	3
500	30	2	6
1,000	45	2	6
5,000	210	15	30
10,000	405	30	60

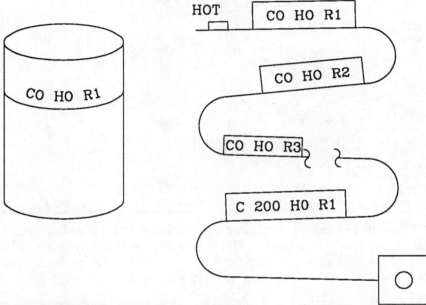

Figure 5.9 Full Volume Backup. The best backup of a volume to have if you have a problem (crash) with a DASD actuator is a full volume backup. Each cylinder, head, and record is copied to magnetic tape. Restoring consists of reversing the process and copying them back to their original locations.

5.3. Protection

If you value your data, you will provide for its protection. This section gives you some of the considerations on how to protect your data, but it cannot build a cost-effective adequate protection plan for your data. You and your company must do that for yourselves.

5.3.1. Full Volume Backup

Full volume backups copy all the data on a DASD to some portable medium such as magnetic tapes.

Introduction to Backups

The best backup would be a full volume backup just before a catastrophic error struck a DASD volume. Full volume backups take 20 to 60 minutes depending on the amount of data to be dumped and the speed of the output device. Unfortunately, the time it takes to do a backup and the interruption it causes to normal accesses on the volume may prevent you from doing full volume backup any more frequently than daily or even weekly.

Figure 5.9 shows a full volume backup of a DASD onto cartridge tape. The first record on the tape is cylinder zero, head zero, and record 1. Each record is copied to tape.

This type of backup, copying record for record, is called a *physical* backup because it transfers records from track to tape. The restore must be done exactly like that, one group of tape records onto one track record. A restore can be done to a different volume of the same DASD model, even if it has different alternate tracks assigned than the backup source volume. This is because alternate track assignment is transparent to channel programs that read and write data.

The disadvantages to physical backups are that you cannot reblock records, restore just a certain data set, or restore to a device with different geometry (number of tracks per cylinder or track size).

Another type of backup, *logical* backup, copies one data set at a time using a utility that understands the composition of the data set. IDCAMS[5] is used for VSAM. IEBCOPY is used for partitioned data sets.

A number of these backup/restore subsystems perform one or both of these type of backups:

---

5   *IDCAMS* is Access Method Services, a utility providing many data set maintenance functions.

DF/DSS

The IBM utility used to make backups of DASD is Data Facility/Data Set Services (DF/DSS). Full volume backups can be made with either physical or logical mode.

CAI: ASM2

The Computer Associates International Inc. program, Auxiliary Storage Manager 2, performs full volume backups similar to the IBM DF/DSS program. ASM2 was available before the IBM product.

DMS/OS

Sterling Software markets a comprehensive DASD archive and backup subsystem. The software performs data compaction, volume recovery, free space management, DASD-to-DASD migration (including 3380 to 3390), and other management tasks in the MVS environment.

Fast Dump Restore (FDR)

Innovation Data Processing markets Fast Dump Restore, a dump restore facility; Compaktor (CPK) for disk reorganization; and Automatic Backup and Recovery (ABR) for archival and retrieval.

5.3.2. Backups and Data Archival

The best defense is a good offense. In the world of DASD, that means having a well-defined and *tested* backup program. How do you test a backup program? The obvious answer is to attempt to restore data sets from an actual backup, but that is not good enough.

The question should really be stated, when or how often do you test a backup program? After losing an HDA is *not* the time to be testing, yet many data centers "test" their backups only when a failure would result in permanently lost data. Let's look at what can go wrong with the backup procedure.

A new version of the program used to perform backups could contain a bug. An old version could contain a bug you have not yet encountered. A new storage controller or HDA could have been installed that reacts badly with the backup program you are using. The tape drive or drives used to write backup tapes could have a hardware problem in which undetected errors make their way to the tape. The tape librarian could have received a new shipment of magnetic tapes that contain manufacturing defects that the tape drive does not detect. One part of the tape library where backup tapes are stored could be subject to a magnetic field on the other side of the wall that induces errors on the tapes.

> ¤ Just about anything can happen to separate you from your valuable data, no matter how conscientious the operations staff is in performing backups. Establish a schedule and perform regular backup tests.

How frequently you test your backups by attempting to restore from them is a judgment you must make, but you must test them. Just as you have a schedule for performing backups, you should establish a schedule for periodically testing them. It may not be practical to test restoring all of the backed-up data, and it may not be practical to test as often as backups are taken. If you cannot afford to test backups, then you might as well not take them in the first place.

In addition to a regular backup test schedule, you might make provisions to test backups more intensely when certain major changes occur at your data center. These changes might include when you install a new DASD or tape drive model, or a new version of the backup software or operating system, or when the tape librarian obtains a new shipment of magnetic tapes or tapes from a different vendor.

Similar concerns exist for *archived* data and transaction journal tapes taken in real time. Data archival is the movement of data sets from their primary location on DASD to a secondary location, such as another DASD or magnetic tape, to make space on the primary DASD for new data. Journal tapes are maintained by many data-base management systems and standalone applications to record changes as they occur, providing an up-to-the-minute backup function.

Archived data is *not* backed-up data. If you archive data to tape and then lose the tape, the data is *gone*. When you archive data, this implies that the data will not be needed for a while. This may be long enough that backup tapes which once contained the archived data set may be recycled through your backup procedures until *no* backup remains of the data set. You may want to consider backing up your archive tapes with a tape-to-tape copy.

Likewise, journal tapes are usually created by applications considered to be important enough that restoring from the last backup would result in the loss of too much data. If the data is that important, you should make sure that the journal tapes being written can actually be read to reapply data base or application updates. If the data base against which the journal is kept is too large for practical testing, the application maintainers might consider keeping a test data base and periodically generating test journal tapes, restoring the data base and applying the test journals, and checking the integrity of the test data base.

> ¤ Be sure you have backups of important archived data. Likewise, ensure that journal tapes taken to avoid loss of data are usable.

The following sections describe various ways to back up and archive data and some utility programs available to accomplish this.

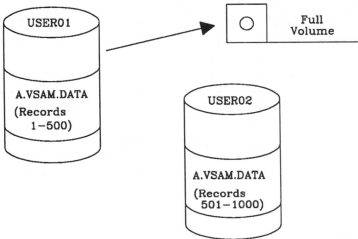

Figure 5.10 Incremental Backup. Once you have a full volume backup of a DASD, you can use a program such as IBM's DFHSM, Innovation Data's Fast Dump Restore, or other programs to search the volume for data sets that have been changed or added since the last full volume backup. This diagram shows the procedure used. A full volume backup is taken at one point in time. At some later time a program is used to scan the volume and copy data sets to tape that are not on the full volume tape. The restore process is to restore the full volume and then add the incrementally copied files. backup;incremental

Incremental Backups

The next best thing to a full volume backup just before a crash is to have a full volume backup at some point in the past *and* have a copy of all the files that have changed since the full backup was taken.

The term *incremental backups* refers to taking a series of backups containing only the data modified since the last full or incremental backup was taken.

Figure 5.10 shows a new data set allocated after a full volume backup has been taken of a DASD. A program can read the inventory information and discover the data sets that have been changed and added after the full volume backup was taken. The full volume backup sets bits in the Format 1 DSCB or elsewhere (this may depend on the backup program used) that indicate that the data set has been backed up. Data sets opened for output and new data sets do not have this bit set. The incremental backup program knows which data sets do not have a proper backup by inspecting this bit.

Incremental backups are usually much smaller than full backups. Thus, they take less time to perform and can be done more frequently than full backups. Restoring from incrementals is more complex than restoring from straight full backups. The latest full backup of a volume must be restored first, then the incrementals must be restored in the order in which they were taken.

Restoring a single data set from incremental backups can be tedious because you may need to search all of the incrementals in the reverse order from that in which they were taken to locate the most recent backup of a particular data set.

For these reasons, incremental backups should be performed by a comprehensive subsystem such as one from the above list. Be sure you understand how to restore a single data set, because that is likely to be the restore task you perform most often. (A good way to do this is to include restoring a single data set as part of your backup test procedures.)

Importance of Synchronization of Data Files

Before we go further, we should remind you that some data sets are actually part of a group of data sets that make up a data base to the end user. DB2 and most data base subsystems are created this way. Several data sets are required to have the information in synchronization.

If either the full volume or incremental volume backups include a part of a data base, then restoring one or more of these parts just scrambles the data.

DB2 and other data base subsystems recommend that you only use the utilities included as part of the data base subsystem to back up and restore data sets that make up a data base. That is good advice! Presumably these utilities would ensure synchronization integrity.

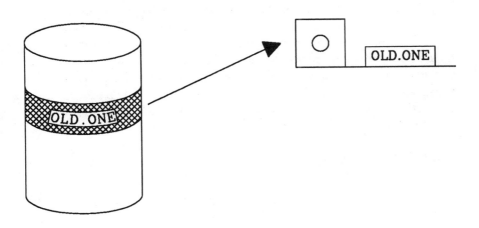

Figure 5.11 Archival of Data Sets. Some programs such as the IBM program product DFHSM will make a backup of a data set and scratch the data set from the DASD.

Application: IEBCOPY, REPRO, xxxGENER, SYNCSORT

The application can use one of the above full volume or incremental backup programs, or it can use the IBM-supplied utility to move the data set. IEBCOPY is used for partitioned data sets. IDCAMS REPRO or EXPORT is used for VSAM, though IDCAMS can also be used for sequential data sets. Sequential data sets can be backed up by IEBGENER.

Sometimes you can use the sort program itself to make a copy if the program supports a *copy* parameter. SYNCSORT makes quick, efficient backups of sequential data sets, primarily because SYNCSORT uses its own optimized channel programs rather than an IBM access method.

SYNCSORT, DFSORT, CASORT, and others can be used as replacements for IEBGENER. IEBGENER is a very slow, inefficient program. The replacements can be installed as a new name (e.g., SYNCGENR), in which case you will have to change the name from IEBGENER to xxxGENER in your JCL. You can also install some of them as front ends to the IEBGENER program. If the program can process the SYSIN cards, it will do so. If it cannot, it passes control to the original IEBGENER program. We have been successful using both techniques. With SYNCGENR, we just replaced IEBGENER and saved millions of I/O operations and countless CPU seconds.

Data Set Archiving

Archiving a data set means making a copy of the data set on another medium (e.g., another DASD or a tape) and scratching (deleting) the data set from the original disk.

The IBM program product *DFHSM* can be used to perform archival and retrieval.

Figure 5.11 shows an old data set that has not been accessed for a specified period of time. An archival program makes a copy of the data set on a magnetic tape and scratches the data set from DASD. Now comes the mirrors and smoke part. The program leaves a pointer in the catalog as if the data set still exists, but it looks as if it were mounted on some strange volume. DFHSM uses *ARCVOL* for this strange volume name.

When the unsuspecting batch job or interactive user tries to access the data set, the archival program seizes control of the open process and reloads the data set from tape onto the same or a different disk.

The requesting program is delayed while the archived copy is found, made available, and restored to DASD. If DFHSM has archived the data to another DASD (level 1) then restoration will be at disk-to-disk speed.

If DFHSM has archived the data to a magnetic tape (level 2), the restoration time includes tape mount and tape-to-disk transfer time. For small data sets, this could be a matter of a few

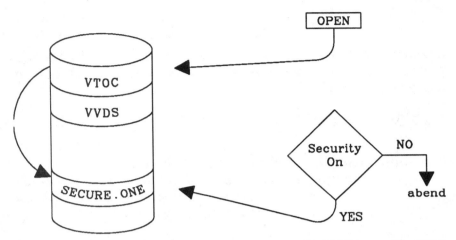

Figure 5.12 Data Set Level Security. Data sets are protected by RACF or one of the RACF look-alikes. In this diagram we simplify the process. If a program tries to access a data set and opens the data set, the security subsystem looks up in a rule book who can access the data set. Read access, update access, and scratch access are the types of protection categories that are controlled.

minutes. For large data sets, it could be a matter of hours. What if the archived copy is in the secret vault several miles away? What if the tape operator is out to lunch or in a shift meeting?

A big problem exists for almost all of the archival programs. Empty data sets or data sets that do not have standard attributes are never archived. The reason given by the developers of these programs is that since they do not know what the end user wants the data sets to look like, they are afraid to move them. The data center gets stuck with much valuable DASD real estate tied up with these strange data sets. On more than one occasion, we have had the dubious task of cleaning up the mess. We usually could not identify the owners or what they intended, so we just scratched them. (Heh, heh.)

Do not forget that archived data sets are not backed-up data sets. Moving them to another DASD or to magnetic tape does not give them magical properties. It can instead increase the vulnerability of the data to loss. If you practice data archival, you also need backups of archived data.

5.3.3. Security

Security of data sets should be a major concern of the data center and could take up a whole book by itself. We shall look only at the types of security you should be considering.

Data Set Security

The operating system provides only data set security. Many computer professionals in the IBM environment do not realize this. The result is that security is checked only at the time a data set is opened. Some authorized programs do not go through OPEN.

In Figure 5.12 you see a graphic representation. When the application issues an OPEN macro, the access method modules issue a macro that calls the resident security modules (e.g., RACF, Top Secret) to compare the security level of the caller and the security level of the data set. If they match, then the OPEN continues. If they do not match, the caller's request is terminated.

RACF is the IBM security package and is implemented with a series of documented module calls. If you purchase and use RACF, IBM supplies your data center with modules to receive those calls and a series of commands to impose security at your data center. If you purchase one of the other security subsystems, they supply you with those security modules (and maybe others) and a different set of commands to impose security.

Your physical and software security stops at your loading platform. Once you sell or transfer devices to someone else, security is gone.

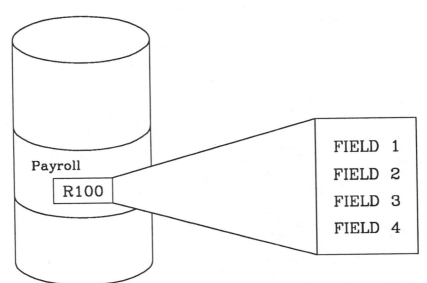

Figure 5.13 Record-Level Security. Record-level security is achieved only by a data base subsystem that can protect specific records from, or allow access to, individuals or jobs.

□ When you dispose of (sell or trade) your DASD, always clear off your disks by writing full track records to the disk on all surfaces to ensure that sensitive data does not fall into the wrong hands. Periodically you will hear of public or private institutions failing to do this, and the data becomes public. Usually the data is of no use to anyone. Sometimes it is sensitive data (payroll information) or highly secure information. *This applies to personal computer hard disks and equipment.* If you discard hard disks when they malfunction, you may want to have the HDAs dismantled and the platters degaussed if the data is sensitive enough to warrant it. **The same goes for magnetic tapes.**

Another consideration for data set security is the downloading of data to a remote location. Once the data is copied out of the

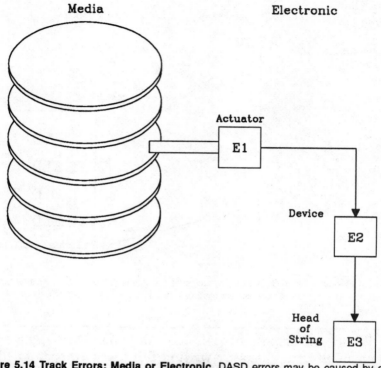

Figure 5.14 Track Errors: Media or Electronic. DASD errors may be caused by either media (platter or head damage) or electronics (cards in the actuator, device, head of string, or even the control unit or channel). Media errors are fatal. You probably cannot recover data on those actuators. Electronic failure may be recoverable.

data center, the host security cannot protect the data because it is out of the control of the security module.

Record Security

Record security cannot be achieved at the operating system or data center level. It must be coordinated as part of the programs that access the records. In most cases, a data base subsystem handles record-level security.

In Figure 5.13 we show one record of a DASD data set. The record is not protected by any operating system security subsystem because the granularity of the data is too small.

Field Security

Field security also must be handled by the data base programs. Again in Figure 5.13, if DASD security methods cannot distinguish between records, they cannot protect fields within the record.

5.4. DASD Error Recovery

DASD errors come in two flavors: electronic-component errors and media errors. Electronic-component errors are caused by some flaw in the circuits that control the flow of data and control information on the channel. The electronics in error could be in the channel, the control unit, the head of string, the device, the actuator within the device, or the cables connecting these.

See Figure 5.14. Media errors are those caused by some problem transferring data from the medium (spinning platter) to central storage. Media errors fall into two categories: the medium has a problem transferring data (bits are dropped) or the medium is totally and positively useless. In the former case, there is hope that you can recover your data. In the latter case, either you have backups of the data or you create it from scratch.

The operating system sees DASD errors as one of two types: **temporary errors** (also called *soft*, or *correctable*, errors) and **permanent errors** (also called *hard* or *uncorrectable*, errors). A temporary error is any read or write that is unsuccessful on the first attempt but is correctly accomplished by hardware or software procedures. A permanent error is any read or write that is **not successfully completed** within a time period (or number of retries) required to exhaust the hardware and software error recovery procedures.

The flow of media error recovery is:

1. **Hardware retry:**
   a. Read or write data. If successful, go to 1f.
   b. Try to recover with Error Correction Codes (ECC). If successful, go to 1f.
   c. Have we tried to recover as many times (e.g., 10) as the designers placed in the design? If not, go back to 1a and try to reread or rewrite the data.
   d. Have we tried to offset the head and read to the right or left of the center of the track more than the designers placed into the design? If not, go to 1a and try to reread.
   e. Signal permanent data check.
   f. Return to the operating system.

2. **Software retry:** repeat 1 above until the number of retries is exhausted.

As you can see, error recovery can cause massive interruptions to normal I/O processing, particularly when the number of software retries is high. In the definition above we used a time period as part of the definition of a permanent error. Some permanent errors disappear. Some permanent errors are caused by faulty electronic components.

For example, on more than one occasion, we have observed faulty electronics present *permanent errors* that the customer engineer stated would require the replacement of the Head Disk Assembly (HDA). We used a program such as Computer Associates' DCR DASDCHEK to read the data, and the data was correct. The channel program ended with a permanent error completion status. We convinced the customer engineer to recheck and replace something in the electronic components (the data could not be unreadable if it was read into central storage successfully). They did. We did not have to replace the HDA. If the customer engineer had replaced the HDA, the problem would probably have recurred, wasting everyone's time and money.

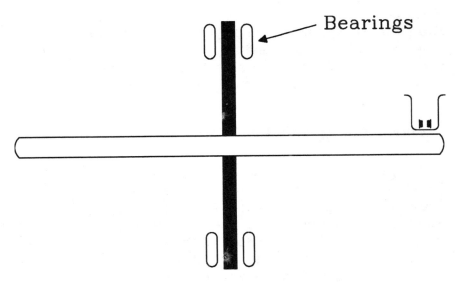

Figure 5.15 Bearings, Shafts, and Small Particles. A number of things can go wrong with a DASD. The bearings can wear out, allowing the entire assembly to move. The shafts can wear out, causing wobble. Particles can get into the device and jam between the fast, low-flying read-write heads, causing damage.

5.4.1. Aging Disk Drives: Risk Placement Analysis

Old DASD is dangerous for your data's health. DASD spins at 3,600 RPM or 4,200 RPM for years at a time. It is only reasonable that eventually the thing is going to wear out. Just as we say one dog year equals seven human years of life, it could be said that one year of a DASD's life is 20 of ours. In any case, DASD is getting old when it is five years old. We are talking about the age of the moving parts and electronic cards. Unlike with us, your vendor can replace everything but the casters in a DASD.

So do not reject older DASD serial numbers unless you know that the components have not been replaced. **Ask the age of components when you are buying used equipment.**

We completely refurbished a group of 3375s over the seven years we owned them, and most of them left our data center with relatively new HDAs. They may last another seven years for another customer. We were just happy to get rid of them!

Bearings, Shafts, and Small Particles

A number of things can go wrong. Figure 5.15 shows one of the first. The shaft of a DASD holds multiple platters in the HDA. There are bearings at both ends of the shaft to hold the shaft in place. As the bearings wear, the entire shaft can wobble and cause the read-write head to touch down on the surface of the platter. This not so gentle event is called *Head Disk Interference (HDI)*, a euphemism for a *head crash*.

The shafts can wear and cause the same wobble. The HDA is a *clean* environment. You cannot squirt oil on the shaft every 3,000 miles. You should now appreciate a bit better the engineering of DASD components. The IBM 3390 devices were delivered several months late in 1989, and one of the reasons given was that the lubrication used was a new formula and was causing early failures.

Small particles also can cause problems. If you inspect vendor's materials about their head-disk clearances you will see that human hair and smoke particles are huge in comparison to the gap.

Particle problems are limited to non-sealed DASD (e.g., 3380s). The filters (5 micron) in these devices should filter out all particles that will not fit between the surface of the platter and the read-write head. In most cases they do. On at least one occasion, the plastic air deflector in the 3380 started flaking off and the particles caused head crashes.

Quite another phenomenon concerns *alpha particles*. Physics theory says that there are particles always passing through the atmosphere and through objects. Very intelligent DASD experts

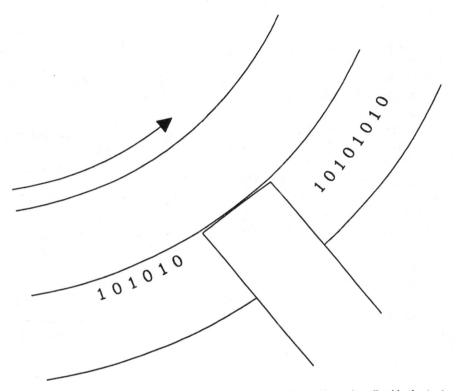

Figure 5.16 Hard Disk Alignment Drift. If one or more of the things described in the text happens, the heads may not align properly on the track. In that case the read-write head may require one or more revolutions to read or write a record. That is a revolving predicament. [Ugh!]

tell us that these alpha particles can and do alter DASD contents, thus forcing temporary errors. We leave this matter to the reader to pursue!

> ¤ It takes a long time to test things that are to last a long time. If it took several months for a problem with the lubrication to appear, how much time will it take to prove that the bearing or shaft components will not fail for some other reason? Most data centers wait for someone else to be on the *bleeding edge* and *find* the errors.

Environmental Damage

All sorts of environmental damage can attack DASD. One type, overlooked by many, is water damage from above the drives. More than once we have seen water leaks from bathrooms, air conditioning water cooling systems, or rain water drop into DASD.

In the aftermath of Hurricane Hugo, one data center lamented that they could have saved millions of dollars had plastic been handy to cover their equipment. Fitted covers are now commercially available in packets that hang from each box in the data center. Do not put the plastic covers on while the equipment is running! It will overheat.

One obscure technical problem caused tin oxide to coat the read-write heads. A chemical used to kill bacteria or algae in air conditioning systems was getting into a gaseous state, passing through the air filters of 3380 devices, and coating the read-write heads. After a period of buildup, the heads crashed, destroying the data. This is not a problem with sealed HDAs, however, and it may have prompted IBM to design sealed systems for the 3390 HDA.

Hard Disk Alignment Drift

You also may experience slow I/O times or data errors reading or writing to a DASD if the heads drift.

In Figure 5.16 we show an up-close and personal look at a track band. The record about to come under the read-write head is centered in the imaginary band on the platter called the track. The record just behind the read-write head is positioned close to the inner limits of the band.

If the head was correctly positioned for the previous record, it may not be able to read the next record, causing at least one RPS miss. Your hardware vendor may tell you this is not a problem because the record is successfully read. How many retries requiring extra revolutions are needed to do so? What caused the drift? Will it drift so far that the records cannot be read? Is this record required in the critical path for acceptable response time?

Management Techniques to Minimize Risk

Several management techniques can minimize your risk. The operative word is *management*. The data center should have in place a plan to detect errors, recover from them, and correct the cause.

1. Understand what errors cost your business. This will give you a basis for how much you should spend on the project. You may find that certain applications are vital and should be protected at all cost. Many applications could suffer outages without major cost.

2. Monitor all errors. Most data centers give the *LOGREC*[6] listing to the customer engineers and wait for them to say, *We need to replace an HDA.*

   This process becomes more and more difficult. You can obtain software systems (e.g., Computer Associates' Reliability Plus) to monitor errors. IBM and other vendors grow weary of being called to task by these comparisons and limit the number and type of errors that get into SYS1.LOGREC. Their reasoning is that the hardware microcode can detect and fix errors without an external interface. Does this make the problem go away, or does it sweep it under the rug where only performance measurements can see it?

3. Develop a disaster recovery plan that takes into consideration local outages (one or more devices fail), building outages (the entire building is damaged), or community outages (the com-

---

6 Refers to the MVS "SYS1.LOGREC" data set containing records of errors and statistics. The contents of this data set are formatted by the *Environmental Recording and Editing Program (EREP)*.

munity is damaged through hurricane, earthquake, or other regional disaster). Consider also simple power outages, normal summer brownouts, and electrical storms.

4. Write and test procedures for recovery. Agencies and other groups concerned with public health periodically conduct simulated disasters because they know this is the only way to ensure that people are properly trained should a real disaster occur. You might consider periodically conducting a simulated disaster at your data center to test the technical and human (e.g., communication) aspects of your procedures. Train people to recover.

> ¤ At some time, we have seen just about every backup subsystem take a backup of data and report normal completion, only to find at a later time that all or part of the data was not backed up or could not be restored. **It can happen to you!** The backup subsystem programmers called it a bug and offered a fix for the problem. We call that a disaster! Be certain you can restore from your backups, and retest this whenever something changes (e.g., a new software release or any new equipment).

5. Reformat DASD actuators periodically. In a relatively large data center, the normal movement of volumes and rotation of DASD into and out of the data center due to lease expirations may provide a reason to reformat actuators. If not, you should consider your own rotation to ensure that actuators get reformatted every three to four years. Do you rotate the tires on your vehicle? Maybe you should do both your tires and your DASD.

5.4.2. Control Unit: Pinned Data

Pinned data is physical blocks of data that were written into cache or nonvolatile storage but have not yet been transferred to the device. The data could be trapped in the control unit because there was a device error (it is very difficult to store data on DASD that is not spinning) or a subsystem error (the control unit suffered a power failure or software error).

Pinned data can be detected by the operator DSSERVE PATHS command and the IDCAMS LISTDATA (STATUS, DSTATUS, and COUNTS subcommands). The IDCAMS LISTDATA PINNED command will report on the pinned tracks.

What can you do about pinned data? Easy: fix the hardware, and the 3990 will destage the data automatically. Otherwise, the data is gone. You do have backups of the data, don't you? If you cannot afford to wait for the hardware fix, or you have a cautious, superstitious, or paranoid nature, you can copy the data to another device with DFDSS or IEBGENER.

You also may use the IDCAMS SETCACHE command with the *DISCARDPINNED* subcommand to eliminate pinned data that you do not need to save. Do something, or the cache allocated to pinned data cannot be used for anything else.

The battery life for NVS is approximately 48 hours. If your system is to be out for longer than that, you should move the data if you can.

Pinned data can be in several different conditions:

- **Retriable,** in which an equipment problem occurred and the data is safely stored.
- **Nonretriable,** in which an error was received from the DASD that is logical in nature (e.g., track overflowed) rather than physical.
- **NVS, Cache Available,** in which the nonvolatile storage and/or cache is available but the image is unusable.
- **Cache Copy Defective,** in which the cache image of a Cache Fast Write block is unusable.
- **Invalid,** in which the 3990 has returned a code that was unrecognizable.

> ▫ Be sure to clear any pinned data before you transfer a 3990 or other cache control unit from your data center. Not only will it be a problem to the installation on the receiving end, but it is a security violation to transfer unknown data to others. Clear off 3990 DASD Fast Write cache before selling control units.

5.4.3. The CONTROL Command

A rare but perplexing condition can appear when a control unit detects a failure and **permanently disables** one or more devices. The result is one or more actuators that cannot be written to or accessed at all.

CONTROL ALLOWWRITE Function

We encountered a problem with writes in the early 1970s with non-IBM hardware, and we have not seen it since. IBM must have had customers with the problem because they added *WRITE PREVENT* and the ability to overcome it for 3880 and 3990 control units.

Suppose a control unit gets confused when asked to write to device 140, cylinder 10, track 5, record 6. Instead, it writes to device 144, cylinder 10, track 5, record 6. Device *144* could report to the control unit that it was not expecting a write. (In the early case we experienced, the control unit sent every write request directed to one device to every device on the string!)

Operating system error recovery procedures (ERPs) detect errors. They isolate the path and retry the write request. In System/370 the same path was used for all the I/O. In Extended Architecture and Enterprise Systems Architecture the path used is the one selected by the hardware for reconnect. A feature called Guaranteed Device Path (GDP) is used for the non-370 I/Os.

If the write error persists, vary that path offline, try another path, and issue a *WRITE PREVENT* command to the control unit. This command may turn off channels, control unit interfaces, or head-of-string interfaces.

A bit is set in the control unit to indicate *Something is wrong, do not allow writes to this drive through this path until a real person looks at the problem.* The symptoms you will see are that certain jobs will fail (anyone trying to update data or allocate a data set) and certain jobs will continue running (anyone with data sets opened for read access only).

The operating system also varies the path in trouble offline to try to prevent further permanent errors.

Call your customer engineers and have them find the error. When they fix the problem, use the following JCL to free up the device:

JCL for Eliminating Write Inhibit
| ```
//STEP     EXEC PGM=ICKDSF
//SYSPRINT DD   SYSOUT=*
//SYSIN    DD   *
 CONTROL UNITADDRESS=(cuu) ALLOWWRITE
``` |

CONTROL CLEARFENCE Function

The 3990 control unit added more error checking for four-way mode. The control unit may also disable or *fence offline* a path to one or more devices.

The term *fencing* in the IBM DASD world means that the hardware and software have isolated a device or actuator and will not allow any I/O operations to it. We got the name from the word *fence*, which means to build a boundary around something. In DASD, however, nothing can get into or out of a fenced device. They did not build gates!

The MVS *DEVSERV PATH* operator command, described later in this chapter, shows device or actuator status. Have your customer engineers fix the device or control unit. Then run the following JCL to access the device(s) through the fixed path:
```

JCL for Eliminating Fenced Devices

```
//STEP      EXEC PGM=ICKDSF
//SYSPRINT DD   SYSOUT=*
//SYSIN     DD   *
 CONTROL UNITADDRESS=(cuu) CLEARFENCE
```

CONTROL RESETICD function

Devices attached to the IBM 3990 model 3 cached control unit can have another disabling condition that requires human intervention. If the control unit tries to read the device's status track and cannot, then the device is placed into the *indefinite status condition*.

You should contact your customer engineer to determine whether something is physically wrong with the device. When all is clear, use the RESETICD parameter to reset the condition. The IDCAMS program may have to be used with the SETCACHE command to destage or discard any pinned data.

JCL for Resetting Indefinite Status Conditions

```
//STEP      EXEC PGM=ICKDSF
//SYSPRINT DD   SYSOUT=*
//SYSIN     DD   *
 CONTROL UNITADDRESS=(cuu) RESETICD
```

5.4.4. DEVSERV PATH Operator Command

The MVS operator command *DEVSERVE (DS) PATH* gives immediate feedback on a volume's status. The output of the command is shown below. Be sure you look up message IEE459I in the appropriate message reference manual for your version of the operating system.

MVS DEVSERVE Operator Command and Sample Output for Device 340

```
DEVSERV P.340.1

IEE459I HH.MM.SS DEVSERV PATHS NNN
UNIT DTYPE M CNT VOLSER  CHPID=PATH STATUS
                  TC  DFW  PIN  DC-STATE    CCA  DDC  ALT CU-TYPE
340.33902.A.ccc.VOLSR1.30=+  31=+  34=+  35=+
                  YY    N        SIMPLEX       40   00       3990-3
```

The above message output has three lines as header information and up to two lines for the data. The first line identifies the message number for the response. You should look in the Messages and Codes manual for your version of the operating system for explanations of the rest of the message. Line 2, and the data for line 2 on line 4, are always there. Lines 3 and 5 are reported if the device is attached through a 3990 model 3 or other cache control unit. The fields in this sample message are:

1. Device address: 340.

2. Device type: 3390 model 2. The DEVSERV command sends commands to the control unit and can display the device type and model.

3. Mode:
   - **A** Device is online and at least one data set is allocated.
   - **O** Device is online but no data sets are allocated.
   - **F** Device is offline.
   - **P** Device is pending offline—probably waiting for some task to close data set(s) on the volume.
   - **M** There is a mount pending for the device.
   - **S** The device is online and allocated, but allocated by an MVS system control address space.

4. CNT: count of data sets open on the volume.

5. VOLSER: volume serial of the actuator.

6. CHPID=a b c d, where up to four paths are displayed. In this example, CHPID 30, 31, 34, and 35 are used:
   - **+** The path is online and available for I/O.

- **.** The path is physically unavailable.
- **X** The status is not known, such as when a dual copy pair is being created.
- **R** The path is available and is reserved for I/O in operation.
- **T** The I/O requesting information did not terminate within a certain time period, and the control unit may be sick.
- **U** Indicates cache or NVS problems.

7. For 3990 model 3 control units, a separate line shows the status of the caching and extended function operations for this device. The appearance of the control unit type on this line indicates that IBM plans to have a series of cache control units. The **TC** is two characters that indicate whether I/Os to the device use the cache:
   - *Y* when eligible for caching and *N* when not.
   - *Y* when caching is active and *N* when not. Both characters must be a *Y* for caching to work.

8. **DFW** for DASD Fast Write and NVS:
   - *Y* when eligible for DFW and *N* when not.
   - *Y* when NVS is active and *N* when not. Both characters must be a *Y* for DASD Fast Write to work.

9. **PIN** indicates whether this device has pinned data. A *Y* indicates that this device has pinned data, an *N* that it does not. If you see a *Y*, get your systems programmer at once. If you *are* your systems programmer, find out what data is pinned and fix it. (The pinned data might be your $10,000.00 pay raise!)

10. **DC-STATE** indicates the dual copy state of the volume:
    - **SIMPLEX.** No dual copy volume assigned to this one.
    - **PR-PNDG.** Dual copy volume copy is in process. This is primary.
    - **SEC-PNDG.** Dual copy volume copy is in progress. This is the secondary volume.

- **PRI-SDPL.** This is the primary volume, and the control unit is in the process of making the operational volume the primary and the nonoperational volume the secondary.
- **SEC-SDPL.** This is the secondary volume, and the control unit is making the operational volume the primary and the nonoperational volume the secondary.

11. **CCA** indicates the channel connection address of the volume.

12. **DDC** (Director to Device Connection) indicates the two hexadecimal digits of the storage director to device address. In this example, we used address *40*.

13. **ALT** indicates the alternate volume address of a dual copy connection. If this volume has no alternate (the case in this figure), then this field is blank. If this is the primary volume, the value here is the secondary volume address. If this is the secondary volume, the value here is the address of the primary volume.

14. **CU-TYPE** indicates the control unit type, in this case the 3990 model 3.

5.4.5. HDA Replacement

Sooner or later you will have to replace an HDA. The reason could be as simple as the lease has expired or your company has decided to sell the device. The reason could be as complex as one actuator on the HDA has become unusable or has errors and you must abandon it to save your data.

A word of caution. Replacing and moving HDAs is serious business. We recommend that you double check each step and use a team approach to this task. Discuss each step with another skilled technical person if at all possible. Do not depend on any set of instructions (even these) and follow them by rote. Before you proceed, be sure you are right. You may not get a second chance.

Replacement Procedure

Be sure of the addresses of the volumes to be replaced. Use the DEVSERV command above to display the operating system and hardware address of the device.

1. Make certain that you must move the data if errors are occurring. This may seem like a trivial step, but there have been occasions when the customer engineer insisted we abandon an HDA, but the problem was electronics in the head of string, not an HDA problem.

2. Move all data off the actuator(s). If you have an active DASD management subsystem [e.g., DFHSM, Fast Dump Restore (FDR)], use the program to archive all data on the volumes. If you are copying to a replacement actuator, you may want to archive off and recall or just use DASD dump programs (e.g., DFDSS or FDR) to move volume to volume.

3. If losing the data would be truly catastrophic to your company, take an extra, redundant backup in case there is a media failure during the restore.

4. Vary all paths to the device offline from all Processor Complexes that may access the data.

5. Ensure that the volume serial number for the actuator(s) is not lurking in Job Control Language that will be run during the time the volume is offline. This is your hardest step. In most cases we skip this step and wait for jobs to go into allocation recovery. We hold the job, reset the job, and cancel the job. In most cases, allocation recovery interferes with other jobs starting and stopping.

6. Have the customer engineer replace the HDA.

7. Format the actuator(s) and test access to them.

8. Place the actuator(s) back in service.

Using Dual Copy to Replace an HDA

One of the problems with moving volumes is that there always seems to be someone with a data set opened on the volume. DASD does not usually break unless you are using it. The solution in the past was to get stand-alone time late at night (or even on the weekend) to isolate the volume and move the data.

If you have an IBM 3990 model 3 control unit or equivalent, you can use the dual copy feature to move volumes if you have a number of conditions met:

1. You have spare, empty, unused volumes (yes, some places do have spare volumes from time to time), of the same geometry (type and capacity) on the same 3990-3 control unit.

2. The receiving actuator can be varied offline to all Processor Complexes.

3. 3990-3 cache and nonvolatile storage (NVS) are active.

Do not use the above as justification for keeping two spare volumes on each control unit. That is not very cost-effective. Instead, strategically allocate actuators that can be sacrificed when the need arises. For example, you could have volumes associated with a test system (or the live system with versions that can deactivate their paging volumes). You could have maintenance volumes. You may be able to shut down portions of your processing to keep the majority alive.

The next steps create a dual copy environment and move the data, active or inactive, to the receiving volume. You next switch the primary volume to the new actuators, and the old ones are ready for service.

1. Use the DEVSERV command to ensure that the M field of the receiving volumes is not allocated. The devices may even be offline. **The volumes must be empty because they will be completely overwritten.**

2. Vary the receiving volumes offline to all Processor Complexes. The *M* field should change to *F*.

3. Establish dual copy pairs.
   a. Execute IDCAMS to establish the secondary volumes. This process will take over 20 minutes depending on activity and parameter specifications. In the following JCL for IDCAMS, the *PACE* parameter specifies how many tracks will be copied before IDCAMS comes up for air (allows others to use the volumes). Replace *volsr1* with the first from volume serial number and *cu1* with the new address. Replace *volsr2* with the second from volume serial number and *cu2* with the new address.

JCL for Using IDCAMS to Create Dual Copy Pairs

```
//STEPNAME EXEC PGM=IDCAMS,REGION=4096K
//SYSPRINT DD   SYSOUT=*
//SYSIN    DD   *
  SETCACHE VOL(VOLSR1) UNIT(DDDD) PACE(1) SETSECONDARY(CU1)
  SETCACHE VOL(VOLSR2) UNIT(DDDD) PACE(1) SETSECONDARY(CU2)
```

---

   b. When the IDCAMS step completes, use the DEVSERV command to be sure the devices are dual copy pairs.

MVS DEVSERVE Command for Old Volumes

```
DEVSERV P.340.2

 IEE459I HH.MM.SS DEVSERV PATHS NNN
UNIT DTYPE M CNT VOLSER  CHPID=PATH STATUS
                TC  DFW  PIN  DC-STATE   CCA  DDC  ALT CU-TYPE
340.33902.A.CCC.VOLSR1.30=+  31=+  34=+  35=+
                YY  YY   N    PRIMARY    40   00   361 3390-3
341.33902.A.CCC.VOLSR2.30=+  31=+  34=+  35=+
                YY  YY   N    PRIMARY    40   00   362 3390-3
```

---

   c. The following DEVSERVE command shows an example of the command for the receiving device, 361:

MVS DEVSERVE Command for Receiving Volumes

```
DEVSERV P.361.1

 IEE459I HH.MM.SS DEVSERV PATHS NNN
UNIT DTYPE M CNT VOLSER  CHPID=PATH STATUS
                TC  DFW  PIN  DC-STATE   CCA  DDC  ALT CU-TYPE
361.33902.N.CCC
```

---

4. Suspend the primary volumes. This task stops activity to the volumes we intend to replace.

   a. Use IDCAMS to *stop using the primary volume.*

JCL for Using IDCAMS to Suspend the Primary Volume (volsr1 and volsr2) on 340 and 341

```
//STEPNAME EXEC PGM=IDCAMS,REGION=4096K
//SYSPRING DD  SYSOUT=*
//SYSIN    DD  *
  SETCACHE VOL(VOLSR1) UNIT(DDDD) SUSPENDPRIMARY
  SETCACHE VOL(VOLSR2) UNIT(DDDD) SUSPENDPRIMARY
```

---

   b. Use the DEVSERV command to be sure the primary devices are now the ones on 361. Note that in the displays below, the DDC addresses *00* and *01* are the old broken devices now ready for service (field M is set to *N*), but the addresses the operating system and all applications use (340 and 341) are operational on DDC addresses *21* and *22*.

   The first- and second-generation DASD had a feature that allowed us to exchange physical addresses. It was known as *popping the plug.* Popping the plug forces a *Device End (DE) signal to the controller, just as an MVS VARY OFFLINE* operator command. That feature is now back! The following shows devices 340 and 341:

MVS DEVSERVE Command. Devices 340 and 341 are Switched with 361 and 362

```
DEVSERV P.340,2

IEE459I HH.MM.SS DEVSERV PATHS NNN
UNIT DTYPE M CNT VOLSER  CHPID=PATH STATUS
                     TC  DFW  PIN  DC-STATE    CCA  DDC  ALT CU-TYPE
340,33902,A,ccc,VOLSR1,30=+  31=+  34=+  35=+
                     YY  YY   N    PRI-SDPL    40   21   361 3390-3
341,33902,A,ccc,VOLSR2,30=+  31=+  34=+  35=+
                     YY  YY   N    PRI-SDPL    40   22   362 3390-3
```

The next box shows devices 361 and 362:

MVS DEVSERVE Command to Look at Old (Broken) Devices

```
DEVSERV P.361,2
```

```
                MVS DEVSERVE Command to Look at Old (Broken) Devices
IEE459I HH.MM.SS DEVSERV PATHS NNN
UNIT DTYPE M CNT VOLSER  CHPID=PATH STATUS
                            TC   DFW  PIN  DC-STATE    CCA  DDC  ALT CU-TYPE
  361,33902,A,CCC,VOLSR1,30=+  31=+  34=+  35=+
                            YY   YY   N    SEC-SDPL     61   00   340 3390-3
  362,33902,A,CCC,VOLSR2,30=+  31=+  34=+  35=+
                            YY   YY   N    SEC-SDPL     62   01   341 3390-3
```

5. Break apart the duplex pairs. Note that in the following we use the volume serial which is being used to access actuators 361 and 362.

```
          JCL for Using IDCAMS to Break Apart the Dual Copy Actuators
//STEPNAME EXEC PGM=IDCAMS,REGION=4096K
//SYSPRING DD   SYSOUT=*
//SYSIN    DD   *
  SETCACHE VOL(VOLSR1) UNIT(DDDD) RESETTOSIMPLEX
  SETCACHE VOL(VOLSR2) UNIT(DDDD) RESETTOSIMPLEX
```

6. Turn off DASD Fast Write and Device Caching. Note that we use the actuator address because they are offline to the operating system. When done, the TC and DFW fields should change to *NY* to indicate that caching is off for this device. **The HDA cannot be replaced until this status is achieved.**

```
          JCL for Using IDCAMS to Set Off DASD Fast Write and Caching
//STEPNAME EXEC PGM=IDCAMS,REGION=4096K
//SYSPRING DD   SYSOUT=*
//SYSIN    DD   *
  SETCACHE UNITADDRESS(361) DFWW OFF
  SETCACHE UNITADDRESS(362) DFWW OFF
```

7. After repair, run ICKDSF INSTALL and a minimal INIT. You will be using addresses 361 and 362.

8. Reset to dual copy status.

```
          JCL for Using IDCAMS to Reset to Dual Copy Status
//STEPNAME EXEC PGM=IDCAMS,REGION=4096K
//SYSPRING DD   SYSOUT=*
//SYSIN    DD   *
  SETCACHE VOL(VOLSR1) UNIT(DDDD) PACE(1) SETSECONDARY(361)
  SETCACHE VOL(VOLSR2) UNIT(DDDD) PACE(1) SETSECONDARY(362)
```

9. Break apart dual copy status. After this successfully completes, you have the actuators back where they were before this started. We recommend putting everything back rather than leaving actuator numbers out of their normal sequence. You must use ICKDSF minimal INIT to reset 361 and 362 because they cannot be used. They still have the volume serial numbers from 340 and 341.

JCL for Using IDCAMS to Break Apart Dual Copy Volumes

```
//STEPNAME EXEC PGM=IDCAMS,REGION=4096K
//SYSPRING DD   SYSOUT=*
//SYSIN    DD   *
  SETCACHE VOL(VOLSR1) UNIT(DDDD) RESETTOSIMPLEX
  SETCACHE VOL(VOLSR2) UNIT(DDDD) RESETTOSIMPLEX
```

5.5. Summary

DASD management is a relatively complex part of a data center's responsibility. In many cases it crosses organizational boundaries in that it consists of configuration planning, software upgrades, hardware installation, and preparation of DASD for use by the data center's end users.

DASD has several facets. The first is the environment, or how much space and air conditioning the devices require. The second is availability, or what percentage of the time the end users can access their data. The third is performance, or how fast the devices can deliver data to the end user's programs. The fourth is capacity and accounting, or who is paying for all these expenses.

Two types of installation exist, disruptive and nondisruptive. With disruptive installation, entire devices are unavailable during the addition or deletion of devices. With nondisruptive installation, the end user may not know that the data center is changing devices.

Initialization with IBM DASD involves the Device Support Facilities (ICKDSF) subsystem. ICKDSF writes the label track and the Volume Table of Contents (VTOC) on uninitialized volumes. ICKDSF also writes records on all the tracks of a volume to prepare it for operating system use.

Several types of initialization can be performed. Minimal initialization writes the label track and VTOC and quickly prepares the tracks for use. Medial initialization performs some verification that the tracks can read and write data. Maximal initialization really works over the tracks to ensure that they can be used. The INSTALL initialization is the same as medial initialization and is used for 3380 and 3390 devices.

Protection of data placed on DASD by the end users and the data center itself centers around full volume and incremental backup philosophies. Full volume copies every record on every track of the DASD to another medium, such as magnetic tape. Incremental backups copy only the changed data sets. In either case, the data must be synchronized with any other data set on other volumes to ensure proper backup.

Another facet of security is field and record security. Neither is protected by operating system backup and restore subsystems because they do not get to field or record levels. They back up data sets.

DASD error recovery considerations require the data center to consider all of the possible problems that could disable spinning DASD from delivering their data. Hardware, electronics, firmware, and software problems can prevent data access.

5.6. Questions

1. What are the primary goals of DASD management?

2. Why should you place DASD on the computer room floor and not move it until you absolutely must?

3. Describe the label track of the IBM standard format DASD. What are the records and their use? When would this track have different records? What is the most important pointer on the label track?

4. What differentiates minimal, medial, and maximal initialization?

5. When is medial initialization usually a waste of time?

6. When would you use the INSTALL function of ICKDSF? What additional function should you perform to prepare a new DASD for use? Why is that important? Why should you not use medial initialization with INSTALL?

7. At what level does the operating system protect data sets? What is the name of the function that supplies the operating system interface?

8. Describe the difference between full volume backup and incremental backup. Why wouldn't you use full volume backup all the time?

9. Suppose an archived data set is destroyed. From where do you retrieve it?

10. Is it important for an application to have synchronized back-ups of its data sets? Why?

11. What are the two components that, should they fail, could produce DASD errors? Which one is really fatal to recovering data?

12. What are the two types of errors that an operating system sees?

13. What makes a permanent error permanent?

14. What is hard disk head alignment drift? Why is it important for a data center to catch this problem?

6

Tuning Considerations

6.1. Monitoring and Measuring

Tuning DASD is similar to tuning anything else. You can be reactive (wait until someone complains) or be proactive (do something). In either case there are several steps. You monitor and measure it, looking for *poor performance*. You form a hypothesis about what causes the poor performance and make a change. You must then measure again and compare with earlier performance to determine whether and how effective the change was.

Monitoring and measuring DASD is a complex topic. One reason for the complexity is the number of data sets to monitor. The average data center may have over 100 actuators and 50,000 data sets online. If several thousand data sets are created (and/or deleted) every day, when do you *run* the VTOCs and count or measure the data sets on each volume? Most data sets are created and moved without regard to performance considerations.

Another reason is the large number and variety of I/O operations performed in a typical data center. Batch jobs and interactive users may dynamically create thousands of data sets and cause thousands of I/O operations against each.

Yet another reason is the complexity of I/O operations. Each access method has a different way of doing I/O. Patterns of I/O by a single access method may change depending on the contents of the data being read and written.

Furthermore, the act of monitoring and measuring may itself affect the statistics. In nuclear physics, this is called the Heisenberg effect, and it can apply to observation of any system: the observer may affect the behavior being observed. Your monitoring could cause performance problems by tying up the devices!

There are two viewpoints on tuning. The operating system may see well-tuned DASD. All devices could be performing each I/O operation in less than 40 milliseconds. The application may see unacceptable slowness, however, if it is doing unnecessary I/O operations because of inefficient algorithms. It is similar to the fable of the blind men examining the elephant. The one that had the leg described the elephant as a tree. The one holding the trunk described the elephant as a snake.

The result is that there are two camps on monitoring and measuring DASD. On the one hand are the theoreticians. They develop models of how DASD should perform, monitor some vital statistics, and predict the performance. On the other hand are the DASD measurement advocates. They summarize statistics over a long period and act on those actuators that do not respond as they should. Both methods provide insight into DASD performance. You should examine the fruit on the trees to see which one is more productive for your needs.

There are a number of things you can do to affect the performance of DASD I/O operations. Hardware can be reconfigured, application software can be redesigned, JCL can be changed to affect performance. So many options, so little time. Just remember one thing:

> ¤ The ultimate goal of tuning DASD is to eliminate the I/O operation if possible, and if not, to minimize the time to read or write the block in question.

We now take a detailed look at how much work goes into a "simple" I/O. Then, having learned how valuable it is to do I/O properly, we look at effective ways to solve your performance problems.

6.2. Anatomy of an I/O

Before we get started on the solutions, let's look at an I/O in detail.[1]

6.2.1. Models of I/O Operations

The classical model for predicting the I/O service time of a DASD I/O can be stated in two different ways: the early model and the recent model.

Early Model of I/O Service Time
Service time = (queue time) + (average seek time) + (device latency time) + (data transfer time)

This is the older form of the model. Nothing measured actual seek time, so the average was assumed to be one-third of the maximum seek distance. The assumption was based on the mathematical theory of a random starting point and a random ending point and each I/O request was unrelated to the previous I/O.

Nothing measured the actual latency, so average rotation was assumed to be one-half of a revolution. The theory was that the access would be random, and the average rotational delay would

---

1 The basis of this section came from Bill Fairchild, author of CA-FASTDASD and CA-DASDCHECK, and co-author of Landmark Systems Corporation's The Monitor for MVS. Bill (Mr. I/O) has been writing channel programs since February 1966. His assistance has been vital to this book.

be one half a revolution. This again assumed a random angular starting point, a random ending point, and unrelated I/O requests.

The data transfer time was computed as *(average block size)/channel data transfer rate)*. An average block size was arbitrarily chosen as 4K.

This model will work for most I/O workloads, but some critical MVS components generate I/O requests that violate the assumptions made in this model. Inaccurate results will occur if the model is used in such cases.

A more recent model, used with XA and ESA operating systems, uses empirical observations instead of theoretical numbers:

Recent Model of I/O Service Time
Service time = (queue time) + (pending time) + (disconnect time) + (connect time)

This model is used with the Extended Architecture I/O Subsystem. The last three of the four components are obtained through the Channel Measurement Facility. Accurate results can be obtained with these measures. Unfortunately, pending and disconnect times can be affected by many different phenomena and may not be repeatable, and it is difficult to extrapolate this form of the model to new workloads.

The basics of an I/O operation depend on the operating system that is in control of the hardware. We will use the MVS example.

One very complex I/O operation, reading and writing the JES2 checkpoint data set, reads and writes data blocks on multiple tracks on a DASD. It is a good study because it embodies a wide range of possible channel program actions.

6.2.2. The I/O Request

An I/O can be started by several methods. An application may either invoke the Execute Channel Program (EXCP) supervisor service directly, as JES2 does, or invoke an access method that, in turn, invokes EXCP. Regardless, a Start Subchannel (SSCH) machine instruction is executed.

Application programs are prohibited from using the hardware instructions to start I/O operations because the operating system must control the environment. Even large portions of the operating system do not issue the real instruction. MVS and VM operating systems have only one of these machine instructions, in the I/O supervisor.

Access Methods

High-level access methods such as QSAM, BSAM, BPAM, BDAM, and ISAM maintain and reference a lot of data to organize I/O activity. All of these access methods require a previously OPENed DCB (Device Control Block) that points to a DEB (Data Extent Block) and a DD entry (Data Definition) within the TIOT (Task I/O Table). The DEB must have a DASD extent entry which points to a UCB (Unit Control Block). The I/O request is represented by an IOB (I/O Block) that points to the DCB and the channel program. The channel program has CCWs (channel command words) that point to I/O buffers.

All these access methods use the slightly lower level EXCP access method to perform the I/O operation once they have constructed the appropriate channel program.

VSAM, on the other hand, requires a previously OPENed ACB (Access Control Block). Also, VSAM has its own IOS Driver defined (the Actual Block Processor).

These access methods are not limited to DASD. EXCP and STARTIO are used for all devices, including tape drives, printers, and communications controllers in the IBM mainframe architecture.

A Typical DASD I/O

Let's look at the steps in a typical DASD input-output operation:

1. The end user issues an I/O request (READ, WRITE, GET, or PUT). JES has a series of macros to call its I/O routines. COBOL and other high-level programs issue READ or WRITE macros.

2. The access method fills in and uses the data structures (control blocks) required by EXCP (DCB, DEB, IOB, virtual CCWs).

3. The EXCP macro causes an SVC 0 interruption to transfer control to the operating system.

4. SVC 0 invokes the EXCP Input/Output Supervisor (IOS) Driver.

5. The EXCP IOS Driver maps the EXCP request into a STARTIO structure (IOSB, SRB, and real CCWs. All of these control blocks are in fixed common pages).

6. The STARTIO service puts the request on an I/O queue (IOQ).

7. If the device is already in use, the I/O request will be in the state known as IOS queuing. This time is not measured by MVS and can only be approximated by a sampling technique.

8. EXCP returns to the end user. The application program has asked for a block to be read, and the I/O operation may not even be started to the device.

9. The end user can do other processing and then issue a WAIT macro when the data is needed.

10. For this example, the I/O has not completed, so another user (address space) is dispatched.

11. The device becomes available and we are next in line. The I/O queue time stops for our I/O operation.

12. The operating system issues a SSCH instruction and the I/O is started. The ORB control block is used to contain information about the I/O.

13. The I/O Channel Subsystem selects a channel path: channel path (CHPID), logical control unit (LCU), physical control unit (PCU), and subchannel. This example assumes the XA or ESA hardware and software. In earlier operating systems, the operating system tried and retried paths.

14. The I/O Channel Subsystem uses the hardware structure of control blocks such as the unit control word (UCW) and channel blocks.

15. The pending time starts being accumulated by the channel.

16. Once a complete path is available from the Processor Complex to the device, the I/O operation starts, the pending time stops, and the connect time starts.

17. The SEEK command causes connect time to stop and disconnect time to start. The actuator moves to the desired cylinder.

18. The SET SECTOR channel command causes the DASD to disconnect from its path and wait until the platter rotates to the desired position on the platter. This is Rotational Position Sensing (RPS). Most DASD hardware takes the user's sector number and subtracts three sectors. These three sectors of rotation are the only time during which the device is even attempting to reconnect.

19. The device attempts to reconnect to a channel path. If it fails to connect, an extra revolution is required. This is called an RPS miss.

20. The device reconnects to the channel. The disconnect time stops and the connect time starts.

21. The record ID search takes place.

22. The device reads or writes the data block.

23. The channel program may transfer control to other commands similar to 17, 18, 21, or 22 if other blocks or tracks are needed. Possible additional disconnect/reconnect operations may be encountered.

24. The connect time accumulation stops.

25. The channel stores measurement data and the status of the I/O operation. Channel End and Device End interrupts are presented to the Processor Complex. The Processor Complex is placed into an interrupt disabled state and the Input-Output Supervisor (IOS) is invoked.

26. The IOS posts the status into the STARTIO control block structure.

27. The EXCP IOS Driver posts the status into the EXCP control block structure.

28. SMF counters are updated unless the access method does not support SMF. Examples of DASD subsystems that do not update the SMF counters are DB2, IMS fast path, Auxiliary Storage Manager (ASM), the media manager, and Storage Management Subsystem.

29. The MVS IOS does a special instruction to see if any other I/O has completed. This Test Pending Interrupt (TPI) is used to take advantage of the fact that IOS is already primed and can process other interrupts if they are ready for processing.

30. IOS transfers control to the dispatcher to transfer control to the highest-priority task. Eventually the application program that requested the I/O is redispatched because its wait is satisfied.

Revisit the Typical I/O

JES2 uses the EXCP access method directly without going through an intermediate access method, such as BSAM. JES2 builds its own channel programs and then issues the EXCP and WAIT macros itself. Many other *subsystem-level* programs also use EXCP.

Whether the end user builds the channel program directly or uses another access method to build it (such as QSAM), an important point to remember is that almost the entire control block structure at the EXCP level is in pageable, private storage, and all address pointers are virtual. Moreover, the only parts of the control block structure that can be trusted, for either validity or security purposes, are the DEB, UCB, and TIOT DD entries, all of which are built and manipulated entirely by *trusted* components of the operating system. These central storage areas are kept secure using hardware-enforced storage protection (keys or read-only attributes).

Once the channel program has been built, the end user issues the EXCP macro. This in turn executes an SVC (Supervisor Call) instruction to switch to authorized routines that are trusted to perform the I/O request. This SVC instruction is the last instruction the end user will execute for some time, and it causes considerable overhead in terms of the application's instruction path length.

First, the processor's status (current PSW and registers) must be saved. Then control is passed to the particular SVC routine needed (SVC 0 in the case of EXCP). The SVC 0 routine first validates all address pointers and control blocks. Next it maps the EXCP-level control block structure into a lower-level structure consisting of an IOSB (I/O Supervisor Block) and SRB (Service Request Block). This is necessary because all I/O requests in MVS must be issued directly by an IOS Driver via the STARTIO macro.

In the old days of OS/360 and SVS (OS/VS2 Release 1), the lowest possible level of I/O access method was EXCP, but now with MVS an even lower level is possible. The EXCP processor in MVS is defined as an IOS Driver, as are also the Auxiliary Storage Manager, VSAM, VTAM, Program Fetch, and JES3, to name just a few.

At the STARTIO macro level, the only control blocks needed are the IOSB and SRB. The channel program also must have real addresses in it, because the DAT (Dynamic Address Translation) technique that maps virtual addresses into central storage for software is not used for channel access of central storage. So at this point the EXCP processor copies the user's virtual channel program to page-fixed storage and translates, using the CPU, virtual addresses to real ones. All pages necessary for the I/O buffers are also fixed because the channel program now references central storage.

This CCW copying and translation, page fixing, and control block mapping can consume considerable CPU time, so one possible source of performance improvement is to use STARTIO directly in an application that has strict response time or CPU time requirements.

Next the EXCP processor issues the STARTIO macro to schedule the I/O operation, which is represented from now on by an IOQ (I/O Queue Control Block). If the device is not in use, the SSCH (Start Subchannel) instruction is executed, which will cause the actual I/O hardware processing to begin.

If the device already has an I/O started by this system and not yet completed, then the IOQ is put on a chain of IOQs for the device. This is the process of software I/O queuing.

One possible cause of queuing is format write commands (e.g., write home address, write R0, write CKD, and erase). These commands cause a Channel End interrupt when the record is written on the track (or immediately in the case of erase), but the Device End interrupt does not occur until the rest of the track has been erased. Another cause is multiple users or systems accessing the same or different data sets on the device.

IOS will not consider this device's last I/O to be complete until it receives the Device End interrupt. In these cases, the I/O request causing the problem will receive what looks like normal service time, but requests from other users will have very large queue times.

To compute the amount of I/O service time required by software queuing, I/O monitors typically use a sampling technique. At frequent intervals (e.g., once a second) the number of I/O queue entries is counted. These counts are accumulated for a longer interval (e.g., a minute), and then the total queued requests are averaged over the longer interval.

This yields a number that is then assumed to be the average I/O queue length. That is, it is the average number of queued entries behind which a randomly arriving request must wait. The length of time the request must wait in the queue before it is serviced is computed by multiplying the average queue length by the device's average service time per I/O request during the same interval.

The device's average service time is computed by dividing the total service time (pending + connect + disconnect) by the number of I/O requests serviced in the interval.

Example of a Model I/O

In the example below, assume the average queue length is 0.1 (sampling the I/O queue finds an I/O queued 10 percent of the time); the device uses 100 milliseconds of pending time, 400 milliseconds of connect time, and 1,500 milliseconds of disconnect time during a 1-minute interval; and 100 I/O requests were processed in the 1-minute interval. Device service time is equal to the sum of device pending, disconnect, and connect time. Then the average device service time per I/O is 2,000 milliseconds divided by 100 I/O requests, or 20 milliseconds. This number, 20 milliseconds, is then multiplied by the average queue length of 0.1 to give an average I/O queue time of 2 milliseconds for this device during this 1-minute interval.

Computing Average Queue Time
Avg. Queue time = (avg. queue length) * (avg. dev. service time) Avg. dev. service time = (pend+disc+conn)/(no. of requests)
Example: Average queue length = 0.1 Total pending time = 100 milliseconds Total connect time = 400 milliseconds Total disconnect time = 1,500 milliseconds Total requests = 100 Avg. dev. service time = (100+400+1,500)/100 = 20 ms Avg. queue time = (0.1) * (20 ms) = 2 ms

What is wrong with the standard model's assumptions so far? The method usually used to compute software queuing time is by sampling, and sampling techniques may miss important events. The only way to obtain an accurate queue time is to intercept both the STARTIO macro and the SSCH instruction for the same request, and then subtract the earlier time from the later time. Tracing SVC 0 (EXCP) interrupts with GTF will give an approximation, but many MVS components do not use SVC 0 to schedule I/O requests. These are IOS Drivers and use the STARTIO macro directly. This path into IOS uses a branch entry point and is not traceable with GTF.

Sooner or later the I/O request will be started with the SSCH instruction. Once again, the I/O control blocks are mapped into a lower-level control block structure. There is only one control block needed for the SSCH instruction, and that is the Operation Request Block (ORB). The ORB is the lowest-level I/O control block maintained by the software.

The channel subsystem (CSS) must now select the appropriate channel path (CHPID), logical control unit (LCU), physical control unit (PCU), and subchannel (represented by a subchannel information block, or SCHIB).

Next the channel subsystem maps the request into a hardware control block structure, primarily the Unit Control Word (UCW). Hardware control blocks are kept in the part of central storage allocated to the Hardware System Area (HSA) and cannot be accessed directly by software.

Hardware queuing may also take place at this time. In XA and ESA the queuing is by logical control unit (LCU). In earlier versions queuing was done at the logical channel (LCH) level. The request is queued by the channel subsystem until a complete path is available. This queuing is also called *device pending time.*

The channel subsystem must send certain electronic signals to the control unit in order to synchronize with it. This process, called handshaking or channel protocol, takes a certain finite amount of time. Although it is very small (about a millisecond) compared with other DASD operations and is usually excluded from models, it can constrain the maximum number of I/O requests per second that can even be serviced. For example, solid-state devices (SSD) have been measured from 1,000 to several thousand I/Os per second, and there are 1,000 milliseconds in a second. It may be physically impossible to drive an SSD any faster because of the handshaking overhead.

When you attempt to drive a device at this fast a rate, you must be concerned with matters that ordinarily are not important, such as channel protocol time, instruction path length to get the I/O started, cache directory search time, etc.

As soon as the SSCH is executed, the Channel Measurement Facility begins accumulating measurement data, in units of 128 microseconds, to be stored in the Channel Measurement Block when the I/O is complete. Three types of time are accumulated, depending on the state of the device. These are pending, disconnect, and connect time.

Causes of High Pending Time

At first pending time is accumulated until the channel subsystem can obtain a complete path to the device. If there is no interference from other Processor Complexes sharing the same DASD, and if there is an available internal path in the control unit, then the pending time will be very short, typically only 0.13 millisecond.

MVS cannot know if the device is really busy to another system, so a very large pending time on a shared device on a noncaching control unit is an indication that the device may be in use by another system much of the time. If the device is not shared and is not on a caching control unit, then the pending time is due to not having enough internal paths in the controller for the workload. If the device is on a caching controller, then the control unit may not have enough internal paths available because of excessive cache slot miss staging, whether on reads or writes (3990-3 only), and whether random or sequential.

The causes of high pending time are many and the following list is a representative sample:

1. The actuator is shared and is busy processing requests from another system. The other system may also have reserved the actuator.

2. No internal path is available in the head of string.

3. Back-end staging by a caching controller causes hidden device-busy time. The following are examples of the type of staging you would get from the IBM 3990 model 3. Other cache control units (e.g., Amdahl and Hitachi) may use different algorithms.
   a. The normal (random) caching algorithm stages all records to the end of the track after the requested record.
   b. The normal (random) caching algorithm stages all records from the beginning of the track to the requested record if a front-end read miss.
   c. The sequential caching algorithm stages all records to the end of the track after the requested record and stages in all of the next track (3990-3 stages in all of next three tracks).
   d. Many types of writes to extended function 3990-3 go into nonvolatile storage (NVS) and will need to be subsequently destaged.
   e. 3990-3 dual copy initialization is taking place. An attempt to access the primary device during this time will cause a pending time of from 17 ms to 20 minutes! (See the IDCAM PACE parameter.)

f. Dynamic reconnect adds 1.8 ms of control unit busy for head-of-string protocol after Device End occurs. This will increase the probability that all internal paths are busy for the next I/O if it happens right after Device End. This may be part of the answer to the observation that a very busy device on a string can elongate I/Os to other devices on the string.

6.2.3. Channel Command Words

Once a path to the device is available, then channel command words (CCWs) can be executed by the control unit and device. The typical channel program assumed by the standard service time model is as follows:

1. SEEK. Move the arm to the selected cylinder.
2. SET SECTOR. Set a counter for the device to use to wake up as the platter spins to a position slightly before it gets to the requested record.
3. SEARCH ID EQUAL. Wait, while connected, for the platter to spin to this spot.
4. READ/WRITE DATA. Transfer the data.

So much for a simple I/O operation. Now let's look at a complex channel program such as the one used by the JES2 checkpoint processor.

1. SEEK cylinder B, track 0
2. SET FILE MASK
3. SEEK cylinder B, track 0
4. SET SECTOR 0D
5. SEARCH ID EQUAL cylinder B, track 0, record 3
6. WRITE DATA length = 1901
7. SEEK cylinder B, track 1
8. SET SECTOR 05
9. SEARCH ID EQUAL cylinder B, track 1, record 1
10. WRITE DATA length = 1000

11. SEEK cylinder B, track 0
12. SET SECTOR 05
13. SEARCH ID EQUAL cylinder B, track 0, record 1
14. WRITE DATA length = 100
15. SEARCH ID EQUAL cylinder B, track 0, record 2
16. WRITE DATA length = 100
17. READ COUNT

The exact channel program generated will depend on what level of DFP is running and to what combination of device and controller the I/O is directed. The channel program shown here was actually generated by JES2 under MVS/XA for a noncaching controller, was traced with GTF, and employs only the count-key-data (CKD) architecture CCWs. If a more modern controller were attached and the proper DFP installed, the channel program would instead use Extended CKD architecture CCWs, and would look like the following:

1. DEFINE EXTENT = 000B0000 to 000B000F
2. LOCATE RECORD cylinder B, track 0, record 3, sector 0D
3. WRITE DATA length = 1901
4. LOCATE RECORD cylinder B, track 1, record 1, sector 05
5. WRITE DATA length = 1000
6. LOCATE RECORD cylinder B, track 0, record 1, sector 05
7. WRITE DATA length =100
8. WRITE DATA length =100
9. READ COUNT

These CKD and ECKD channel programs are functionally the same as far as both accessing data and timing are concerned. The timing may change with asynchronous control units.

Once a complete path is acquired, the device starts out connected to the channel path, and the Channel Measurement Facility stops accumulating pending time and begins accumulating connect time. The device stays connected until something happens to disconnect it. Then it stays disconnected until something happens to require reconnection.

Let's look at each channel command word (CCW) of the CKD channel program in detail.

CCW 01: SEEK

The first CCW is a SEEK command. Assume the last I/O request on this device left the access mechanism positioned on cylinder B (as determined from the GTF trace data). This SEEK causes no arm motion, completes immediately, and does not cause the device to disconnect from the channel path. Only SEEKs that cause actual arm motion will also cause the device to disconnect. Since this device is shared, the other system may have moved the arm, in which case we would disconnect and start the arm moving to cylinder B.

How long would a seek motion take if it were necessary? Seek times on a 3380 vary from a minimum of 3 to a maximum of about 30 milliseconds. The average seek, as reported by the hardware vendors, is about 16 milliseconds. What is an *average* seek? Mathematically, it is one-third the maximum distance. This is the value sometimes assumed in the standard model for service time. The problem with this model is that the mathematical, theoretical average is not very typical in most workloads. Normally, an *average* seek of one-third the maximum will occur, followed by a burst of several more I/O requests to the same cylinder. Such access patterns reduce the time for an average seek in the real world. Access patterns vary considerably from device to device, depending on the workload. Unless the device is active to more than one Processor Complex, a safe assumption is probably one-fourth the time of the vendor's average, or one-twelfth the maximum seek time.

CCW 02: SET FILE MASK

Next is a SET FILE MASK CCW. This is added in front of all channel programs processed by EXCP for file integrity purposes. The effect of this CCW is to prevent one I/O request from accessing data in a different data set, and also to prevent writing into a data set opened for input. This command ends instantly and the device stays connected.

CCW 03: SEEK

Next is another SEEK command for the same cylinder and track number. Again, this SEEK does not cause arm motion, so the device remains connected.

CCW 04: SET SECTOR

The next CCW, SET SECTOR, causes the device to disconnect from the channel path and the control unit to begin looking for angular sector number 0A (3 less than the user's sector number of 0D). When sector 0A is detected, the control unit begins attempting to reconnect the device to the channel path. There is only a three-sector window in which the reconnection may occur. On an IBM 3380 device spinning at 3,600 RPM and with a total number of 222 sectors per revolution, a three-sector window is equivalent to 225 microseconds of elapsed time.

Now we must enter the world of probability theory. Since the channel path was disconnected at the beginning of the SET SECTOR command, the same channel path may now be in use by another device. Newer control units and the XA I/O hardware allow the device to attempt to reconnect to any available channel path connecting the processor with the control unit. If no available channel path can be found during this 225-microsecond interval, then the control unit stops trying to reconnect, waits for a complete revolution of the device, and then searches for sector 0A again. This phenomenon is known as a missed RPS (Rotational Position Sensing) reconnect or an RPS miss.

IBM control units will continue this process indefinitely. Some of the plug-compatible vendors take the approach that the control unit will allow only two missed RPS reconnects to take place, after which the controller will continuously attempt to reconnect, regardless of the current sector number, and will then remain connected until sector 0D is found. This approach does not guarantee that you will never miss more than two revolutions, but it does guarantee that after two revolutions have occurred, the minimum possible number of additional revolutions will be required for a reconnection.

According to probability theory, as the all-channel-path-busy percent increases, the probability of a successful RPS reconnect decreases. Assuming only one channel path is available, at 33% busy, one-half of an extra revolution will be required for a successful reconnection. At 90% busy, nine revolutions are required. The exact formula for only one possible channel path to reconnect to is given as:

Number of Revolutions Missed
Number of revolutions = (percent busy)/(100 - percent busy)

For a controller connected to more than one channel path with dynamic reconnect, a different formula has to be used, but the simple formula already given will approximate the results of the other, more complex formula. For two channel paths to a controller, both channel paths could average 50% busy before one-half of an extra revolution would be required for reconnecting. For a controller with four channel paths, all four channel paths would have to average about 70% busy before the reconnection would require an average of one-half revolution.

Computing the Number of Missed RPS Reconnects **(Assuming Only One Possible Channel Path to Reconnect To)**
No. of misses = (percent busy)/(100 - percent busy) Example: Assume 33.3% busy on the only path No. of misses = (0.333)/(1 - 0.333) = 0.333/0.667 = 0.5 revolution Example: Assume 90% busy on the only path No. of misses = (0.9)/(1 - 0.9) = 0.9/0.1 = 9 revolutions

A major shortcoming of the classical model for predicting service time is revealed by this JES2 checkpoint channel program, and that is the assumption that there is only one point in the channel program at which the device must attempt to reconnect to the channel path. There are three such points in this sample channel program (CCWs 04, 08, and 12 in the CKD variation).

At each of these three points, the probabilistic effect of missed RPS reconnects must be considered. Each of these three points is mutually independent of the other activity on all the channel paths connected to the device, so the total effect is cumulative. If all the connected channel paths are averaging 33% busy, then this channel program will require 1.5 additional revolutions just for the missed RPS reconnects (one-half revolution for each of the three disconnect/reconnect points). At 3,600 RPM this translates into an additional 25 milliseconds.

The classical model was designed to describe *most* I/O requests, which are well behaved and have only one reconnect point. The model can be applied to all devices in a configuration and yield fairly accurate results. When you attempt to apply a general model to a specific device, you must understand the characteristics of the I/O workload on that particular device.

Some devices have very critical, complex, lengthy, specialized channel programs running on them and very few of the normal, simple, well-behaved channel programs. Other notable examples of channel programs with multiple reconnect points are paging I/O (with a possible maximum of 30 reconnect points) and certain DB2 operations. If you intend to model I/O on devices with workloads such as these, you must take multiple reconnections into account.

The following are some of the causes of high disconnect time.

1. Long average seek distance.

2. All channel paths busy, causing many missed RPS reconnects.

3. Multiple disconnect/reconnect points in one channel program.

4. Data sets being erased as part of a security specification. RACF (and the RACF look-alikes) have an option that will rewrite all the tracks of a data set if it is ever scratched. This option may be chosen for specific, highly sensitive data sets. It should **not be specified** for a large number of data sets.

5. Device error recovery.

6. Controller microcode bugs.

CCW 05: SEARCH ID EQUAL

Sooner or later we find we are at sector 0D and are also connected to a channel path. We then begin to search for record 3 (see CCW 5).

In Figure 6.1 you see a DASD platter rotating. The area between the SET SECTOR being started and the requested sector being reached is where the channel and control unit are available for other operations. After the requested sector is reached, the device is connected to the channel and control unit. All search operations are always connected. In fact, the only three CCW commands that can cause disconnection are a motion SEEK, a SET SECTOR, or a LOCATE RECORD command (which embodies a seek, set sector, and sector function).

If the sector number has been calculated incorrectly and is slightly higher than where record 3 really begins, we will have a connected search of one entire revolution. When writing DASD channel programs, it is important that you calculate sector numbers correctly or else use a READ SECTOR command if the records are not all the same size. One possible cause of otherwise inexplicably high connect times could be an incorrectly calculated sector number.

CCW 06: WRITE DATA

At this point we must also consider the effects of being on a caching control unit. On a cached controller, every transfer of data must begin with a search of the cache directory despite the caching algorithm in use. A SEARCH command requires the control unit to orient to a particular part of a particular record, so the cache directory is searched. Searching is a read-only operation as far as the cache is concerned. We will find that the

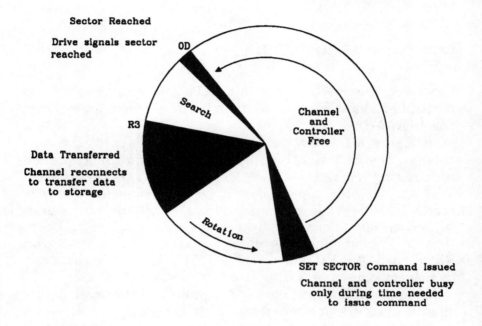

Figure 6.1 SET SECTOR Reconnect. This figure represents the channel, control unit, and device activity for a SET SECTOR operation. Note that the channel and control unit are free to do other things until the desired sector is reached. Then the three act together to read or write the records.

record is either in the cache (a hit) or is not in the cache (a miss). Let us assume that record 3 is found in the cache. Since this CCW is writing the data, this will be a DASD Fast Write hit (assuming a 3990 model 3 with extended function).

Once record 3 has been found, we now begin the actual transfer of data. Since the CKD channel program does not have a DEFINE EXTENT CCW in it to specify a caching algorithm, the defaults are used, which are random (normal) caching with DASD Fast Write (DFW) allowed. CCW 06 causes 1901 bytes to be transferred from central storage both to the cache storage and simultaneously to the nonvolatile storage (NVS). This slot is marked as needing to be copied to the real DASD (staged) whenever the controller can get around to it. Meanwhile, there is a permanent copy of the data in NVS in case the controller loses power.

The following are the most likely causes of high connect time. If all the data accessed is found in the cache, only the first two of these causes can apply.

1. Large average block size being transferred

2. Many blocks being transferred

3. Long searches (multitrack keyed, typically)
   a. VTOC (use indexed VTOC)
   b. OS CVOL (use VSAM/ICF catalogs)
   c. PDS directory (use PDSE)
   d. ISAM (use VSAM)

4. Incorrect sector number

Since the next CCW is another SEEK command, it is time to update the cache counters. Why not wait until the end of the channel program? A little-known "feature" of IBM cache controllers is that one channel program can actually appear to the cache counters as multiple I/O requests.

The 3880 model 23 started a new *command chain* whenever a SEEK or LOCATE RECORD CCW is processed. It is not clear whether the SEEK had to be a motion SEEK or not, so we infer that any seek will commence a new command chain.

Therefore this JES2 checkpoint I/O with its four SEEK commands will cause the value 3 to be added to the number of non-read-only requests (CCWs 06, 10, and 14 are WRITE DATA commands). Since no data was actually transferred between central storage and the actuator for CCWs 01 through 03, no counters are incremented for the first two CCWs.

This feature can cause some unexpected results if you are monitoring a cache control unit's performance. The total number of I/O requests performed by a cached controller can often be the total number of I/O requests issued by the processor, as measured either by EXCP counts or through the Channel Measurement Facility.

To make cache performance even more difficult to measure, the cache storage and counters are shared by other systems. So our MVS system may do only one I/O to a cached controller, but the counters might increase by several hundred because another system is using the same controller much more intensely. In a case such as this, you would expect to see a high pending time on any I/O to this device, as it would be busy much of the time to the other processor.

The total number of cache requests can be compared to the total number of I/Os as measured by the Channel Measurement Facility and a ratio computed. If the ratio ever changes dramatically, then you would be best advised to study the new I/O workload presented to this control unit by all processors to which it is attached. Knowing what percent of all I/O to a cache is from one processor lets you know how much to trust the hit percentages. But if the hit percentages are very close to 100, they can be trusted, no matter how much I/O to the cache is from any processor.

CCWs 07–17: Completion of the I/O

The rest of this JES2 channel program is just more packets of CCWs doing the same things that we have already discussed, so we may assume that the I/O has ended. It is time now to signal the processor that the I/O is complete via the I/O interrupt process. The control unit passes status information to the channel subsystem, which then attempts to interrupt the processor.

What if our I/O interrupt is pending but all the processors are disabled for I/O interrupts? Or what if our MVS is running under PR/SM or VM, and the control software has made the virtual MVS machine nondispatchable? We wait, of course. This phenomenon can and does happen in MVS. Unless MVS is damaged, the length of time we must wait will be very short: MVS is probably disabled for I/O interrupts only because it is processing a previous I/O interrupt.

The exact amount of time spent waiting for a pending I/O interrupt to be fielded can be computed by tracing I/O with GTF and using the "time stamp" option. First, subtract the SSCH time stamp from the I/O interrupt time stamp. This represents the I/O service time but also includes any possible interrupt pending time. Second, add the pending, disconnect, and connect time from the channel measurement block together to obtain the actual device response time. These numbers are hard to get for an individual I/O request, and may require an additional I/O trace facility, as GTF only reports on the device connect time. Subtract the channel measurement time from the I/O response time, and the result is the interrupt pending time. This may be zero or as much as 50 ms (the PR/SM default).

An advantage of running on MVS/XA or MVS/ESA is that on a multiprocessor (MP) configuration, the I/O subsystem can interrupt any processor that is enabled for I/O interrupts. We do not have to interrupt the same processor on which the I/O was started. However, only one processor might be capable of handling I/O interrupts.

IBM deliberately designed the I/O Supervisor (IOS) in MVS/XA and MVS/ESA to work this way because of lessons learned from the high-speed cache storage in the processor (not DASD cache). When a task switch occurs, such as an I/O interrupt, much of the contents of processor cache is no longer valid for the new task. Also, the translation lookaside buffer (TLB), designed to speed up the DAT feature, must be purged to ensure storage integrity. The net effect is that many highly specialized and complex features of the processor hardware designed to make instructions execute more quickly are ineffective until the new task runs long enough to establish its new working set of instructions and data in the processor cache and translated virtual addresses in the TLB.

MVS normally attempts to run with the smallest possible number of processors enabled for I/O interrupts in order to minimize the impact of this task-switching overhead on the instruction processor. The percentage of I/O interrupts detected by the Test Pending Interrupt (TPI) instruction compared to all interrupts over an adjustable threshold causes MVS to dynamically enable one more processor in an MP configuration. See the CPENABLE parameter of SYS1.PARMLIB(IEAOPTxx) in the Initialization and Tuning manual for your release of MVS for a further explanation of how to adjust this parameter. When the TPI percentage decreases below another threshold value, then MVS will dynamically disable processors for fielding I/O interrupts one at a time until only one processor is left to handle I/O interrupts.

The length of time we may have to wait while the interrupt is pending is not measured anywhere. It is assumed to be negligible in our JES2 example. However, it may not be. Research from one user shows as much as 3 milliseconds of I/O elongation on a 3090-600 because of this phenomenon and because of PR/SM. The user now runs with the CPENABLE parameter set so that all six processors are always enabled for I/O interrupts. Again, this phenomenon usually accounts for only a small elongation of I/O service time, but as devices become faster and total I/O response times decrease, small phenomena become significant.

Causes of High I/O Interrupt Pending Time

The following are likely causes of high I/O interrupt pending time:

1. All processors are disabled for I/O interrupts (usually normal; adjust CPENABLE).

2. VM has made MVS (running as a guest operating system) nondispatchable.

3. MVS running in a PR/SM partition. PR/SM may make an MVS partition nondispatchable even if that partition is enabled for I/O interrupts.

4. A vendor product or authorized user program has disabled the CPU with a module that has a long instruction path length.

Sooner or later, the interrupt occurs, IOS obtains the full status information for the interrupt by using the Test Subchannel (TSCH) instruction, and the status is stored in the Interrupt Response Block (IRB). Then IOS maps the status information back into the IOSB and informs the IOS Driver that the I/O is complete. The IOS Driver (EXCP in this case) then maps the status back into the EXCP control blocks (IOB and ECB) and informs the access method that the I/O is complete. The access method will then map the status into any higher level of control block structure, if it exists (e.g., QSAM). Ultimately, the end user is made aware that the I/O request is complete and has access to the status information to determine if the data was correctly transferred. Remember the I/O we started with EXCP pages ago? It has just ended.

6.2.4. Conclusions

A DASD I/O operation is very complex, and it gets more complex with each new version of MVS, DFP, device, or control unit. Those of us in the performance measurement business must understand how this all works if we are to be able to tune an I/O workload with any degree of success. And there are some critical system I/O workloads that violate the assumptions made by the classical model for predicting I/O service time. These include JES2 checkpoints, paging, and some DB2 I/O requests. If you are modeling a device whose I/O is predominantly one of these types (and to make the system perform optimally you have probably excluded as much other I/O as possible from that device anyway), then you must take into account the deviations from the standard model originally introduced.

The following phenomena were not addressed in detail in this chapter, but the performance specialist must understand them: dynamic pathing, use of the suspend/resume feature, error detection and recovery, all cache internal algorithms, asynchronous control units, and general tuning methodology.

The source of the measurement data must also be considered. Different parts of the I/O path may count the same event differently. Not all EXCPs are accounted for by SMF. The only I/O requests counted in the SMF control block structure are those performed by the EXCP and VSAM IOS Drivers. Other drivers may or may not choose to account for their I/O requests.

Additionally, if you ever have to design an application with a critical response time requirement, you must be aware of anything which can elongate the I/O service time by even a fraction of a millisecond. The currently known phenomena in this category are CPU time to process the I/O request, channel protocol time, cache directory search time, and I/O interrupt pending time. These phenomena are generally ignored today because they are not measured anywhere and are typically of very short duration. If you are trying to drive a solid-state device, however, at 1,000 or more I/O requests per second (which we have done), then you must concern yourself with these more esoteric phenomena. At these higher I/O rates, the anatomy of an I/O can easily become a pathology instead!

6.3. Types of Monitoring Programs

Monitoring DASD is an important part of a data center's responsibility. Some are very complex to use. This section will cover some of the most popular. It is not designed to be all-inclusive.

6.3.1. OS Monitoring Programs

Several types of rudimentary programs are provided by the operating system as part of the distributed, or for-fee, subsystems from the vendor.

Tracing Facilities

One of the most detailed, but hard to use, is the detailed trace facilities of the operating system. VM has the Program Event Recording (PER) command to trace I/O operations. MVS has the GTFTRACE subsystem to capture all activity to a device.

The VM PER command is interactive. You enter the command and watch what is captured. Because PER is a CP command to inspect a virtual machine, it is limited to the DASD that the user ID can access.

The MVS GTFTRACE is a combination of a started system task (GTF) and batch jobs to print the data captured. GTFTRACE may not be supported by IBM in future releases; we infer this because the documentation for ESA removes the function from supported programming interfaces.

The GTFTRACE facility gathers data from hooks installed in the various device drivers. They also generate so much output that the data volume makes the end result difficult to reduce and use. Moreover, they are dependent on your ability to spot a problem and start the detailed trace facility.

Monitoring Programs

One widely used type of program is provided by most of the IBM operating systems. VM has the performance monitor. MVS has the Resource Measurement Facility (RMF). Reports from these program products allow you to specify an interval of time for the report. For MVS, the interval is specified in the RMF parameters in SYS1.PARMLIB.

These programs change with every version of the operating system, so examples are not shown here. We suggest you get the user manual for your version of the operating system and monitoring program, create some reports, and start to track the numbers.

You will quickly find that these reports are usually just a print of the data captured or calculated. For example, in almost all the versions of RMF, the DASD activity report shows each device, the I/O rate per second, some version of the response time and its components, and other information (e.g., percent allocated, open data sets).

The I/O queuing activity report shows the measurements obtained from the logical control unit (LCU) perspective. Remember, LCU is a term brought forward by the original operating systems and is used to represent one or more physical control unit pairs. Logical control units are the control units that access the same DASD.

Don't get us wrong. You should start now so you can begin to understand what these numbers should be during *normal* time periods. We recommend you plot (even by hand or in a PC spreadsheet) the response times and components until you **really understand** the numbers and what they mean in your data center. It is hard work, but someone must do it.

You will quickly want to customize reports to indicate problem areas. This is not an easy task with the operating system monitor reports.

Several companies (e.g., Landmark, Candle, Boole and Babbage, Goal Systems) provide interactive monitoring programs that give the end user the opportunity to display DASD as it is executing. The time frame may be either real time, as it is happening, or near real time (activity in the last several minutes or hours).

6.3.2. Cache Controllers

Cache controllers are a special concern. They are expensive pieces of hardware and are designed to improve performance of DASD accesses. If you cannot measure the cache usage, then you are not getting the most benefit from the cache. As with the rest of the DASD environment, there are a number of options for reports.

IDCAMS

IBM provides an IDCAMS command to report on their cache usage. Most of the other vendors also provide minimal reporting. Many also have cache reporters that manage the data from the controllers better than these raw reports.

The following table shows the result of an IDCAMS *LISTDATA COUNTS FILE(PROD01) DEVICE* command.[2]

```
┌─────────────────────────────────────────────────────────────────────────┐
│                  Output for LISTDATA COUNTS Command                       │
├─────────────────────────────────────────────────────────────────────────┤
│ 3990 STORAGE CONTROL MODEL 03                                             │
│                  SUBSYSTEM COUNTERS REPORT                                 │
│              VOLUME PROD01   DEVICE ID X'80'                               │
│              SYBSYSTEM ID X'0012'                                          │
│                                                                           │
│                              CHANNEL OPERATIONS                            │
│         ......SEARCH/READ.....    ................WRITE .............     │
│                TOTAL   CACHE READ        TOTAL     DASDFW CACHE WRITE      │
│                                                                           │
│ REQUESTS                                                                  │
│ NORMAL      3439831  3031454          721491         0          0         │
│  SEQUENTIAL    5913     5462            1319         0          0         │
│  CACHE FAST WRITE 0       0               0        N/A          0         │
│                                                                           │
│ TOTALS      3445744  3036916          722810         0          0         │
│                                                                           │
│ REQUESTS              CHANNEL OPERATIONS                                   │
│                                                                           │
│  INHIBIT CACHE LOADING           2742                                     │
│  BYPASS CACHE                     100                                      │
│                                                                           │
│ TRANSFER OPERATIONS       DASD/CACHE     CACHE/DASD                        │
│                                                                           │
│  NORMAL                     411138          0                             │
│  SEQUENTIAL                   4074        N/A                             │
│                                                                           │
│ DASD FAST WRITE RETRIES         0                                         │
│                                                                           │
│ DEVICE STATUS        CACHING:        ACTIVE                               │
│                      DASD FAST WRITE: DEACTIVATED                         │
│                      DUPLEX PAIR:    NOT ESTABLISHED                      │
└─────────────────────────────────────────────────────────────────────────┘
```

The same report is obtained when *device* is replaced by *SUBSYSTEM,* in which case you would get one page for each actuator on the string. The output of this command shows the actuator

---

2 IBM still uses the term *device* to refer to an actuator. They also use the term *device* or the term *unit* to refer to the entire box on casters. We think it is confusing to have the same term refer to both a part of the whole and the whole. We prefer their term, started with the 3380, *actuator* to refer to a single, addressable volume.

volume serial and the counters that have accumulated since the control unit was reset. It also shows the device status for caching, DASD Fast Write, and duplex pairs.

The following table shows the result of an IDCAMS *LISTDATA STATUS FILE(PROD01)* command. The cache statistics for the whole 3990 are listed; the amounts of installed cache (*subsystem storage*) and nonvolatile storage are printed. The portions of these that are currently available, pinned, or offline are displayed.

```
               Output for LISTDATA STATUS Command

3990 STORAGE CONTROL MODEL 03
            SUBSYSTEM STATUS REPORT
        VOLUME PROD01  DEVICE ID X'80'
        SYBSYSTEM ID X'0012'

           ..........CAPACITY IN BYTES.........................
            SUBSYSTEM STORAGE                 NONVOLATILE STORAGE
CONFIGURED       33554432                          4194304
AVAILABLE        33275904                             N/A
PINNED                  0                               0
OFFLINE                 0                               0

RETURNED STATUS   0-19 00804001 008000000 00000200 000001FB C0000000
                 20-39 00000000 000030000 00400000 00000000 00000012

SD CACHING CONDITIONS:      CACHE FAST WRITE ACTIVE

NVS STATUS:                 DEACTIVATED-HOST OR SF

DEVICES WITH STATISTICS:    64

STATISTIC SETS/DEVICE       1

DEVICE STATUS
  FOR DEVICE IS X'80'  CACHING:          ACTIVE
                       DASD FAST WRITE:  DEACTIVATED
                       DUPLEX PAIR:      NOT ESTABLISHED
```

LANDMARK's MVS Monitor

Landmark Systems Corporation's TMON/MVS software monitor displays the I/O subsystem and cache controllers in an interactive manner rather than requiring you to run a batch job and look at the output.

The next few figures in this part of the book are screen captures using the product at one of our data centers.

Figure 6.2 contains a print of the TMON/MVS Caching Logical Control Unit Activity screen. It shows volume *PROD02* having no caching activity at all.

Look at the column to the right of center titled *CACHING DATA*. Three of the four devices have percentages in the *RD%* (read percentage), *R H %* (read hit percentage), and *W H %* (write hit percentage) columns. Also note that the service time for the three cached devices is between 3 and 9 milliseconds.

By using the cursor to select the line with device 392, PROD02, you get the menu *DEVICE DETAIL SELECTION MENU*.

Figure 6.3 shows a historical perspective for our volume. The service times for each second are in the 20-millisecond range. That is relatively good for 3380 DASD, but the accounts payable application end users are reporting 8 to 10 seconds response at their terminals.

From this monitor, you can select *cache detail* to get more detail about the volume. Figure 6.4 shows no caching activity at all.

The problem here is that a volume attached to the 3990-3 had become disabled for caching operations and was not caching any I/O requests. The IDCAMS command to restore caching to the volume is *SETCACHE VOLUME(PROD02) UNIT(3380) SUBSYSTEM ON*.

Doing so in the example returned 2–3-second response times to the accounts payable users. They were happy again. We never did find out why the caching was turned off for this device. That makes you think you should have a way to check caching for all your actuators such as an exception processing system to watch for the unexpected. Again the Landmark TMON/MVS subsystem has an exception processing system to do this. Other monitors may also have such a feature.

```
JOBNAME: TMONMVS1   CACHING LOGICAL CNTRL UNIT I/O ACTIVITY   DATE: MM/DD/YY

SYSTEM : SYSB                                                 TIME: HH:MM:SS

COMMAND: _____  CYCLE: MMSS
    SRM STATS:  CPU= 66.87  UIC=255  DPR= 32  TPR= 69  PDT=111
SSCH/SEC: 73.1 CTL UNIT: 3990-03 LCU AVBSY:  0.0 CACHE AVL:  31.7 MB
         DEV  RESP. COMPONENTS SERVICE      CACHING DATA     QUEUE # OPN % DEV
VOLSER  NUM   PEND  DISC  CONN   -10--20 RD % R H %   W H % ? LNGTH DSETS CONN

SYS057 0390   0.0   0.1   3.1    3.28  75.5 87.4   39.4 Y     0    20   4.8
TEST03 0391   0.1   3.4   5.6  ===9.04  77.2 86.4   17.3 Y   3.4    41   5.3
PROD02 0392   0.0  19.1   3.0  ==22.08                       16.0   16  20.7
DB2001 0393   0.0   0.0   2.8    2.84  74.2 84.7   50.6 Y  23.5    22   8.5


    HELP INFORMATION = PF1                    PF KEY ASSIGNMENTS = PA1
```

Figure 6.2 Caching Logical Control Unit I/O Activity. This figure shows a single 3380-AK4 with three of the four actuators getting caching results. Note the device is doing I/O and has a queue length (third column from right) of 16.0.

> ▢ What if you see caching activity on a volume that is not supposed to have cached data sets? The VTOC, the VTOC index, and the VVDS are always cached, even in an SMS environment, since you cannot assign storage classes to these.

6.4. Hardware Solutions: Configuration Analysis

In many cases, tuning DASD means taking a close look at the hardware configuration and applying some common sense and analytical techniques to what you see.

```
JOBNAME: TMONMVS1          DEVICE ACTIVITY HISTORY          DATE:   MM/DD/YY
SYSTEM : SYSB                                               TIME:   HH:MM:SS
COMMAND:  _____              CYCLE: MMSS
    SRM STATS:  CPU= 74.37   UIC=255   DPR= 47   TPR= 76   PDT= 43
DEV: 0392 VOL: PRODO2
           RESP.   COMPONENTS SERVICE TIME IN MILLISECONDS SSCH/ % DEV QUE OPN
  TIME     PEND  DISC  CONN 10----20---30---40---50-- SECND  BUSY LEN DS
08:45:05    0.0  21.4   2.7 ==========  24.13            39.5  95.2  0 14
08:45:04    0.1  20.2   3.2 ========    23.51            26.4  61.8  0 14
08:45:03    0.1  15.2   3.6 ======  18.87                 9.8  18.4  0 14
08:45:02    0.0  18.6   3.2 ========= 21.81              12.9  28.2  0 14
08:45:01    0.1  25.0   2.2 ===========  27.26            0.8   2.2  0 14
08:45:00    0.0  16.5   2.3 ======  18.82                 4.1   7.7  0 14
08:44:59    0.0  24.7   2.1 ==========  26.75             1.2   3.3  0 14


  HELP INFORMATION = PF1          TMVSO1          PF KEY ASSIGNMENTS = PA1
```

Figure 6.3 Device Activity History. The device activity shows that the device is getting 19-26 millisecond response time. None of the disconnect times is in the zero to nine millisecond time range which would indicate caching.

6.4.1. Which Additional Hardware?

In one case we have observed, a data center tried to configure the least-cost method to provide the number of megabytes needed for an application. Their failure can help us on a universal scale.

The data center configured hardware and wrote software to drive an inventory system at 400–500 transactions per minute. The results of their tests, as the system was about to be installed, were that they could not get more than 150 transactions per minute through the system.

In Figure 6.5, you will see the 3083 class of Processor Complex connected to one 3880 control unit and two strings of DASD. The DASD provided the number of megabytes, but the channel paths (two) were totally inadequate.

Conversion to the automated system was delayed for a year. The bad part was that the capacity planners wanted a larger CPU; the network planners wanted new communications controllers; the systems programmers wanted software monitors

```
JOBNAME: TMONMVS1                  CACHE DETAIL               DATE:  MM/DD/YY
SYSTEM : SYSB                                                 TIME:  HH:MM:SS
COMMAND: _____        CYCLE: MMSS

DEV: 0392 VOL: PROD02 DEV TYPE: 3380-AK4 CTL UNIT: 3990-03 STATUS:   DISABLED
TIME 5---10---15---20---25---30---35---      MEGABYTES CACHE SIZE:
TOTL    .00                                     CONFIGD:  32.0 PINNED 0.0
PEND    .00                                     OFFLINE:   0.0 AVAIL  :   31.7
DISC    .00
CONN    .00                                     MEGABYTES NVS SIZE:
        TOTAL I/O RATE PER SECOND:              CONFIGD:   4.0 PINNED 0.0
THIS CPU:      0.0 CTL UNIT:   56.2
READ  NORMAL         :   0.0  (       % HIT)  TOTAL I/O HITS :        %
READ  SEQNTL         :   0.0  (       % HIT)  TOTAL READ HITS:        %
WRITE NORMAL         :   0.0                  HITS PER SECOND:
WRITE SEQNTL         :   0.0                  HITS PER STAGE :
INHIBIT CACHE LOAD   :   0.0
BYPASS CACHE         :   0.0                  CACHE TRANSFERS PER
SECOND:
CACHE FAST WRITE     :   0.0  (       % HIT)  DASD-TO-CACHE       :
CACHE FAST WRITE READS:  0.0  (       % HIT)  SEQNTL DASD-TO-CACHE:
DASD FAST WRITE NORMAL:  0.0  (       % HIT)  CACHE-TO-DASD       :
DASD FAST WRITE SEQNTL:  0.0  (       % HIT)
DASD FAST WRITE FORCED:  0.0
   HELP INFORMATION = PF1           TMVS01          PF KEY ASSIGNMENTS = PA1
```

Figure 6.4 Cache Detail. We see the cache detail for device 392 (*PROD02*) and note that the control unit has activity but the device is not cached at all.

(they were right, monitors will give you answers if you know how to use them) and the newest cache DASD controllers. Management had over $5 million in requests to fix the problem!

6.4.2. Cost/Performance Evaluations

It did not take long to determine that the problem was an I/O bottleneck. The cost of newer (e.g., 3390) devices and cache controllers was beyond the budget of the data center. Yes 3390s would be a much faster solution. Yes, cache control units would make the I/O almost disappear as a part of the problem. The data center could not afford that solution.

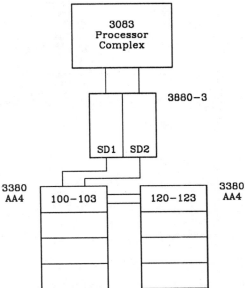

Figure 6.5 An Example of an Inadequate Device Configuration. The 3083 Processor Complex was configured with two channels to one 3880 model 3 control unit. Only two strings of 3380 devices were attached. The bottleneck is the two paths to all of that DASD.

No problem. The older 3880 and 3380 devices could be obtained for a very small monthly sum. A 3880 control unit (to give four paths to all devices) and two short strings (an AA4 and a B04) were ordered. The result was drastically reduced I/O queuing time. The result was over 400 transactions per minute.

> ¤ You can throw money at a problem (always buy the newest and fastest) or you can invest in knowledge. We do not agree with just throwing money at a problem!

6.5. Job Control Solutions

Another way to tune DASD is to have individuals tune DASD for their jobs by I/O elimination.

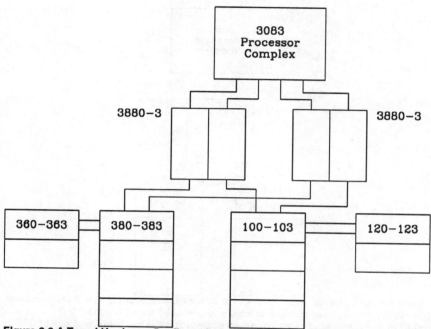

Figure 6.6 A Tuned Hardware Configuration. This example shows short strings of DASD for data sets that should not be obstructed and long strings for large, less important data sets. The reader should note that this may not work for all DASD installations, but is certainly better than the previous figure.

6.5.1. Buffer Considerations

You can use JCL and buffering techniques to save I/O operations. In Figure 6.7, you see the JCL to tell the operating system to use ten buffers instead of the default of five. We have seen up to 100 buffers improve the elapsed time and the resources used by a batch job.

Watch out, though, if your paging subsystem performs poorly: indiscriminately increasing buffers uses more virtual storage resources which must be backed by central storage page frames.

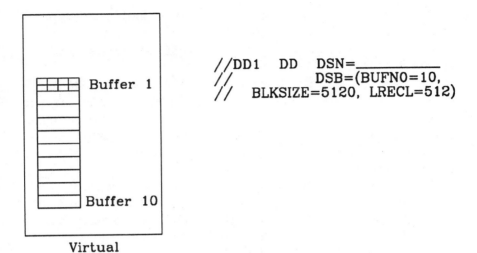

Virtual
Storage

Figure 6.7 An Example of Tuning I/O Access with JCL. In this example, JCL is used to expand the default (five buffers) to minimize I/O transfers. Buffering techniques are very beneficial for sequential access.

6.6. Programming Solutions

The systems analyst can also affect the number of I/O opera-tions. We have seen very successful tuning efforts accomplished by the analyst changing the program flow.

6.6.1. Data Access Methodology

Figure 6.8 shows a very successful application. The program in question was to read transactions, go out to a file to get the name and address of the vendor, and write a report. Over the year, the number of transactions would grow very rapidly. The number of vendors would grow and level off. I/O activity to the vendor master file became huge.

The program was changed to read the vendor names and numbers into a COBOL table. The table was searched for a vendor and almost all I/O operations were eliminated from the vendor names file.

As with most tuning efforts, it worked for a while. The table grew past the COBOL limit (32 Kb). The data center had not converted to COBOL II (in which the table can be a much larger size). The programmer placed two tables in working storage and continued to read values into the table even after it went past the 32-Kb size limit.[3]

He read records into the table only when they were needed. One pitfall of this technique is that you may try to read in whole tables only to find that certain executions of the program require only a few of the table entries. You will have read more records than if you just read the necessary ones.

6.6.2. Program Redesign Considerations

Another successful technique is to ensure that your applications are not reading a file further than they need to read it. In Figure 6.9, a file was read and compared against transactions to print a report. After the transaction file was complete (and all the lines were printed that were to be on the report), the program continued merrily along until it finished reading the master file.

The application manager discovered this and made a change to the program to quit reading both files. This was a simple change, but one that saved many thousands of I/O operations.[4]

---

3 Many thanks to Jim Thompson for showing that when systems programmers and hardware purchasing fail to get the job finished, the programmer can come through!

4 Thanks to Richard Milazzo for his eagle eye at tuning!

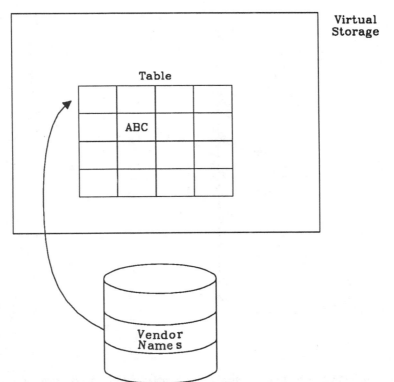

Figure 6.8 Tuning with Tables. Another method frequently used to avoid I/O operations is to read a file or a portion of a file into storage. This could be as simple as reading information into a COBOL table or as complicated as reading an entire data set into one or more hiperspaces.

This is a simple example, but there are many ways you can check your application to ensure that they are not doing unnecessary I/O operations. In the world of data base tuning unnecessary I/O operations (e.g., sorts) complicate the transaction process.

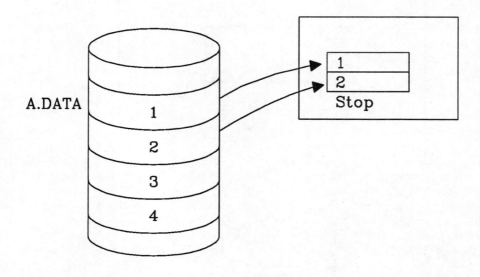

Figure 6.9 Tuning by Stopping. A frequently overlooked method of preventing I/O operations is to ensure that you stop reading input files when no more processing needs to be
done. One example eliminated thousands of I/O operations by detecting the end of the
input transactions (for a report) and terminating the job before the entire master data set was
processed.

6.7. Summary

Monitoring and measuring DASD is simple in concept and complex in practice. The first reason is the number of data sets in
your installation. There are probably thousands of data sets! The
second reason is the number of I/O accesses to those data sets.
The third reason is the complexity of a single I/O operation.

Tuning should be done in two arenas. The first is by averaging
the accesses to a single DASD actuator and determining
whether, on average, the device is not getting good service. The

second is to look indepth at the device during peak times and determine on a microscale if the individual I/O accesses are acceptable.

There are two models for predicting I/O service time. The first one added the time the I/O request was queued in the operating system plus the average seek time plus the device latency plus data transfer time. The second, for use in XA and ESA subsystems, adds queue time plus pending time plus disconnect time plus connect time. The hardware is now really timing the I/O operation and giving us some rudimentary measurements.

Pending time is one of the most perplexing parts of the equation. The actuator could be shared by another Processor Complex or PR/SM LPAR. The internal paths could be busy in the head of string. Back-end staging could be taking place on a cached control unit.

As the operating system and hardware evolve, the I/O operation becomes more complex. We must still understand it to see if it needs attention. We must really understand it if we are to tune it and get more performance from our operating system and hardware.

The operating system provides some monitoring programs (e.g., RMF and GTF). Vendors provide more sophisticated monitors. One monitor, Landmark's TMON/MVS, provides a number of online, interactive viewpoints for DASD monitoring.

Tuning can be done with hardware solutions. You could buy hardware until the pain stops (at least in your I/O subsystem, if not your pocketbook). You can solve your problems with software. Changes to Job Control Language or program changes can drastically reduce your I/O requirements.

6.8. Questions

1. Explain the reasons DASD tuning is difficult.

2. Describe the classical model for predicting I/O service times. Does this model work in all ESA environments?

3. Describe the XA or ESA model for predicting I/O service times. What hardware change made this model practical?

4. Which programs use the hardware STARTIO or Start Sub-channel (SSCH) instructions? Why are they limited to those programs?

5. Describe the typical DASD I/O operation.

6. Describe the causes of high pending time.

7. What does the SEEK channel command do?

8. What does the SET FILE MASK command do?

9. What does the SET SECTOR command do?

10. Explain the difference between operating system monitoring programs (e.g., RMF) and tracing programs (e.g., GTF).

11. What items should you monitor for cache control units? Why?

12. What hardware solutions do you have for tuning DASD?

13. Describe several software solutions you have for tuning DASD.

Shared DASD Considerations

7.1. Sharing Data in an IBM Environment

Sharing data between multiple Processor Complexes is a perplexing and complicated part of data processing. The IBM mainframe environment does not have a complete solution. Personal computers and most minicomputers did not have the problem when they started out because they did not share their data. Evolution of sophisticated data sharing has come faster with small computers because of their inherently distributed nature.

7.1.1. Non-IBM Mainframe Environments

The end user in these non-IBM mainframe environments could make a copy of the data on another medium and sneaker-net the data to another processor. Most mini- and microcomputer users also have excellent file transfer capabilities over phones. Ma Bell is just wearing the sneakers.[1]

---

1   The term *sneaker net* refers to moving a copy of the data to a portable medium (e.g., tape or diskette) and running (therefore the sneaker) the data to another location.

Although these seem like simple operations, a problem invariably arises. With data in two places, which copy is more up to date? If both are updated differently, neither is the "correct" copy. Is there a reader who has not accidentally used a back-level file or made different changes to two copies?

PCs and minis have been the most successful at solving this problem. Instead of sharing DASD at the I/O interface, as the IBM mainframes do, the most common means for smaller computers is through shared file systems using server computers on Local Area Networks (LANs).

Examples of this are Sun's Network File System (NFS) for the Unix environment and Novell Netware for the PC environment (and many others as Portable Netware is propagated to different operating system architectures). These have a single computer system to maintain DASD, and other computers send and receive data using LAN protocols. Although this is flexible, a price can be paid in performance: DASD I/O through a server can be affected by LAN transmission speeds and traffic levels.

Stratus minicomputers, marketed as System/88 by IBM, can use a high-speed, dedicated network to share DASD. They also can use public packet switching networks when performance is not an issue.

Digital Equipment Corporation (DEC) superminicomputers, a few models of which have in recent years qualified as mainframes, also use a hybrid approach for DASD sharing. For performance, DEC VAXes can be "clustered". This connects Processor Complexes using a private, high-speed bus. Sophisticated supervisor functions control not only DASD sharing but all aspects of interactions between multiple copies of operating systems running in separate processors.

DEC has also built their proprietary network, DECNET, into the VMS supervisor services that applications use to access DASD. Thus, DASD can be accessed over DECNET as if it were local. The operating system provides locking services to coordinate I/O over the network.

Both simple data set and field locking and full transaction protection services are available on almost all microcomputer and minicomputer platforms. Transaction protection services allow an application to declare that it is initiating a transaction, perform I/O operations, and then declare the transaction complete. The processor that directly controls the DASD also coordinates transactions by applying and removing locks and keeping track of all I/O activity performed for a transaction. If a transaction aborts (or is perforce backed out), the transaction services undo all the I/O operations (even to different data sets on different actuators) back to the start of the transaction.

Thus, in most cases, any outages are recoverable. This includes distributed workstation and server failures as well as many kinds of application failures.

7.1.2. IBM Mainframe Environments

Of the many operating systems that can run System/370 to System/390 Processor Complexes, MVS has the most advanced data sharing capabilities. There still are a large number of considerations.

Since the data is read-only, the only concern is where the data is. Unfortunately, we keep insisting that we want to *update* the data.

Think about the process of updating data. The data resides on a disk platter. It is read into control unit cache storage (if available) and then into Processor Complex storage. The data is then modified and rewritten.

That process sounds like it takes a very short time. Any time is too long if others are trying to update simultaneously. Some processes (text editors) copy the file into storage or temporary data sets until the entire update process is completed, which could be minutes or even hours later.

> ◘ As a rule, if a single operating system controls the data, and that operating system enforces data sharing rules, then data is somewhat safe. Unfortunately, the IBM operating systems leave data sharing to the data center to enforce.

7.2. Shared DASD: Hardware Control

The System/370 and System/390 hardware platforms provide a simple data protection architecture. Unfortunately, it is at the level that the hardware understands: the actuator level.

> ◘ Hardware shared DASD protection is limited to protecting entire actuators. The actuator is either available (any Processor Complex can read or write to the actuator, one at a time) or reserved (reads and writes are allowed from only one Processor Complex).

7.2.1. Physically Separate Processor Complexes

The most common hardware configuration you will encounter with shared DASD is two separate Processor Complexes (e.g., 3090-200J and ES-9000) on the same computer room floor. Both have a physical path to a control unit with DASD. Just consider the hardware configuration for the time being and ignore which operating system is running.

The term used for this configuration is *loosely coupled Processor Complexes*, because they do not share central storage or central processor capabilities. In a *tightly coupled* configuration, these resources are shared, and several CPUs act more like a single CPU.

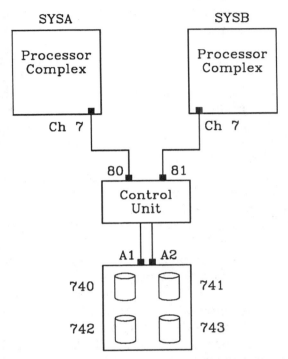

Figure 7.1 Multiple Processor Complex Sharing. Two Processor Complexes (SYSA and SYSB) can access all the data contained on devices 740 through 743. In this case, both use channel path 7, but that is not required.

In Figure 7.1 you see a Processor Complex on the left labeled *SYSA* that uses channel 7 to get to a control unit containing four DASD actuators. The device type does not matter for any of these examples. All control units implement only one type of sharing: minimal! A second Processor Complex, on the right, is labeled *SYSB*. It uses its own channel 7 to access the same control unit and DASD.

A program running on *SYSA* could read a data set from actuator 740, and start to update the data. A second program running on *SYSB* could want to read and/or update the same data set.

> ¤ Failure to protect against simultaneous updates is a serious matter. Think of this as a **last-in-is-only-one** update process.

If two or more programs read in the same records and then update the DASD file, then the last one to write to the file wins: the last update replaces the earlier ones. The first program's **updates are completely lost.** The beauty of DASD is fast, direct access. The beast of DASD is that you can directly update a record, but something must coordinate the updates.

For this example, assume SYSA is running a version of MVS. Any program running under MVS follows the MVS conventions. A data set on actuator 740 is opened for output. MVS JCL and data set allocation routines issue an *ENQ* supervisor call to build a control block in virtual storage that indicates which task has the data set opened for output. No I/O is initiated by SYSA through channel 7, path 80 during this process, so the operating system on SYSB does not know that the data set is opened, much less that it may be updated in the future.

There are two types of data locks available in the System/370 or System/390 environment. Hardware locks use the Reserve/Release channel command to lock the entire actuator. In the example in Figure 7.1, if an editor on *SYSA* used the hardware reserve for a data set on actuator 740 for one track, then all the tracks on 740 would be unavailable from *SYSB*. For the want of an track, the actuator is locked: pretty drastic.

The second type of data lock is a software lock. These require that the same type of operating system (e.g., MVS and MVS) be running on both sides and that the operating system have, and be using, software protection. The Enqueue supervisor service is an example of a software locking service. It must be propagated to other systems (via Global Resource Serialization or another service).

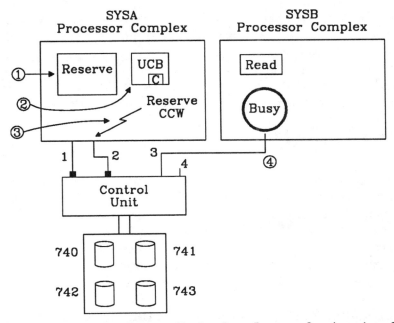

Figure 7.2 Split Processor Complex Sharing. Some Processor Complexes (e.g., 3084 and 3090-400) can be physically partitioned to form two separate hardware platforms. Each side can have an operating system running the show. The operating systems do not need to be the same type. *SYSA* above could be running MVS and *SYSB* could be running VM or VSE.

7.2.2. Reserve/Release

Considerations

Hardware protection is implemented with two channel commands that set indicators in the control unit and/or head of string that indicate that a particular actuator can be accessed only by a single path or group of paths. A single path can be connected to only one Processor Complex. If a single path can be used, then only the tasks on the operating system running that Processor Complex can access any part of that actuator while the hardware protection is in effect.

One CCW is *Device Reserve* (set the protection on) and one is *Device Release* (set the protection off). The Device Reserve command reserves the actuator on the channel path through which the command is issued, or on all the channel path groups if dynamic path selection is operating. The Device Release command removes the hardware lock on the actuator and notifies all channel paths that it is now available.

Device Reserve CCW

In Figure 7.2 at point *1*, the operating system determines that a Device Reserve channel command must be issued. A nonzero count in the reserve count field of the control block is found (for MVS it is the Unit Control Block, UCB, at *2*). We will discuss how it became nonzero shortly. (The Device Reserve CCW must be at the front of a channel program.) The channel program cannot even have a SET FILE MASK command in front of the Device Reserve CCW.

In Figure 7.2 path 2 is used (at *3*) for this particular I/O. Paths 1 and 2 are used from SYSA and paths 3 and 4 are used from SYSB. After the successful Device Reserve, only paths 1 and 2 can be used to access 740.

In Figure 7.3 you see a closeup of the paths to the control unit. The control unit and head of string process the Reserve CCW by locking onto the path(s) that issued the Reserve CCW.

Any I/O operation attempted by the operating system running on Processor Complex SYSB (path 3 or 4) will result in an *actuator is busy* status returned to SYSB. It is easy to see that this is a very crude protection scheme. If the actuator on 740 has 500 data sets, then *all of the data sets are considered busy until the update completes and the actuator is released.*

The multiple path operations depend on the version of operating system you have and the type of DASD. The earliest versions locked onto one channel. If something happened to the Processor Complex or to that channel, then the actuator was just out to lunch permanently. As DASD evolved and operating systems matured, the microcode was changed to recognize that several

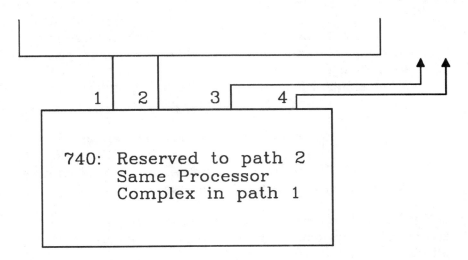

Figure 7.3 Reserve Bit in Hardware. A bit is turned on in the hardware to indicate the path(s) that can access a reserved device.

paths might come from the same copy of an operating system. MVS was updated so it could use an *Unconditional Reserve* CCW to free up a stuck I/O operation.

Unconditional Reserve CCW

The Unconditional Reserve is used to recover from hardware malfunctions in that it forces the actuator to become reserved. The operation is valid only on the storage control through which the I/O operation passes. What if another Processor Complex has an I/O operation in progress?

- If the actuator was reserved from the other system, then that reservation is reset and the Processor Complex issuing the Unconditional Reserve gets control of the actuator. This is useful if the other Processor Complex died in the middle of an I/O operation and still had control of the actuator.

- If the actuator has an I/O operation in progress and is in between channel commands, the I/O is aborted and the Processor Complex that initiated the I/O will lose the interrupt that would have occurred later in channel program execution. This is not good for any operating system.
- If the actuator is active, a recoverable equipment check is presented to the other Processor Complex. It will look like an I/O error.
- If the actuator is idle and not reserved, it will be reserved to the Processor Complex that issued the Unconditional Reserve CCW. In this circumstance, an Unconditional Reserve behaves like a normal Reserve.

The Unconditional Reserve command should be issued only by the operating system, because it must also handle these side effects.

Device Release CCW

The Device Release CCW is issued when all processing completes for a particular volume that requires the volume to be reserved. The Release CCW is usually the result of a dequeue (DEQ for MVS, the opposite of ENQ). A DEQ decrements the reserve count in the Unit Control Block (UCB for MVS). The operating system issues a stand-alone channel program with this as the only CCW when the reserve count becomes zero.

In Figure 7.4 you see the same Processor Complexes as in Figure 7.2. Actuator 740 is reserved. The operating system (at *1*) processes a DEQ for the actuator and the UCB reserve count is one. It decrements the UCB count to zero (at *2*) and sends a Release CCW to the actuator (at *3*). The operating system starts an I/O operation with a Device Release CCW to free up the actuator.

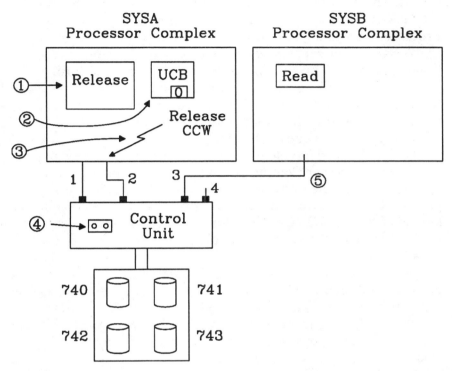

Figure 7.4 Device Release CCW. The Device Release CCW turns off the bit and sends a Device End indication to all paths to wake up any waiting task.

The control unit and/or the head of string processes the Device Release channel command and *sends a notice to all attached paths.* That notification allows access to any Processor Complex that is waiting because it got a busy condition on a pending I/O operation, to restart the I/O.

If two Processor Complexes are of substantially different speed (e.g., 308x and ES-9000 classes), then the faster Processor Complex may hog the actuator. If both get the notification that I/Os can be started, the faster central processing unit (in this case four times as fast) will likely get the actuator because it can execute the instructions in the I/O supervisor or channel subsystem faster. There is no mediation to ensure that the slower Processor Complex gets fair access to the actuator.

We have seen reports of uneven access when the Processor Complexes are different distances from the control unit. Until now we were limited to placing Processor Complexes within a few feet of each other. With ESCON considerations, the Processor Complexes may be miles apart! This may become a much more important concept in the future.

The CPU speed problem is only important where you have dissimilar Processor Complexes, but in that circumstance, it is a big problem for the data center. We have heard of, and seen in person, I/O response times of **10 seconds**! Let us repeat: 10 seconds for each I/O operation. For a CICS transaction with ten DASD I/O operations, that is 1 minute 40 seconds just to read data blocks.

There is nothing you can do about this situation to remove the problem. You can minimize the effect by isolating actuators to certain Processor Complexes or only going to the DASD infrequently (buffering in virtual storage). A cache control unit can help: read hits are processed without disconnecting the channel from the control unit. If the record is in cache storage, it will be read quickly at least.

7.3. Shared DASD: Operating System Control

All System/370 and System/390 operating systems have software implementations of the hardware protection. Your data center can use the hardware protection, it can use software protection, or it can do synchronization within the application to protect the integrity of data on shared DASD.

The latter option, though risky, is in use today. We know several data centers that share DASD and do not have protection. This is dangerous. It is definitely not recommended by the authors. It may be the only cost-acceptable solution, however.

Now let's look at the software or systems implementation of the hardware protection features. For example, MVS contains macros and supervisor services to indicate that a resource is to be reserved for a period of time. These services are called *ENQ* and *DEQ*.

MVS has a *RESERVE* macro that is only a call to the ENQ service with SYSTEMS (described below) specified. In the following discussion, RESERVE and ENQ are considered the same operating system service.

7.3.1. ENQ and DEQ

Protection of data resources in a shared DASD environment really only means serialization of accesses to the data for update or write mode. If all data sets were read-only, then protection would not be needed. If one is going to update a data set, then reads and writes must be coordinated within the system.

The name of the macro and the name of the supervisor service that protects a resource is *ENQ*. The name of the macro and the name of the supervisor service that frees up a resource is *DEQ*. The end user can specify read (*S=shared*) or update (*E=exclusive*) access in these macro calls.

In Figure 7.5, an application issues the ENQ macro with a parameter, *SYSTEMS*, to indicate that the service should include protection from other operating systems on other Processor Complexes. MVS increments a counter to indicate that the actuator is to be reserved. If the count was zero and changed to one, MVS inserts a Device Reserve CCW at the start of the next I/O to protect future I/O operations.

Why would an application in a Processor Complex want the entire actuator? One example is for allocation of new data sets or scratching data sets off a volume. VTOC records are read into

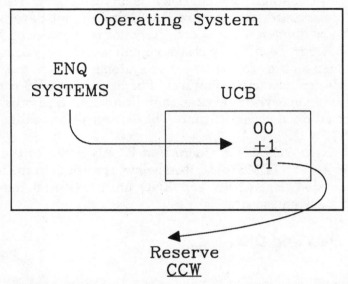

Figure 7.5 ENQ/DEQ. Application programs use the MVS ENQ and DEQ services to activate protection within a copy of the operating system and force Device Reserve and Device Release CCWs to hold and free shared actuators.

storage and altered. During the read, update, and write process, the volume should be locked from any other operating system in any other Processor Complex. The elapsed time to process VTOC modifications or catalog updates is relatively short.

The Linkage Editor performs a reserve while it is processing its output data sets. The program minimizes the time the reserve is outstanding, but it may cause problems, as some modules require from several seconds to over a minute to process.

Another somewhat longer process could be editing a data set. End users would logon to the operating system's time sharing subsystem (for MVS this is TSO). They would enter the editor and specify a data set to modify. They could go on coffee break for minutes or to lunch for an hour. All the while, the data set would need to be reserved. The DASD actuator would be reserved.

Fortunately, few data centers operate that way. Either they use editors that do not issue Reserves (dangerous) or they use software to propagate ENQs from Processor Complex to Processor Complex.

7.3.2. Deadly Embrace

One problem that can occur with hardware reserve/release is called *deadly embrace*. The situation occurs when two applications (batch jobs, TSO address spaces, etc.) issue reserve commands out of order.

Typically what happens is that one application issues an exclusive ENQ against two resources. For example, job HOLDEM issues an ENQ for resource GETME.FIRST and then resource GETME.SECOND. But job WAITEM issues the ENQ backwards. First it ENQs for GETME.SECOND and then it issues an ENQ for GETME.FIRST.

In most cases the jobs will run separately and not get into trouble. Sometimes when the two jobs run at the same time, there is trouble. Look at the following chronological list of events.

1. Job HOLDEM is running and gets the first resource.

2. Job HOLDEM is interrupted.

3. Job WAITEM starts and gets the GETME.SECOND resource.

4. Job HOLDEM tries to get GETME.SECOND but cannot because WAITEM has it.

5. Job WAITEM tries to get GETME.FIRST but cannot because HOLDEM has the resource.

6. Both jobs wait until an operator cancels one or the other.

That is what makes the deadly embrace so hard to find and fix unless you have a software monitor such as the monitors from Candle, Goal, or Landmark Systems Corporation.

7.3.3. Shared DASD Serialization

Subsystems

All shared DASD serialization subsystems run a copy of the serialization software in each copy of the operation system. Unfortunately, different platforms do not share such software. Thus VM and MVS software protection does not cooperate.

Moreover, VSE does not use Reserve/Release except to access its lock file or to update VTOCs. There is a lock manager in VSE that maintains an internal lock table. Each entry is given a 12 byte resource name. The operating system and applications (through supervisor calls) can use the table, but name selection must be coordinated. The lock table is maintained in a data set and is the only DASD sharing that exists in VSE.

Another common attribute is that the subsystems must have a method to communicate resource allocation and deallocation. Communication can be non-DASD-based or DASD-based.

These subsystems also have a performance implication in shared DASD environments. Properly configured, they can eliminate Device Reserve and Device Release CCWs from the DASD subsystem. Protection is performed by proper use of the serialization subsystem.

Global Resource Serialization (GRS)

The IBM MVS solution is the Global Resource Serialization (GRS) subsystem. It is a subsystem of every MVS system. Each version (370 to XA to ESA) gets better and more responsive to medium to large production environments. GRS uses a non-DASD communication medium. A channel-to-channel adapter (CTCA) dedicated to GRS connects two Processor Complexes. GRS coordination is accomplished by communication through these channels.

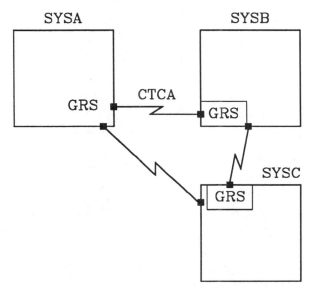

Figure 7.6 IBM: Global Resource Serialization. The IBM solution to serialization is a ring connection for the GRS software.

In Figure 7.6 we see three Processor Complexes labeled SYSA, SYSB, and SYSC. Each Processor Complex has a copy of the GRS subsystem, and it collects ENQ and DEQ requests. When set up properly, GRS periodically passes its collected inventory and updates among all Processor Complexes.

The configuration is called a *ring* because all Processor Complexes are strung in serial fashion. The figure shows the path a Reserve or exclusive ENQ request in Processor Complex SYSA would use to go to SYSB and then to SYSC. Only after the request came back without conflict would the application continue.

Early GRS implementations suffered from performance problems with the CTCA concept. CTCA recovery is both simple and complex. If only one path exists, then availability is a real problem. CTCAs have high availability only on the ES/9000 product line, where ESCON channels can emulate CTCAs. CTCAs con-

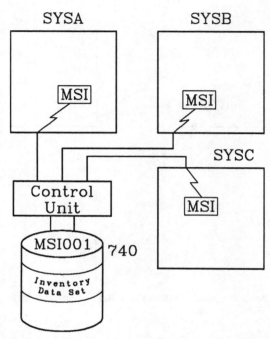

Figure 7.7 Non-IBM: MSI. Several non-IBM subsystems such as Legent's Multiple Systems Integrity package use shared DASD to protect shared DASD requests.

figured on channels that contain other highly active devices cause performance problems. Finally, the volume of data passed around the ring caused early versions to choke.

Non-IBM Solutions

Several other subsystems or vendor products are available to the data center to eliminate Device Reserve/Release lockouts and to propagate protection among shared DASD systems. Most of them do not use the channel-to-channel adapter to communicate.

Instead they use a data set on one of the shared DASD volumes. They would not be needed, after all, unless there were shared DASD volumes in use.

Figure 7.7 shows one, the Multiple Systems Integrity subsystem from Legent Inc. MSI uses an inventory data set on a shared volume that is read and written to by all participating systems. Whoa! Who is watching the fox watching the chicken house? If MSI is protecting data sets on shared DASD, who is protecting the MSI data set?

The answer is, of course, that MSI (and the rest of the DASD based software solutions) uses the real Device Reserve/Release hardware protection to protect its data set. Early versions of JES2 used Reserve/Release for its checkpoint data set.[2]

The result in Figure 7.7 is that MSI on SYSA would reserve the actuator at address 740 with a volume serial of MSI001. The software would add and remove ENQ and DEQ requests. SYSA would then release the volume, and the other two could access the volume in the same manner.

In most cases the DASD-based (non-IBM) protection schemes for shared DASD have outperformed the non-DASD (e.g., GRS). Recent papers suggest that GRS has caught up with the DASD implementations. Moreover, GRS is *free*: it comes bundled with the MVS code at no extra charge.

7.4. Shared DASD: Application Control

What is issuing the ENQ and DEQ macros for data sets and other resources? Applications or subsystems can and do combine hardware and software solutions to data sharing.

---

2 JES2 now uses a lock record that is the equivalent of the compare and swap instruction. There is a 1-byte lock record on the track. The channel program does a search key and data equal on that byte. If the byte is equal, the channel program changes the byte and then JES2 is free to use the whole data set. If the byte is not equal, JES2 waits 5 seconds and retries the I/O operation.

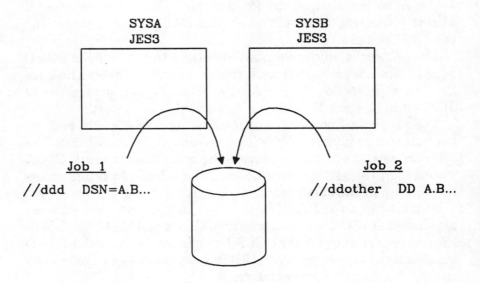

Figure 7.8 JES3 Implementation. The JES3 subsystem has its own way of protecting batch jobs. JCL specifies share (SHR) or exclusive (OLD) access to data sets. JES3 keeps a data set inventory and will not release jobs that conflict.

7.4.1. Application Program Use of ENQ/DEQ/RESERVE

Any application program can issue the ENQ or DEQ macro if the application is written in assembly language or calls an assembly language subroutine.

If the program issues an ENQ macro with the SYSTEMS parameter or the RESERVE macro, then a Device Reserve will occur for the next I/O operation.

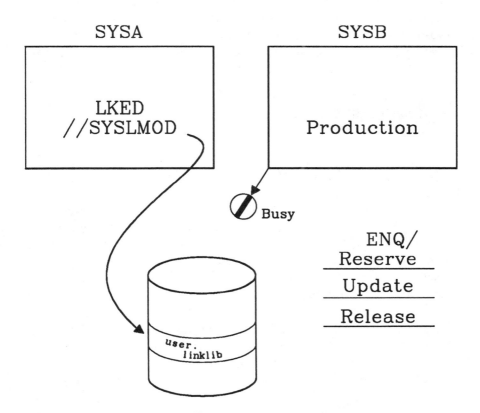

Figure 7.9 Program (LKED) Use of Reserve. Some program products such as the IBM linkage editor specifically ask MVS to reserve volumes such as the program library as it is being updated.

7.4.2. Job Entry Subsystem 3

JES3 processes all JCL for batch jobs and controls read-write access for SHR or EXCL operands for the DISP= parameter. Jobs do not get started until they have all the resources needed for the job.

Figure 7.8 shows two JES3 Processor Complexes. Two jobs are trying to access the same data set. If both want the data set for read-only (DISP=SHR) access, then both can start (assuming no other task has the resource). If Job 1 specifies DISP=OLD and starts, then Job 2 waits for the completion of Job 1.

7.4.3. Linkage Editor

At least one IBM utility, the linkage editor (LKED), issues the RESERVE macro to protect data: SYSLMOD is LKED's output. In Figure 7.9, the linkage editor issues the ENQ/RESERVE, updates the data set, and then issues a Release for the data set.

Here, one of the software solutions identified above could save you large DASD delays in a shared DASD environment. If one system is used for development or production preparation, it could lock out volumes for long periods.

Take the example in Figure 7.9 again. Suppose a large number of programs are available for production turnover. The data center has a policy to recompile each module and link it into the production library to ensure consistency between source and load modules. On the test system, SYSA, a large number of compile and link jobs are released. If the linkage editor is reserving the volume often and for somewhat long periods, then production access to the volume could be delayed.

7.5. Other Shared

Configurations

Your data center does not need to have different Processor Complexes to discover the joys of shared DASD. Hardware and software can emulate having multiple Processor Complexes.

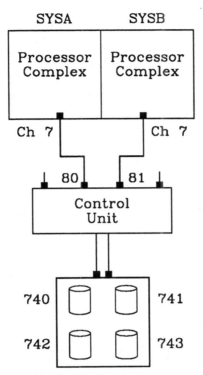

Figure 7.10 Split Processor Complex. Some Processor Complexes can be divided down the middle to form two sides, each with half of the resources. A different version of the operating system can run on each side. Some data centers run this way all the time.

7.5.1. Physically Partitioned Processor Complexes

One hardware configuration is the physically partitioned Processor Complex. Figure 7.10 shows a typical configuration. A 3084 or 3090-400 class processor can be physically partitioned to make two *sides*. Each side can have a different operating system running on it.

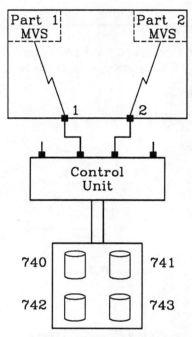

Figure 7.11 PR/SM. The data center of today can have shared DASD excitement with a single Processing Complex with a single central processing unit (CPU). The PR/SM feature of IBM Processor Complexes or the Amdahl Multiple Domain Feature can logically partition resources to run several copies of the operating system.

The most common application is for the systems programmers to split a large machine to allow them to IPL a test or building-production version of the production operating system. Sometimes data centers must run such a machine split because of virtual storage constraint problems.

Another reason to run split is to run two completely different operating systems, such as MVS on one side and VM or VSE on the other.

The same rules apply to physically partitioned Processor Complexes as to two completely separate systems. Either software or hardware protection methods must be used to protect data from last-in-is-only-one updates.

A physically partitioned machine is likely to get the data center into trouble unless the physical partitioning is done to run two different production operating systems. What usually happens is that the second side (partition) is used for testing, and protection is not in effect.

7.5.2. PR/SM Separated MVS Systems

On the newer Processor Complexes, the Processor Resource/Systems Manager (PR/SM), a part of the hardware, emulates the shared DASD environment. In Figure 7.11 we see a PR/SM Processor Complex such as a 3090 or ES/9000 with two partitions active.

PR/SM is functionally equivalent to the Amdahl Multiple Domain Feature. Amdahl calls its partitions *domains*. Both domain configurations divide resources on the Processor Complex into parts. Physical processor(s) of the Processor Complex may be shared among multiple partitions or domains or they can be dedicated to one partition. If central processing units are shared among partitions, each gets a time slice to process instructions.

Both require that channels be dedicated to a partition. Thus they avoid the Reserve/Release coordination. I/O performance is affected, though the channels are dedicated. The I/O must be processed by the operating system's input/output supervisor. If the partition is not active when the I/O completes, then the I/O will be elongated by the time it takes to dispatch the partition.

> ▢ Some monitors (e.g., Landmark's The Monitor for MVS) report on this metric. This is one of several things that can cause elongated response times. If you have this configuration, watch for it.

Reserve/Release works properly in this environment. Suppose an application running in partition 1 issues a Device Reserve CCW for actuator 740. Path 1 is dedicated to partition 1, and

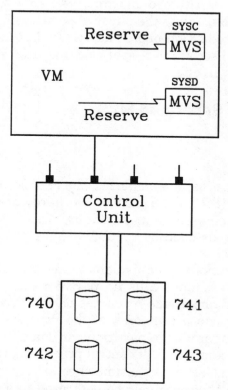

Figure 7.12 VM Split. The IBM operating system VM also logically divides resources for multiple copies of operating systems. VM handles some Reserve/Release commands and passes others on to the hardware.

thus actuator 740 is reserved to partition 1. Any I/O from partition 2 will be marked as busy until the software in partition 1 releases the actuator.

PR/SM I/O service time elongation does not happen if the Processor Complex is logically partitioned, because the channels and central processing units are dedicated to an operating system.

7.5.3. Virtual Machine Partitioned MVS Systems

VM is not so much an operating system as an operating system enabler. VM is useless by itself; it gives the appearance of many virtual Processor Complexes in which other operating systems run (e.g., MVS, VSE, AIX, simple monitors such as CMS, or VM itself). Multiple copies of MVS can be running under VM. As each issues the Device Reserve CCW, VM processes them and emulates the result.

Figure 7.12 shows one possible configuration. Two copies of MVS are *sharing* volume 740. The virtual machine SYSC, running MVS, issues a Reserve. VM intercepts the channel program, marks its Real Device Block (the equivalent of the MVS UCB) that a Reserve is issued, and waits for the next I/O to the actuator. If the MVS system marked SYSD tries to access actuator 740, then 740 will appear busy until SYSC frees the actuator.

VM can operate multiple preferred guests and thus can support several high-activity operating systems. VM can use the logical partitioning (LPAR) features of PR/SM to allocate resources.

> ¤ Be careful when configuring both PR/SM and VM LPAR systems. The performance and management of the combination is a relatively complex topic.

7.6. Shared DASD Performance Considerations

Shared DASD always performs slightly slower than nonshared DASD because the operating system requires extra instructions and even extra CCWs for shared DASD. Some performance tuners have speeded up all I/Os in a data center by marking all volumes nonshared in the operating system I/O configuration. Of course, there were no other Processor Complexes nearby: overhead accrues just because DASD is marked as shared, though it is not actively shared.

> ¤ Be very careful when you begin sharing (e.g., PR/SM or a new processor). VTOCs can get destroyed in a hurry if you do not specify the correct parameters.

What we are really concerned about is not the incremental, very small increase in response time, but the really big increase in response time because one system is interfering with another system's access to a DASD actuator.

7.6.1. Performance in Partitioned Mode

DASD performance to and from a partitioned operating system is affected by the configuration. That should not be a surprise to anyone this far in the book, but it is surprising that some ignore configuration when they are planning DASD.

Performance can vary because of real contention as the other system(s) read and write to the shared volume. It can vary because of reserve/release considerations. It can vary because of arm movement. It can vary because control unit cache is affected.

Real Contention

It is relatively obvious that if another Processor Complex or partition is using the same volume as the one your application wants, then your response time will be elongated. The hard part is to discover when those sneaky uses pop in. With hundreds and thousands of data sets on a volume, it becomes a management nightmare to control and monitor them.

Whenever you have shared DASD, you will have this problem. The best solution is to have a monitor that will pop up a display when critical DASD response times get elongated.

Reserve/Release

Reserve/release problems should not occur. If your data center is using shared DASD, it should implement GRS or one of the non-IBM products to remove all Reserve/Release channel commands unless they are for one of the subsystems that is protecting the empire, such as JES or RACF.

Your job is to ensure that data sets do not get assigned on the same volume as these must-reserve volumes. If you place a data base data set on the JES2 checkpoint volume, you are only asking for massive delays in data base I/O activity.

Arm Movement

A subtle problem is arm movement. If one system thinks it has the arm positioned at cylinder 10, and another Processor Complex moves the arm to cylinder 910, then the next I/O from the first Processor Complex will do a 900-cylinder seek.

Almost all IBM control units now move the arm asynchronously to eliminate disk surface problems.

Nothing can be done about this problem except to watch it and continue trying to eliminate I/O operations to the DASD in the first place. What usually happens is that one system (maybe the test system) starts a job that does many extra I/O operations and causes each I/O on the production system to be elongated. Elongation is caused partially by device busy and partially by the arm movement or seeking.

Cache Considerations

Cache is a finite resource. If more than one Processor Complex shares the finite resource, then it may be depleted sooner. This is true of cache controllers.

In one case study in which we participated, the nonvolatile storage was overrun by a nonproduction Processor Complex. This caused widely varying response times for DASD Fast Write accesses within the production Processor Complex.

7.6.2. Data Consolidation: System Timer

It is difficult to correlate performance data about shared DASD. System/370 and System/390 Processor Complexes all come with separate time-of-day clocks. Think of your trying to meet friends at a certain place and a certain time. If your watch is a few minutes slower than theirs, they will think you are late.

In the world of milliseconds, it is impossible to synchronize time-of-day clocks. The System/390 Sysplex timer makes it possible to have one clock drive all connected Processor Complexes. It can even be synchronized to the government's standard clock!

Why do we care, you ask? If you are trying to look in detail at the effect of response times on shared DASD, you will need to trace the I/O on each Processor Complex and place the I/O operations in time sequence. Without the Sysplex timer, you can only guess.

7.7. Summary

Sharing data on DASD requires that multiple Processor Complexes have a channel/control unit path to a single DASD volume. The term used for this is loosely coupled Processor Complexes.

Sharing data in an IBM environment is a very important and viable activity. Within a single copy of the operating system, data sharing is a piece of cake. Shared DASD adds some excitement to the venture, but it is still easy to do.

As we move to Processor Complexes with more partitioning capability, shared DASD becomes easier for more of us to do, so this chapter is vital to current and future configuration considerations.

If no one wrote to data sets, then we would not have a problem. Updates require coordination to ensure that a record can be read, updated, and rewritten without losing the update because a copy of the record existed somewhere else.

Hardware protection is limited to whole actuators. The Device Reserve CCW is used to lock out all accesses from other Processor Complexes until the read-update-write process completes. The Device Release CCW is used to unlock the connection and allow other Processor Complexes to access the volume.

For MVS, the ENQ and DEQ services process the request to lock out access to DASD and free the resource when done. Shared DASD serialization subsystems remove the hardware lockouts and coordinate the access through software means.

The IBM solution is called Global Resource Serialization (GRS) and uses channel-to-channel adapters to pass information about serialization requests. Several non-IBM solutions exist that use software to control shared DASD (and other ENQ requests).

Originally, shared DASD was only for large, complicated data centers that had multiple Processor Complexes and DASD farms. Today, the ES/9000 line of Processor Complexes includes the PR/SM feature, and now all of us can enjoy the excitement of shared DASD.

Shared DASD performance is affected by several factors. Activity from another Processor Complex, of course, affects response times. Head movement, reserve/release activity, and the cache controller also can affect the final response times. It is somewhat like living in the same room as your siblings. Deals have to be made.

7.8. Questions

1. Why is shared DASD an important option with today's computers?

2. What is "sneaker net"?

3. Describe the Device Reserve process and its effect on another Processor Complex.

4. What does the Device Release CCW do?

5. Why was the Unconditional Reserve CCW created by IBM?

6. Is there a problem with different speed Processor Complexes sharing DASD? If so, explain.

7. Describe the two shared DASD serialization techniques and give examples of how they pass data from one copy of the operating system to another.

8. Describe the things that affect DASD performance when running from a partitioned (IBM) or domain (Amdahl) Processor Complex.

DASD Types

The next section contains information on the several generations of DASD that developed over the history of the modern IBM systems. A careful look at the past reveals what the future will be. Generations of DASD have progressed in a predictable pattern.

The first chapter covers the first three generations of DASD. These three have both removable and fixed Head Disk Assemblies (HDAs) to contain the data. The second chapter covers the IBM 3380 and compatible devices, called the fourth generation because they gave us a decade of upgrades in performance and capacity. The fifth generation, the IBM 3390, at first seems like an extension of the 3380 line. Indeed, the 3380 xK4 devices could be configured with four paths just like the 3390. But the 3390 class devices are really a departure in that they are sealed, smaller, and almost plug-in-and-go devices. The same sort of upgrades will be seen for the 3390 class of device.

The last chapter covers all the DASD look-alikes. Mass storage devices attempt to emulate DASD by fooling the operating system into thinking a certain device is available at an address. Solid-state devices are limited in size but very fast. Optical devices have been promised for over a decade and are available. Redundant Array of Independent Devices (RAID) promises unlimited capacity at never-fail reliability. All of these special-purpose devices fill a nitch to eliminate one or more DASD limitations.

8

IBM DASD: Introduction and Pre-3380 Types

8.1. How to Interpret Specifications

As with other components of computer systems, we cannot directly perceive what DASD do. They are hidden from view inside boxes; they do things far too quickly for our sluggish senses. We see them only indirectly through their effects. The various DASD models have more in common than not. Fortunately, there are measures of capacity and speed the vendors love to display that make comparison easy. Or so it would seem.

In these next three chapters, we are going to look at the characteristics and effects of many DASD to understand and compare them. This information will be useful for the particular DASD you have at your installation, of course, but it also shows trends in DASD evolution. You will get only a partial benefit if you skip reading about all but your DASD.

You will notice that, with the exception of solid-state DASD, only DASD that has been marketed and manufactured by IBM is in the tables. IBM is not the only vendor that provides DASD for the IBM-compatible mainframe environment.

We concentrate on IBM for several reasons. First, we get a clearer view of technological progression over a long time by concentrating on one vendor's equipment. Second, other vendors must be *plug compatible* to enable data centers to use the non-IBM DASD because IBM provides the operating system and thus dictates the geqmetry of the devices. Other vendors make their products compatible with IBM's by necessity: IBM controls the operating system architectures and the commonly used access methods.

IBM was the only vendor of IBM-compatible DASD from 1964 until the middle 1970s. From then until now, the non-IBM vendors have emulated the IBM architecture from its external operation. Internally, their DASD were smaller and faster with more/different features. In the 1990s, the non-IBM vendors will have DASD with noncompatible external features.

Although you have learned much of the terminology used to specify DASD already, we review it here to emphasize the meaning behind the numbers.

8.1.1. Specification Terminology

DASD specifications are in three broad categories: functions, data storage capacity, and speed. You should already be familiar with most of the terminology, but we review the terms briefly while supplying context appropriate for comparing different DASD models.

Functional Specifications

These are DASD functions not directly concerned with writing data to and reading data from DASD. These specifications determine how you can configure a *DASD subsystem*. Specific DASD models require certain storage controllers and specific operating system software releases. You can install certain combinations of different models within DASD strings and together on the same storage controller.

We are not going to dwell on these functional specifications and requirements. You are better off getting these from the "horse's mouth", and the installation planning documentation does a fairly good job of rattling off the list.

One common feature is emulation. Some DASD can emulate earlier models to aid migration to newer models. We recommend that you not use this emulation. It almost always wastes storage capacity otherwise available when using the device in its native mode and renders ineffective some useful features you have paid for. It defers (possibly indefinitely) the inevitable conversion to native mode use, which in the long run is not cost-effective. Migration procedures themselves can be complex and are not easily automated. Finally, development of emulation by vendors can delay introduction of new technology and diverts their resources from other areas that would better benefit the industry. If you do not use emulation, maybe natural selection will take its toll on it.

Perhaps the real reason you might feel forced into emulation is that you do not need the newest and best after all but are unwilling to accept that. Many data centers are highly successful using older machinery. The only way the vendor can force you to upgrade your equipment is by effectively dropping operating system support or hiking up maintenance fees. Aside from that, you should make your upgrade decisions from the standpoint of what is really cost-effective for your enterprise.

Storage Capacity Specifications

DASD geometry is the arrangement of cylinders, tracks, and read-write heads on magnetic platters for a particular DASD model. A *track* is the data that one read-write head can access over a spinning platter without moving the head. A *cylinder* is all the tracks that can be accessed with all the user data heads without moving them. The geometry for each DASD type is listed. The number of tracks per cylinder includes only user data tracks and excludes tracks reserved as alternates or for servo data.

If you multiply the number of data bytes that can be stored on a track, the number of tracks per cylinder, and the number of user data heads per volume,[1] you get the maximum number of data bytes that the volume can hold. We supply these figures in tables for each IBM DASD model.

Storage capacity is potentially the most misleading of the specifications because 100% utilization of the DASD is nearly impossible. A vendor can say, "X of these babies gives you 22.7 gigabytes of storage space", but what they do not say is "if the block size of every data set is Y and you fill every track". We look at this detail more closely shortly.

Speed Specifications

No vendor can tell you, "this model will service your application at X transactions per second" without disclaiming liability should the device not deliver that level of performance. Many factors go into the performance soup, including operating system performance, the design of each application, how many applications are competing for use of the same device or paths to the device, data transfer rates at various points in the path, the access method used, data set record size and blocking, how the data is laid out in the record, and so on.

What the vendors *can* tell you is how fast the platters spin, how long it takes to move the read-write heads from cylinder to cylinder, how fast data can be transferred from the DASD to its control unit and on the channel. It really is much like making homemade soup: the ingredients taste different separately than they do when combined and cooked for a while.

Like the vendors, we do not know what your installation is like. We cannot tell you how effective a particular DASD model will be in your environment. We can tell you what the ingredient

---

1 Remember, not all read-write heads are for user data. Some DASD reserve a head for servo feedback to aid actuator positioning.

measures are for each model and guide your interpretation of them.

We call the time it takes the platter to make a complete revolution the *RPS miss* measure. This is more commonly called the *rotational latency*, but we prefer to emphasize the penalty for overallocating the I/O capacity of a DASD. (More on this later.) A derivative measure used in simple performance modeling is *average latency*, or *average rotational delay*, the average length of time it takes for desired data to spin under the head. This is one-half the rotational latency because, on average, the data you need is on the other side of the spindle. (Isn't life like that?)

Three numbers are commonly given for seek times: minimum, average, and maximum. A *seek* is the movement of the heads in the actuator from one cylinder to another. The *minimum seek* time is how long it takes to move the heads from one cylinder to an adjacent cylinder. More precisely, this is the time interval beginning when the channel issues a *SEEK* command and ending when the DASD responds with a *Seek Complete* to the storage control unit. (Or so IBM leads us to believe.)

This value is larger than you would think because it does take time to get the actuator moving. If it took no time, the acceleration would be infinite, the actuator arms would buckle, and the heads would slam into the surface of the platter!

The *maximum seek* time is as you would expect: the time it takes to move the heads from the innermost to the outermost cylinder, or *vice versa*. (This is also the penalty for improperly administering your DASD.)

The *average seek* time is a bit more complex. Most of the industry believes average seek time is the time to move one-third of the maximum number of cylinders. Mathematicians prove that, given a random starting cylinder and a random ending cylinder, the average value is an infinite series which converges to one-third of the maximum. For example, if the number of cylinders is 1,113, then the average seek time is equal to the time it takes to move 367 cylinders. It is usually not one-third of the maximum seek time because of acceleration and deceleration considerations.

IBM (and other vendors) does not define how they reach their timings. They could execute a channel program that seeks to a cylinder x, then, for every other cylinder y, seeks to y and then back to x. This pattern could be repeated for every cylinder x on the volume. The entire test could be timed in a nonshared environment and the average calculated from all these measurements. We just do not know how the numbers are calculated.

8.1.2. Vendor Announcements

As you may have noticed, vendor announcements and documentation for products do not take great pains to describe how measurements were calculated. Do vendors lie about their devices? That is highly unlikely. Do vendors attempt to mislead you? No, what they try to do is to *influence* you to purchase their wares, as every red-blooded American business does. Statistics are great for influencing people.

One fine example is the use of the term "megabyte". We all know that engineers consider the prefix "mega" to mean $1,000 * 1,000 = 1,000,000$, or a million. To us in the computer industry, however, a "mega" is $1,024 * 1,024 = 1,048,575$. If we mean a million bytes, we say that.

The IBM *Storage Subsystem Library: IBM 3380 Direct Access Storage Introduction* (GC26-4491-1) lists the capacity for a single-density 3380 as 47,476 bytes per track, 15 tracks per cylinder, 885 data cylinders per device, and 630 megabytes per device. Multiply these and you get 630,243,900. That is about 630 million bytes, *but it is only about 601 megabytes.*

Likewise, the IBM International Technical Support Center *3390 Direct Access Storage Migration Guide* (GG24-3373-00) lists 902 megabytes as *0.94 gigabytes*. Where did the extra 40 megabytes go? What is the meaning of cost per megabyte when the number of megabytes that may have gone into the calculation is incorrect?

The first published clarification we have seen appears in the *3390 Storage Reference Summary* (GX26-1678-04), where a footnote has been added which states "MB equals 10^6 bytes". It is now more accurate, but we still retain two interpretations for "MB", one for DASD and the other for central and expanded storage.

Another example is the average seek time. Vendors state this figure, and most people take it on faith that it is correct. Empirical evidence shows that they are in the right ballpark. These figures are used in activities such as DASD configuration and tuning, and if the figures were wrong, we would see the inconsistency.

What could be wrong with the average seek time figure, then? Suppose you wanted to conduct a test and calculate this yourself. You could write a channel program as described earlier and time repeated test runs. You would then need to adjust the raw data to compensate for characteristics of the test. If the figure measures "movement from every cylinder to every other cylinder", you need to subtract the movement to the "every cylinder"; otherwise your figure is slightly inflated. Watch out for "fence post" errors! There are many ways to make honest mistakes.

What about fixed-head cylinders? Some DASD, such as the 3350 "F" models, contain fixed heads over two cylinders. Positioning to these cylinders takes zero time. How much time does it take to position from these cylinders to others? Including the fixed heads in your measurements can deflate your figures. When IBM calculated the average seek time for the 3350, which models did they use? If they used an "F" model, did they allow for the fixed heads?

> ◻ The lesson here is that you may be comparing apples with oranges when evaluating the specifications of different DASD models and DASD from different vendors unless you do some digging. Your time is better spent, perhaps, conducting actual benchmarks in your own environment with your own data: taste the soup, not the ingredients.

Maximum storage capacity measurements are easy enough to verify by doing the math; real capacity measurements require a lot more math and data that only you and your installation can supply.

IBM user group surveys throughout the 1980s indicate that the average block size in the average data center is **3.8 kilobytes**. This yields 85% to 90% utilization *if all the tracks are fully utilized. Many tracks are unused. The bottom line is that our DASD is* **usually only 50% utilized!**

8.1.3. Why Capacity Is Not Concrete

Can a 22.7-gigabyte DASD subsystem ever contain 22.7 gigabytes of your data? The answer is "rarely." With little hesitation, we might even say "never." Even if you use automated storage management techniques, you will probably never reach this. Is this a bad thing? "Probably not." Read on.

When is a triple-density DASD smaller than a single-density DASD? The answer is not "never." The reason is that there are really two kinds of capacity. Data storage capacity is the amount of data that a DASD can hold. That is what most people think of. The other kind of capacity can wipe out the benefits of higher data capacity: the I/O capacity of a DASD subsystem.

Data Storage Capacity

As mentioned before, you can calculate (or a vendor representative will bark gleefully to you) the maximum capacity of a DASD by multiplying track sizes and cylinder counts. How realistic is this figure? What can affect the difference between the potential and actual utilization of that space?

The most common way we can waste storage capacity is with inappropriate block sizes. A block, or physical record, is the unit of data that is read or written at one time; it usually contains one or more data records for an application. Each block is preceded by an inter-record gap, required to give DASD electronics time to coordinate data transfer and give the channels time to fetch the next CCW (in non-ECKD mode). If your block size is too small, you can lose most of your capacity to dataless gaps. For example, an 80-byte block size on a 3380 loses almost 85% of the track to gaps.

Likewise, large block sizes can waste capacity. A block must be fully contained within a track; it cannot cross a track boundary. Moreover, at this writing, IBM access methods limit the maximum block size to around 32K. If you use the access method maximum block size of 32K on a 3390 DASD track of 56,664 bytes, you are wasting over 23K, about 42%, of the capacity of each and every track, simply because the block size requires over half the track.

As you will see, DASD track sizes are different for different models and have tended to increase with each generation of DASD. The most space-efficient block size depends on the kind of DASD. Space efficiency is not always best, however, because the block size also can affect how quickly the data can be accessed.

I/O Bandwidth Capacity

Bandwidth is a communications term that denotes how much intelligence can be transmitted using a medium in a particular amount of time. The idea is applicable to the amount of data that can be read from or written to a DASD subsystem. A 22.7-gigabyte storage subsystem does you no good if it cannot perform the necessary I/O fast enough to meet your response time service levels.

Note the use of *subsystem*. Your DASD may be capable of data transfer at 4.2 million bytes per second, your channels may support that rate, and your operating system may be tuned to drive the DASD subsystem at that rate, but that is not enough. Many installations find that 80% of their I/O operations are for 20% of their data. If there is an I/O bottleneck in the path to access that 20%, then the bandwidth capacity of that path has been exceeded.

These numbers may be misleading. The rated channel data transfer speed is the speed at which the channel can transfer a block of data. But you cannot drive channels anywhere near that rate for a sustained period of time. Channel protocol overhead, I/O interrupt processing time, missed revolutions, etc. interfere.

There are several ways to utilize your I/O bandwidth more effectively. One way is to properly configure your DASD paths to balance the load or to make judicious use of storage controller cache and dynamic path features to avoid bottlenecks. (We dealt with this in Chapter 4. You did read from the start of the book, didn't you?) Another is to distribute critical data sets throughout the DASD subsystem. This can be done through manual DASD administration or with the help of automated storage management software.

A third way is to carefully select block sizes for your data sets. Reading and writing longer blocks takes longer than for smaller ones. An oversimplified example would be to use larger block sizes for sequential, batch processing and smaller block sizes for random, interactive processing.

There are circumstances in which you would place a single, small, critical high-use data set (such as the JES checkpoint data set) on a volume all by itself, wasting most of the volume's data capacity, in order to meet I/O capacity (and hence throughput) requirements. That is one reason models of even the latest DASD (3390) are available with relatively small data storage capacity.

8.1.4. Benchmarks: The Only Real Measure

The foregoing discussions are meant not to intimidate you with the complexity of DASD subsystems but to hammer home the important lesson that there is only one way to determine whether a particular DASD configuration will work for you. The vendor's performance figures are not enough. Modeling using vendor facilities is helpful but not enough. There is too much potential for unforeseen bottlenecks and operational details to conclude with confidence that a hypothetical configuration will work for you.

Though they may be difficult to set up and conduct, you should run benchmarks using your applications, your data, and your system configuration when deciding to upgrade or augment your DASD subsystem.

8.2. First Generation: 2311, 2314, 2319, 2321

The first generation was characterized by *removable media*. The 2311 and 2314 (and an "enhanced 2319") had removable media. These do not contain a Head Disk Assembly (HDA), because the heads remained in the DASD and the *disk pack* of platters was removed from the device.

The benefits of this architecture were that the data center could have more direct access files than they had drive hardware. You could have, and many did, an entire master file on one set of removable media and another entire master file on another set, processing against one or the other at different times.

The liabilities were that the volumes were susceptible to dust and other contaminants (and being dropped or lost!). For that reason, the distance between the head and the surface of a single disk platter had to be relatively large. Also, different sets of heads in different disk drives would read and write the same data. Slight misalignments between disk drives could cause read or write failures. The best practice is always to use the same set of heads for a disk pack, a practice enforced by today's HDAs.

Remember that earlier in this chapter we discussed the different meaning for "MB". For central and expanded storage a megabyte is 1,024 * 1,024 bytes, or 1,048,576 bytes. For DASD most vendors use "MB" to mean *one million bytes*. Our tables use "MB" to mean 1,048,576 bytes for all storage, whether DASD, central, or expanded storage. You may find our capacity numbers different from those in other tables.

The following table provides information about the geometry for devices in this group. The DASD model, number of HDAs per device (unit), the number of actuators per HDA, the megabytes per actuator (given maximum block sizes), the number of cylinders per actuator, the number of tracks per cylinder, and the number of bytes per track (count-key-data format) are provided.

First-Generation DASD: Geometry						
DASD Mdl.	HDA/ unit	Act./ HDA	Mb/act. max.	Cyl./ act.	Trk./ cyl.	Bytes/ trk.
2311	2	1	6.9	200	10	3,625
2314	2	1	27.8	200	20	7,294
2319	2	1	27.8	200	20	7,294
2321	10	10	3.81	400	5	2,000

The following table provides information about the performance for each DASD model in this group. The RPS miss time in milliseconds, the average latency in milliseconds, the minimum seek time (for one cylinder) in milliseconds, the average seek time in milliseconds, the maximum seek time, and the data transfer rate in megabytes per second is included.

First-Generation DASD: Performance						
DASD mdl.	RPS miss (ms)	Avg. lat. (ms)	Min. seek (ms)	Avg. seek (ms)	Max. seek (ms)	Xfer. rate (Mb/s)
2311	25	12.5	25	75	135	0.13
2314	25	12.5	25	60	130	0.30
2319	25	12.5	25	60	130	0.30
2321	N/A	N/A	95	173	600	0.5

8.3. Second Generation: 3330, 3333, 2305, 3340, 3344

The second generation was characterized by the addition of *Rotational Position Sensing (RPS)*. The head of string and control unit were much "smarter": the control unit of the 3330 was approximately the power of a System/360 model 30. Second-generation DASD also had removable media (except 2305) and are thus not said to contain HDAs.

Of course, with removable media, you need one model number for the disk drive and another for the disk pack. The 3330 was the drive, for example, and the 3336 was the pack.

The 3330 was released in single capacity (3330-1, 100 megabytes per actuator) and dual capacity (3330-11, 200 megabytes per actuator). There are two actuators in each device, one on top of the other, but the actuators are independent of each other and electrically separate.

The 2305 model 2 has 96 "cylinders" and 8 tracks per cylinder, but since it has fixed heads, the cylinder concept is stretched a bit. All tracks can be accessed without moving the arms. We wonder why IBM did not state that it had 1 cylinder and 768 tracks.

Channel programs for the 2305 made it even more complex. The channel was always supposed to be zero and the track number from zero to 767. Maybe that was why IBM's architecture included a 2-byte track number in 1964 and we have been stuck with carrying an additional byte for tracks ever since.

The 3340 is a hybrid. The 3340 was the only one of the group to offer Rotational Position Sensing as an option. The heads are integrated into the disk pack instead of remaining in the disk drive when the pack is removed. In this way, the 3348 disk pack was a precursor to the modern HDA. The 3348 was available in two models: the 3348-35 had 348 cylinders with a volume capacity of 34,944,768 bytes, and the 3348-70 had twice the cylinders, 696, for twice the capacity, 69,889,536 bytes per volume.

The following table provides information about the geometry for devices in this group. The DASD model, number of HDAs per device (unit), the number of actuators per HDA, the megabytes per actuator (given maximum block sizes), the number of cylinders per actuator, the number of tracks per cylinder, and the number of bytes per track (count-key-data format) are provided.

Second-Generation DASD: Geometry						
DASD mdl.	HDA/ unit	Act./ HDA	Mb/act. max.	Cyl./ act.	Trk./ cyl.	Byte/ trk.
3330-1	2	1	95.4	404	19	13,030
3330-11	2	1	190.8	808	19	13,030
2305-1	1	1	5.2	48	8	14,136
2305-2	1	1	10.7	96	8	14,660
3340-35	1	2	33.3	348	12	8,368
3340-70	1	2	66.7	696	12	8,368
3344	1	2	266.6	2,784	12	8,368

The following table provides information about performance for each DASD model in this group. The RPS miss time in milliseconds, the average latency in milliseconds, the minimum seek time (for one cylinder) in milliseconds, the average seek time in milliseconds, the maximum seek time, and the data transfer rate in megabytes per second is included.

Second-Generation DASD: Performance						
DASD mdl.	RPS miss (ms)	Avg. lat. (ms)	Min. seek (ms)	Avg. seek (ms)	Max. seek (ms)	Xfer. rate (Mb/s)
3330-1	16.67	8.33	10	30	55	0.77
3330-11	16.67	8.33	10	30	55	0.77
2305-1	10	5	0	0	0	2.86
2305-2	10	5	0	0	0	1.43
3340	20.24	10.12	10	25	50	0.885
3344	20.24	10.12	10	25	50	0.885

8.4. Third Generation: 3350, 3310, 3370, 3375

The third generation DASD have nonremovable media: the disk platters are sealed inside HDAs and can be replaced only by placing a service call to the vendor's customer engineer.

An option available with the 3350 "F" models was fixed heads for two cylinders, 1 and 2. Seeks to those cylinders required no actuator movement and so zero seek time. It was common to place the volume's VTOC on those cylinders because the VTOC is frequently accessed and a two-cylinder VTOC was about the right size.

That the cylinders were 1 and 2 brings up a warning to the reader about paying attention to the meaning of specifications. In the early days of the 3350, one data center had 3350s with the fixed-head option. They had set up data on the first two cylinders and noticed that the response time for those data sets was higher than expected. After researching the problem, they realized that the fixed heads were over the *second and third* cylinders. The first cylinder is called zero!

You would never make a mistake like that, right? Okay, tell us how much you know about your million dollar 3390 model 3! What data do you think is being cached? What data is actually benefiting from cache? You should know that!

The 3350 also could be configured as two 3330-1s or as a dual-capacity 3330-11. The hardware mapped the 19 heads of the 3330 onto the 30 heads of the 3350. This was an expensive solution (to develop) for an upward compatibility issue. As we know with 3390 emulation of the 3380, this unfortunate tradition carries on. Do not rely on vendors to do this with every new model, however: minimize your data's dependence on DASD geometry and make it a non-issue at your installation instead.

The 3310 does not use the count-key-data architecture but rather the *fixed-block architecture (FBA)*. The 3310 is a fixed-media subsystem with 512-byte physical blocks. It was usually attached to 43xx Processor Complexes. It is not used with MVS but was widely used in VM and VSE operations.

The 3370 is also a fixed-block architecture device. All blocks are 512 bytes long. IBM targeted this DASD primarily at small and midrange customers. VM supports this device. Although MVS does not support it for user data, the 3370 is an integral part of one of the 309x: a 3370 stores the microcode and diagnostic programs for this Processor Complex.

Why did IBM pick 512 bytes instead of 1 Kb or 4 Kb for the fixed-block size? Perhaps they learned the lesson from other manufacturers of small and midrange computing systems. Most minicomputers use a 512-byte fixed-block size on their disk drives because it is a good compromise between efficiency and disk fragmentation for the kinds of data small users tend to keep. Most small users can justify only a couple of disk drives for their installations, and their files tend to be small and numerous (files of text, for example). Increasing the block size would waste too much space at the end of the last block of each file.

Berkeley used a 1-Kb block size in their version of Unix™. To overcome the fragmentation problem, they came up with an elaborate scheme to suballocate portions of blocks into "frags", effectively combining the ends of several text files into a single block. IBM apparently chose not to go this route when adding 3370 support to VM.

Some models of the third generation, the 3370 and 3375, are the first to support a diagnostic took for the IBM customer engineer. This *Maintenance Device (MD)* (also affectionately called the *Mighty Dog*) is a hand-held microprocessor that plugs into the Storage Control Unit or the DASD. The MD leads the CE through diagnosis and replacement of actually or possibly failing *Field Replaceable Units (FRUs)*. It performs the following functions:

- Automatically executes diagnostic routines.
- Re-creates and isolates failures.
- Analyzes *Fault Symptom Codes* generated by the hardware.

The Mighty Dog is not used for 3390 DASD, which has a built-in service interface and notifies the operator of problems using *Service Information Messages (SIMs)*, introduced with the 3390.

The following table provides information about the geometry for devices in this group. The DASD model, number of HDAs per device (unit), the number of actuators per HDA, the megabytes per actuator (given maximum block sizes), the number of cylinders per actuator, the number of tracks per cylinder, and the number of bytes per track (count-key-data format) are provided.

Third-Generation DASD: Geometry						
DASD mdl.	HDA / unit	Act./ HDA	Mb/ act. (Max)	Cyl./ act.	Trk./ cyl.	Bytes/ trk.
3350	2	1	302.8	555	30	19,069
3370	1	2	272.5	750	12	31,744
3375	2	2	390.9	959	12	35,616

The following table provides information about performance for each DASD model in this group. The RPS miss time in milliseconds, the average latency in milliseconds, the minimum seek time (for one cylinder) in milliseconds, the average seek time in milliseconds, the maximum seek time, and the data transfer rate in megabytes per second is included.

Third-Generation DASD: Performance						
DASD mdl.	RPS miss (ms)	Avg. lat. (ms)	Min. seek (ms)	Avg. seek (ms)	Max. seek (ms)	Xfer. rate Mb/s
3350	16.67	8.33	10	25	50	1.14
3310	19.2	9.6	9	27	46	0.98
3370	20.2	10.1	5	20	40	1.77
3375	20.20	10.10	4	19	38	1.77

8.5. Staged DASD: 3850 Mass Storage Subsystem

The 3850 Mass Storage System (MSS) is a hybrid device. To the Processor Complex, it has the appearance of a 3330-1, 3330-2, or 3330-11 DASD but provides access to far more data than a 3330 could contain. The 3850 does, in fact, contain a 3330 DASD, along with a 3851 Mass Storage Facility (MSF). The MSS is, then, a second-generation DASD.

The MSF can contain 236 billion bytes stored on tape cartridges. Each 2" by 4" cartridge holds 50.4 million bytes on a spool of tape 770 inches long (with 677 usable inches). Two cartridges are the equivalent of one 3336-1 disk pack.

On demand, the MSS transfers data in eight-cylinder units between the tape cartridges and the 3330 DASD. This activity is called *staging*. The data is then accessible from the Processor Complex on the 3330. The primary significance today of the MSS is the experience gained through the design of MSS staging: similar operations are necessary in DASD controller cache for 3380 and 3390 DASD. We will look at the 3850 in greater detail in the chapter on miscellaneous DASD.

8.6. Storage Control Units

Storage Control Units (SCUs) act as an interface between the Processor Complex's channel and one or more DASD heads of string (HOS). The split of responsibility between these devices in a DASD *path* varies somewhat with the Processor Complex, controller, and DASD.

Historically, the line between SCU and DASD has become blurred as DASD HOS have become more intelligent. SCUs have not decreased in complexity, however, because they have been enhanced to offload work from the Processor Complex and to provide DASD configuration features to increase I/O throughput.

Responsibilities for DASD I/O operations can be grouped as:

- *Processor* functions: store channel program, status, and data.
- *Channel* functions: fetch channel command words (CCWs) and data; control data transfer.
- *SCU control* functions: interpret channel programs; control channel and Direct Access Storage (DAS) interface; perform controller and DAS diagnostics.
- *SCU data* functions: serialize and deserialize data; detect and correct errors; add and strip parity bits used in Processor Complex central storage.
- *DAS* functions: respond to controller commands; control actuator movement; select read-write head; read and write data; Rotational Position Sensing (RPS).

The 2820 SCU performs SCU control and data functions for the 2311 DASD, 2321 Data Cell Drive, and 2303 Drum Storage. Likewise, the 3830-1 controller performs both SCU control and SCU data functions for 3330 DASD.

The 2314 is a self-contained control unit. Additional 2312, 2313, and 2318 DASD can be attached to it. A second control unit, the 2844 Auxiliary Storage Control, could be attached to the 2314; this provides access to the DASD through a second channel for improved performance and reliability.

The 2835 SCU provides control functions for the 2305 Fixed Head Storage Facility. The 2305-M2 DASD provides data control functions. One or two 2305s could be attached to the 2835.

With the 3340-A2 and 3350-A2 DASD, SCU data functions are performed in the head of string itself. 3835-M2 and 3830-2 SCUs are attached to these heads of string.

Some Processor Complex models contain an *Integrated Storage Control (ISC)* that combines a channel with an SCU. System/370 models 148, 155, and 168 could be configured this way, as can the 4331 with its *Direct Attachment* option.

3370 and 3375 third-generation DASD could take advantage of the 3880-M1 and 3880-M2 SCUs.

8.7. Summary

DASD specifications for capacity and speed are never concrete. The capacity of a particular model depends not only on its maximum track capacity, the number of tracks, and the number of cylinders, but also on how efficiently the space is used. Improper block sizes can waste the majority of the available storage capacity.

I/O capacity is the level of service a DASD can provide within the context of the DASD subsystem in which the DASD resides. It is sometimes desirable to trade I/O capacity for data storage capacity or vice versa.

Vendors publish specifications for their products to influence you to select them instead of their competitors'. You should accept these with a critical eye and verify their accuracy if possible. The best verification is to conduct your own benchmarks using as much of your actual environment as possible. Only then can you know how a particular DASD will perform for you.

We can classify DASD models into generations based on temporal proximity and on significant characteristics present in DASD within each generation. The first generation had removable media, in which the actuator remained in the disk drive, and the disk pack containing the magnetic platters could be removed.

The important RPS feature heralded the second generation. This permitted DASD to disconnect from a path during periods of rotational latency, increasing I/O concurrency over the first generation. Even though RPS was available in the early 1970s, we had to wait until ten years later (until MVS/XA and 370/XA) to have the ability to measure connect time and disconnect time. Will we have to wait ten years to get the proper metrics for cache control units?

Third-generation DASD contained HDAs, which sacrificed some flexibility and data center storage capacity but had the advantage of improved reliability.

The next two chapters consider the fourth and fifth generations, DASD that is most commonly used today.

8.8. Questions

1. Describe the term *plug compatible* and what it means in the DASD environment.

2. Can you use 100 percent of the DASD space advertised for a particular DASD? If not, explain why not.

3. What three time estimates are associated with seek time? Explain how each is used.

4. What is the most common way we waste DASD capacity?

5. Explain an example of good DASD capacity management that allowed a DASD volume to be partially allocated (e.g., a few cylinders) and the rest of the space never used.

6. What is the distinguishing characteristic of the first generation of DASD (e.g., 2311, 2314, or 2321)?

7. What is the distinguishing characteristic of the second generation of DASD (e.g., 3330, 2305, 3340, and 3344)?

8. What is the distinguishing characteristic of the third generation of DASD (e.g., 3350, 3310, 3370, and 3375)?

9

IBM DASD: 3380

9.1. Unto the Fourth Generation

The 3380 family of DASD spans the 1980s and provides a wide range of storage devices that contain from 630 Mb to 1,890 Mb per actuator. The size range allows the data center to configure a device for either I/O capacity (performance) or data storage capacity.

The 3380 is more reliable than any of the previous DASD generations. On average, one error occurs for every trillion bits of data processed. In perspective, that is like publishing a 50-page daily newspaper for 2,000 years with only a single incorrect letter.

Interestingly, the 3380 is a step backward in one way. Unlike earlier DASD such as the 3350, no 3380 model is available with fixed heads. The 3380 was delivered one and a half years later than was announced, and a common assumption was that IBM could not get fixed heads to work on the 3380. IBM's intent to do so is clear because some of their published literature specifically mentions A4F, AAF, and B4F DASD with the fixed-head feature.

For comparison with the other four DASD generations, here are the statistics for the 3380 models available. Remember that in previous chapters we discussed the different meanings for "Mb". For central and expanded storage a megabyte is 1,024 * 1,024 bytes, or 1,048,576 bytes. For DASD most vendors use "Mb" to mean *one million bytes*. Our tables use "Mb" to mean 1,048,576 bytes for all storage, whether DASD, central, or expanded storage. You may find our capacity numbers different from those in other tables.

The following table provides information about the geometry for 3380 devices. The DASD model, number of HDAs per device (unit), the number of actuators per HDA, the megabytes per actuator (given maximum block sizes), the number of cylinders per actuator, the number of tracks per cylinder, and the number of bytes per track (count-key-data format) are provided.

Fourth-Generation (3380): Geometry						
DASD mdl.	HDA/ unit	Act./ HDA	Mb/act. max	Cyl./ act.	Trk./ cyl.	Bytes/ trk.
3380-A04	2	2	601.0	885	15	47,476
3380-AA4	2	2	601.0	885	15	47,476
3380-B04	2	2	601.0	885	15	47,476
3380-CJ2	1	2	601.0	885	15	47,476
3380-AD4	2	2	601.0	885	15	47,476
3380-BD4	2	2	601.0	885	15	47,476
3380-AE4	2	2	1,202.1	1,770	15	47,476
3380-BE4	2	2	1,202.1	1,770	15	47,476
3380-AJ4	2	2	601.0	885	15	47,476

Fourth-Generation (3380): Geometry						
DASD mdl.	HDA/ unit	Act./ HDA	Mb/act. max	Cyl./ act.	Trk./ cyl.	Bytes/ trk.
3380-BJ4	2	2	601.0	885	15	47,476
3380-AK4	2	2	1,803.1	2,655	15	47,476
3380-BK4	2	2	1,803.1	2,655	15	47,476

The following table provides information about the performance for the 3380 devices. The RPS miss time in milliseconds, the average latency in milliseconds, the minimum seek time (for one cylinder) in milliseconds, the average seek time in milliseconds, the maximum seek time, and the data transfer rate in megabytes per second is included.

Fourth-Generation (3380): Performance						
DASD mdl.	RPS Miss (ms)	Avg. lat. (ms)	Min. seek (ms)	Avg. seek (ms)	Max. seek (ms)	Xfer. rate (Mb/s)
3380-A04	16.67	8.33	3	16	30	2.86
3380-AA4	16.67	8.33	3	16	30	2.86
3380-B04	16.67	8.33	3	16	30	2.86
3380-CJ2	16.67	8.33	2	12	21	2.86
3380-AD4	16.67	8.33	3	15	28	2.86
3380-BD4	16.67	8.33	3	15	28	2.86
3380-AE4	16.67	8.33	3	17	31	2.86
3380-BE4	16.67	8.33	3	17	31	2.86

Fourth-Generation (3380): Performance					
DASD mdl.	RPS Miss (ms)	Avg. lat. (ms)	Min. seek (ms)	Avg. seek (ms)	Max. seek (ms)	Xfer. rate (Mb/s)
3380-AJ4	16.67	8.33	2	12	21	2.86
3380-BJ4	16.67	8.33	2	12	21	2.86
3380-AK4	16.67	8.33	2	16	29	2.86
3380-BK4	16.67	8.33	2	16	29	2.86

9.1.1. Design, Manufacturing, and Maintenance Advances

The first wave of 3380 devices had a number of improvements over the third-generation devices. Perhaps the most important are the path enhancements that make it easier to balance I/O load over the DASD subsystem: Dynamic Path Selection and Device Level Selection. These are described in the next section.

The 3380 was the first IBM DASD model that allowed nondisruptive DASD installation. With the model combinations that allow four paths to DASD strings, additional units can be added to a string without disrupting operation of the other units. A single path is made unavailable during installation, so the payment is a slight degradation of service instead of a complete one during installation.

Another distinguishing characteristic of the fourth-generation 3380 is that media maintenance shifted to the data center. It is true that ICKDSF began with the 3350, but the 3380 was the first device IBM delivered and turned over to the data center for installation and diagnostics.

IBM began to shift responsibility for media maintenance from the customer engineer to the customer. IBM customer engineers provided all maintenance functions for the first three DASD generations. They installed devices and performed error correction by assigning alternate tracks and skip displacements. With the 3380, IBM provides a utility program, Device Support Facilities (*ICKDSF*), that allows the customer to analyze and correct errors on the disk surface (ICKDSF is used with 3350 DASD, but IBM performed skip displacement analysis with the 3350). As we shall see in the discussion of fifth-generation DASD, yet more responsibility has shifted to the customer as the maintenance reporting functions have been integrated into the system operator interface.

3380s can be upgraded in the field, though upgrades can be made only between models in the same model group. This idea was taken further in fifth-generation DASD: the 3390 can be field upgraded with few restrictions.

Other improvements that came with the Standard 3380 models include the following:

- Thin-film head technology
- 12 million bits per square inch
- Film head slider
- Thicker magnetic disk
- Simple spindle bearing support
- X-wing linear actuator
- Bearingless actuator carrier
- 2 actuators per HDA
- Compact voice coils
- New encoding scheme and ECC
- Head offset
- Maintenance device

A second wave of 3380 devices, the *Extended Capability* "D" and "E" models, carried more improvements:

- Improved film head [more read-write coil turns ("E" only)]
- Improved disk coating ("E" only)
- 23 million bits per square inch
- Smooth electrophoretic head carrier coating
- More powerful voice coil magnets
- Improved 3880 storage control function

- Fast path microcode
- Denser circuit packaging
- Redesigned read-write channel
- Simplified cable interconnections
- Improved power supply
- New operator panel

9.1.2. Path Enhancements

Two path enhancements introduced in the 3380 are Dynamic Path Selection and Device Level Selection.

Until the fourth generation, the HOS was little more than an electronic traffic cop to connect a DASD to a controller. With the 3380, the HOS became an intelligent controller in its own right.

Dynamic Path Selection (DPS)

Dynamic Path Selection (DPS) is a combination of four functions for 3380 devices that are connected to one or more SCUs with at least two paths:

1. *Alternate Controller Selection* is the ability of the 3380 to use two paths for transferring commands and data.

2. Simultaneous data transfer can occur over the two paths *if the actuators are on separate paths.*

3. Volumes can be reserved by path groups. All DASD supports *volume reserve* to protect data when one Processor Complex is updating data in the VTOC and other common areas. The 3380 can be reserved on one path, have that path fail, and continue the operation on another path without interruption.

4. *Dynamic Path Reconnect* (starting with XA) allows the 3380 to interrupt the control unit over any active path when trying to reconnect to transfer data or status.

All models except the A04 provide two or more paths to access the data on the actuators. You cannot, therefore, make use of DPS on that model. The 3380 model CJ2 contains a DPS array, but it is in the storage control.

A single HOS can be connected through control units to multiple Processor Complexes (up to eight when the proper features are present). The HOS must be informed of and keep track of which paths go to which Processor Complex. Path data is kept in an area in the HOS (for 3880 control units and 3380 devices) or the control unit (for 3990 control units) called the *DPS Array*.

DPS is another name for *multiple pathing*. Several of the OEM second-generation devices allowed multiple concurrent I/O operations to the actuators in a string. Almost all of the OEM third-generation 3350 equivalents supported multiple paths. Examples are:

- Control Data Corporation (CDC) called its version the "Dual Access Facility".
- Storage Technology Corporation (STC) called its version the "Dual Port Feature".
- Memorex called its version the "Intelligent Dual Interface (IDI)".

The third-generation 3375 can be configured with a special "last" device, a D2 unit, that allows two concurrent I/O operations for up to eight 3375 devices, but the IBM 3380 family was *designed* to allow multiple I/O operations on a single string. The 3375 "second path" is not the same as DPS.

Dynamic Path Reconnect (DPR)

In all third-generation devices preceding the 3380, once an I/O operation is started, the I/O operation must continue using the same path selected at the start of the I/O. Normally this is not a problem, but what if there were a problem reconnecting at an RPS disconnect? The result would be at least one 16.7-millisecond delay, an RPS miss.

With MVS/XA as the operating system driving the 3380, RPS misses can be avoided by a DPS feature called *Dynamic Path Reconnect (DPR)*. With DPR, the 3380 attempts to reconnect to all paths attached to a single Processor Complex at the same time. The first path that responds is used for the reconnect. This feature allows MVS/XA to attempt more I/O operations per second with fewer long delays.

Device Level Selection (DLS)

Device Level Selection (DLS) is an extension of DPS, in that DLS allows two simultaneous I/O operations *on any path to the head of string*. DLS is available only on IBM models AD4, AE4, AJ4, and AK4. (Most of the OEM products include true dual pathing in both their second- and third-generation hardware; there are no limitations on internal pathing.)

Another helpful feature of DLS 3380s is *Beejay switches and lights*. The Standard 3380 devices only have a power-on light and an enable/disable switch for the entire string. The DLS 3380s have a ready light and an enable/disable switch for *each actuator* on the string. In 1982, one of the authors visited the San Jose Laboratories in California to discuss his experiences with Standard 3380s installed at a large data center. He explained to the engineers and IBM management that operators and data center managers needed to know which actuator had a problem, not just that some actuator had a problem.

The Beejay switches and lights appeared on the DLS devices shortly thereafter. We have heard many "war stories" about how the presence of the lights and switches minimized outages and diagnostic time. The most significant one happened when a JES2 SPOOL volume was damaged. JES would not initialize after that. By disabling the device with the Beejay switch, the system could be started, and service was restored to thousands of terminals. The volume was repaired with normally scheduled maintenance.

Device Level Selection Enhanced (DLSE)

Device Level Selection Enhanced (DLSE) is an extension of DLS. The IBM 3380 models AJ4 and AK4 can be connected to a second AJ4 or AK4 to permit four paths to each actuator.

This was the first time IBM allowed nondisruptive installation. Up until DLSE, if the data center was to add a device to a 3380 string, it would have to have all operating systems disconnected (all volumes offline) and the *entire string* powered down. With DLSE and four-path connection, the customer engineer could take two paths at a time and connect or disconnect a device.

9.2. 3380 Models and Features

There are twelve 3380 models in four groups:
- *Standard* models.
- *Extended Capability* models (AE4, BE4) can provide concurrent transfer with any two devices in the string, each using one of two paths.
- *Enhanced Subsystem* models have a smaller average seek time and can provide even higher performance when connected to certain models of the 3990 SCU.
- *Direct Channel Attach* models (i.e., CJ2) contain an integrated SCU for direct attachment to a 4381, 9370, or 30xx Processor Complex.

The 3380 models span three data storage capacities: single, double, and triple capacity. All four groups are available in single capacity, the Extended group is also available in double capacity, and the Enhanced group is also available in triple capacity.

Regardless of total actuator capacity, the HDAs of all 3380s have the same physical dimensions. Likewise, they have the same track geometry: the same number of bytes per track

(47,476) and tracks per cylinder (15). They differ only in the number of cylinders per actuator, or volume, and in the density with which the data is stored on the platter surfaces.

The model numbers for the 3380 family indicate the capacity and features of the unit:

3380 Model Numbers and Capacity		
First character	**Second character**	**Third character**
A: Head of string	**0** or **A**: single-capacity Standard model	**2**: One HDA with two actuators for two logical volumes
C: Head of string with the Direct Channel Attach feature (integrated SCU)	**D**: single-capacity Extended Capability model	**4**: Two HDAs with two actuators each for four logical volumes
B: A secondary unit that must be attached to a head of string (HOS) to be used	**E**: double-capacity Extended Capability model,	
	J: single-capacity Enhanced Subsystem model,	
	K: triple-capacity Enhanced Subsystem model,	

For example, an *AE4* is a dual-capacity, Extended Capability, four-actuator HOS and can attach directly to a Storage Control Unit (SCU). A *BE4* is also a dual-capacity, Extended Capability, four-actuator DASD but is secondary and must be attached behind an HOS such as an *AD4* or *AE4*. This is called "filling out" the string.

The following table summarizes the available combinations:

3380 Capacity			
3380 model	Single capacity	Double capacity	Triple capacity
Standard	A04 AA4		
Extended Capability	AD4 BD4	AE4 BE4	
Enhanced Subsystem	AJ4 BJ4		AK4 BK4
Direct Channel Attach	CJ2		

9.2.1. 3380 Strings

A head-of-string device, such as the AD4, can have attached up to three add-on units. The group of units is referred to as a *string*. The HOS and the SCU to which it attaches determine whether the device can have one, two, or four data paths active simultaneously.

The 3380-A04 can have only one connection to an SCU. Because this is the same architecture as second-generation DASD, the only reason to consider A04 is the price. Performance with an A04 HOS will not be as good as for the rest of the 3380 family.

The reason is quite simple: servers. Did you ever go into a supermarket and find five people waiting for one checkout clerk? If you were fourth in line, you knew you might not go out before 1, 2, and 3 were finished. If there were two checkout clerks, however, you might choose the wrong one and wait much longer than if you chose the other one, but in the end, two "servers" will outperform a single server.

A 3380-AA4 can have two paths: two actuators can be simultaneously active as long as they are not on the same path.

The Enhanced Subsystem 3380s (AJ4, BJ4, AK4, and BK4) can have two HOS butted together, and then any four of the actuators on the two strings can have concurrent I/O operations.

This is *Device Level Selection (DLSE)*, defined earlier. Four-path strings can be configured only when attached to a 3880-M2 or 3880-M3 SCU with the proper microcode and operating system support.

There are rules about which 3380 models can be attached to other models. B04s cannot be attached to AD4s because a DLS HOS requires DLS units. AE4s can be attached to AD4s because both support DLS. Be sure to consult with your customer engineer in the installation planning stage: if the CE cannot hook it up, it probably is not worth purchasing the unit!

9.2.2. Internal Paths

Each 3380 HOS (except the A04) contains two sets of control unit logic, and each control unit has four paths for accessing the actuators on the string. There are two kinds of internal paths: those for the Standard models and those for the Extended Capability and Enhanced Subsystem models.

The Standard models (e.g., AA4) limit which actuators can have concurrent I/O operations. The following table shows the limitations. The best performance can be had by not putting data sets that are likely to be accessed at the same time on the same internal path.

3380 Standard Internal Path Limitation			
Internal path	Device	Device	Device	Device
1	xx0	xx1	xx8	xx9
2	xx2	xx3	xxA	XXB
3	xx4	xx5	xxC	xxD
4	xx6	xx7	xxE	xxF

The drawback to this architecture is that if you have I/O operations that might happen one right after the other, placing the data sets on actuators that are on the same internal path can cause a delay for the second I/O. We are back to the single checkout clerk: I/O becomes single-threaded even though the noninternal paths are configured for concurrent use.

One of the early mistakes we made was to place swap data sets on consecutive 3380 volumes. Internal pathing delays doubled the time for a swap because the MVS Auxiliary Storage Manager (ASM) would start all the swap I/O requests at the same time. The first one would start (e.g., on 380) and the second one (e.g., on 381) would wait for the first to complete.

We went to great lengths to put swap data sets on even/odd pairs until we discovered this little trick!

As you add B04 units, the situation gets a little bit better. Look at the whole string. If the HOS does random I/O operations for all the actuators on the string, then the probability of a bottleneck is slightly lower, but it remains a limiting architecture. None of the OEM manufacturers made the mistake of internal path restrictions.

The Extended Capability models (AD4, AE4) and the Enhanced Subsystem models (AJ4 and AK4) eliminated the architectural limit of the Standard model. Any path can be used to access any actuator on the string.

9.2.3. Upgrade Paths

IBM can upgrade certain single-capacity devices (AD4 and BD4) to dual-capacity devices (AD4 and BE4) and certain single-capacity devices (AJ4 and BJ4) to triple-capacity devices (AK4 and BK4). Upgrading is a cost-effective conversion, but it is less expensive to get the size you will need in the first place.

In addition, there is a very large penalty for upgrading in terms of timing and effort. The data center must remove all data from the single-capacity device (2.56 Gb), wait approximately 24 hours to allow for installation of the upgrade and actuator reformatting, and then restore the 2.56 Gb. The least painful time to accomplish upgrades is when the data center has at least four single-capacity actuators as excess capacity at the time of the conversion. (Thus, "the rich get richer" in the DASD world.)

9.2.4. Recommendations

The hardest part of all is to decide what is required for your application. IBM no longer sells 3380 devices. When they stopped selling the standard devices, a large third-party market sprang up. The success of the 3380 line will ensure that they are available, probably through the end of the century. But which ones to buy?

The easiest answer is, of course, to get all Enhanced Subsystem devices (AJ4, BJ4, AK4, and BK4) from day one, but that is also the most expensive option. You do not have to have all of the same type DASD. A mix and match philosophy is the most cost-effective method of managing your DASD resources.

Here are some guidelines for you to use to evaluate what is right for your situation:

1. Do not choose A04 unless you must for financial reasons. The A04 is just not acceptable because it has only one path for four actuators.

2. Select Standard models (AA4, B04) when you are constrained for money. They are very good units and can be obtained through third-party leasing companies for the best price per megabyte. Remember your goal: price/performance.

3. Select double and triple capacity for very large files. Your company may have several files that are larger than a single capacity actuator. The double- and triple-capacity actuators are ideal for these files. The theory behind this rule of thumb is that large files are normally accessed randomly, and the amount of data accessed is usually small—last year's historical records, for example. Multiple volume data sets are more difficult to manage than data sets that fit on one DASD volume. Larger DASD will minimize the number of multiple volume data sets or will minimize the number of volumes required for a single data set.

4. Select Enhanced Subsystem models (AJ4, BJ4) for data that must be accessed with a minimum of delay. Usually, these files are read or written so often that every improvement in I/O access time can be seen by your end users. The concept here is I/O loading, that is, how much data you can put on a volume before you overrun the capability of the drive (and string, control unit, and channel) to deliver blocks of data in a timely manner.

5. Design some strings with only a single Ax4 HOS. These strings should contain paging and swapping data sets for your operating system or indexes for your data base system. You cannot afford to have any other I/O contending for the HOS of these high-activity data sets.

6. Design all other strings as full strings. For the 3380, this is 4 units containing 16 actuators. This rule applies in almost all data processing centers. The very small center running a 4381, for example, cannot afford to have too many control units. Large data centers can afford to have many control units because they usually have many 3380 devices. The random pattern of access to files will minimize the drawbacks of having so much data on four double- or triple-capacity devices on each HOS.

7. Upgrade single-capacity units to double- or triple-capacity when you are growing at a steady rate. Delaying the additional storage capacity results in substantial savings of lease/purchase money for the DASD space.

These are general guidelines and should be put into place only if you have a firm grasp of the DASD considerations and the tools to monitor the response time not only of your users, but of the DASD subsystem itself.

9.3. Summary

The fourth generation, containing twelve models of 3380 DASD, brought improvements in nearly all aspects of DASD performance and management. A broad range of data storage capacity and performance options allows a data center to configure DASD for I/O or data storage capacity.

Important improvements were made in a 3380 DASD subsystem's ability to make the most use of its paths to Processor Complexes. Dynamic Path Selection and Device Level Selection allow several actuators to have I/O in progress and to share a pool of paths, relieving path constraint.

Also with the 3380, IBM began to shift the responsibility for media maintenance from the IBM customer engineer to the customer. As we shall see, this trend continues with the 3390 as IBM places even more DASD maintenance and management on the customer while attempting to build assistance into its operating systems.

9.4. Questions

1. What is the range, in megabytes, of the fourth generation of DASD (e.g., 3380)?

2. Explain Dynamic Path Selection.

3. Explain Device Level Selection.

4. What was the first IBM DASD model to allow nondisruptive installation?

5. What is the distinguishing characteristic of the fourth generation of DASD (e.g., 3380)?

6. Explain Extended Capability 3380 improvements.

7. What is a DPS array?

8. What is the importance of Dynamic Path Reconnect to DASD performance?

9. Explain the significance of Device Level Selection Enhanced to the availability of 3380 devices.

10. Why did the early 3380 internal path limitations cause performance problems for some installations?

11. Why would placing two MVS swap data sets on 3380 Standard devices 380 and 381 be counterproductive?

10

IBM DASD: 3390

10.1. The Architecture of the Nineties

In November of 1989, IBM announced a new series of Direct Access Storage, the 3390. Why do we think the 3390 will be the DASD of the 1990s? For starters, the 3380s lasted the decade of the 1980s. Both started out with few real advantages over the previous generation. The advantages billed over the previous generation, 3380 DASD, can be summarized:

- Increased performance
- Decreased cost per gigabyte
- Decreased real estate per gigabyte
- Increased reliability and data availability

10.1.1. Performance Improvements

Channel path improvements through Device Level Selection Extended (DLSE) were available through the 3990 SCUs and particular configurations of 3380-AJ4 and 3380-AK4 DASD, and this four-path feature is carried forward as a standard feature of all 3390 DASD models: 3390 is a DLSE-only subsystem. The primary performance improvements made in the 3390 over the 3380 are, then, increases in the raw statistics.

First, the platters are made to spin faster. The 3390s spin at 4,260 RPM, while the 3380s amble along at a mere 3,600. If the medium rotates faster, then rotational latency decreases; the result is that the 3390 has an average rotational delay of 7.1 milliseconds verses the 3380's 8.3.

Second, the platters themselves are physically smaller, at 10.5 inches verses the 14 inches of previous DASD. As you might expect, seek times dropped. 3390 seeks range from 1.5 to 18 (x1x) to 23 (x2x) milliseconds, while the 3380s range from 2 to 31. Average seek times for the 3390 are reduced to 9.5–12.5 milliseconds from the 3380's 12–15.

Third, maximum channel throughput for the 3390 is 4.2 million bytes per second (4 Mb/s), whereas that for the 3380 is 3 million bytes per second (2.8 Mb/s).

The 3990/3390 configuration also has a Dynamic Path Selection (DPS) array. The array is implemented in the 3990 storage control unit to provide a faster, better implementation for tracking which Processor Complexes can control a device.

If you are currently running 3380 DASD, what would the 3390 speed improvements mean to your applications if you replaced all your 3380s with 3390s? Unfortunately, the answer can range from a decrease in DASD subsystem response time to an increase.

10.1.2. Storage Capacity Improvements

As with all other progressions from one DASD generation to another, the 3390 brings increased data density on the magnetic media. Thin-film heads, introduced in the fourth-generation 3380s, are more precise in the 3390, allowing more density of data within the track (therefore the larger track capacity) and allowing the tracks to be spaced closer together (therefore the reduced platter diameter).

IBM initially offered the 3390 in two models for data storage capacity purposes: model 1 (x1x) and model 2 (x2x). Model 1 devices have 1,113 cylinders per actuator, and model 2 devices have 2,226. Although some 3380 DASD have more cylinders per actuator (2,665 in 3380-xK4), the track capacity is increased in the 3390 to 56,664 from the 3380's 47,476.

Do not be deceived by all this smoke and mirrors into thinking that you are getting more storage on an actuator with a 3390 than with a 3380, because that is not necessarily the case. The maximum data storage for a 3390 model 2 actuator is about 1,804 Mb, and for a triple-density 3380 (xK4) you get 1,802 Mb, for a maximum capacity increase of 2 Mb per actuator!

Considering that the track size is larger on the 3390, and end users probably will not be significantly more effective at choosing block sizes, you may find that less real data fits on a 3390 actuator than on a 3380. Perhaps this was intentional on IBM's part to influence data centers into giving serious though to Storage Management Subsystem.

The real storage capacity improvement with the 3390 is in terms of real estate. Whereas eight 3380 boxes are required to house 32 actuators, only three 3390 boxes are required for the same number of actuators. This means that less floor space, power, and air conditioning are required for each gigabyte of storage capacity.

10.1.3. Availability Improvements

Reliability translates directly to availability (a dead DASD is an unavailable DASD), so we consider both at the same time. The primary reliability feature is that nondisruptive maintenance can be performed on 3390 strings. Not only can strings be upgraded, but HDAs can be replaced without making the still-functional HDAs unavailable to the system.

3390s are physically more reliable than their predecessors. Direct drive motor mechanics are used, so there is no more belt to become loose or break. Fewer logic cards are required—less than 25% of those required for a 3380 xKx string if you count them per gigabyte of storage capacity.

The same serviceability feature that allows field upgrades, namely separate power facilities for each HDA, also functions to improve availability. Failure of the component supplying one HDA should not affect the other HDAs in the DASD unit.

Let's stretch it here and say that the smaller HDAs make it less likely that one will be dropped during shipment. Hey, these things happen. (Want to buy a few used 3390 actuators, cheap?)

On the software side, the 3390 is the first IBM DASD to use the 3990 *Service Information Message (SIM)* capability. The 3990 is supposed to diagnose DASD problems automatically and report them to the operator through the SIM interface. SIMs provide notification of the severity of the failure, its impact on DASD function, and recommended actions. Also, the 3390 contains a built-in service interface, so no more Mighty Dog![1]

Media maintenance can be performed on a 3390 concurrently with certain other kinds of processing. (This is supported by ICKDSF Release 11 and later.) A track may be INSPECTed if the track is not in a data set, or the data set is non-VSAM and not in use; if it is VSAM, the device must be offline. Media Maintenance Reserve can be used to copy a track to an alternate track, perform maintenance on the original track, and then release the track. Data would be referenced on the alternate track during maintenance on the primary track.

10.1.4. Physical Planning

The equivalent number of 3390 actuators requires about a third the floor space of the 3380, and one 3390-2 string uses about two-thirds the power of a 3380-xKx string. A 3390-2 string pro-

---

1 Maintenance Device, introduced with the 3380s.

duces only about two-thirds the heat of a 3380-xKx string, but the watts per *square foot* are greater for the 3390 than the 3380. If you fill up the room with 3390s, you may need to increase the room's electrical and air conditioning capacity.

The 3390 uses the same cables from the control unit as the 3380, which simplifies replacement of 3380s: the cable distance limitations are the same. 3390 cabinets are the same height and depth as 3380 but are narrower by about 4 inches. The 3390 requires no end service clearance; service is performed from the front and back, but only one door can be opened at a time.

The 3390 and 3380 devices are about the same weight (approximately 1,000 pounds, depending on the model). The 3390 contains more data for that weight. You may need to rework the floor cutouts a bit; the cutout is at the rear of the 3390-Axx, whereas it is at the front of the 3380.

10.2. 3390 Models and Features

This section discusses the models and features that are available for the 3390 DASD. Remember that in previous chapters we discussed the different meanings for "Mb". For central and expanded storage a megabyte is 1,024 * 1,024 bytes, or 1,048,576 bytes. For DASD most vendors used "Mb" to mean *one million bytes*. Our tables use "Mb" to mean 1,048,576 bytes for all storage, whether DASD, central, or expanded storage.

The following table provides information about the geometry for devices in this group. The DASD model, number of HDAs per device (unit), the number of actuators per HDA, the megabytes per actuator (given maximum block sizes), the number of cylinders per actuator, the number of tracks per cylinder, and the number of bytes per track (count-key-data format) are provided.

Fifth-Generation (3390): Geometry						
DASD mdl.	HDA/ Unit	Act./ HDA	Mb/ act. (Max)	Cyl./ act.	Trk./ cyl.	Bytes / trk.
3390-A14	2/4	2	902.2	1,113	15	56,664
3390-B14	2/4	2	902.2	1,113	15	56,664
3390-A18	4/8	2	902.2	1,113	15	56,664
3390-B18	4/8	2	902.2	1,113	15	56,664
3390-B1C	6/12	2	902.2	1,113	15	56,664
3390-A24	2/4	2	1,804.4	2,226	15	56,664
3390-B24	2/4	2	1,804.4	2,226	15	56,664
3390-A28	4/8	2	1,804.4	2,226	15	56,664
3390-B28	4/8	2	1,804.4	2,226	15	56,664
3390-B2C	6/12	2	1,804.4	2,226	15	56,664
3390-A34	2/4	2	2,706.5	3,339	15	56,664
3390-B34	2/4	2	2,706.5	3,339	15	56,664
3390-A38	2/4	2	2,706.5	3,339	15	56,664
3390-B38	4/8	2	2,706.5	3,339	15	56,664
3390-B3C	6/12	2	2,706.5	3,339	15	56,664

Note in the above table that each unit can have a different number of actuators. You can fully populate the device at acquisition time or you can wait to add DASD modules at a later time.

> ◻ If you must upgrade the device within 12 months of acquisition, it is usually not cost effective to to upgrade— get the capacity installed when you get the device. The increased price of the upgrade is more than you will save in finance costs for that short period of time.

One distinguishing characteristic of the fifth-generation (e.g., 3390) DASD is that you can have devices on your computer room floor that DASD actuators can be added to at a later date.

The following table provides information about the performance for the 3390. The RPS miss time in milliseconds, the average latency in milliseconds, the minimum seek time (for one cylinder) in milliseconds, the average seek time in milliseconds, the maximum seek time, and the data transfer rate in megabytes per second is included.

DASD mdl.	RPS miss (ms)	Avg. lat. (ms)	Min. seek (ms)	Avg. seek (ms)	Max. seek (ms)	Xfer. rate (Mb/s)
3390-A14	14.1	7.1	1.5	9.5	18	4.0
3390-B14	14.1	7.1	1.5	9.5	18	4.0
3390-A18	14.1	7.1	1.5	9.5	18	4.0
3390-B18	14.1	7.1	1.5	9.5	18	4.0
3390-B1C	14.1	7.1	1.5	9.5	18	4.0
3390-A24	14.1	7.1	1.5	12.5	23	4.0
3390-B24	14.1	7.1	1.5	12.5	23	4.0
3390-A28	14.1	7.1	1.5	12.5	23	4.0
3390-B28	14.1	7.1	1.5	12.5	23	4.0

Title row: **Fifth-Generation (3390): Performance**

Fifth-Generation (3390): Performance						
DASD mdl.	RPS miss (ms)	Avg. lat. (ms)	Min. seek (ms)	Avg. seek (ms)	Max. seek (ms)	Xfer. rate (Mb/s)
3390-B2C	14.1	7.1	1.5	12.5	23	4.0
3390-A34	14.1	7.1	1.5	15.0	33	4.0
3390-B34	14.1	7.1	1.5	15.0	33	4.0
3390-A38	14.1	7.1	1.5	15.0	33	4.0
3390-B38	14.1	7.1	1.5	15.0	33	4.0
3390-B3C	14.1	7.1	1.5	15.0	33	4.0

IBM offers the 3390 in two primary model families, model 1 and model 2. The actual three-character model numbers have a regular pattern that is simplified over that of the 3380. In 3390-*ABC*, "abc" has the following meaning:

- **A**: A for A unit (HOS) or B for secondary unit.
- **B**: 1 for model 1, 2 for model 2, or 3 for model 3.
- **C**: the number (in hexadecimal) of actuators that are installed in the unit.

10.3. Attachment Options

3390 DASD can be used with Processor Complexes that support the 4.2 million byte per second (4.01 megabyte per second) channel rates required by the 3390. These include the IBM ESA/9000, 3090, 3090E, 3090S, and (with the appropriate RPQs) 308x (except 3081D).

Another distinguishing characteristic of the 3390 is that it can transfer data at 4.2 million bytes per second. It can transfer up to 6 million bytes per second with later releases.

It is important that 3390s *cannot* be used with the 43xx Processor Complex. "So what," you say, "our production system is a 3090." Okay, what is your test system? Is any of your 3090 DASD shared with a 4381?

Channel attachment requires a 3990 model 2 or model 3 SCU. (A dual diskette reader is required, and your 3990 might also require a microcode upgrade before attaching 3390 DASD to it.) A full string of 3390 DASD consists of one A unit and two B units. Up to two full strings can be attached to each 3990 SCU.

3380 DASD strings can coexist with 3390 strings on the 3990 SCU provided certain rules are followed. 3380 Standard models *cannot* be used. (That is a good reason not to purchase any more Standard models if you were planning to do so!) A 3390 string can be mixed with the following 3380 string configurations on a 3990:

- One four-path string of Enhanced Subsystem (DLSE) 3380s (xJx or xKx);
- One or two two-path strings of Enhanced Subsystem 3380s;
- One or two two-path strings of Extended Capability (xDx or xEx) 3380s; or
- One Enhanced Subsystem (DLS) two-path string and one Extended Capability string.

10.3.1. Software Support Requirements

There are software support requirements for 3390 DASD. If your operating system or utility software is out of date, you will need to update these before installing any 3390s. For example, for MVS environments, you should confirm with IBM that you have the appropriate releases of EREP, ICKDSF, MVS/DFP, DFDSS, DFHSM, and DFSORT.

For VM environments, confirm EREP. VM/XA SP Version 2.0 is required if you run MVS as a guest SCP; in this case, dedicate the 3990 strings to the guest, and VM does not have to know about them. VM/XA SP 2.1 is required for "native" (e.g., minidisk) use. VM/SP HPO Releases 5 and 6 can be used with the appropriate PTFs (Program Temporary Fixes). Additionally, if you use DFSMS, you need DFSMS/VM 1.1.

10.3.2. Upgrade Paths

Upgrading possibilities for 3390 DASD are flexible and can be done in a nondisruptive manner provided there are four paths from the 3990 controller to the HDAs that are not involved in the upgrade; one of the paths is quiesced during the upgrade, and the noninvolved HDAs are accessed using the three remaining paths. The primary reason for this is that the power and service boundaries designed into the 3390 are separate for each HDA.

The following installations can be performed in a nondisruptive manner:
- A second 3390 string can be attached to a 3990 SCU.
- **B** units can be attached to an **A** unit.
- A model 1 can be upgraded to a model 2.
- Additional HDAs can be added to appropriate units.

Upgrading from a model 1 to a model 2 to a model 3 requires replacement of all the HDAs, as you can infer from the capacity tables. *A* units can be upgraded from 2 to 4 HDAs, and *B* units from 2 to 4 HDAs and from 4 to 6 HDAs. For an example, the upgrade paths for models 1 and 2 are summarized in the following table.

3390 DASD Upgrade Paths for Models 1 and 2
A14 - A18 - A28
A14 - A24 - A28
B14 - B24 - B28 - B2C
B14 - B18 - B1C - B2C
B14 - B18 - B28 - B2C

10.4. Migration to the 3390

A recurrent theme throughout this book, and indeed throughout the history of IBM, is *migration*. More than any other vendor, IBM has staunchly supported upward compatibility for application software. In theory, this is great, because it helps preserve resources invested in applications. In practice, it is only imperfectly accomplished.

Regardless, it is there for everything but DASD. Yes, the count-key-data architecture has survived the decades. Each DASD generation, and each model within a generation, however, is so different (from a simple geometric perspective) that Job Control Language for an application, and also some applications themselves, must be changed to use the new DASD. Migration of data and applications from one DASD model to another is rarely painless.

True, IBM provides "compatibility modes" in its DASD. The newest model can sometimes be configured to look like the model it replaces (e.g., 3350 and 3390 devices). This is upward compatibility at great expense: a customer purchases a new DASD generation but cannot get all the benefits from it without a costly migration effort.

If you believe that necessity is the mother of invention and that natural selection is a force in technology as it is in nature, it was inevitable that the trend toward Storage Management Subsystem had to occur. Looking at it from another perspective, IBM has taken us through a series of migration efforts, and we are ready for the software to make this process easier.

10.4.1. 3380 Track Compatibility Mode

If you are migrating from 3380s to 3390s, you could use the 3380 track compatibility mode. It is called *track compatibility* for a good reason: the amount of data per track is the same with emulation as with real 3380s, but the number of cylinders per actuator remains that of the native 3390. The following table compares 3380 *native* maximum capacity and the 3390 *native* maximum capacity.

3380 native vs. 3390 emulation of 3380		
	3380 AE4	**3390 model 2**
Bytes per track	47,476	47,476
Tracks per cylinder	15	15
Bytes per cylinder	712,140	712,140
Data cylinders per actuator	2,655	2,226
Mb per actuator	1,803.1	1,511.8

The number of bytes per track and bytes per cylinder is the same for the 3380 and the 3390 compatibility mode. Almost 9 Kb of each native 3390 track is wasted. There is no 3390 configuration that matches the number of cylinders per actuator (volume) of the 3380. You waste 291.3 Mb of data space in this example comparing the 3380K to the 3390 in native mode.

This is why we do not recommend that you use DASD compatibility mode except in special circumstances. If you do not need to make application programming changes to use the 3390 in its native mode, you should take the plunge and migrate to that mode instead of wasting the storage capacity for which you have paid. Some of the special circumstances may be device-dependent applications that you cannot afford to upgrade or critical third-party software that has not been upgraded. You should question why your data center is dependent on such limited software.

10.4.2. Migration to Native 3390

If you are going to migrate directly from 3380 or earlier DASD to 3390 native mode, you must accommodate the changes in geometry between the old and new DASD. We speak as if you are migrating from a 3380, but the issues are the same if you are migrating from a 3350 or other CKD DASD.

The 3390 has a larger track size and therefore a larger maximum cylinder capacity. Capacity planning is complicated by data set allocations that explicitly specify old model tracks or cylinders: more capacity is allocated for the same amount of data. Moreover, explicitly specified block sizes that are optimal for the old DASD can result in better or worse capacity utilization on the 3390. In general, a 3380 track would hold more data than a 3390 native track for block sizes less than 276 bytes.

There are better utilities today than were available for previous migration efforts, but you and your users must be properly *positioned for Storage Management Subsystem* to take advantage of DFDSS, DFHSM, ISMF, and DFSMS/VM. DFDSS will copy between unlike devices at the data set or volume level, and it will take care of catalog entries and RACF if applicable. DFHSM supports 3390 native mode for migration and backup activities.

If you have implemented Storage Management Subsystem, you can replace a Storage Group and move data a pool at a time. If you have not implemented pooling, the effort depends on whether all data sets are catalogued. If data sets are not catalogued, you will most definitely be forced to modify JCL. If data sets are catalogued, how much JCL you must modify depends on how carefully the jobs were written to avoid unnecessary references to volume names; allocation space changes will likely be required as well.

If you have positioned data, you can use DFDSS and DFHSM to move some data (e.g., system, some DBMS, TSO, and some batch data sets). IMS and DB2 utilities can be used for much of their data. Nonpositioned data must be moved using more human-intensive methods involving JCL and possibly application changes. VM data can be moved with VM/DFSMS.

If you can afford to keep the old DASD while rolling in the new 3390s, you might choose a "gradual" migration strategy in which you establish procedures for your users that conform to Storage Management Subsystem and have them minimize new allocations on old DASD. This is expensive in equipment and environmental terms, but perhaps less so in disruption of service. It also gives systems support personnel a chance to learn along with the users.

The extra time you get from a gradual migration can be applied to increasing device independence at your data center. You can either determine compromised block sizes that efficiently utilize storage capacity over several DASD generations or let SMS calculate block sizes. For example, you can achieve over 90% capacity utilization with a block size of 6,233 or 8,906 for 3350, 3380, and 3390 DASD, or you can use 10,796-byte block sizes for 3380s and 3390s. Applications that are necessarily device dependent can use controller facilities such as *Read Device Characteristics* and calculate DASD parameters instead of "hard coding" them into applications.

There are other things to think about. BDAM data sets may contain data that is sensitive to DASD architecture, so data conversion would be required along with application modifications. Volume name references and multivolume data sets need to be handled. Empty, never-opened data sets cause problems with migration aid utilities. Operational time needs to be allocated to execute data base migration utilities and for unload and reload of KSDS data sets.

The time of your systems staff and users is probably best spent as an investment in your next migration. Solve this migration and make the next one a lot easier.

10.5. Summary

3390 DASD is not significantly larger than the previous generation of 3380. The track capacity is about 19% larger, as is the cylinder capacity, but a 3390 device contains about the same capacity as a triple-capacity 3380 (xKx) but has fewer cylinders (2,226 versus 2,655). That is, the actuators have about the same capacity. 3390 DASD subsystems provide much more capacity per square foot than 3380 because many HDAs can be installed in each 3390 cabinet.

3390 DASD is somewhat faster than 3380 if you look at low-level measurements. These performance improvements are offset somewhat because all this extra data can be accessed through only four channel paths.

3390 reliability, availability, and serviceability are increased over all previous DASD generations. This is important as more and more data centers move to 24-hour online service and can be a factor in the trend toward "lights out" operations, in which the DASD farm may be located miles from the Processor Complex.

Distinctions between the first through fourth DASD generations were characterized by technical improvements to the devices. The 3390 fifth-generation devices also carry technical improvements, but they are the first to be designed specifically to support Storage Management Subsystem. 3390 can take full advantage of 3990 model 2 and 3 *Service Information Message (SIM)* facilities, continuing the trend introduced in the 3380s to shift media maintenance responsibility from the customer engineer to the customer.

Unlike migration between devices in previous generations, there are more tools available with the 3390 to make your data center and its applications less dependent on DASD architecture. If you are going to go through a migration effort to the 3390 architecture, you might as well position (or continue positioning) your data center for Storage Management Subsystem, both to improve day-to-day DASD management and maintenance and to make the next migration less painful and expensive.

The next chapter describes "other" DASD, those not composed, or not entirely composed, of spinning platters. Following that, we address Storage Management Subsystem, into which IBM is gently but firmly pushing us all.

10.6. Questions

1. Describe the availability improvements of the 3390.

2. Is the geometry of the 3390 the same as that of the 3380? If not, what is different?

3. What model DASD can the 3390 emulate?

4. What are the two different model families of the 3390, and what differentiates the two families?

5. What are the distinguishing characteristics of the fifth generation of DASD (e.g., 3390)?

6. When would you choose 3380 emulation for the 3390 DASD?

7. Why is emulation of previous generation DASD usually not a good idea?

11

Other DASD Types

11.1. 3850 Mass Storage Subsystem

In 1974, IBM introduced a device that was to combine the advantages of DASD and magnetic tape devices. DASD, as we know, allows rapid and random access to a large amount of data. Magnetic tape allows slow and sequential access to a huge amount of data. Aside from speed, the primary difference is one of cost: magnetic tape is less expensive than DASD if calculated in dollars per megabyte.

Back in the 1970s, before DASD farms grew out of control, real estate on DASD was (and still is) at a premium. Data centers kept the most important, most frequently accessed data on DASD and everything else on tape. The price paid for economy was, as usual, time.

To use a tape, it must be mounted on a tape drive. A task had to wait for a tape drive to become available, and the system had to ask a human being to go find a particular tape and mount it on the drive. Because tapes are accessed sequentially, tape drives could not be shared by more than one task, and some tasks required simultaneous use of more than one tape drive at

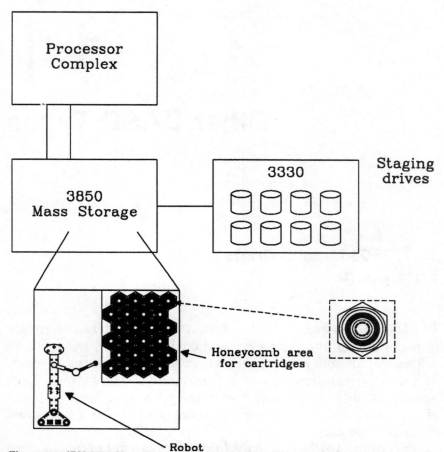

Figure 11.1 IBM 3850 Mass Storage Device. The IBM 3850 Mass Storage Device created the concept of virtual drives. Data sets were cataloged to DASD volumes that existed on tape cartridges stored in a robot-controlled environment. When a data set was opened, the data set was *staged from the cartridge to 3330 DASD. This process took several seconds to several minutes.*

a time. The throughput, or amount of useful work, of a system sometimes depended not on how powerful the system was but on how many tape drives were needed and available.

IBM's solution was a device that looked like a DASD, had the capacity of a tape library, required no human intervention to make data volumes available, and cost significantly less than the equivalent DASD. The result was the **3850 Mass Storage Subsystem (MSS)**.

Figure 11.1 shows a simplified view of an MSS. The MSS stores data on thousands of tape cartridges in a library accessed by a kind of robotic arm. The arm moves the cartridges between the honeycomb where they normally live and a read-write station. Data is moved on demand between the cartridges and specially prepared 3330 DASD, an activity called *staging*, and applications can then access the data on the 3330 *staging drives*. Data modified on the staging drives is copied back to the cartridges in an operation called *destaging*.

In short, the 3850 MSS almost gives the appearance of many "virtual" 3330s using a handful of real 3330 DASD and a magnetic tape backing store.[1]

The configuration of devices making up an MSS is a little more complex than Figure 11.1 indicates. The box that contains the data cartridges is the **3851 Mass Storage Facility (MSF)**. One MSF can contain up to 225 gigabytes of data, and up to two MSFs can be included in an MSS. The MSF connects to the Processor Complex with a byte multiplexor channel. A **3830-3 Storage Control Unit** connects to the Processor Complex with a block multiplexor channel. The MSF and SCU are also connected to each other with data and control paths.

Staging drives are connected to the 3830-3 SCU through normal means. Strings of actual 3330 DASD or 3350 DASD emulating 3330s are connected to the SCU. The 3330s are not connected directly to the 3851 MSF, but are accessed by the 3851 through 3880-3 using the data and control paths. Individual 3330 actuators become staging drives for the MSS by configuration and preparation, not because they are cabled differently from other actuators.

---

1 IBM called the 3850 MSS *virtual DASD*, the DASD equivalent of virtual storage inside a control unit. The 3850 implemented a new term, *cylinder fault*, which indicated that a cylinder was needed but not on real DASD. This was similar to a page fault for central storage.

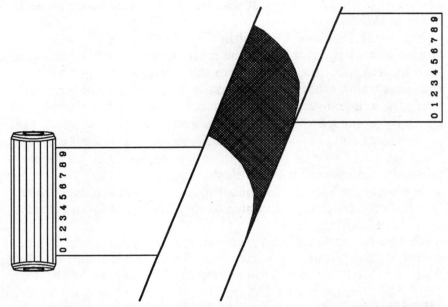

Figure 11.2 Data Cartridges. Each 3850 data cartridge holds approximately half of a 3330 single-density volume. The recording technique made several advances in the format of the data stored on tape.

11.1.1. Data Cartridges

The data cartridges stored in the MSF are 2 inches in diameter by 4 inches long and contain 770 inches of tape, of which 677 are usable. Each data cartridge holds 50 million bytes, and two cartridges hold the equivalent of a 3336-1 disk pack.

A pair of cartridges is called a *Mass Storage Volume (MSV)*. Up to 2,360 MSVs can be accessed by a single MSF, so 4,720 MSVs can be accessed by a single MSS. Although 450 gigabytes is now not considered a vast amount to have online, it certainly was back then.

To read or write a data cartridge, the robot assembly moves it into a *Data Recording Device (DRD)*, where the tape is unwound in a helical manner around a read-write mandrel. Unlike conventional magnetic tape, in which data is recorded in parallel tracks down the length of the tape, the DRD records data as diagonal stripes on the MSS tapes.

Figure 11.2 shows the cartridge and stripes. Each stripe contains servo data, including a stripe number, to aid tape positioning. 67 stripes store a 3330 cylinder; of these, 4 are alternates and 1 is a separator. Count, key, and data are recorded on the tape, as is an end-of-track marker. Home address, gaps, and DASD error correction code are not recorded.

11.1.2. Staging DASD

The MSS uses 3330 or 3350 DASD to emulate many virtual 3330-1 volumes. The actual staging DASD may be 3330-1, 3330-2, 3330-11, or 3350 DASD emulating 3330-11.

A 3336-1 equivalent DASD volume becomes an MSS staging volume by virtue of its preparation. All such volumes have the first four characters of the volume serial in common, and the last two characters identify the MSS. The VTOC must be placed on cylinder 0, track 2.

The VTOC is initialized to indicate that the entire volume is filled by a single data set. This has the effect of reserving the volume for use by MSS and prevents the system from allocating any other data sets on the volume. Although a staging volume is otherwise no different from any other volume, neither a staging volume nor a normal volume can be used for the other purpose without being reinitialized.

11.1.3. Operation

A system task called the *Mass Storage System Communicator (MSSC)* runs in the primary host Processor Complex. It maintains a *Mass Storage Volume Inventory (MSVI)* on DASD that tracks the presence of tape cartridges and whether they are part of a volume or are available for assignment to a new volume.

(The MSSC also keeps a journal of changes that can be used to reconstruct the MSVI in case it is corrupted.)

The MSSC coordinates virtual volume mount requests with the 3851 MSF, which controls the tape cartridge library. The MSF communicates with the 3830-3 SCU to stage and destage data on the 3330 DASD reserved for such activity.

Several varieties of data staging can occur. The variety employed depends on the access method used by the application. The minimum unit of data staged or destaged (that is, transferred between tape cartridges and staging DASD) is one cylinder.

The entire data set can be staged at OPEN time, or cylinders can be staged on demand, an activity called *cylinder faulting*, as they are referenced after the OPEN. Figure 11.3 shows demand staging of three cylinders from volume VOL100 and one from VOL120. Destaging can be on demand using a least recently used (LRU) algorithm on a cylinder basis, for the entire data set at CLOSE time, or controlled by *binding* the data set; in this case, the data is not destaged until the data set is *unbound*.

IBM updated BSAM, QSAM, BDAM, BPAM, and EXCP to support staging at OPEN time; the entire data set is copied from tape cartridge to 3330 DASD, and modified portions are destaged at CLOSE time.[2] In other words, neither cylinder faulting nor binding is possible with these access methods.

ISAM data is accessed only with cylinder faulting because IBM made no change to ISAM. A severe price in performance is paid for this if the MSF is frequently shuffling data cartridges between their resting places and the read-write station. This was a convenient tool for IBM to force customers to migrate from real ISAM to VSAM's emulation of ISAM.

IBM modified VSAM for MSS more than the other access methods. Staging could be controlled. A data set could be designated to be staged entirely at OPEN time or gradually staged using cylinder faulting, or the data set could be staged and

---

2   Linear data sets and Data in Virtual also update the data set at the time the file is closed.

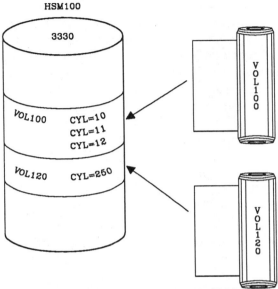

Figure 11.3 Mapping Virtual to Real Cylinders. Many virtual volumes' data could be stored on a real 3330 volume. This figure illustrates that virtual volume *VOL100* could have cylinders 10–12 online while virtual volume VOL120 could have cylinder 250 online. Mapping of virtual to real volumes always was on cylinder boundaries.

bound at OPEN time. Destaging could be synchronous, at CLOSE time, or asynchronous, in which cylinder attrition would occur as the LRU algorithm forced cylinders to be destaged.

11.1.4. Why It Failed

IBM has stopped selling the 3850. It was a very effective, if frustrating, device. We used one for five years, and when it was working, data would be available in less than a minute, but when it was not working, a huge volume of data was totally unavailable.

All that data was dependent on too many moving parts. As we shall see, optical disk *jukeboxes*, serving a function similar to the MSF, have that same problem. In all fairness, we never personally lost a byte of data that was stored on the 3850. Regardless, we are glad we do not have to support one now.

The MSS would have another problem were it in common use today. The problem was not so bad in the 1970s. Here in the 1990s, we are more dependent than ever on online applications, and poor response time is perceived as costly for an enterprise. Staging entire data sets might have been effective in an environment in which batch jobs predominated, but more of our data is required for simultaneous online access today than two decades ago. Imagine having to tune an MSS to maintain an average subsecond response time to interactive users!

IBM has a manual to help data centers migrate off the 3850: the *3850 MSS Migration Guide* (GG24-1716). In our experience, this is the only book IBM ever published to help its customers stop using an IBM product! Enough said.

The MSS was not a total loss, however. The experience lives on in at least two ways. First, to help the data center manage all that data, IBM produced the *Hierarchical Storage Manager (HSM)* to assist space management, backup, and recovery functions. The MSS gave IBM and their customers a taste of what it is like to manage a very large amount of data, and that experience lives on in the utilities we use to manage our large 3390 DASD subsystems.

Second, the logic used to stage data between two levels in the data hierarchy, DASD and tape, is similar in principle to that required in the newer cache control units. There, the two levels are high-speed RAM instead of DASD and DASD instead of tape, but the issues are similar. IBM learned to move staging down to the level of DASD architecture instead of trying to implement it at the data set and access method level. How much of the 3851 MSF microcode do you suppose lives on in the 3990 SCU?

11.2. Solid-State Devices

Unlike the other "other types" of DASD, *solid-state devices (SSD)* look, feel, and act just like conventional magnetic DASD except that they are much faster, because they operate at electronic and not mechanical speeds; more reliable, because they typically have no moving parts to wear out; and much smaller, because the density of silicon chips is much higher than that of magnetic substrate.

SSDs are designed to masquerade as 3380 or 3390 DASD subsystems. They do so at the channel program level, so they are usable without modification of access methods, utility programs, or applications with any device dependencies except timing. (Yes, it is possible to see a bug only when your DASD runs faster.) If the emulation is done properly at the hardware level, SSDs can be used with any operating system—MVS, VM, VSE, TPF, and Unix—, and do not require modification of it. Compare this with the 3850 MSS, which required changes throughout these software levels; MSS was usable only on an OS/VS (MVS) system.

Unlike magnetic media, dynamic RAM does not retain its data if it loses power. That is a scary prospect, so the SSD vendors have expended a lot of effort to ensure that their devices are *nonvolatile*. All use self-contained battery backup systems, but these can maintain power for only up to about 48 hours. Some SSDs contain Winchester disks and use the backup battery power to copy the contents of RAM to this backing store.

So far, so good. One characteristic that SSDs do not share with spinning DASD is that SSDs can force a change in operational procedures. Blocks of storage on SSD are relatively expensive, byte for byte. Blocks that are allocated and never used cause the cost-conscious part of us to become concerned.

One use for SSDs is for very fast operating system paging space. Part of the IPL for MVS allocates pages for the start-up programs that are never referenced for hours, days, or even months (until the next IPL). If you allocate these on magnetic DASD, you are merely wasting 3380 or 3390 space. If you allocate these on SSD, then you are wasting precious real estate.

Likewise, once the system is operating normally, the MVS Auxiliary Storage Manager (ASM) calculates a *burst size* to determine how many pages are written at once to each of several paging data sets on different actuators. These calculations depend on the device type and are designed to take device architecture and timing into account. If your SSD is emulating a 3380, then the calculated burst size may be inappropriate for that device, or ASM might rely less on the SSD than it should to get the best paging performance.

Various zaps have been available to overcome these problems, and IBM has modified the ASM algorithms over the years. The important thing to remember, though, is that history does repeat itself. It takes careful and comprehensive observation to ensure that the system is indeed using your expensive toy as you intended.

11.2.1. Alternatives to SSD

In yesteryear, the storage hierarchy was simple. There was fast central storage, not so fast DASD, and slow magnetic tape. The 3850 MSS blurred the line somewhat between DASD and tape by combining the two. Then SSD blurred the line between central storage and DASD by combining those.

The lines are fading rapidly. We now have *Expanded Storage*, which is like central storage but with more overhead. (Early System/360 devices had a large storage system called LCS which was larger than central storage yet cheaper. The more things change, the more they stay the same.) We have cache buffers inside controllers which can help speed DASD accesses if used properly. The components are getting more complex, the issues more difficult to address, and the system more difficult to measure.

Figure 11.4 shows the difference between RAM in cache on the left and RAM as DASD on the right. Cache controllers attempt to keep the most used data readily accessible at RAM speeds. This is dynamic selection of data to be stored in high-speed RAM. The SSD on the right *is* the DASD: all data is stored in high speed RAM. Which is the best arrangement?

Cache is more expensive per byte than an SSD, but a smaller cache can potentially improve all DASD accesses. An SSD im-

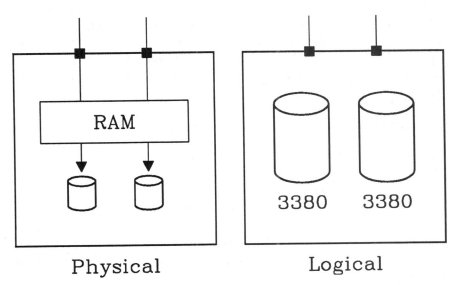

Physical   Logical

Figure 11.4 Solid-State Devices. Solid-state DASD (SSD) emulate all the channel commands for real DASD. The difference is that the data is stored in Random Access Memory (RAM) instead of on spinning DASD. The result is speed. While the end user (or operating system) thinks it is accessing cylinders and tracks as the logical representation above shows, the SSD has the data in RAM ready to go without disconnects or waiting for rotation. Some SSD have real DASD to keep a copy of the data in case of failure. These are not used for access.

proves access to data sets stored in the SSD. This, in turn, can improve DASD performance by relieving path constraint to the DASD. Cache is only as effective as the caching algorithms and placement of data sets to make the most effective use of those algorithms. SSD is only as effective as placement of data sets within the SSD. Since the SSD is usually smaller than all the DASD behind a cache control unit, the SSD implementation usually requires more tuning effort than the cache implementation.

Figure 11.5 shows three approaches to getting the most out of a DASD subsystem. *A* in Figure 11.5 shows two 3880 SCUs used to access 3380 strings. The primary danger is path constraint, exhausting the I/O bandwidth of the DASD subsystem. Two SCUs with four paths each provide eight channel paths, but only two paths between the SCU and the string. *B* in Figure 11.5 shows a 3990 controller with the same eight channel paths, though these are faster than the 3880 channel paths. Four paths are available to the 3390 DASD actuators. *C* in Figure 11.5 shows a hypothetical SSD with the same eight channel paths and two "paths" to emulated 3380 strings.

Which configuration gives better I/O response time? There is not enough data available to answer that question. We have no idea what data sets are located where or what their access patterns are. All we can do, and all any vendor can do, is generalize. We can say that the 3390 configuration is faster than the 3380 because there are more paths between the SCU and the actuators and the 3390 can have cache installed. The 3390 can potentially have much more data stored among its actuators, however, so the extra I/O bandwidth could be negated by the larger volume (pardon the pun) of data accessed through those paths.

Likewise, the SSD is always fastest, right? Yes, *provided the proper data is stored on it*. If high-access data makes its way to conventional DASD, the SSD is not being used. In the case of the SSD, no I/O is too little I/O.

SSD vendors work harder than ever to convince you to purchase their wares. They commonly do this by computing and comparing the cost per second of ownership of SSD versus DASD with subsystem throughput, or the number of I/O operations per second. SSD is usually more expensive than DASD in cost per megabyte. SSD can be shown with carefully constructed statistics to be less expensive than DASD in cost of ownership if you value time.

A favorite trick of SSD vendors is to bring in a utility program that measures the actual DASD use at your site to form a model, then modify the model by "moving" your high-hit data sets to a model of their SSD. Invariably, the output of the utility proves that your overall response time and throughput will improve. By judicious application of these numbers, the vendor can further prove that you will save the equivalent of the purchase or lease

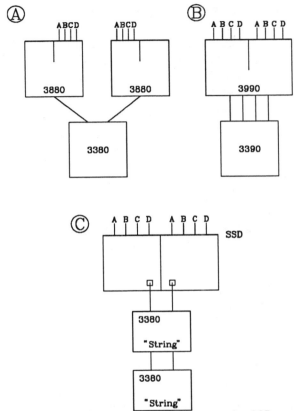

Figure 11.5 Alternatives to SSD. Alternatives to fast, expensive SSD or cache controllers may be innovative configurations. In *A* above a single device is used on a path to minimize path delay. In *B* above the same thing is accomplished with 3990 and 3390 DASD. It is a more expensive option. Finally, at *C* the SSD is emulating two strings of DASD in RAM.

price of the SSD in *X* months. It's your data and your access measurements, but it's their model and their calculations.

We are not trying to denigrate SSD vendors here. Far from it: SSD can be an efficient, cost-effective, viable solution for many data centers. It is a wonderful idea, and if the cost of dynamic RAM keeps dropping, it will become even better.

What we are saying here is that an SSD vendor's models cannot take the place of your own understanding of your data center. Unless you have an in-depth knowledge of how and why your DASD subsystems perform, you cannot make informed decisions about SSD, caching controllers, or any other technology. None of these technologies is a cure-all for a poorly managed (which usually means just a poorly understood) data center.

The other side of this is that you cannot reject these technologies outright if you expect to learn how and when to apply them. No amount of theoretical study, statistics, or projection can fully meet your need to understand your data center. Sometimes you have to take the risk, install the equipment, and experiment with it. Just remember that your job does not end with installation. You must study the equipment's effects, experiment with it, and interact with your peers elsewhere in the industry to improve your own understanding. Eventually these will not be black boxes to you but pawns that you control to get the effect you require.

11.3. Optical Storage

If you listened to the entrepreneurs as they went about raising capital for their new ventures, optical storage was to be a breakthrough in technology that would replace paper shuffling forever in the conduct of business. Optical storage media are cheap and can hold a lot of data. They can hold so much data, in fact, that it was to be feasible to store not only character data but also images of documents.

When a piece of paper entered a building, it was to be scanned by a mechanism like an office copier but with a data connection to a computer. The computer would store the digital image on an optical mediuim. Later, the document could be selected by anyone on the data network and displayed on a high-resolution workstation or sent to a laser printer to obtain a paper facsimile of the original.

First, we look at the technology to see what all the hoopla is about. Then, we look at why the promising, and promised, optical storage has failed so far.

Writing   Reading

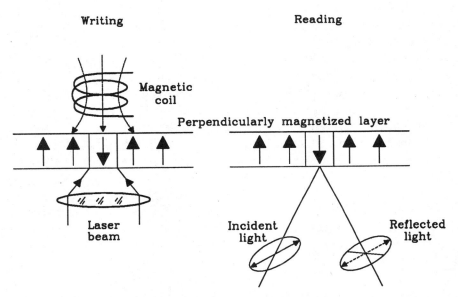

Figure 11.6 Optical DASD. Optical disks have been "coming" for two decades. The technique for writing and reading involves laser beam technology, which has been slow to develop. A typical optical drive is much slower than the rotating DASD because the mirror movement is slower than actuator head movement.

11.3.1. The Technology

The principle behind optical disks is quite simple. A reflective substrate is sandwiched between two layers of durable plastic. Binary data is written by scarring the substrate with a laser mounted on an actuator arm. The data is read by using a lower laser power and reflecting it off the reflective substrate; where it reflects a lot is a zero, where it disperses the light is a 1. Figure 11.6 shows this writing and reading activity.

Because light is used and not magnetic flux, it is possible to store data on an optical disk platter with a much higher density than on a magnetic platter. A 14-inch optical platter can store a gigabyte or two of data on a side. That's a lot of data.

This density requires precise control over the laser light. Figure 11.7 shows typical components. A diode laser is directed through a beam splitter. Most of the beam is directed through a mirror and a polarizer onto the surface of the substrate, and part of the beam is reflected back to a detection assembly.

When writing, the laser power is increased to a level adequate to alter the substrate surface. When reading, the laser power is lowered and reflected off the substrate, back through the polarizer. Most of the reflected beam goes straight through the beam splitter, through the polarizer, and into another beam splitter. The split beam is aimed at two light-intensity detectors. Comparing the outputs of the two detectors allows differentiation between a zero and a 1. Servo data recorded on the substrate during manufacture aids positioning of the actuator with respect to the rotating platter. This is common among all optical disks.

Optical disks come in two flavors and drives in three. *Write Once Read Many (WORM)* disks are like punched paper tape (if you are old enough to remember that). The act of writing data permanently deforms the substrate. You can only add more *1* bits; you can never change them back to zero.

WORM media are produced in different ways for two different kinds of drives. The first kind is as just described. The second is less expensive: optical media are mass produced with prerecorded data using a lithographic process similar to that used by musical compact disks. The drive hardware used for these only allows reading the disks, not writing data to them.

Write Many Read Many disks operate on a principle similar to pasting the holes back into a paper tape: the areas of the substrate deformed by a laser can be "repaired" and rewritten. These devices are more expensive than WORM devices.

Some vendors have made WORM disks look as if they are reusable. With logical mapping of data onto the surface, data is "rewritten" by writing the new data on a virgin area of the platter and remapping references to the data to its new location. Unlike with magnetic DASD, however, as you update data with this arrangement, your optical disk gets smaller. If you do it

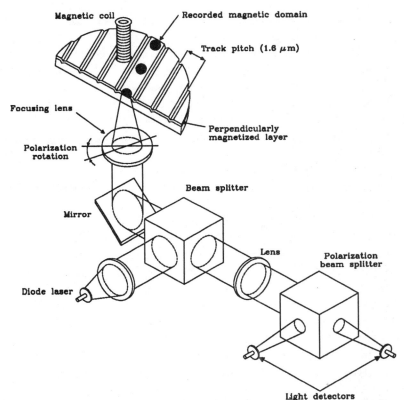

Figure 11.7 Laser Components. Laser beams are focused with lenses and mirrors to detect surface recordings on the optical platter.

right, you can end up with an optical disk that is full but has almost no data on it!

11.3.2. The Reality

As with most technologies, optical storage is useless unless it can be used. One would think this idea is so simple that it need not be actually stated. Doing so insults one's intelligence. Ironically, this inability to use optical storage in real-life circumstances has given it a rocky history.

The perceived advantage of optical storage over conventional magnetic DASD is that each medium can hold a lot of data, usually about a gigabyte per platter. This was to make storage of digitized images practical for the first time. A digitized image could require from several hundred kilobytes to over a megabyte per page, depending on the resolution of the digitizer, whether the image was to be black and white or halftone, and whether data compression is used. This makes conventional DASD uneconomical for image storage: too much of it is required to hold a file cabinet's equivalent of paper.

There are technical problems every step of the way. The first problem is that the information on paper has to be *digitized* before it can be stored. The scanning technology used for this is equivalent to that used in office copiers. If it is good enough for copies, it should be good enough for data archival, correct? Not quite. We accepted the limitations of bad copies in exchange for convenience. A bad copy was just a bad copy, and one could always refer to the original if part of the copy was unreadable.

The idea of archiving document images is to get the original into digital form and discard (or store in a conveniently inaccessible place) the original. Then you use the digital form for all your business purposes. Well, if you cannot clearly read the digital form, you cannot use it.

The second problem is *identification*. Once a digitized document is in the system, it cannot be used until it can be retrieved. How do you identify a piece of paper? You do so by referencing what is on it. Some form of index must be constructed so that a request for the document from a computer would be satisfied by its retrieval. From where does the index data come?

At first, the allied technology of optical character recognition (OCR) was tried. Have a computer analyze the digitized image and extract the relevant data to use in the index. If the digital form is so bad that a human cannot read it, then a computer is certainly going to have problems. Moreover, OCR has big problems dealing with all the ways we write or print characters on paper.

Never mind handwriting, a simple enough example is typesetting. Whereas a typewriter or simple computer printer deposits characters separately on a piece of paper, typesetting makes them "beautiful". For example, "f" and "l" are usually typeset so that they flow together; this is called a *ligature*. A single graphic represents two characters. OCR systems designed to accept extreme variations in how individual characters appear get terribly confused by such things as ligatures.

Okay, so you pay a clerk a pittance to sit there, scan each page, and enter index data manually. What? A clerk paid a pittance does not know or care enough about the business to identify the important index data? (Do you blame the clerk?) You cannot get a person skilled in your business to sit there all day indexing papers. You have a problem.

The third problem is *workstation hardware*. Even though you may have a good digital copy of a document and can index it effectively so it can be retrieved, the digital copy must appear somewhere so that it is readable. Most computer workstation displays have resolution, or the number of picture elements displayed, far too small to read the full image of a page comfortably. No one wants to look at a page through a peephole. The first thing you must do is to replace those cheap VDTs with very expensive, high-resolution, large-format monitors and connect them to very expensive, high-resolution monitor adapter cards.

The fourth problem is *network throughput*. You cannot circulate optical media as you do the paper originals because, ironically, too much data is stored on each. It is impractical to distribute a single page on a medium that holds thousands of pages. The obvious solution is to store the optical media in a central location and access them through a Local Area Network. What? Your network only transmits 10 megabits per second at best? How many digitized pages can you transmit at once before the network slows to a crawl?

The fifth problem is *media handling*. You are not going to purchase a device to read each optical disk you record. That would be too expensive. Instead, you are going to use a *jukebox*, a device that has a couple of readers, storage for a lot of media, and a robot assembly that carts media between their storage slots and the reader. But wait, we have seen this before. Didn't IBM's 3850 MSS use the same principle with spools of tape instead of optical platters? Didn't it fail as a usable technology because a failure of one of many moving parts made a large amount of data inaccessible?

Are you crying "uncle" yet? Optical storage holds such promise but comes with so many problems to solve before those promises can be kept. Why hasn't the industry given up on it as a problematic technology? There are two reasons. First is the perseverance of those trying to make it work. Second, and most important, it is a technology that is easy to explain to the accountants that are responsible for watching your company's spending.

It is easy to demonstrate. It is easy for anyone to understand taking a picture and storing it on this shiny disk. It is easy to equate shiny disks with file cabinets. It is easy to severely underestimate the costs required to make it work. Optical disks will not go away. We will make them work if it kills us.

Another reason is that multimedia storage is vital to our end users. Think about the last automobile accident you had. (If you have not had one, ask a friend!) Reports were taken, signatures obtained, maybe photographs or even videos recorded the scene. These are not just the letters A–Z and numbers 1–9. As our end users need to store multimedia information, our computing systems will need to respond.

The legal profession must come to grips with acceptance of stored information. That is not simple. On the PC I am using to type these words, I can scan in a document and change it. So much for evidence and procedure! We have a long way to go.

11.4. Redundant Arrays of Inexpensive Disks

As Ford and Winchester discovered long ago for cars and guns, mass production using an assembly line makes for affordable goods. "Economy of scale" is not just a business term, it is part of our popular culture.

If a very large number of people want something, ways can be found to manufacture a very large number of them, and when healthy competition exists between the manufacturers, it is justifiable to make a lot less money on each unit. A million nickels is five million dollars.

When VCRs were first available in the consumer electronics market, they were expensive. As more and more brave souls placed their kilodollars on the barrelhead, the price of VCRs began to come down to the point at which almost anyone could afford one.

A similar thing happened with personal computers, which these days straddle the border between true computer equipment and consumer electronics. At this writing, you can get a reliable, fast computer with a large fixed disk in a market where the price is dropping and the size is increasing.

A group of researchers in academia, for example at the University of California at Berkeley, the birthplace of BSD Unix, have been investigating the use of cheap personal computer DASD to construct large DASD subsystems. Dubbed *RAID*, for *Redundant Array of Inexpensive Disks*, these store data on arrays of tens to hundreds of these disks.

Having an array of actuators handy makes for some interesting data configurations. Three which may be found in RAID are data shadowing, striping, and bit slicing:

- *Mirroring* or *shadowing* is writing the same data to two or more actuators so that if one actuator utterly fails, the data stored on it is available without interruption from another actuator. (The IBM 3990-3 dual copy feature is an example of mirrored disks.)

- *Striping* is splitting a block to be written into several pieces and writing each piece to a different actuator on sectors in the same position across the disks of the group. Error correction data in addition to the ECC data stored on each actuator is written to an additional actuator should a data actuator be unable to supply a correct stripe.
- *Bit slicing* is writing each data bit and the parity bit to different actuators.

Combinations of these data configurations spring immediately to mind. Figure 11.8 shows a simple combination. Each data block is split (striped) onto four actuators, 0 through 3, with extra error correction ("P" for "parity") written as a bit slice to an additional actuator. Furthermore, each stripe is shadowed onto additional actuators, 4 through 7 plus a redundant parity actuator. Berkeley personnel have defined seven *levels* of RAID to facilitate discussion of these. These are:

- **RAID-0.** This has striping without redundancy and without extra error correction data. The stripe is large compared to the size of the data block. The usable capacity is the capacity of the entire subsystem.
- **RAID-1:** This is *Mirrored Disks* where volume shadowing or mirroring without extra error correction data is used to gain reliability. It is widely used in minicomputers (e.g., Tandem Computers) and microcomputer Local Area Networks (e.g., Novell) to provide fault-tolerant systems. Each write to a disk is duplicated to a second disk, maybe through entire duplicated paths. The usable capacity is half the capacity of the entire subsystem. RAID-1 is most appropriate for high transaction rate processing where the cost can be justified.
- **RAID-2.** This is *Bit Interleaved Array* which is is similar to central and expanded storage protection where a group of disks has extra disks associated for error recovery. A single parity disk can detect a single error, but more disks

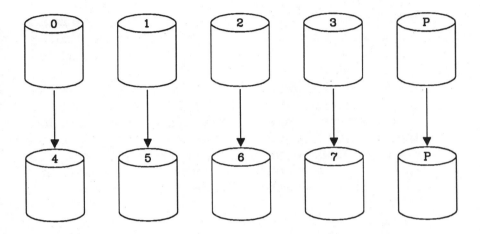

Figure 11.8 Redundant Arrays of Inexpensive Disks (RAID). This figure shows a simple configuration of one method to place one bit from each byte on different small disks. Bits zero through 3 are written to RAID DASD 4 through 7. Parity bits are stored on another RAID disk.

are needed for recovery. The number of extra disks varies, for example, from 4 for a group of 10 disks to 5 to cover 25 disks.

- **RAID-3.** This is *Hard Failure Detection and Parity* which has striping with extra error correction data; it assumes that the DASD, using traditional techniques, can determine where the bit is that failed. The stripe is small compared to the size of the data block; that is, the data block is split over more actuators than in RAID-5. The usable capacity is better than that of RAID-2 because only one disk is used to maintain the integrity of a group of disks. RAID-

3 is better for supercomputer applications than for transaction processing systems.

- **RAID-4.** This is *Intragroup Parallelism* where blocks can be spread across a group of disks to reduce the transfer time by exploiting the bandwidth of the group. RAID-4 is better than RAID-2 for small blocks because sectors are scattered, not just bits. Unlike with RAID-2 and RAID-3, more than one I/O at a time can be active at one time to a group of disks.

- **RAID-5.** This is *Rotated Parity to Parallelize Writes* which is like RAID-3 but stripes the data block over fewer actuators. The usable capacity of the subsystem is larger than that of RAID-3 because fewer actuators are reserved for error correction data. RAID-5 is better at writes than RAID-4 because more than one write can take place at a time. RAID-5 is therefore most appropriate for mixed environments.

- **RAID-6.** This is *Two-Dimensional Parity for Even More Reliability* which is a two-dimensional disk organization (devices are one level and sectors on the device are another). RAID-6 adds a third dimension by having two levels of disks with the sector being the third dimension. The benefit is that RAID-6 should be able to recover from a loss of any two disks as well as many losses of three disks. Writes are still a problem, as the overhead to synchronize those levels is high.

Berkeley has identified two configurations as the most likely candidates for actual use. RAID-1, also called *Mirrored RAID*, makes the best use of subsystem capacity because actuators are not reserved for extra error correction data. RAID-5, also called *N+1 RAID*, allows adjustment of the amount of error correction data by storing more or less error correction data.

Why all this concern over redundant data and error correction? Although PC disks are often rated with a Mean Time Between Failure (MTBF) comparable to that of mainframe DASD, around 30,000 hours, empirical evidence suggests that the failure rate is much higher. Moreover, if the data block is split and stored on several actuators, failure of one actuator can result in loss of many more data blocks than the capacity of that actuator.

The MTBF of N actuators is the reciprocal of the sum of their individual MTBFs. For example, assume the actuators have an MTBF of 30,000 hours. If you depend on two actuators, the probability is that one of them will fail before 15,000 hours and one after 15,000 hours. Okay, the sample size is small here, so maybe both will fail after 20,000 hours. What is the subsystem MTBF for 50 or 100 actuators, however? In other words, what is the probability that one of those actuators will fail much sooner than the rated MTBF? The probability is *scary*.

Suppose the unreliability of the individual actuators can be overcome by mirroring or extra error correction. That leaves another big problem with RAID: **performance**. Remember the discussion of channel reconnection and RPS miss, how extra platter revolutions spell the death knell for DASD response time? Remember how challenging it is to configure DASD subsystems so RPS miss is avoided?

The problem can be worse with RAID. With shadowing, striping, or bit slicing, a single I/O request depends on the revolution of media not under one actuator but under two or more actuators. The response time of N actuators is the worst-case response: the I/O cannot be completed until all the data is read or written from all the actuators involved. For example, if the first, third, fourth, and fifth stripes for a read request are available immediately but the data for the second stripe just passed under its actuator, the entire read request is held up until the second stripe's data passes under the second actuator.

This is why any practical implementation of RAID will have to have actuator-level buffering or caching with nonvolatile storage.

The problem is made worse with the extra error correction data. Figure 11.9 shows data stripes as crosshatched boxes and the extra error correction with "+" boxes. To read a block requiring a stripe from actuators 2 and 3 with error correction from 4

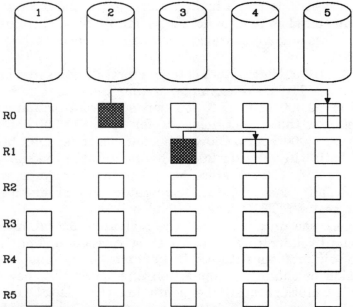

Figure 11.9 Troubles with RAIDs. As extra error correction techniques are applied, mapping bits onto RAID devices becomes more complex. In this case the data bits and parity bits are separated to different volumes. If the parity bits and the bits for a byte are stored on the same device, performance suffers as bit retrieval becomes serial, not parallel.

and 5, the timings of four actuators affect the response time of the request. If the request is large enough and parity blocks are scattered throughout the data actuators, it is possible that a data block must be read from an actuator and then a parity block must be read from the same actuator. What a nightmare!

Okay, maybe we can fix this by synchronizing platter rotation. Make all the actuators involved in the stripe or shadow operation spin at exactly the same rate over time. Some RAID products do synchronize spindle revolution. If this is done successfully, the "RPS miss" of a RAID configuration need not be worse than that of a single actuator. Now, however, you have reengineered the actuators. You require a *different product* from the manufacturer. You no longer have the advantage of using inexpensive, off-the-shelf actuators. You now have *RAED*. (redundant array of *expensive* devices).

The preceding notwithstanding, RAID is a promising application of DASD technology, though probably more so for workstations than for mainframe environments. It is the first technology to bring large-scale mainframe data storage capacity down to an affordable level. This makes it viable for smaller computers such as minicomputers and especially microcomputers. Study and development of RAID is just beginning. As it matures, it will likely make it easier for an organization to move away from centralized computing and more towards distributed computing.

The IBM 9570 Disk Array Subsystem is the IBM entry into RAID-3 technology. It attaches to IBM Processor Complexes via the industry-standard High Performance Parallel Interface (HIPPI).

Access is provided through an industry-standard interface for the multiple record transfers with a single Intelligent Peripheral Interface-3 (IPI-3) command set. (Is this the 1990s version of the HIPPI-IPI weather man?) MVS/ESA applications will be supported through the Parallel I/O Access Method (PIOAM). (VM/XA and AIX/ESA come later).

The first version can transfer data at rates of 50 million bytes per second and provide high data availability for the customer.

11.5. Summary

We have looked at alternatives to the conventional DASD with a spinning magnetic medium. The 3850 MSS combines disk and tape. Optical disks have much higher density than magnetic disks but are less flexible and fraught with related technical problems. SSD and related technologies blur the lines between primary and secondary storage. RAID uses conventional but inexpensive DASD in the unconventional configuration of an array of devices managed like a single device.

The IBM 3850 Mass Storage Subsystem attempted to combine the advantages of DASD's direct access with the large data storage capacity and the potential to automate tape libraries. Unfortunately, the MSS had too many moving parts and too many points of exposure in which a failure would prevent access to a lot of data. IBM no longer sells this device.

Optical disks use lasers to record data by scarring reflective media. Precise control of light is easier to accomplish than precise control of magnetic flux, so optical disks can store vastly more data than their magnetic counterparts. This gives optical technology great promise for office automation tasks that heretofore were not economical, such as digitizing the vast amounts of paper that flow through any organization.

Unfortunately, as with most promising technologies, the hidden costs of optical disks are many. These range from inadequate allied technologies such as digitizing, optical character recognition, network throughput, and insufficient workstation hardware to more human concerns such as the lack of effective workflow management. Someday optical disks may be commonplace in our businesses, but someday is not today.

Solid-state devices (SSD) directly emulate conventional magnetic DASD subsystems. Instead of using rotating magnetic media, they use solid-state dynamic RAM. The subsystems are made nonvolatile by using batteries and relatively inexpensive backup media.

SSDs were the first application of RAM to secondary storage as an alternative to central storage in a Processor Complex. Other alternatives are now available, including expanded storage inside the Processor Complex and cache storage inside conventional storage control units. These technologies are expensive, and it is difficult to decide the best application of them to a particular data center. They should be applied judiciously and with a good understanding of the data center that can only be developed through your attention over time.

Redundant Arrays of Inexpensive Disks, or RAID, are being researched as a way of getting a lot of DASD storage relatively cheaply. RAID has three big problems. The first is availability: each data block depends on a number of devices functioning properly. The second is performance: you get the worst-case performance on every I/O. The third is architecture: unless the standard CKD (count-key-data) architecture is emulated by a

RAID subsystem, it is unlikely that RAID configurations will make inroads into the mainframe arena.

11.6. Questions and Exercises

1. Why did the IBM 3850 MSS fail as a viable technology? Identify two important characteristics that contributed to this failure.

2. What legacies did the 3850 leave us?

3. There are successful companies that market optical disk subsystems. Research them and determine how, and how well, they solved the problems we identified for the technology.

4. Draw a diagram illustrating the conventional storage hierarchy from central storage to magnetic tape and identify where the lines between levels of the hierarchy have become blurred. Can you predict whether and how the lines will become less distinct in the future?

5. Locate a technical article giving benefits of an SSD vendor. Question the assumptions by replacing them to show that an SSD is not cost-effective under the circumstances.

6. Perform thought experiments with various RAID configurations. Pick theoretical values for average latency and average seek times and calculate average and worst-case access times for striped configurations. Are there ways to organize application data that overcome RAID performance limitations?

7. Visit your local college library or contact the University of California at Berkeley and obtain their papers on RAID technology. Determine how much remains theoretical and how much has been tried on actual RAID configurations.

8. Contact manufacturers of inexpensive disks and obtain their Mean Time Between Failure ratings, then acquire empirical measures of observed failure times. Correlate them. Are MTBF figures accurate or optimistic?

4

Storage Management Subsystem

Storage Management Subsystem is the term used by IBM to categorize operating system and other types of software that allow the installation to automate some decisions concerning allocation and use of data. In other literature you may see the terms Storage Management Subsystem and systems managed storage capitalized or in lower case. IBM originally announced Storage Management Subsystem as a part of their MVS operating system, so some capitalized the term as part of a major function provided by IBM. IBM then renamed Systems Managed Storage to Storage Management Subsystem. Since it comes as part of IBM's data management software Data Facility Product, it is also known as DF/Storage Management Subsystem.

The subject will be in a state of flux throughout the remainder of this century, so we have decided to use systems managed storage for the generic topic and DF/Storage Management Subsystem for the IBM implementation.

SMS is a marginally defined function because IBM has taken the approach that SMS will start out nondisruptive and be **evolved** over the 1990s. Both hardware and software will be needed to implement a managed storage subsystem fully. The

IBM MVS version 4.2 operating system was a start in the direction of the software changes in that this version rewrote the operating system Input/Output Supervisor.

Why all the interest in systems managed storage? Consider:

1. 50% of the average annual MIS budget is storage costs.

2. In 1987, more gigabytes of DASD were purchased than in the entire 3350 line from 1975 until 1982.

3. It is common for an installation's storage capacity to grow 30–40 percent per year.

In other words, DASD costs a lot of money, and that is of interest to us all. We do know that as anything grows, it becomes more important for us to manage it in an automated fashion. The mainframe environment has the best tools for managing data, but even it needs improvement. Thus we have Storage Management Subsystem.

IBM and other vendors have marketing approaches that predict savings if you install their software. IBM's SMSVALUE claims that annual savings average from $195,000 for a 100-gigabyte data center to $1,152,000 for a terabyte data center. Those are actual dollar savings annually! Do we have your attention?

A word of caution. The age-old question often asked is: When do you stop dancing with a gorilla? When the gorilla wants to stop. The IBM DF/SMS load module is *IGDZILLA*. Some user groups adopted a godzilla type figure to represent DF/SMS. The DF/SMS question could be: When do you stop installing, tuning, and tweaking DF/SMS? The answer could be when DF/SMS wants to stop!

12

Data in a Pooled Storage Environment

12.1. Introduction to Pooling

Up to now we have concentrated on the raw material of the DASD storage media family: DASD as equipment. We now shift our perspective to the strategic place it holds in the data center: DASD as a tool of business.

With each generation of operating systems from IBM, the operating system itself has automated more and more of the process of DASD data management. The early techniques were simple ones suitable for the relative simplicity of data centers in their time. Data centers have become so large, complex, and difficult to manage that many of them go essentially unmanaged. Lately, IBM has made much fanfare about Systems Managed Storage, or SMS, claiming it will straighten out this problem so you can forget all about your data management woes.

As we shall see, it is certainly no panacea and has the potential to become a Pandora's Box to your data center. You have little choice, however, because the costs of not managing your data far exceed the pain required to establish sound management. It seems so obvious but is worth stating that a computer cannot do something if we cannot tell it how to go about it.

This chapter is about identifying the characteristics of data set requirements and use so you can construct rational storage management practices, whether or not you choose to use IBM's products to accomplish them. No software, not IBM's, not anyone's, can read your or your end users' minds. Any claims to the contrary should be identified and evaluated rationally.

Keep in mind why we have DASD: to make information available to our customers in a timely, efficient, and cost-effective manner. How do we go about allocating DASD space for data storage? A brief look at history shows that SMS is the natural extension of a trend with roots in the earliest days of data processing.

In the early beginnings of IBM operating systems (under DOS), the end user selected a volume and the cylinders or tracks that the data was to occupy and started writing. Those times were really exciting. Someone had to keep track of every track in the data center lest one's turf become confused with another's. The reason this method was acceptable then was that there were few volumes, and the number of tracks was manageable.

IBM later introduced OS/Primary Control Program (PCP) and Job Control Language, and through these the operating system could decide where space is allocated on the volumes. Hundreds of volumes could be supported in this manner. Someone still had to manage the volumes, but less bookkeeping was required than under DOS. This "management" consisted mostly of figuring out what to do when volumes became full. Someone had to decide whether to move or scratch old data or to obtain additional volumes. The latter solution was always welcomed by the DASD salesman!

After that, operating systems such as Multiprocessing with Variable number of Tasks (MVT) and Multiprocessing with Fixed number of Tasks (MFT) allowed the data center to associate a name with a set of volumes. End users could request allocation using this name, and the operating system would select the specific volume for the data. This is none other than the simplest DASD pooling.

Pooling does not refer to a body of water. Anyway, it would be dangerous to have DASD standing in water with all that high-power electricity running through it. Pooling is the gathering of resources (e.g., DASD space) according to their characteristics and the method of acquiring resources from the pool. The resources could then be allocated according to some rules. Pooling has thus been around for years. (Sorry to all of you selling systems managed storage, but it is just an old idea that is evolving into a better, more efficient product!)

In this chapter, we will look at DASD in the total storage hierarchy and look at the concepts important to understanding pooled DASD resources.

We say it again. In order to manage data sets, you need to have rules that can be codified by whatever SMS you decide upon. Planning up front will pay off in a successful management of storage. Lack of planning will doom your efforts, and no amount of technology will save you.

12.2. Life Cycle of Data in Depth

The first place to start is to look in detail at the life cycle of data, for that is what SMS is all about.

12.2.1. Allocation Time

The data set name is used by MVS to point to a catalog that contains the rest of the information about where a data set resides. All data sets should be cataloged. All data sets must be cataloged with DF/Storage Management Subsystem.

The organization of the data is probably predetermined by the application. For example, if the contents are going to be load library members, then the data set will be a partitioned data set.

The logical record size (LRECL) is also predetermined by the application. The logical record size determines the bounds of the physical block size (i.e., it must be some multiple of LRECL).

The end user chooses the space required for the data. Space requirements vary over the lifespan of the data. The amount needed for the first group of records is the minimum amount needed. The amount for all records that the data set will ever contain is the maximum amount needed.

The end user can specify a retention period on the JCL, but this feature is practically worthless. It almost works for tape volumes, but for DASD data sets, all a retention period gets you is operator messages as you try to update it. Generation data sets (GDGs) have an implied retention (e.g., keep the last x versions of this data set). What is missing is an effective method for the end user to specify, "Keep this data set as long as I am testing version 1.0 of the payroll modules."

Finally, the end user specifies where the data set is to be allocated. In pre-SMS environments, this placement specification has implications. The DASD volume has certain performance and space characteristics. Nonspecific allocation can be requested, but then the end user is playing the lottery with data set placement and the data set's resultant performance and contention with other data sets.

12.2.2. Active Time

For illustration purposes, we consider an active data set as one that has been read from or written to within the last seven days. Your time frame might be different, but we have seen many indicators that a weekly cycle is a good time frame to use for *active*.

Response

What response times do we require for accessing the data? Response times can vary over the lifetime of the data set. Initial response times are monitored most closely because we tend to look more closely at something new than at something that has been around for a while. Response time requirements may change over time as well: if the data center upgrades a Processor Complex, its users would expect faster response for their data accesses.

Response times after initial monitoring may vary, because things change. The data set may have been moved to a volume other than the one on which it was initially observed. If the data set did not move, the mix of the other data sets on the volume may have changed. The only way to ensure that response times do not vary is to isolate the data set to a volume and a path and never allow any changes. That, of course, is impossible. We are heading, with SMS, to a time when we can specify a response time target, and the system will make changes to achieve the target. In effect, SMS will be able to compensate for changes that affect response time goals set for the data.

That utopian goal will never be completely realized. The only way to affect response time positively is to remove delays. The data set may need to be moved or other work rerouted.

Frequency of Use

How frequently will the data set be used? If the data set is an online, highly active data set, then it will be available all the time. If it is needed constantly, the records probably should be in central or expanded storage for minimum response times.

Access Pattern

How will the data set be accessed? What security will be required for the data? Will it need to be available constantly, or will the data be needed for predetermined periods of time—each Saturday, for example?

Who will want to share the data? Will multiple terminals from within a communications subsystem (CICS, IDMS, etc.) want to access the data? Will multiple TSO users want to share the data? If so, sufficient paths to the data should be available to satisfy the concurrent users.

How and when will maintenance be applied to the data? If it is a customer data base, new customers will need to be added and old ones deleted.

Growth

What growth is expected for the data set? We have seen data sets for a large company grow from a few cylinders to several dual capacity volumes over the course of the year. Should you allocate two whole volumes in January or allocate just part of the final volume and risk running out of room in October or November?

Backup and Recovery

Who is responsible for backup and recovery? If the data set is part of a data base, its maintenance must be coordinated with that of the others that constitute the data base.

12.2.3. Inactive Time

At some point, there will be a period of time since the data set was last accessed. This time is called the inactive time because no task needed the data during this period.

Migration and Recall

With the exception of data sets used in regularly scheduled, periodic processing, a data set that has been inactive for a while will probably not be referenced for a while longer. Maybe it will never be used again. The data center can and should migrate the data set to a non-DASD medium when its access pattern no longer requires DASD residence.

The most convenient way to "move" the data out of the way is to scratch it. The problem is that the data center does not know for certain that the end users will not come back and want the data. Instead of deleting the data, the data center can *migrate* it to DASD upon which fewer performance demands are placed or to secondary storage such as magnetic tape.

A *recall* function would move the data from secondary storage back to DASD should the end user require it. If the recall function is automatic upon reference to the migrated data set's catalog entry, the end user may not realize that the data center reused the DASD space the data set occupied before it was migrated.

Retirement

Data sets can be retired semipermanently. Archiving them to an offline medium is a theoretical solution, but it suffers from the requirement to know where the data is if it is to be used. You might as well scratch the data set. The difference between migration and retirement is thus one of convenience. Both techniques allow reuse of DASD space, but migration gives the user a better chance of retrieving the data once it is moved.

In the PC environment, archiving is unfortunately one of the few methods of clearing off our fixed disks. We have hundreds of floppy disks with back levels of our files. If we need to get to them, the process is manual.

Deletion

Finally, data sets get scratched. The space they were occupying is now available for other data sets.

> ◘ Two basic truths relate to data. **Locality of reference** means that if data in one place is referenced, chances are good that nearby data will be referenced in the near future. **Data reuse** means that data being used now may be reused by some subsequent job or job step. The probability that it will be reused decreases dramatically with time since its last use.

12.3. Storage Hierarchy

Why are we so interested in the way we store data? The answer is that there is more data to store than places to put it, and storage media are becoming a larger slice of our data processing budget as our data centers continue to mature.

At the growth rate over the last decade, the entire planet may be neck deep in 3390 spindles shortly after the start of the new century. (You will be able to tell a DASD salesman reading this by the dollar signs that replace their eyeballs!)

12.3.1. Cost of Storage

Many studies show that the total data storage budget is **50% of the total data processing budget.** Management and stockholders alike are learning that there is an information explosion and that information is expensive to maintain.

In 1978, 1980, 1984, and 1988, IBM and the GUIDE and SHARE user groups performed surveys of the DASD in a sampling of data centers. The results were surprising: the numbers changed each year, but they maintained similar proportions. The 1988 surveys estimate:

1. The "average" data center had over 200 gigabytes of DASD storage.

2. The "average" data center had over 50 MIPS of Processor Complex power.

3. The gigabyte per MIPS ratio has remained nearly constant at around 3.8 Gb/MIPS.

4. The average number of data sets was over 43,000 data sets.

5. The average number of DASD volumes was over 200 per data center.

6. **The average volume was only two-thirds allocated.**

If you have read this far into this book, you are certainly interested in DASD, so what does this have to do with your installation? NOTHING! Averages and rules of thumb are useful to you in a practical application only if you can take the information and use it successfully where you are. Let's try:

1. Total storage in gigabytes. What is the size of the online storage in your installation? What is the growth rate? What are your plans for the future? What data lies waiting in the wings? One of the worst times we faced was at a large government data center. We had a relatively stable, growing DASD farm. A large lawsuit became a reality, and it was dictated that we kept large volumes of the information in a data base, online. The amount of data stored on DASD doubled in two years! Surprise!

2. MIPS. What is your total capacity to process instructions? The fact that the "average" is growing at a certain rate is of no use to you and your loved ones. Plot your MIPS growth rate (probably a step chart) for the last several years.

3. Gb/MIPS ratio. What is the Gb/MIPS ratio? Since your MIPS rate jumps from one plateau to another, it may be interesting to see how it is at year end for your company.

4. Number of data sets. How many data sets do you have? What is the history of this growth?

5. Percent allocated. What percentage of the total capacity of your DASD volumes is allocated? Remember that this is only the tip of the iceberg. If someone allocates 10 cylinders for a

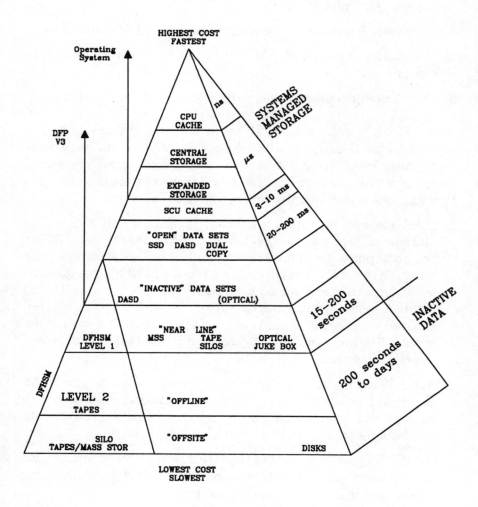

Figure 12.1 Storage Hierarchy. Data storage can be grouped into systems managed storage and inactive groups. The front face of this pyramid shows all the flavors of storage where your data may reside. The right face shows the approximate time to access the data. At the top is the highest cost and fastest data: inside the Processor Complex ready to be used. At the bottom is the lowest cost, yet slowest to access. Human and mechanical travel takes time.

data set and then only uses 1 track, there is a large volume of "free space" that appears as "used", meaning *allocated*, in the VTOC. VSAM files also have "free space" in the form of empty space in control intervals and control areas.

Armed with the above information, you can do some real cost justification of systems managed storage.

> ¤ One of the most common mistakes made in performing a storage management task is to underestimate the manpower needed to make it successful. The people on the task force are the ones who must make it work. The people must be experienced, or they will need time to become trained.

Take the number of gigabytes in your DASD subsystem. Multiply that by the percentage of unallocated storage. Multiply by the cost per gigabyte that you are experiencing. The number is the maximum savings you could achieve if you could fully allocate all DASD.

That is not possible. If you tried to reach 100% capacity in DASD (unlike MIPS), you would have so many production problems (abnormal terminations) that you would probably be run out of town on a rail. So what is a good number? Answer: somewhere between where you are now and the maximum.

12.3.2. DASD Pyramid

DASD storage is only one part of the story. In Figure 12.1 we see the hierarchy of data storage. The DASD pyramid is a three sided figure.

On the front face is the type of data storage. On the right face are typical access times for each data storage group. At the top of the pyramid is the fastest access, and at the bottom the slowest. On the left face are the parts of the operating system that control access to the data.

Active Data

Active data has been accessed sometime within a relevant period of time. For CPU cache, this might be within the last few nanoseconds; for slower devices, this might be within the last few days. Active data is managed by the operating system. A program can access data within an active data set by reading or writing to a block.

The term "accessed" usually refers to the OPEN macro issued to allow the operating system to take control and update the last-access date in the VTOC or system catalog. In most circumstances, simply allocating the data set (e.g., Job Control Statements) does not cause the last-accessed date to be updated. The following devices contain active data:

1. **CPU cache**. Each central processing unit (CPU) has a very fast buffer containing instructions and data that instructions act upon. Access to data cannot get any faster than this. (One exception is placing data in a CPU register and using register-to-register instructions, but that is splitting hairs.)

2. **Central storage**. Each Processor Complex contains many megabytes of storage that contain data read from and written to peripheral devices. Data in central storage is shared by all CPUs in the Processor Complex.

3. **Expanded storage**. Expanded storage in the Processor Complex is a slower storage medium than central storage. For Processor Complexes predating ES/9000, the I/O subsystem cannot access expanded storage. (By the time you are reading this, we may have I/O instructions for E-Storage.) Expanded storage is accessed by the *move page* instruction and is accessed in 4,096-byte units called "pages". Some data in cache, central storage, and expanded storage is never read from DASD nor any I/O device and may never be written. Program-originated data such as control blocks and work areas reside in these areas but are never stored in a data set.

4. **Storage control unit cache.** Outside the Processor Complex, data could exist in a storage control unit cache such as is found on the IBM 3990 model 3 or the 3880 model 23. Although the components that make up SCU cache typically have very short access times, access to this data from a task in the Processor Complex takes around 3 to 10 milliseconds.

5. **Peripheral devices.** The rest of the *open* data sets either reside on solid-state devices or DASD or are duplexed onto several DASD volumes using the 3990 dual copy feature. Open data sets have control blocks in virtual storage that describe the data's location and attributes.

Inactive Data

Some data is not currently available to programs and is called "inactive" because no control blocks are available to the operating system to reference the data. Catalogs may point to the data, but they would have to be accessed to find these data sets. Inactive data may not have been accessed for a period of time ranging from days to years. We can classify inactive data as follows:

1. **Inactive online data sets.** The data set could be on DASD but not available to any task running in the Processor Complex. These are also referred to as *closed* data sets. It may not been accessed for some period of time, say from seven to twenty days. The data is still on DASD, available for an OPEN to locate the data set and make it available. Most likely the data exists on spinning, magnetic DASD, but it could reside on an optical or mass storage DASD. An online data set is readily available to a task.

2. **Near line.** Some data has been compacted and moved to another DASD device, but is not in a form usable by the normal access methods. The data is said to be "near line", because the operating system can recover the data from

DASD by transforming it back to the original access method format before the application's OPEN macro ends. The data may be in DFHSM level 1 format, on a mass storage device tape silo, or on an optical juke box in which a mechanical contraption must move an optical platter into the optical actuator assembly. A near-line data set requires some kind of conversion processing or time-consuming mechanical movement before it is available to a task, but this requires just a few seconds to accomplish.

3. **Offline.** Some data has not been used for some longer period of time and has been moved to non-DASD storage, such as a tape reel or cartridge. The data can be restored to a format acceptable to the normal access method, but it requires a tape mount on a device. A person (tape operator) may or may not be required. If the device is located in one of the automatic tape cartridge subsystems, then a tape mount could occur without a real person handling the tape. Most backups are offline, but a data set's primary location may also be offline. Offline data can require minutes or hours before it can be accessed.

4. **Offsite.** Data at two extremes of importance are stored offsite. Data that is old or has just enough potential importance to save it from being scratched may be stored offsite where real estate is less expensive. Data that is important to the continued function of the enterprise must be stored offsite where a local disaster would not affect it. Offsite data access time can be affected by local traffic conditions.

The "site" in "offsite" means the location of the data relative to its usual storage location, not necessarily to that of the Processor Complex. Data stored in a DASD farm remote to the Processor Complex is "onsite", or online, with respect to the Processor Complex.

DFHSM Managed Data

One part of systems managed storage implementation is a near-line data manager. The IBM solution is DFHSM, shown as the bottom left corner of the storage pyramid. DFHSM maintains data on two levels:

1. **Level 1** keeps a copy of the data on near-line storage in a compressed format. The application program cannot access the data directly because it is in encoded format, but DFHSM can recall the data to online DASD quickly.

2. **Level 2** holds data on magnetic tape, which can be kept offline or migrated to offsite storage.

12.4. Pooling Considerations

Pooling data sets on DASD is a challenge because the tools are there for us to start today, but the techniques and experience are not. Pooling DASD is often a hit or miss situation. The literature mill is churning out theories, strategies, and vendor-inspired techniques.

Unfortunately for you and me, the data itself plays a large part in what must be decided at a specific data center. Data sets are a lot like people. There is one of every kind.[1]

There are a many ways to look at your data sets. Each has its benefits. Several are presented here to prompt your thoughts about data sets for which you are responsible.

---

[1] Thanks to Dr. Rich Olcott for his many articles and papers which force us to think of new ways to look at data. Dan Kaberon and H. Pat Artis have also been instrumental in our understanding of alternate DASD locations and SMS in particular.

Vertical Pools

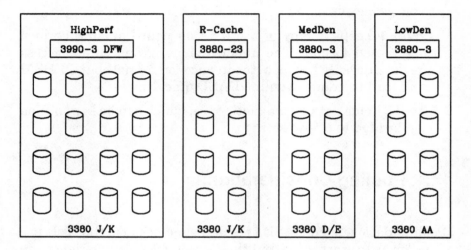

Figure 12.2 Vertical Pools. Actuators may be viewed vertically. High-performance volumes could be all the volumes attached to a 3990-3 cache control unit and accessed with DASD Fast Write.

> ¤ Remember, the first step in analysis of your data sets is to collect information about them. You may want to view your data sets from their access patterns, size, or other characteristics. You may have to view them from several viewpoints to understand how to approach systems managed storage.

12.4.1. Types of Pools

Figure 12.2 shows the first of two types of organization for your volumes. Vertical pooling implies that you dedicate strings of DASD to a specific use. In the figure, a pool is created that contains all the high-performance data sets. The pool is on 3380 devices behind a 3990 model 3 cache control unit with DASD Fast Write.

Figure 12.3 shows a different type of organization. Each type or work or business unit has a need for quick-response volumes (again on the cache control unit) and for other, slower volumes.

12.4.2. Pooled Data Sets: Access Patterns

The unit of measurement and manipulation for SMS is the data set. We are concerned with the life cycle of the data set from the time it is created until it is scratched, never to return. Some of us in the space management business think the latter never happens. We are certain that data sets get created, but that nobody scratches them!

An SMS pool is a collection of data sets grouped together on DASD because some software subsystem told the allocation manager to place them on the same DASD volume or group of DASD volumes. Does the access behavior of the data give us a way to group data?

Always Active

The first access behavior pattern pool contains the data sets that are always active. Either online systems have them allocated or some batch job is backing up or reorganizing the data set.

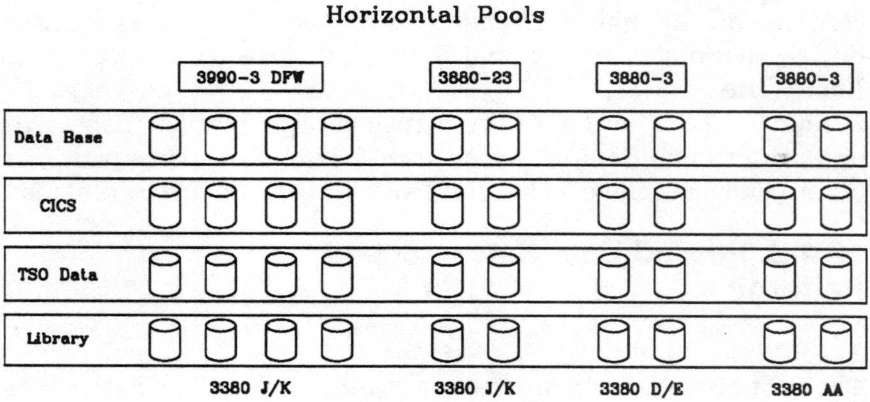

Horizontal Pools

Figure 12.3 Horizontal Pools. Actuators may be viewed horizontally. Data base volumes may be on the 3990-3 cache controller or on regular 3380 DASD attached to the older 3880-3 control units.

It is clear that online DASD must be available to contain these data sets. In some cases the data will be so active that it must be isolated for performance reasons. In some cases the data will be part of a large data base that experiences random access patterns, possibly over its entire contents.

A "data base" is a collection of data related by logic and not by its appearance within a single data set. It is obvious, then, that the contents of a data base are stored in more than one data set. Does your storage management system know this? Have you ever restored one part of a data base and found, later, that the data base was no longer self-consistent? Your idea of a unit of data and the storage manager's may not be the same.

Single Shot

These data sets are similar to a backup data set. They are created to be used "when something goes wrong." Often they are generation data group (GDG) data sets. These usually should be archived immediately if possible.

A second type of single-shot data set is one that is created as an intermediate place to hold data. It is read back in, and the data is moved to another data set, probably in a different format.

It is not so clear how to handle these data sets. Maybe they should be pooled together, with the slate periodically wiped clean. Keep in mind that many end users are unaware of DASD management issues, particularly those users unfamiliar with your site or even with IBM operating systems in general. In despair and ignorance, they may request (or allow default) allocation of important data to the most generic storage pool.

It is tempting to "punish" ignorance, but in the end something is wasted: time and money at the least. (Some might say that is enough!) Some end users cannot become educated because of their own capabilities or simply because of their work circumstances. When designing your storage management practices, you should consider human issues in addition to purely technical ones. You may want to move all these data sets to near-line or offline storage, for example, discarding the data after a time.

There is a subtle and related concern for single-shot data sets. Making single-shot data sets easy to allocate, use, and deallocate encourages experimentation by the end user. People who experiment with the system can make more sophisticated, reliable, and effective use of it. This has unquantifiable but certain benefits for your data center and your enterprise.

Temporal

Temporal data sets are created to be used within a fixed time after which they become useless. In some cases, they may be used several times over the next day or two, for example a DASD copy of a report. Some are re-read every week or month. One example is a weekly data set that is gathered for some month-to-date reporting scheme. If the SMS routine tries to archive this type of data set each seven days, and it is accessed on the seventh day, the operator can be saved a trip to the tape library.

The data set may be accessed in a chaotic manner. A data set could be created for each of a large population of customers. Only if a user asked for information about a particular customer would that data set be accessed. You should be wary of chaotic accesses. You may not know the pattern, but there could be a correlation that predicts the accesses.

This is where coordination of DASD management and production design and control pays off. As the DASD manager, you can either keep yourself educated about production applications and their cycles or ensure that production management staff is educated about your storage management practices.

For example, it is possible that production control has the wherewithal to supply you periodically with a list of customers against whom DASD activity is unlikely, perhaps because their credit is no longer good. The data sets associated with these customers could be moved from online to near-line storage with a positive impact on access times for the remaining customers.

The educational process can go the other way, too. Having noticed chaotic accesses among a large number of data sets, you could approach production control personnel and initiate changes to the application that would make its use of DASD more efficient. You may be greeted with a "no time, no money" defense, but successes cannot be had before opportunities are created.

12.4.3. Pooled Data Sets: Size

Another way to look at data sets is to group them by size for pooling guidance.

Why Size Is Important

Size is important for pooling, because each DASD volume is a fixed-size bag. We cannot put more into the bag than it can hold. What's worse, data sets are limited by a fixed number of extents (e.g., 16 extents for non-VSAM data sets on a single volume).

Fragmentation problems occur quickly when you mix large and small data sets on the same volume. For example, on a single capacity volume with 885 cylinders, a single 500-cylinder data set could be allocated comfortably if the volume were empty or nearly so. If hundreds of 10-track data sets were allocated and scratched without defragmentation, the 500-cylinder data set allocation could easily fail, even if 500 cylinders' worth of data is free (spread over more than 500 cylinders) on the volume.

Another fragmentation problem occurs when a data set is expanded by the application as it adds data. In many cases the larger the data set, the more likely the amount of data added will be a large volume. For example, with our 10-track data sets above, if they double in size (the end user missed by 100% in the primary allocation), the total size will be 20 tracks, but the secondary extent could be allocated on a previously free cylinder. The 500-cylinder data set may not be extensible in cylinder units for lack of completely free cylinders.

12.4.4. Pooled Data Sets: Access Speed

Some data must be accessible in the minimum amount of time and so must be placed on cached DASD volumes or solid-state devices. The opposite is true for non-DASD online storage. There may be a group of data sets that are never needed quickly. These could be routed to mass storage, tape silos, or optical devices.

12.4.5. Pooled Data Sets: Data Set Organization

Another way to look at pooling DASD is to consider the data set organization as a divider. Partitioned data sets are clearly program or source libraries and usually have their members accessed, not the whole library at one time. (OK, we know about backups and reorganizations!) The access patterns are relatively predictable. For a read, the directory is read to find the member, and then the member is read. For a write, the new member is written to the free space and then the directory is updated. Either the old entry is updated with the new location of the module or a new entry is created.

Sequential organization also has a predictable pattern: read the data set until the end is reached or some stopping point is found. Unlike with other data sets, the entire data set is likely to be accessed, once started.

VSAM, ISAM, BDAM, and other *data base-like* data sets probably have a random access pattern. That is, after all, why the data set organization was chosen. VSAM has several flavors of sequential access possibilities, such as entry sequenced (ESDS), relative record (RRDS), and linear (LDS), and they are becoming more popular.

12.4.6. Data Set Naming Conventions

The primary piece of data supplied to the SMS routines is the data set name. Remember that the shortest JCL statement contains the DSNAME and DISP parameters.

This will be your most challenging part of systems managed storage implementation.[2] What are your data set naming conventions? If you do not have any now, you will have them. If you

---

2 Of all the challenges we face, data set naming seems always to pop up as top priority. Thanks to Bob Rogers of the IBM Systems Center for his several presentations that help us focus on what the considerations are in this complex topic.

do have them, you will be changing them. The data set group most likely to be pooled first is temporary data sets. Why do you suppose this is so? Temporary data sets have have the most stringent data set naming conventions: you have no choice when the IBM operating system decides the name for you!

In the SMS environment the name may have to provide all of the "5 Ws": *who* owns it, *where* did it come from, *what* is it, *when* will it go away, *why* does it exist (e.g., what response time, locality of reference is expected)?

> ▫ We recommend that you provide for information about the owner of the data set and the type of use expected for the data set as part of the name. The owner of the data set is a complex decision. Some data sets should be owned by a person (e.g., memos, utility jobs, etc.) and some should be owned by the department (e.g., source and production JCL libraries). The type of use should be "quick access index" or "audit trail file" and not "put it on a device behind cache".

What Is a Data Set Name?

The above is a lot to ask of a data set name. For starters, the data set name has a different meaning in different platforms. As we grow, the name may be transported across networks. Several of the international standards organizations are struggling with this question. Among them are the International Organization for Standardization (ISO) and the American National Standards Institute (ANSI).

In MVS, the data set name can be a maximum of 44 characters consisting of eight-character chunks, or qualifiers, separated by periods. The name must begin with an alphabetic letter (A through Z) or one of the *National Standard Characters* ($, @, or #). The rest of the name can be alphanumeric (A-Z, 0-9, or National).

In VM, the name can be up to 168 characters. The name may incorporate references to a directory, a subdirectory, a file pool ID, a file name, and a file type. All characters can be National or alphanumeric.

The personal computer environment under DOS limits the name to 12 characters—eight for a name, a period, and a three-character "extension", or type—but device and subdirectory may appear using punctuation such as the colon and backslash, forming a "path name" of up to 63 characters. Alphanumeric and a wide range of special characters can be used for the name.

The personal computer environment under OS2 and the AIX environment allow any 254 characters including blanks, and some non-IBM operating systems such as Unix allow file specifications of up to 1,024 characters, each of which may be any of 255 characters! For networks of heterogenous systems, the location of the data set is often encoded in the "file name", as is (indirectly) the owner of the data.

Does anyone out there wonder why we are having trouble interconnecting these environments? The bright side of this is that IBM operating systems have traditionally imposed the most stringent restrictions on data set names, so most non-IBM systems sporting IBM connectivity have facilities to translate their names into forms suitable to IBM. This is handled, however, on an implementation-by-implementation basis and not through standard practices.

Who Is the Data Set Owner?

Another question you may want to have answered is: Who owns the data set? Typically data centers will encode the identity of the owner in the data set name. For example, if a data set belongs to the accounts receivable department, then the high-level (first) qualifier may begin with "AR" or some other notation. Another common practice is to have all privately owned data sets begin with a universal constant character, followed by an account number identifying the individual or work group.

With personal TSO data sets, it is convenient to have the high-level qualifier be the user ID of the person creating the data set. (The Interactive System Producivity Facility, ISPF, assumes this to be the case.) The problem with that is that TSO user IDs are created in strange ways. Some of us create department IDs such as SYS056. Who is SYS056 anyway? You need a chart or file to cross-reference. What if the person who is SYS056 goes to the payroll department? Do you rename all the files PAY056? What if there already is a PAY056? Some create IDs with the person's name. What if MSMITH gets married and now is MJONES?

The problem here is that people have personal data sets and they have department data sets. Before SMS, we could just weed them out as necessary. Now we are trying to automate the process of device allocation and manage the data based on rules and the data set name. Is this getting complicated yet? Are we having fun yet?

You may also have the security system designate the owner. For example, the RACF DSOWNER parameter can control which RACF resource is the owner of the data set.

Where Is the Data Set?

Some part of the name may specify where the data set exists. Part of the company could be moved or sold to another company. What happens when the workload shifts to another resource provider within the company?

Another aspect of *where* is: Where is the data set going? Some of us add a part to the name to indicate offsite storage.

What Is the Data Set?

The next consideration for a data set naming convention is to carry an indication of the file's contents. Some of these conventions are imposed in the PC, MVS, and VM worlds because the programs that usually read or write the data set add or assume "default" suffixes on their own. One example of that in the mainframe world was VSAM KSDS names. Most of us ended the name of the data portion of the file with ".DATA" and ended the name of the index portion of the file with ".INDEX". Eventually, IBM changed the software to do this for us automatically. Your data set naming conventions must accommodate such impositions.

You may want to have the relative importance of the data specified. Many of us use a "P" for production and "T" for test data sets. We may use other characters to indicate whether the data set contains the real data or a backup copy.

You may want to indicate the cycle in which the data will be used: daily, weekly, monthly, quarterly, or annually, for example. That would certainly help the automatic subroutines decide what to do with the data set at archive decision time. If a weekly data set is created on Saturday, and the routine is running on Sunday, then it would be a pretty good bet to archive it, lacking other input that it will be used again, if at all. Conversely, it would not pay to archive a weekly data set created last Saturday if the routine runs on the following Friday.

Avoid trying to encode characteristics that may change. (We know that almost all of the attributes may change!) The classic example is the tape or disk designation. For years we specified "D" for disk and "T" for tape, only to discover to our horror that we had to change a lot of JCL to move the data from one medium to another.

Another seemingly reasonable characteristic to encode is the service-level specification. The second- or third-level qualifier could contain "cache" to ensure that the data set is cached. Soon, however, almost all of the data set names will contain this special code!

Conclusions

We have asked a lot of questions in this part. Unfortunately, this is the most important part of SMS. After the planning and structure is complete, implementing SMS is almost an anticlimax.

One important piece of advice that can span all installations is to keep the high-level qualifier of the name unique across all your systems. Remember that your data center (and its data sets) may be combined with another data center. (Alas, corporate acquisitions are a fact of life these days.) At the very least, you may be asked to *share* data with another center, and making your names unique in the universe only helps to ease this process.

12.5. Summary

Systems managed storage is the term used to describe the automation of data set management. If DASD is the primary repository for data, then the operating system components that affect DASD are affected by SMS.

Allocation of a data set is the primary area for control. It is the place where DF/Storage Management Subsystem gets control to apply the rules defined by the data center.

After the data set is allocated, it may be active for some period of time. Applications can read from or write to the data set at this time because it is on online DASD. At some point, the data set becomes inactive and may have to be migrated to near-line or offline storage to allow reuse of valuable DASD space.

Data set backup and recovery routines are needed to ensure continuity of the data in case something happens to the physical media. It is particularly important to maintain the integrity, or self-consistency, of logical sets of data that span the actual data sets managed by SMS.

The storage hierarchy can be described by a pyramid showing the parts of the operating system and program product extensions that control data. If the data is active, it may be in the Processor Complex as CPU cache, central storage, or expanded storage. The data may be in storage control unit cache or online in peripheral devices. If the data is inactive, it may be in online devices or it may be in one of the several near-line or offline media.

Pooling considerations are as varied and depend on the data being described. Some methods of looking at your data are:
- Access patterns of the data.
- Size of the data set.
- Speed of access requirements for the data.
- Data set organization.

Data set naming conventions are an important part of the SMS environment. Data set names vary widely from platform to platform, yet in an SMS environment the data set name is the key to management. Even within the IBM platforms, the number of characters, levels, and valid characters vary crazily.

It is important to know who owns the data sets you manage. You would not want to scratch the president's data sets!

Where the data set is and what is in the data set are important pieces of information you will need to know in order to make intelligent, automatic decisions about the data set.

12.6. Questions

1. Explain the concept of *pooling*.

2. What are the major parts of the life cycle of data?

3. Which part of the IBM architecture controls the *active* data? What are the different places an active data block could exist? Are there differences in the time it takes to access the data? If so, what causes these differences?

4. What part of the IBM architecture controls *inactive* data? Explain the response time differences for inactive data. Give examples of the type of data that would be contained in each inactive data area.

5. What is the significance of the DASD data set name in a systems managed storage environment? What do you do if you have a well-entrenched data set naming convention?

6. When do the DFSMS routines get control in an MVS environment?

7. Why would you archive data sets to near-line or offline media?

13

IBM DFSMS (IGDZILLA)

13.1. Definition of DF/Storage Management Subsystem

Systems managed storage is a generic term for the automation of allocation and control of data sets on DASD. On February 15, 1988, IBM announced Enterprise System Architecture/370 (ESA/370) as an extension to the 370-Extended Architecture. Part of that announcement was MVS/Data Facility Product (MVS/DFP) Version 3, which implements systems managed storage.

DFSMS is the IBM implementation of SMS. Although this chapter concentrates on the MVS operating system, the authors believe that IBM is committed to DFSMS, and that the MVS, VM, and VSE implementations will become one. The DFSMS/VM subsystem has already been announced. It varies substantially from the MVS implementation because VM allocations are still possible in minidisk units. DFSMS/VM supports only Shared File System (SFS) allocation because that is the only way VM can support allocation in DASD pools.

Why would IBM be committed to implementing a single data management subsystem? The answer is simple. IBM wants to sell hardware and software. They want to protect their investment in operating system development. One way to do that is to replace the data management subsystems in all the operating systems. The replacement can be *Object Code Only (OCO)*. We leave out the TPF and Unix environments for the foreseeable future; they are just too different. With these exceptions, we will have one world of DASD data!

As usual, IBM creates new terminology to describe the DFSMS environment. The noun *constructs* describes the logical specifications and rules for four groups of routines required for systems managed storage. These groups of routines are named *Data Class, Storage Class, Management Class,* and *Storage Group.* DFSMS will evolve, but we expect these constructs to remain the same. They can be thought of as the external specifications for data as contrasted with the internal specifications for how the data is represented and organized. We will look at these constructs in the next chapter, but first you need to be up to speed with the relevant terminology and the historical progression that spawned it.

Two stages of development occurred for DFSMS. In the first, IBM created vehicles through which DFSMS would be used and supplied partial SMS functions. In the second, IBM built new storage management functions into the infrastructure created in the first stage.

13.1.1. Stage I: Simplify Interfaces

Before DFSMS was announced, a number of program improvements were delivered to the MVS operating system. In some cases, the new function was included as part of a new release of software at no extra charge. In other cases, IBM charged additional fees for a group of programs.

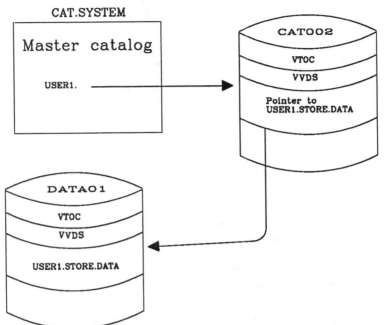

Figure 13.1 Non-SMS: Single-level Alias. With pre-DFP Version 3 (non-SMS) levels of MVS, only a single level of a data set could be referenced by an ICF catalog.

Interactive Storage Management Facility (ISMF)

ISMF is supposed to be a user-friendly interface to SMS functions provided for DFSMS. It runs as a dialogue under the
TSO/ISPF subsystem and combines, but separates, the data administrator functions and the end user functions. Here is where
DFSMS claims a reduction in personnel time to perform data
management tasks. With an automated, interactive methodology, fewer hours are required to accomplish the desired level of
management, and it is easier to train personnel to handle the
task.

ISMF was introduced with MVS/XA as a data set management
aid. Before MVS Data Facility Product (MVS/DFP) Version 3, it
provided primitive storage management functions. The an-

nouncement of MVS/DFP Version 3 in February 1988 added new capabilities to ISMF. Applications for the definition, alternation, deletion, and listing of data classes, storage classes, management classes, and storage groups were added to ISMF. Users could display data sets or move data sets in a user-friendly manner.

ICF Catalog Recovery Enhancements

The Integrated Catalog Facility (ICF) was introduced with MVS and is a significant improvement over previous catalog structures. To be managed by the IBM DFSMS environment, all data sets except temporary data sets must be cataloged. The catalog must be the ICF catalog and not one of the older VSAM catalogs or CVOL environments. Some data centers are still using those old architectures. The time to change is well before you start systems managed storage.

The catalog contains all information about the data set, including the constructs associated with the data set. Said another way, the catalog changes. One of the "war stories" about DFP 3's early implementation was that if you brought up a test version of the system, it **contaminated every catalog it accessed.** The result was that a test time slot left the entire production system in an unusable state. Program Temporary Fixes (PTFs), of course, fixed the problem then. *What about the next time your data center is installing a new version of DFP?* Shouldn't you anticipate the possibility that this problem could recur by running the new system, accessing only a test catalog, and then bringing up your production system to ensure that the old and new work together? This is a "must" for anyone out there who is going to upgrade a very old copy of MVS to a current version.

Another thing that must be eliminated before SMS implementation is JOBCATs and STEPCATs. The MVS operating system has long allowed the end user to specify another path to *find* a data set. This was never a great idea and was implemented only because the catalog structure did not allow the flexibility needed to generate itself with more than a single level

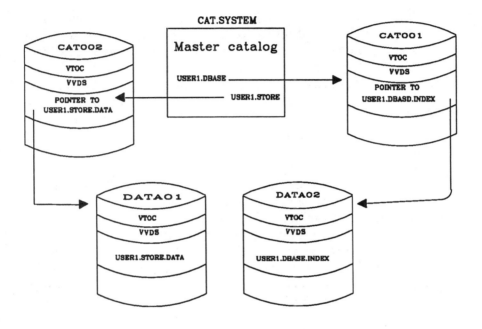

Figure 13.2 SMS: Multilevel Alias. With DFP Version 3 and later, multiple alias levels are supported. In this case, the files of a user are in multiple catalogs.

of catalog access. Find and remove all JOBCATs and STEPCATs.

One important catalog enhancement is **multilevel aliasing**. Aliasing is the MVS catalog standard that allows the systems administrator to place a pointer (alias) in one catalog that references another catalog. In subsystems prior to DPF 3, only a single level of the data set name could be used for this pointer.

In Figure 13.1, you see a master catalog, *CAT.SYSTEM*, directing all references for data sets with a high-level qualifier of *USER1* to a user catalog on volume *CAT002*. In that catalog, the entry for data set *USER1.STORE.DATA* references volume *DATA01*. The operating system supports single-level alias pointers.

With DFP Version 3 and later, the data center can have multi-level alias pointers. In Figure 13.2, you see a master catalog, but in this case, there are two pointers for the high-level qualifier, *USER1*. The first one directs all references to data sets beginning with *USER1.DBASE* to the catalog on volume *CAT001*. The user catalog on that volume has a pointer to the *USER1.DBASE.INDEX* on *DATA02*. The second alias in the master catalog is for data sets that begin with *USER1.STORE*. It directs references to these to the catalog on volume CAT002.

Another improvement in ICF catalog processing for system data sets (e.g., SYS1) and generation data groups (GDGs) allows the use of universal characters in addition to alphabetic and national characters in the alias name. By specifying *SYS**, for example, the data center can alias SYS1 data sets.

Generation data groups (GDGs) are a special type of data set. All of the levels of the data set name except the last are in the catalog. The last level is of the form "G*nnnn*V*mm*", where *nnnn* is the generation number, and *mm* is the version of that generation.

GDGs on DFSMS volumes can, of course, be cataloged only in an ICF catalog. **There is another big difference.** Before DFSMS GDG processing, the full name was not cataloged until the job ended. Jobstreams referred to *GDGs in the making* by appending a *(+1)* to the end of the highest-level qualifiers. The DFP software kept the fact that a generation was being built in the GDG's sphere record.

With DFSMS GDG processing, the fully qualified name is cataloged when it is created. There are two phases in the life of a GDG being created. When the job that is creating a GDG terminates, the fully qualified name will be *rolled into* the sphere record. The fully qualified name is deleted. If the GDG limit is reached, the oldest one will be *rolled out* as a fully qualified name.

One of the benefits of ICF catalogs over the older VSAM catalogs was the use of the sphere record to reduce the number of records created and scratched in the catalog. The ebb and flow of records often caused the catalog to experience control interval splits and caused degradation in catalog access. You should watch your catalogs if you implement DFSMS.

If all of this gets you confused, as you know will eventually happen to the operating system, you will be happy to know that IDCAMS has a new *ROLLIN* function. You can use the ROLLIN function to manually roll in the data set if it ever seems stuck. Another good thing about this update to the GDG processing is that the old pattern DSCB is not supported for GDGs in DFSMS. The Data Class takes the place of a pattern DSCB. Now what will we do with all of those empty, funny data sets we have spread over our DASD volumes? [1]

Disaster Backup Support

Data Facility Hierarchical Storage Manager (DFHSM) has long been the IBM inactive data mover. Originally DFHSM used its own routines to make copies of data sets for backup or archive.

DFHSM was changed to call Data Facility Data Set Services (DFDSS) directly for data movement. The reason probably was that DFDSS supported physical (track for track) and logical (by data set) movement of data sets. Why reinvent the wheel?

DFHSM and DFDSS can provide two tapes for backups. The first one, to be kept on-site, is used to restore data sets as needed. The second set is a duplicate, backup, copy of the data intended to be sent to an off-site location in case a local disaster occurs *in the building that houses the computer center*, or more precisely, when remote DASD exists, in the building that houses the DASD.

---

1   For those of you just joining us, you may want to look up GDGs in an old JCL book. The rules were that you must code the name of a *pattern DSCB* or the name of a data set with the default characteristics of a new GDG data set. Most of us set up a few empty, cataloged, data sets with no attributes (no use setting defaults no one wanted!).

Erase on Scratch

Another improvement to data management was the addition of *erase on scratch*. Some data is so sensitive that just erasing the VTOC pointer to the data is not enough. The track must be overwritten to destroy the records that were contained in the data set. Examples are payroll records, password files, and client information.

The problem this tries to overcome is the potential breach of security inherent in the DASD tracks of scratched files. Access security is normally supported by marking the VTOC entry for a file and having a subsystem such as RACF intercept OPEN attempts for the file. If any program or user tries to access the file, RACF is queried and the access is allowed if the requestor has proper authority. When a file is scratched, the VTOC entry is removed. In fact, if another file is allocated in the same location on that DASD, then *any program that can access the new file can access the old data.*

This situation has occurred, and not just on MVS. We have seen sensitive data displayed because sensitive files were not "erased" but "scratched". (This applies equally to our PC fixed disks. It may be preferable to eat a dead disk than to send it away for replacement or reconditioning, depending on what was stored there.)

Erase on scratch should be controlled. It is expensive, because it takes time to overwrite data. For example, if the sensitive file were 100 cylinders of a 3380, and the file were scratched (probably as normal daily maintenance reorganized the file), then 100 cylinders of empty, dummy records would be transferred to DASD. The erase operation would then take *at least 25 seconds* of elapsed time and maybe as long as 50 seconds!

Should DASD used for one-shot data sets be erase on scratch? Is sensitive data stored there during normal processing? Perhaps care should be taken in allocation of temporary data sets when sensitive data is processed.

□   Sensitive data can lose the protection of security systems
    when its data set is deleted. Erase on scratch avoids this
    breach but is an expensive operation, and its use should
    be carefully controlled. Consider also temporary data sets
    containing sensitive data in your analysis and proce-
    dures.

13.1.2. Stage II: DF/Storage Management Subsystem

DF/Storage Management Subsystem
DFSMS spans two areas of the operating system: the Logical
Data Manager (LDM) and the External Data Manager (EDM).
In fact, this incorporates the same functions that have been
around since PCP days but with a new name. The LDM is really
the access methods, and the EDM is the operating system routines (e.g., EXCP, EXCPVR, and STARTIO routines) that support them. These were called the logical and physical data management routines before they assumed new marketing significance.

These names came from the DOS/360 Logical I/O Control
Supervisor (LIOCS) and the Physical I/O Control Supervisor
(PIOCS). MVS is steeped in heritage, and components of other,
older operating systems seem never to die.

Logical Data Manager (LDM)

The LDM routines are concerned with the attributes of the data
set, the management of records, and the access security of the
data set. None of this is seen by the COBOL or assembler routines that open data sets and read or write them. The goal is to
be compatible at the access method level. Remember that there
are millions and maybe billions of preexisting data sets and
programs that open, write, and read data. Upward compatibility
must be maintained to keep them from becoming a maintenance
nightmare.

External Data Manager (EDM)

The External Data Manager is the owner of the physical DASD. The EDM is concerned with things such as the space for a data set, the performance of the I/Os to the DASD, the availability of the DASD, and device installation.

Object Access Method (OAM)

One of the newly introduced concepts which begins life without much to do is the Object Access Method. Until now we have processed bytes of data which were characters or numeric values or something that can be represented by a byte. The world really has other objects. OAM is designed to process these.

One of these *other* types of data is images captured for storage. One example would be a photograph of someone or something or a digitized representation of a paper document. Today, we store the image as a large file of bytes that describe each pixel or picture element (dot) on the image. Future data storage will require many more of these types of graphic objects. OAM is the designated access method for them.

13.2. Non-DFP Components

Figure 13.3 shows the outboard utilities, or "Independent Vendor Utilities", that handle the four functions of SMS that are not part of the operating system. These are the inactive data mover, the active data mover, the sort function, and the security subsystem. In the early 1990s IBM came to grips with the realization that some independent vendors had wonderful software. Also, if they were to convert the entire IBM community to SMS, they would at least have to carry on these vendors, and maybe get some help from them.

The best news is that IBM announced an open system architecture for DFSMS. The goal is to make it easier for data centers

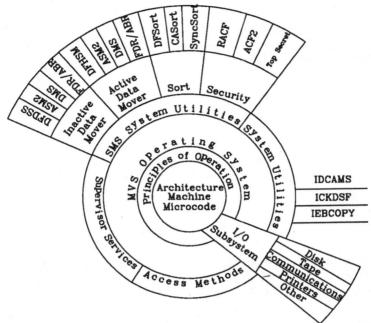

Figure 13.3 SMS Outboard Utilities. Four groups of utilities support DF/Storage Management Subsystem management of data.

to take advantage of new technology in both hardware and software. This is not a ploy to sell more hardware and software as such. IBM and the rest of us are in a bind. We have end users out there building data faster than we can react!

13.2.1. Active and Inactive Data Movers

Almost all of the active data movers also operate as inactive data movers. It just makes sense: if a subsystem is going to move data sets around the DASD farm, then it probably has the capability to scratch unused data sets and to migrate data sets to near-line or offline storage.

The following are a few of the active and inactive data movers on the market today. They are primarily oriented to MVS, but the functions are also needed for VM, Unix, and other platforms (or operating systems). The list is not complete, nor is it intended to be. If you are reading this, there are two possibilities.

First, you are in a data center that has one of these or an equivalent from a competitor. If so, you should concentrate on the documentation for your product. Do not forget the user groups. Your vendor will not tell you all the tips and techniques you will need to know to survive.

Second, if you are going to select a data mover as a new or replacement subsystem, make a list of your requirements, then make a search of the available products for your operating system environment. See how the products honor your requirements.

Again, do not forget the user groups. Ask your prospective vendors for a list of clients with whom you can discuss the products under consideration. Spend some time with the people on the list. We have even made trips to customer data centers to get an in-depth look at how they performed their data management.

To help you construct your list of requirements, let's look at the functions a data mover might be asked to do.

1. Backup:
   a. Full volume backup: make a full copy of the volume on magnetic tape.
   b. Incremental backup: backup only data sets changed or created since the last backup.

2. Restore and recovery:
   a. Restore a data set or a whole volume.
   b. Recover a group of data sets and one or more volumes.

3. Archive: make a copy of the data set on tape and then scratch the DASD copy.

4. Compression and space release: the subsystem may be asked to compress partitioned data sets or reorganize VSAM data

sets as it restores the data set. It may also be asked to free allocated but not used space at restore time. The advantage is that unused space is recovered. The disadvantage is that an application may expect the unused space to be there at some future time. By freeing unused space, you risk the application's failing at some future time because space is not available. If the program can reblock on restore, the size will also be affected.

There is an interesting twist to incremental backups. If you have never done them, you may be in for a surprise if you attempt to restore a volume from a baseline full backup and its associated incremental backups. You may find that the restore operation fails for lack of space on the volume! How can this be?

Suppose you have a full backup and three incrementals to restore. A user created a large data set before the first incremental was taken, then deleted the data set afterwards. A user created another large data set that spans the second incremental, and so on. If the utility responsible for managing incremental backups does not keep track of which data sets were deleted in addition to which were created or modified, you will have trouble. Precious few backup utilities in the entire computer industry do this; an exception is that available with the Berkeley flavor of Unix.

We will not be able to take full advantage of incremental backups until the utilities do the job properly. That will only arise from pressure from you, the customer. It is no wonder that many data centers rely exclusively on full backups, but how much of your operations schedule is occupied with these, and how does it affect availability of data to your end users?

Now let's take a brief look at some of the players.

IBM: DFDSS/DFHSM

The IBM solution is two program products. Data Facility Data Set Services (DFDSS) is the data mover. It is the *high-speed* data mover which copies data from DASD to magnetic tape (or other

DASD) in either logical or physical format. Data Facility Hierarchical Storage Manager (DFHSM) is the backup, archive, and recovery subsystem. DFHSM maintains a catalog of data sets and their location on offline storage volumes. This feature is called Aggregate Backup and Recovery Support (ABARS).

One of the benefits of DFHSM is a feature called *Small Data Set Packing*. Remember that the smallest unit of space that you can allocate on DASD is one track. If you only have a few bytes of data in your data set, you will use over 47,000 bytes on a 3380 or 3390 volume. DFHSM combines multiple small data sets into track-length compressed data sets. The savings can be very large for data center with many small data sets.

CAI: ASM2

Computer Associates International sells a subsystem for backup, archive, and recovery and calls it Auxiliary Storage Manager 2 (ASM2). We have wondered what happened to ASM1. All of the functions listed above for DFDSS are available with ASM2.

Sterling: DMS/OS

The Sterling Software product *DMS/OS* is a data storage management system that contains all of the needed functions for Storage Management Subsystem.

DMS/OS has a very useful feature called *Sequential Migration to Tape*. Most archival routines make a copy on tape that may be in the original format or in a compressed or encoded format. In either case, no application program can access the data directly from the tape because the catalog is pointing to a virtual volume. If an application tries to access the data, the archival program must recall the data to online DASD.

In the case of DMS/OS, you can ask that a sequential data set be moved to magnetic tape and the catalog changed to reference the magnetic tape. Any subsequent accesses by an application would go directly to magnetic tape. With this feature, you could implement a policy that says something like "All data sets over 10 megabytes will be on magnetic tape". The disadvantage is that you will be using one whole magnetic tape for a data set that probably is only a small part of the tape. The advantage is that you do not have these very large data sets clogging up your online DASD volumes.

Innovation Data: FDR

Innovation Data's Fast Dump Restore, COMPAKTOR, and FDR/ABR also have all the needed Storage Management Subsystem functions.

Problem Areas

Remember that all of these subsystems were around for years before DFSMS (FDR since 1974). Most of them have been around since before VSAM Integrated Catalog Facility (ICF) catalogs were implemented by IBM. These are the problem areas for third party data movers.

The first problem encountered by most DASD managers is the empty VSAM data set. For some reason, almost all of the data movers have or have had trouble deciding what to do with empty VSAM data sets. It seems perfectly obvious to the most casual observer that data movers should treat them just like VSAM data sets containing data, but they don't. Some data movers just leave them on the DASD.

A similar problem is the multivolume VSAM data set. The data mover is usually concentrating on a single volume. For example, in Figure 13.4 the data mover is backing up volume *USER01* and comes across a VSAM data set *A.VSAM.DATA*. The first half of its records are on volume *USER01*, and the second half are on *USER02*. *USER02* may be further down the string or even on another string of DASD. If the data mover stops and goes to retrieve the second part of the data set, what happens when

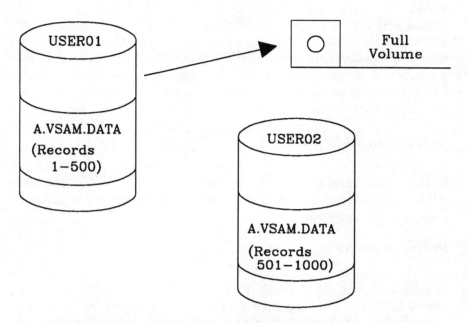

Figure 13.4 Multiple-Volume Data Sets. One of the problems data mover subsystems get into is what to do with the multiple-volume data set. In this example, the subsystem is backing up volume USER01. One of the data sets, *A.VSAM.DATA,* has part of the data set on this volume and part of the data set on volume USER02. Should the data mover stop and jump over to volume USER02? What if the data mover is asked to restore volume USER01? Should it also restore part of volume USER02? What if the two parts have different last-used dates? Complex, isn't it?

the data mover is asked to back up (or restore) volume *USER02*? Should it go back to volume *USER01* to make a second backup? Should it ignore it?

Most data movers backup the data set but refuse to archive the data set because the process seems too complex. Many data movers refuse to archive the data set even if the data set is only on one volume *but has candidate volumes to which it could expand!*

Another problem area is data sets that do not have the proper data set attributes assigned in the VTOC. This is not supposed to happen, but over the course of months and years, system outages and other abnormal things leave data sets without block sizes, logical record sizes, or data set organization. Again, it seems obvious to us that the data mover should just copy the name to the archived tape with whatever attributes were in the VTOC. If necessary, the tracks could be moved to tape. We have never seen a single instance, however, where these data sets are anything more than space holders that waste DASD.

13.2.2. Sort

The sort component is the high-speed *data arranger.* Again, there are a number of these on the market. IBM's entry is DFSORT; Computer Associates markets CA-SORT; Syncsort markets SYNCSORT. If you are in a data center, you may have more than one of these. They tend to be acquired as part of a package or merger. Each has its own attributes.

The sort function as a part of SMS is the weakest link. Sort, after all, is just another application program. You or I could write one, but it would not be nearly as efficient as the ones on the market with their decades of experience in sorting algorithms. It would also be very much more expensive for us to write our own sort.

So why is sort one of the four non-DFP components? The answer is that the the sort function uses a lot of DASD for intermediate work space. It makes sense that one of the biggest players would be invited to the party. Until now, the sort just asked to write and read blocks of data. But with SMS, the sort can ask to use new Processor Complex instructions to sort the data in central and expanded storage, and the sort can tell the DASD subsystem to use cache fast write for its I/O operations.

If possible, benchmark the different products. Beware: the sorts leapfrog each other in performance claims and results. Also be wary of the vendors' benchmark results. One benchmark some years ago reported comparison of before and after improvements without disclosing that many megabytes of expanded storage were added for the *after* jobstream that were not available for the *before* jobstream. You may be better off selecting one product and sticking with it, allowing market competition to yield your performance improvements. The authors have been very successful using the SYNCSORT product.

13.2.3. Security Subsystems

A whole book could be written about security subsystems. In the old days, RACF was so slow that the non-IBM competitors, Computer Associates International's Top Secret and ACF2, were always a better choice. RACF today, using generic profiles, gives the other subsystems a real run for their money now, however.

The best method to use (for software to snowshoes), if you are selecting one is to make a list of your requirements and match the requirements to the security subsystem. As with sort subsystems, you should choose one and stick with the vendor. Moving from one to another is a nontrivial task.

13.3. DFSMS Requirements and Considerations

The first implementation of DFSMS required an MVS/ESA environment. IBM explained that DFP Version 3 required the use of the data spaces and hiperspaces available with ESA but not XA. We do not know whether IBM intended to bring the implementation back to the MVS/XA environment from the beginning, but they eventually did. Today, DFSMS is running effectively in many XA shops.

13.3.1. Hardware Requirements

Originally, the installer of DFSMS had to have ESA and an ESA-level Processor Complex to work with DFSMS. Today, people are installing DFSMS on 3084 Processor Complexes running under MVS/XA.

It is clear that having cache control units, expanded storage in the Processor Complex, and a DASD farm that can be divided into storage classes are hardware *requirements*. But do not stop if you do not have this *state-of-the-art* or leading edge hardware. You can still benefit from DFSMS.

13.4. DFSMS Planning

Planning for DFSMS is dependent on your installation's practices and requirements, so the following will be general guidelines for you to consider as you move toward systems managed storage.

13.4.1. Decide on the Goal

The first part of any planning is to agree upon the goals of the project. In the case of DFSMS, there are a number of goals that can be achieved. You should rank these in the order of importance to your data center, as they will color your implementation plan:

1. Better people productivity.

2. Improved service.

3. Higher utilization of storage space.

4. Faster device migration.

5. Strategic positioning for future software releases.

13.4.2. Position Yourself for SMS

When we moved from MVS/370 to MVS/XA, the key term was *positioning*, which meant that you must get your software to a level that would tolerate both the 370 version and the XA version of MVS. Once you accomplished that feat, the conversion was relatively painless. (I hear you out there with complicated data centers who had a lot of problems with the conversion: hold that thought.)

The same can be said for SMS implementation. The following positioning actions could make your life easier:

1. Get executive direction and control of the project.

2. Convert to all ICF catalogs and ensure that all data sets are cataloged.

3. Convert all DASD to indexed VTOCs.

4. Establish service-level contracts or change the ones in effect to be meaningful, with allocation and performance standards included.

5. Remove all JOBCATs and STEPCATs.

6. Really look at all your catalogs. Are they the right ones? Are they the proper size? Do they allow for expansion?

7. Define data set naming conventions or reevaluate yours to ensure that you have names that convey the necessary char-acteristics of the data set.

8. Begin to use pooling instead of volume allocation. If you have non-DFP pooling products, review their use. You may already be close to systems managed storage.

9. Define DFSMS constructs for **a very small population of your data.** Most begin with temporary data sets and then tackle one application at a time.

13.5. Summary

Systems managed storage is a generic term for the management and control of DASD data set allocations. On February 15, 1988, IBM announced their version of SMS and called it DF/Storage Management Subsystem.

Constructs refers to logical specifications and routines to implement DFSMS. There are four of them: Data Class, Storage Class, Management Class, and Storage Group. They will be fully explained in the next chapter. The specifications for these constructs are created using the Interactive Storage Management Facility (ISMF).

Improvements to the DFP components make storage management easier. All data sets must be cataloged. JOBCATs and STEPCATs are not allowed in DFSMS environments. The data center can implement multilevel aliases to subdivide end user data sets into multiple catalogs. Up to four qualifiers may be used.

Generation data groups (GDG) are changed. The fully qualified data set name is cataloged as it is created.

Access methods are given a new name. The Logical Data Manager (LDM) is the collection of access method routines concerned with the data set attributes and buffer management. Likewise, the External Data Manager (EDM) is the operating system components concerned with the physical attributes of the DASD volume that contains the data.

A new access method, the Object Access Method, is introduced to provide access to whole objects, such as graphic images.

The non-DFP components are separated into four functional areas. The first two are active and inactive data movers. Examples are IBM's DFHSM, CAI's ASM2, Sterling's DMS/OS, and Innovation Data's FDR. The third area is the sort. Examples are IBM's DFSORT, CAI's CA-SORT, and Syncsort's SYNCSORT. The last group covers security for SMS. IBM's entry is RACF. CAI has two: Top Secret and ACF2.

Planning for and implementing SMS requires a number of steps be taken to ensure that the proper environment exists for the implementation.

13.6. Questions

1. What are the two parts of DFSMS?

2. What is a DFSMS construct?

3. What are the four constructs?

4. What is ISMF, and when would you use it?

5. What different processing takes place with generation data groups between non-DFSMS environments and DFSMS environments?

6. What is multilevel aliasing?

7. What is the Logical Data Manager (LDM)?

8. What is the External Data Manager (EDM)?

9. Name the four non-DFP components of DFSMS.

14

SMS from the User Perspective

14.1. DFSMS Constructs

At most data centers today, the end user is the source of information about data sets as they are created. How systems managed storage is employed is determined primarily at *allocation time*. Job Control Language (JCL) is spread throughout the end user's libraries. JCL today contains information about size, attributes, and (the worst part) where the data set is to be placed. Systems managed storage in general, and DF/Storage Management Subsystem in particular, is about moving that knowledge from the end user to the data center and, more importantly, automating the process.

The IBM vehicle for this movement is the set of DFSMS *constructs*, or parameters, that decide and direct allocation of DASD data sets. The optimum we strive for is for the end user to specify minimal information, such as the data set name and the disposition. If the disposition is *OLD* or *SHR*, then the operating system will find the data and make it available. If the disposition is *NEW*, then the operating system will allocate space on the *appropriate* DASD and allow the application to begin writing.

It is the word "appropriate" that causes trouble. What is appropriate for one installation or circumstance may be inappropriate for another. Sometimes, your decisions about how to employ DFSMS constructs arise from objective reasoning. Other times, the best you can do is to make subjective decisions or rely on your intuition and experience. To make your task more challenging, you must also take into consideration that circumstances change, and some of your decisions may become inappropriate in the future. You may find yourself deciding to use DFSMS constructs in such a manner that you insulate yourself and your users from the effects of change.

The IBM DFSMS constructs we discuss in the remainder of this chapter find application in several areas:

1. DFSMS constructs make decisions on behalf of users who are cavalier in their placement of data sets, too busy with other things to be concerned with data set placement, or just plain unaware of the impact their placement decisions have on themselves and each other.

2. By forcing you to classify your data and codify the classifications to direct data set placement, DFSMS constructs force you to think hard about your installation's present and future needs. You should feel encouraged to get out there and visit with members of your user community: ignorance goes both ways. If you are unaware of your installation's data access patterns, needs, and trouble areas, now is the time to educate yourself.

3. Making a serious effort to use DFSMS for all its worth positions your installation to take advantage of enhancements IBM makes to SMS in the future. If you use DFSMS half-heartedly, you are not only deferring work but possibly compounding its difficulty down the road. You must balance this, however, with the effects DFSMS will have on data set allocation overhead. If you lack the wherewithal necessary to convert your entire data center to DFSMS control, you may decide to phase it in gradually.

First you must learn what you can control through the DFSMS constructs. Second, you must analyze your data sets with these controls in mind. You will look for *patterns* in types of data, how it is accessed, when it is accessed relative to other data, and its life cycle. Third, you will either decide against DFSMS or make it part of your data center's operation. Fourth, you will find ways to measure DFSMS' effectiveness. Finally, you will repeat the entire process, successively refining your use of DFSMS to use it more effectively and to manage changes in your data center's workload.

14.1.1. Automatic Class Selection (ACS) Routines

There are four Automatic Class Selection Routines. One is for the Data Class. One is for the Storage Class. One is for the Management Class. One assigns the Storage Group. Each of these can change only the *construct name* for its area. For example, the Storage Class routine is allowed to change only the Storage Class name.

> ¤ Data class, storage class, and management class define the logical requirements of a data set. Storage group describes the physical DASD environment for the data set.

In Figure 14.1 you see the flow for new allocations. A request comes in from the left and goes through the Data Class routine. Parameters (discussed later) are examined and the data class variable, *DATACLAS*, is set or not. The Storage Class routine is entered and decides whether it should continue or allow non-DFSMS allocation to continue processing the request. The *STORCLAS* variable is set. If this is to be a DFSMS allocation, then the Management Class routines are processed, and the *MGMTCLAS* variable is set. Finally, the Storage Group routines are entered, and the *STORGRP* variable is set to indicate the Storage Group of DASD volumes to be used for allocation.

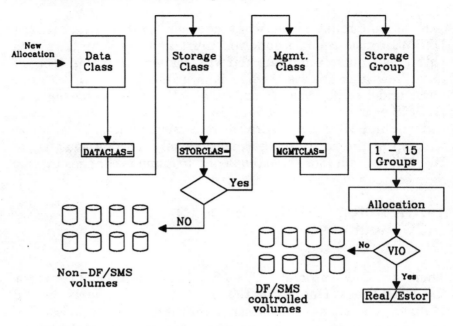

Figure 14.1 Automatic Class Selection Flow. This figure represents the flow from the beginning of allocation to the decision to place a new data set on DFSMS volumes or on non-DFSMS volumes.

ACS routines are expressed in a CLIST-like language and are installed using ISMF. They control the decision-making processes for DFSMS.

> ▫   Every allocation goes through these routines. Do not make them too complex or you will consume too many CPU cycles at allocation time.

14.1.2. Data Class

Data Class answers the question: What does the data set look like? Data Class variables are like a template to define the allocation attributes for a new data set. Most of us have a fixed idea of what a source data set should look like. LRECL should be set to 80 and BLKSIZE should be set to some multiple, say 8,000. The DSORG should be partitioned. These routines also automate the selection of space and block size estimates based on the geometries of the receiving DASD.

Data Class is used only at *data set allocation time*. It can be specified in JCL, on ISPF/PDF panels, or in Access Methods Services (IDCAMS) control cards. Data Class may be overridden by the external ACS routine.

A Data Class is not necessary, even for DFSMS data sets. If you are serious about DFSMS controlling your DASD allocations, you should at least plan for and define the requirements of the Data Class attributes.

One of the new features of DFP Version 3 and later is the ability to set the block size to a default *optimum value*. If the requested block size is set to zero **and** the record format is set to fixed blocked, then the value is used. You may want to write an exit to force a zero block size for new data sets.

One question may be in your mind. Why can't IBM make a zero block size the default so you automatically get the optimal BLKSIZE? The answer, of course, is that IBM (and other software vendors) do not like to force options on their users, even if that would seem best. The practice helps sell iron and ensures that we remain very important to our companies.

Data Class variables are:
- Data set type.
- Record length.
- Space information.
- Expiration and retention information.
- VSAM key placement information.
- VSAM subparameters such as control interval size, free space, share options, and index options.

The following is an example of a Data Class routine. This is a very simple example that sets the Data Class to the one specified, if it exists.

```
                          Data Class Example

PROC 1 DATACLAS
/•••••••••••••••••••••••••••••••••••••••••••••••••••••••••••••••/
/*   ACS ROUTINE TO SELECT DATA CLASS                          */
/*        CHANGE HISTORY                                       */
/*   DATE       WHO  COMMENTS                                  */
/*   MM/DD/YY   NNN  IF DATACLAS IS NOT BLANK THEN USE THE     */
/*                     DATACLAS SPECIFIED.                     */
/•••••••••••••••••••••••••••••••••••••••••••••••••••••••••••••••/
IF &DATACLAS NE '' THEN
   DO
     SET &DATACLAS = &DATACLAS
     EXIT
   END
   END
```

14.1.3. Storage Class

Storage Class answers the question: What service is required for
this data set? Storage Class attributes define the processing
requirements of the data, such as the service levels and availability of the data set. The Storage Class ACS routine receives
control after the Data Class ACS routine and is the proper place
to determine which data sets will be SMS-managed and which
will not.

The Storage Class is used only at *data set allocation time.* It
can be specified in JCL, on ISPF/PDF panels, or in Access Methods Services (IDCAMS) control cards. It may be overridden by
the external ACS routine. RACF can be used to control access to
Storage Classes.

> ¤   The No Storage Class specification means the data set is
>   not DFSMS-controlled.

If *AVAILABILITY=CONTINUOUS* is specified in the Storage
Class, the data set must be placed on a DASD attached to a
3990-3 class control unit with dual copy enabled. If there are no
such devices, then the allocation will fail. The original and
backup volumes must also be in the same Storage Group.

Examples of the Storage Class attributes are:
• Availability of the data set.

- Guaranteed space (not really guaranteeing space, as you might imagine, but saying that DFSMS will not select the volume: it will use the specified volume instead).
- Millisecond response time requested for direct access and sequential access.
- Probable read-write bias for cache selection.

The following is an example of a storage class routine. This example shows all nonDASD allocations are excluded, storage classes on DFHSM recalls are allowed, storage classes specified on JCL are allowed, all temporary data set allocations are forced to *WORK*. When those conditions are not met, the storage class is set to nulls meaning allow the allocation to continue to non-SMS DASD volumes.

Storage Class Example

```
PROC 1 STORCLAS
/*.........................................................*/
/*  ACS ROUTINE TO SELECT STORAGE CLASS                  */
/*     CHANGE HISTORY                                    */
/*  DATE      WHO  COMMENTS                               */
/*  MM/DD/YY  NNN   ADD COMMENTS HERE                     */
/*.........................................................*/


/*.........................................................*/
/*   FILTER DASD UNIT NAMES                               */
/*.........................................................*/
  FILTLIST DASD_UNITS INCLUDE ('3380','SYSDA','SYSALLDA','VIO'
/*.........................................................*/
/*  EXCLUDE NON-DASD ALLOCATIONS                          */
/*.........................................................*/

   WHEN (&UNIT ^= &DASD_UNITS) SET &STORCLAS = ''


/*.........................................................*/
/*  WHEN RECALL OR RECOVER AND STORCLAS NE ''            */
/*     SET STORCLAS = STORCLAS                           */
/*.........................................................*/
  WHEN ((&ACSENVIR='RECALL' ] &ACSENVIR='RECOVER') && &STORCLAS ^= '')
     SET &STORCLAS = &STORCLAS


/*.........................................................*/
/*  ACCEPT STORCLAS CODED BY USERS                       */
/*.........................................................*/

   WHEN (&STORCLAS ^= '') SET &STORCLAS = &STORCLAS
```

Storage Class Example

```
/•••••••••••••••••••••••••••••••••••••••••••••••••••••••••••••/
/*  SET TEMPORARY DATASET TO STORCLAS = WORK                  */
/•••••••••••••••••••••••••••••••••••••••••••••••••••••••••••••/

    WHEN (&DSTYPE = 'TEMP')
       DO
          SET &STORCLAS = 'WORK'
          WRITE 'STORCLAS ASSIGNED TO (' &STORCLAS ') BY ACS ROUTINE'
       END


/•••••••••••••••••••••••••••••••••••••••••••••••••••••••••••••/
/*  DEFAULT TO STORCLASS = ''                                 */
/•••••••••••••••••••••••••••••••••••••••••••••••••••••••••••••/

    OTHERWISE
       SET &STORCLAS = ''
END
END
```

14.1.4. Management Class

Next, the data set allocation passes through the Management Class ACS routine. Management Class answers the question: What service is required? The migration, retention, and backup requirements of the data set are specified here. The *inactive data mover* (e.g., DFHSM, FDR/ABR, or DMS/OS) is the non-DFP component that will perform the stated objectives.

Examples of the types of information provided by the Management Class are:
- Retention period.
- Number of backup copies retained.
- Backup frequency.
- GDG processing options.
- Free space release.

The Management Class is used only at *data set allocation time.* It can be specified in JCL, on ISPF/PDF panels, or in Access Methods Services (IDCAMS) control cards. It may be overridden by the external ACS routine. RACF can be used to control access to Management Classes.

The following is an example of the management class routine. Certain data sets with a high-order identifier of *USER01* will be given a management class of *STANDARD*. If a data set is being recalled by DFHSM, it will be given the management class assigned before recall. Temporary data sets get no management class assigned. The default is to set the management class to *STANDARD*.

Management Class Example

```
PROC 1 MGMTCLAS
/*•••••••••••••••••••••••••••••••••••••••••••••••••••••••••••••••••••••*/
/*  ACS ROUTINE TO SELECT MANAGEMENT CLASS                            */
/*     CHANGE HISTORY                                                 */
/*  DATE      WHO   COMMENTS                                          */
/*  MM/DD/YY  NNN   COMMENT HERE                                      */
/*•••••••••••••••••••••••••••••••••••••••••••••••••••••••••••••••••••••*/


/*•••••••••••••••••••••••••••••••••••••••••••••••••••••••••••••••••••••*/
/*  FILTER LIST FOR DATASETS                                          */
/*•••••••••••••••••••••••••••••••••••••••••••••••••••••••••••••••••••••*/
 FILTLIST ARHIST INCLUDE('USER01.*')


/*•••••••••••••••••••••••••••••••••••••••••••••••••••••••••••••••••••••*/
/*  CHECK FOR RECALL OR RECOVER AND MGMTCLAS NE NULLS                 */
/*•••••••••••••••••••••••••••••••••••••••••••••••••••••••••••••••••••••*/
 SELECT
   WHEN ((&ACSENVIR='RECALL' ] &ACSENVIR='RECOVER') && &MGMTCLAS ^= '')
     SET &MGMTCLAS = &MGMTCLAS

/*•••••••••••••••••••••••••••••••••••••••••••••••••••••••••••••••••••••*/
/*  IF AR HISTORY FILE THEN SET MGMTCLASS = STANDARD                  */
/*•••••••••••••••••••••••••••••••••••••••••••••••••••••••••••••••••••••*/

   WHEN (&DSN = &ARHIST)
     SET &MGMTCLAS = 'STANDARD'

/*•••••••••••••••••••••••••••••••••••••••••••••••••••••••••••••••••••••*/
/*  SET TEMP DATASETS TO NULL MGMTCLAS                                */
/*•••••••••••••••••••••••••••••••••••••••••••••••••••••••••••••••••••••*/
   WHEN (&DSTYPE = 'TEMP')
     SET &MGMTCLAS = ''

/*•••••••••••••••••••••••••••••••••••••••••••••••••••••••••••••••••••••*/
/*  DEFAULT MGMTCLAS = STANDARD                                       */
/*•••••••••••••••••••••••••••••••••••••••••••••••••••••••••••••••••••••*/
   OTHERWISE
     SET &MGMTCLAS = 'STANDARD'
   END
END
```

14.1.5. Storage Group

Storage Group answers the question: Where is the data set to be placed? The Storage Group ACS routine selects a target DASD for the allocation by nominating one or more Storage Groups. The literature seems to imply that the end user can specify high-performance DASD such as cached volumes, or regular activity such as DASD, or even near-line or offline places for data. The implementation current at this writing does not yet do all of that.

The output of the Storage Group routine is a list of the possible Storage Groups on which the data set can be allocated. The STORGRP list can contain from 1 to 15 names, and the order does not imply any priority for selection.

> ¤   These are candidate recommendations. A DASD volume may belong to one and only one Storage Group, and a data set may be allocated only in one Storage Group. The data set may span volumes, but all the volumes must be in the same Storage Group.

A storage group should contain only one device type. The reason is that, under MVS, a data set cannot span unlike device types. This is not new with DFSMS, but has been around since the first releas of OS/360 in the middle 1960s. If a data set was allowed to have one part on one geometry and another part on another geometry, the control blocks would have to be updated with new tracks per cylinder and track size parameters. End of volume routines were not designed to do that. Remember *upward compatibility* is vital to this architecture.

Three types of groups are defined. **DUMMY** and **VIO** groups are not real DASD. **POOL** volumes are real DASD volumes.

Dummy Storage Group

The DUMMY storage group is thought of as a migration aid but may be inportant for years after you implement DFSMS. If existing JCL has DISP=OLD or DISP=MOD (when the data set exists) and the old volume no longer exists, the system would fail the request. Place the removed volume serial numbers in the DUMMY groups and DFSMS will allow the allocation and find where the data set really exists.

VIO Storage Group

If the data set is a temporary data set, it may be allocated to VIO if the requested size is less than or equal to the VIO size (VIO-MAXSIZE parameter) specified in the VIO Storage Group Define. At last we have a control for the size of VIO data sets. In previous versions you specified a *device type* for VIO allocation and the maximum size was the maximum number of bytes for that device type. Most of us depended on the small size of a second-generation 2305 drum! VIO can even be disabled by specifying *DISABLE(ALL)*.

VIO data sets are not allocated to DASD but are virtual data sets emulated by control blocks and buffers in central and expanded storage. Thus, the selection of VIO remains installation-dependent. Your specifications will select VIO regardless of the status of the Processor Complex storage and the responsiveness of the paging subsystem. Someday we may be able to take into consideration the Unreferenced Interval Count (UIC) and the Migration Age of the pages in storage before we assign VIO.

POOL Storage Group

POOL storage group specifications are for real DASD allocations. How you group your volumes is very important because you are now affecting where data sets will reside for the important first days of their lives.

> ¤   The device selection process takes place during data set creation, recall, and recovery. All rules are applied during this time, even if it is 3:00 a.m. in the morning!

Storage Group specifications for a pool of DASD volumes contain information such as:

- The volume serial of the DASD volumes that make up the pool or Storage Group.
- The volume status: a volume may be specified as available for new allocations, available for *OLD* allocations only, or not available.
- The Processor Complexes that can access the group.
- Space allocation thresholds.
- Migration, backup, and dump characteristics.
- Virtual I/O (VIO) limits for data sets allocated on the group.

> ¤   The Storage Group cannot be specified by the end user on JCL. If you want more than one Storage Group specified, you must write the Storage Group ACS routine to select among them. If you need only one Storage Group, then you do not need SMS!

The following table is an example of a storage group. A specified storage class of *CRITICAL* will be assigned to a group of volumes in the *SGBASE* pool. If *PRODNORM* or *WORK* is specified then two storage groups are available—*SGBASE* and *SGTEST*. If *DBTEST* or *NORMAL* is specified then *SGTEST* is selected. The default will be *SGBASE*.

Storage Group Example

```
PROC 1 STORGRP
/*..............................................................*/
/*    ACS ROUTINE TO SELECT STORAGE GROUP                       */
/*        CHANGE HISTORY                                        */
/*    DATE      WHO  COMMENTS                                   */
/*    MM/DD/YY  NNN  ADD COMMENTS HERE                          */
/*..............................................................*/
```

Storage Group Example

```
SELECT

/•••••••••••••••••••••••••••••••••••••••••••••••••••••••••••••••••/
/•• IF STORCLAS IS CRITICAL THEN SET STORGRP TO SGBASE ..........••/
/•••••••••••••••••••••••••••••••••••••••••••••••••••••••••••••••••/
  WHEN (&STORCLAS = 'CRITICAL')
      DO
          SET &STORGRP = 'SGBASE'
          EXIT
      END

/•••••••••••••••••••••••••••••••••••••••••••••••••••••••••••••••••/
/•• IF STORCLAS IS WORK THEN SET STORGRP TO SGBASE AND SGTEST  ••/
/•••••••••••••••••••••••••••••••••••••••••••••••••••••••••••••••••/
  WHEN (&STORCLAS = 'WORK')
      DO
          SET &STORGRP = 'SGBASE','SGTEST'
          EXIT
      END

/•••••••••••••••••••••••••••••••••••••••••••••••••••••••••••••••••/
/•• IF STORCLAS IS PRODNORM THEN SET STORGRP TO SGBASE AND SGTEST ••
/•••••••••••••••••••••••••••••••••••••••••••••••••••••••••••••••••/
  WHEN (&STORCLAS = 'PRODNORM')
      DO
          SET &STORGRP = 'SGBASE','SGTEST'
          EXIT
      END

/•••••••••••••••••••••••••••••••••••••••••••••••••••••••••••••••••/
/•• IF STORCLAS IS DBTEST THEN SET STORGRP TO SGBASE ..........••/
/•••••••••••••••••••••••••••••••••••••••••••••••••••••••••••••••••/
  WHEN (&STORCLAS = 'DBTEST')
      DO
          SET &STORGRP = 'SGTEST'
          EXIT
      END

/•••••••••••••••••••••••••••••••••••••••••••••••••••••••••••••••••/
/•• IF STORCLAS IS NORMAL THEN SET STORGRP TO SGTEST ..........••/
/•••••••••••••••••••••••••••••••••••••••••••••••••••••••••••••••••/
  WHEN (&STORCLAS = 'NORMAL')
      DO
          SET &STORGRP = 'SGTEST'
          EXIT
      END

/•••••••••••••••••••••••••••••••••••••••••••••••••••••••••••••••••/
/•• SET DEFAULT STORGRP TO SGBASE                          ••/
/•••••••••••••••••••••••••••••••••••••••••••••••••••••••••••••••••/
  OTHERWISE
          SET &STORGRP = 'SGBASE'
  END
END
```

POOL Device Selection

The device selection process for a new, permanent data set in the DFSMS envrionment is different from previous allocation methods. A list of eligible volumes is created by the DFSMS subsystem from the possibilites defined by the POOL storage group in the storage group Automatic Class Selection (ACS) routine. Each volume is further screened to determine if its connectivity, freespace, performance, and availability satisfy the data class, storage class, and managment class attributes requested.

The ACS routines builds a volume candidate list based on the storage group definitions. Ineligible volumes (attributes of DIS-ABLE, DISABLE(NEW), NOTCONN, or OFFLINE) are removed from the list.

Each volume is examined to ensure that the space available will satisfy this request. Volumes with insufficient space are removed from the list. If the request does not exceed the DASD volume's storage group high allocation threshold, the volume is placed on a *primary list*. If the request exceeds the volume's requested threshold, it is placed on a *secondary* list.

If the request contains *AVAILABILITY=CONTINUOUS* then all but duplexed, dual-copy volumes are discarded. If there are no dual copy pairs, then the allocation is failed.

The performance objective requested is checked next. If a DASD volume in the primary list is meeting the expectations, it is retained in the primary list. Otherwise, the volume is moved to the secondary list. If there are no volumes left, the best performing volumes are retained in the primary list. Volumes are associated with their control unit. If a volume is not specified for caching or DASD Fast Write (DFW) it is still considered as having those attributes.

The final primary list of DASD volumes meet *all* of the following cirtieria:

- Storage group enabled.
- Volume enabled and online.
- Volume has enough space for the primary request.

- Volume meets the availability requirement.
- Volume meets or exceeds the data set's storage class performance objectives.

The secondary list contains the DASD volumes that meet all of the following requirements:
- Volume is online.
- Volume can satisify the data set's availability requirement.

The secondary list must also meet at least one of the following:
- Volume can contain the primary space request but it will exceed the high threshold.
- Volume does not meet the performance objective.

These lists are passed to the Systems Resource Manager (SRM) for the final selection. SRM starts with the primary list. Allocation continues as it did before DFSMS. If the primary list is exhausted before the SRM can pass it (e.g., space was consumed by another Processor Complex), then the secondary list is used. The volume with the most freespace is tried first.

> ¤   If the data set is being extended, the same storage group is assigned for the extension. All volumes in a given Storage Group must have the same device geometry (track size and tracks per cylinder). If unlike devices are in a storage group, requested extensions to a data set may fail.

GUARANTEED SPACE

Specific volume requests are provided for by the GUARANTEED SPACE attribute in the storage class definition. The volume specified will be used for the primary space allocation. The data set allocation will fail if:
- All specified volumes are not in the same storage group.
- The volume fails the availability requirement (e.g., it is not a dual copy volume).

- The volume is marked DISABLE, DISABLE(NEW), NOTCONN, or OFFLINE.

14.1.6. ACS Input and Output Parameters

Figure 14.2 shows the flow of parameters available to the ACS routines and the four outputs of the ACS routines that are used by the DFSMS allocation routines. These could be grouped in a number of ways, but we have chosen to use the groupings suggested by H. Pat Artis in his studies of data set allocation under DFSMS.[1]

Data Set Variables

The most important input variable is, of course, the data set name. Other interesting parameters, such as the data set organization and maximum size, could be used to set the Data Class.

Installation Variables

The job, step, and DD names are available but should be used only if you really must. These are volatile and probably should not be used for any judgments. Account codes for the job and step may be of some use. These can be controlled by SMF exits and often map to functional areas of the company.

---

[1]   See *Data Set Allocation and Performance Management Under Systems Managed Storage*, CMG 90, December 1990, p. 736.

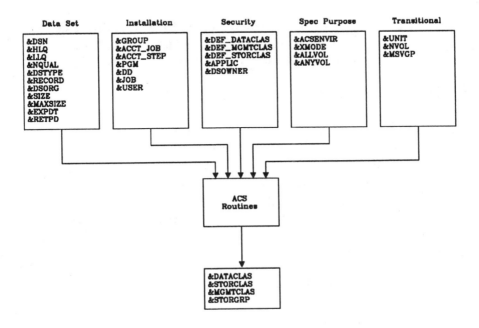

Figure 14.2 Input Variables to ACS Routines. This figure groups the input variables to the ACS routines into five logical groups.

Security Variables

Some installations are successfully using RACF or the RACF-like subsystems to specify information about the default Data Class, Management Class, and Storage Class. This has some merit in that you probably already have logical groupings for your RACF groups, and these may map into service-level or business unit associations.

Special-Purpose Variables

Some variables give the routine a clue as to why the routine was entered. One important one is the suggested allocation boundaries from the requesting task.

Transitional Variables

As you recall, DFSMS is an evolving subsystem. Some variables may not be there in the future as we tighten down the screws to automate allocation tasks. If we are trying to get away from the unit specification of old days, then the &UNIT parameter is clearly doomed. Likewise, the number of volumes (who has not been caught by underspecifying or overspecifying the number of volumes) and the Mass Storage (yes, Virginia, the 3850!) Volume Group will go away someday.

14.1.7. Writing ACS Routines

ACS routines are written and stored in partitioned libraries with the ISPF/PDF editor. They are translated by the ISMF routines and placed into the Source Control Data Set (SCDS). The new specifications are then tested against the defined classes and groups to see if you have made a mistake specifying the variables.

14.2. What DFSMS Is Not

DFSMS is not for every data set in your facility, and it is not for every data processing facility. If you listen to the non-IBM vendors that have years' head start on SMS pooling concepts, then you will never need DFSMS; just use their version of systems managed storage. For now, let's concentrate on DFSMS.

14.2.1. Not for All Data Sets

The current implementation of DFSMS, and probably all future versions through this century, will have allocations that do not belong in a general-purpose, automated system. There are probably several data centers out there that will completely switch to all SMS volumes. We would guess that they have minimized their SMS gains by such an action because they have oversimplified the representation of their data center's needs to SMS.

Not for GUARANTEEDSTORAGE=YES

Some data sets are so large or so important that they require you to place them on DASD volumes yourself. Data base files are examples of very large data sets. We have seen a single VSAM data set span more than four dual-capacity 3380 volumes. You certainly do not want DFSMS, DFHSM, or any other automatic routine trying to manage that gorilla.

Some data sets *must* reside on different volumes because one is the audit trail of another. You could place specific references in your ACS routines, but then you are maintaining a list of data sets used in programs. That has never been a good practice, and this continues to be true with ACS routines.

Examples of separate data sets are data base logging files, the tape management file and its audit file, and the DFHSM inventory and audit files. These should all be specified with GUARANTEEDSTORAGE=YES to let the normal allocation routines find the volume specified.

Not for ISAM

DFSMS does not support ISAM. Convert it to VSAM, use the VSAM emulation of ISAM, or purchase a non-IBM product to emulate applications' ISAM calls.

14.2.2. Not for the Faint-Hearted

Implementing DFSMS or any of the non-IBM systems managed storage products is an exciting adventure. You will be taking control of the allocation and space management domain that has been the domain of others.

The good news is that most end users do not want the responsibility. As the old marketing saying goes, "The people who buy drills do not really want a drill, they want holes." End users want a place for their data that is responsive to their needs.

The other good news is that you cannot mix DFSMS volumes with non-DFSMS data sets (you can with the non-IBM solutions). You start by allocating a number of DASD volumes to DFSMS (the end user already realizes that the "system" takes most of the DASD storage anyway). You then give the end users space on the volumes, and they are happy.

Fortunately, most of you who have been in the DASD management business for a long time have developed tough skins and know you are ultimately responsible for all that DASD data.

14.3. DFSMS Implementation

Now we turn to a brief overview of the IBM DFSMS implementation. This brief overview should not be just that. If you are at the point at which you must install or fully understand this concept, you should turn to the manuals that apply to your version of DFSMS. DFSMS will change and grow each year, and you must understand what your version of DFSMS can and cannot do.

14.3.1. DFSMS Address Space

Three control data sets are required to implement DFSMS. These are the Source Control Data Set (SCDS), the Active Control Data Set (ACDS), and the Communications Data Set (-COMMDS).

Source Control Data Set (SCDS)

The SCDS contains the input parameters for the ACS routines and the configuration information for the Processor Complex.

Active Control Data Set (ACDS)

The ACDS contains a copy of the interpreted and activated SCDS member for each of the constructs. One ACDS is used by all the copies of MVS running on all the Processor Complexes in a data center that uses DFSMS.

Communications Data Set (COMMDS)

The COMMDS provides a common data set for all the DFSMS routines in all the processor complexes.

14.3.2. DFSMS Initialization

DFSMS is started by creating a subsystem using the SYS1.PARMLIB IEFSSNxx member and by specifying initialization parameters in the IGDSMSxx SYS1.PARMLIB member. The latter specifies the data set names for the ACDS and COMMDS data sets. The following is an example of member IGDSMSxx:

```
            DFSMS parameter member IGDSMSxx In SYS1.PARMLIB

SMS ACDS(TSV1.SMS.ACDS)
    COMMDS(TSV1.SMS.COMMDS)
    INTERVAL(15)
    DINTERVAL(150)
    REVERIFY(NO)
    ACSDEFAULTS(YES)
    TRACE(OFF)
    SIZE(128K)
    TYPE(ALL)
    JOBNAME(*)
    ASID(*)
    SELECT(ALL)

/* DESELECT(...) NOT SPECIFIED                                      */
  /*                                                             */
  /* LIB: SYS1.PARMLIB(IGDSMS02)                                 */
  /* GDE: CBIPO MVS CUSTOMIZATION                                */
  /* DOC: THIS MEMBER SPECIFIES SMS INITIALIZATION INFORMATION   */
  /*      ALL ENTRIES ARE USING DEFAULTS                         */
```

The SMS address space is started by issuing the **SET SMS=xx** operator command. Parameters are changed by issuing the **SETSMS** command. Storage Group and volume status are changed with the **VARY SMS** command. The status of DFSMS can be displayed with the **D SMS** operator command. Individual volumes can be inspected using the **DEVSERV SMS** command.

14.4. Converting DASD to DFSMS

DASD controlled by DFSMS must have a VSAM Volume Data Set (VVDS), an indexed VTOC, and new fields in the FORMATx records in the VTOC.

14.4.1. Gradual Conversion

Prudent readers will consider a gradual migration to DFSMS control of the data in the data center. For example, the following groups could be converted in this order:

1. Yourself. Pick a group of users such as yourself and your departments (or maybe your worst enemy) and convert their data sets. The good news is that whoever it is will have all that DFSMS DASD volume to themselves.

2. Temporary data sets. Next easiest is to allocate new SYSDA volumes and point to them all. One problem with this is that you will need to get control of all the temporary data volumes to make the conversion. You should know that this did get one user into trouble, as there was a bug in DFSMS early on that allowed a data set to span multiple volumes upon creation, but quit reading after the first volume was read. This made for wonderful data-lost scenarios.

3. Test and development applications. These are the most aware end users of the data center. Once you have their confidence, you should bring your friends to the party.

4. Data base management data. These are not the very large data sets but all of the extra data sets that data base systems seem to carry with them.

5. Production applications. Finally, the rest of the world should be introduced to the future.

14.4.2. Copy-and-Go Conversion

Some data centers have just converted whole volumes to DFSMS and successfully converted a lot of data in a very short time. You may be able to do that too; it is just too risky for our blood.

14.4.3. Cache Control Unit Considerations

One of the Storage Class specifications is to control dynamic data set caching. The user is cautioned to watch the specifications we include below. The research we did for this work is reported here

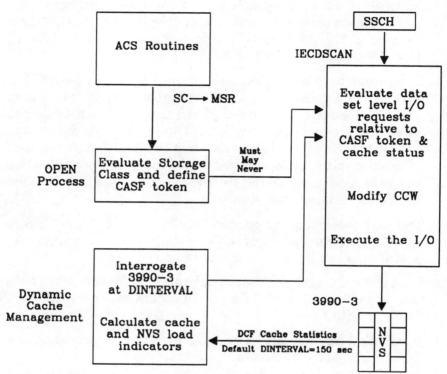

Figure 14.3 To Cache or Not to Cache. Caching is turned on or off at the CCW level. This example shows a flow from the OPEN process to the CCWs being modified. Periodically the cache controller is interrogated for statistics (approximately every 150 seconds) and the load and responsiveness is determined.

but IBM promises to change the DFSMS defaults and rules as they go. Partially, they want freedom to make the most intelligent decision for all users. Partially, they want to control their cache control units.

Figure 14.3 shows one representation of the flow for dynamic cache. The major point to note is that the decision to allow cache access is controlled as the CCW is going out the channel. If the cache is behaving in an acceptable manner (not overloaded) then caching is allowed for all operations. This is great. If nothing is

Must Cache Data Sets
3380 Class Devices

	Read Bias Sequential	Read Bias Direct	None specified	Write Bias Sequential	Write Bias Direct
3880-13	14<=MSR<25	14<=MSR<25	14<=MSR<25	N/A	N/A
3880-23	10<=MSR<25	10<=MSR<25	10<=MSR<25	N/A	N/A
3990-3 DFW	10<=MSR<25	10<=MSR<25	10<=MSR<25	6<=MSR<25	6<=MSR<25

Figure 14.4 Must Cache Data Sets. The millisecond response time (MSR) is a parameter used by SMS to convey the data center's desires for I/O service time.

going on, your batch jobs will gain immense benefits. I your online systems are operating, you should have them use the cache and let batch go directly to and from the spinning DASD.

There are three levels of cache control for a data set: never cache, may cache, and must cache. Figure 14.4 gives the possibilities.

Never Cache

A millisecond response (MSR) target of 999 milliseconds will get your data set a specification that prohibits data set caching if the data set is on a volume behind a 3990 model 3 control unit.

All volumes are either cached or not cached depending on IDCAMS commands to the 3990-3 or 3880-23 control unit. For data set level caching, you must turn on the volume for caching and let DFSMS set bits in the Define Extent CCW to indicate caching or no caching.

The 3990 model 3 allows data set level caching because the control unit can give information and take Define Extent commands to turn caching on or off for each channel program.

The 3880-23 cached control unit can be used to specify very fast response times but suffers from the fact that caching is specified only at the volume level. All data sets on the volume must be cached or none of them.

◻   We do not recommend *never cache* for most data sets.

May Cache

A MSR of between 25 and 999 milliseconds will get you a specification that allows the DFSMS routines to either turn on or turn off data set level caching.

◻   We recommend *may cache* for almost all data sets.

Must Cache

A MSR of less than 25 milliseconds indicates that you want these data sets always to use cache. You can also indicate a write bias value. If you do, DFSMS will allocate to volumes behind 3990-3 control units because the 3880-23 and 3880-13 do not support write caching.

◻   We recommend you limit the use of *must cached* to a very few data sets that are very small in size. If you have too many must cache data sets then you limit the ability of the system to respond to cache overloads.

14.5. Moving DFSMS between Processor Complexes

All shared volumes must be accessed by at least MVS/DFP Version 3 and later software. Failure to do so may result in disaster. There always is the possibility for bugs in the software and you are gambling you company's data.

14.6. Summary

DFSMS is implemented with a series of Automatic Class Selection (ACS) routines. There are four of these routines or constructs. Every allocation in your data center goes through these routines, so do not make them very complicated.

The first is Data Class, which controls the data set characteristics such as block size, logical record size, and space. Data Class specification is not necessary but desirable.

The second is Storage Class, which controls the service the data set is to get or whether the data set is to be controlled by DFSMS at all. If no Storage Class is assigned, then DFSMS is not in control. If you specify AVAILABILITY=CONTINUOUS, you must have dual copy running on a 3990-3 control unit, or the allocation will fail.

The third is Management Class, which covers parameters passed to the inactive data mover part of the non-DFP portions of DFSMS. Items like the retention period, the number of backup copies kept, and GDG processing options are specified.

The final one is Storage Group, which gives a list of volume pools on which DFSMS can allocate the data set.

There are a number of input variables to the ACS routines, but only four are allowed to be changed. &DATACLAS, &STORCLAS, &MGMTCLAS, and &STORGRP are the four, and each can be changed only by its routine. Writing ACS routines is done using the ISPF/PDF editor and implemented through the ISMF screens.

DFSMS is not for everyone and not for every data set. Large data sets should probably not be under DFSMS control. Some system data sets cannot be controlled by DFSMS. ISAM is not supported.

Cached control units can be controlled by DFSMS routines, and, with DFSMS controlling the volumes, we finally get to determine caching at the data set level rather than the volume level on 3990-3 control units.

There are three states of caching specification: never cache, maybe cache, and always cache.

14.7. Questions

1. Name the four DFSMS constructs. What are their purposes?

2. How do you enter DFSMS ACS routines into the MVS system?

3. What are the four variables that can be changed by ACS routines?

4. How do you specify that a data set should never be cached? How do you specify to sometimes cache a data set? How do you specify to always cache a data set?

5. How can the cache specification implicitly select the volume where a data set will be allocated?

A

Glossary

The glossary in this book concentrates on the terms used in the data processing industry in connection with Direct Access Storage Devices. It is not meant to be a complete glossary of data processing terms. Could there ever be one, Mr. Webster?

Many have more meanings or more general meanings than are expressed here. You should consult other dictionaries of computing terms for other meanings.

A-unit. A DASD that contains actuators and the electronics and cables for communications with control units. B-units may be attached to A-units. Sometimes these are called a head of string.

ACDS. The Active Control Data Set contains information about the DFHSM or the DFSMS subsystem. See also COMMDS and SCDS.

ACS. Automatic Class Selection. The name given to IBM's DFSMS routines.

Actuator. The read-write heads, arms that they are attached to, and electronics for head selection during I/O processing. In MVS the actuator is pointed to by the unit control block (UCB).

Alternate track. When one area on a platter surface of a DASD has so many errors that the data is declared to be unusable, the DASD administrator can assign an alternate track from several provided on the surface of the device. This practice should be a very rare occurrence, and you should be suspicious of any device that needs an alternate track assigned.

Authorized program. A state, indicated in the program status word (PSW), indicating that the program can issue instructions that would otherwise not be valid instructions.

B-unit. The designation of a DASD device that contains actuators but does not contain the electronics or cable connections to control units.

BCDS. Backup Control Data Set. The DFHSM data set used to keep information about backed-up data sets and the volumes that contain the data sets.

BDAM. Basic Direct Access Method.

Block length. The size in bytes of a physical block transferred to and from DASD devices.

BPAM. Basic Partitioned Access Method.

BSAM. Basic Sequential Access Method.

C-unit. A name used for DASD that connects directly to the channel and performs both control unit and head of string functions. B-units may be attached to C-units.

Cache. Random Access Memory in a Processor Complex, storage control unit, or DASD actuator used for faster access than the other components positioned further away can provide.

Cache Fast Write (CFW). A form of write where the data is written into the cache RAM and control returned to the access method as if the data had been written to the spinning DASD. CFW should only be used for temporary data which can always be recreated from input (e.g., sort work files).

CCHH. Cylinder (2 bytes) and head (2 bytes). An address for a DASD track.

CCHHR. Cylinder (2 bytes), head (2 bytes) and record (1 byte). An address for a physical record on a DASD track.

CCW. Channel command word. An 8-byte value built by applications or the operating system to command the channel to perform a read, write, sense, or diagnostic action. One or more CCWs make up a channel program that directs reads, writes, sense, and control operations for control units and I/O devices.

CFW. See Cache Fast Write.

Channel End . CE is one of the statuses presented during an I/O operation involving transfer of data or control information between the I/O device and the channel. CE indicates that the subchannel is available for another operation. There is only one CE for an operation.

CHPID. Channel path identifier.

CKD. Count-key-data format. Most DASD are formatted using a variable format which allows each block on the DASD to be specified by the application. The other format is called fixed-block architecture (FBA). Examples of CKD format DASD from IBM are 2311, 2314, 3330, 2305, 3340, 3344, 3350, 3375, 3380, and 3390 devices

CLIST. A list of commands which emulate TSO commands and logical control information. A CLIST is used in TSO or ISPF/PDF to perform a function.

COMMDS. Communications Data Set. A shared DASD data set used by DFSMS programs to communicate among multiple Processor Complexes and control DFSMS actions. It contains the name of the ACDS and current utilization of the DFSMS controlled volumes. See ACDS and SCDS.

Control unit. The hardware device between the Processor Complex and DASD.

Count-key-data (CKD). A DASD with records physically recorded on the track that identify the cylinder, record, record contents, and other information about areas on the track. CKD is an attribute of a particular DASD model. The other type is fixed blocked architecture (FBA). A CKD device cannot operate in FBA mode and vice versa.

Cylinder. A cylinder is the logical grouping of all the tracks accessible with the read-write head stopped at a position on the disk platter surface.

DADSM interrupt recording facility (DIRF). Bit 5 of the DS4VTOCI field of the format-4 DSCB is turned on when the MVS Direct Access Device Storage Management (DADSM) program is started as a flag that the free space (format 5) DSCBs are being changed. Some vendor-supplied software turn on this bit. To turn off the bit, just allocate a new data set on the volume and MVS will detect the problem and rebuild the format-5 DSCBs. It may also be on if the volume has indexed VTOCs.

DASD. Direct Access Storage Device.

DASD Fast Write (DFW). A form of writing to DASD attached to 3990 model 3 (or equivalent) control units which writes the block into control cache and a special nonvolatile storage. The application program is signaled (e.g., Device End) to continue as if the data was placed on the spinning DASD volume.

Data Facility. The name IBM assigns to a group of modules that are part of the operating system (e.g., DFP) or utility programs (e.g., DFHSM) used to supplement operating system functions.

Data Facility Product (DPF). The name of the IBM software that controls access to I/O devices. There are versions for MVS/370, MVS/XA, and MVS/ESA.

Data set. The unit of data storage on DASD devices. If you are looking this one up, you may need to start from the beginning. Find a copy of *MVS Concepts and Facilities*.

Data set changed indicator. Bit 6 of the DS1DSIND field of the Format 1 DSCB (data set record) of the VTOC. It is set to 1 by OPEN when a data set is opened for OUTPUT. Many incremental dump programs look at this bit to see which data sets are changed. The program turns off the bit after it makes a backup copy of the data set.

Data spaces. ESA allows a 2-gigabyte address space that can be used for data storage only.

DD. Data Definition. One Job Control Statement (JCL) used to define the location and attribute overrides of an existing data set or the attributes and place to put a new data set.

Device. The term device may mean a single, uniquely addressable part of a DASD as in *accessing the device*. This book uses the term to mean a box you purchase from IBM (e.g., 3380 or 3390 device).

Device End (DE). DE is one of the device statuses set at the end of device activity for each channel command. One of the meanings indicates the completion of a command. There is only one DE for an operation. The device is ready for another CCW (if command chaining was specified). When DE is presented with Channel End, the I/O operation is complete.

Device level selection (DLS). A term used for 3380 models AD4, BD4, AE4, BE4, AJ4, BJ4, AK4, BK4, and CJ2. DLS implemented all paths to all devices by both of the head of string paths.

Device level selection enhanced (DLSE). A term used for properly configured 3380 models AJ4, BJ4, AK4, and BK4 and all 3390 models. DLSE implemented four path access to all devices by all four paths of the head of string(s).

DFDSS. Data Facility Data Set Services. The IBM program product used to copy, move, dump, or restore individual data sets or whole DASD volumes.

DFHSM. Data Facility Hierarchical Storage Manager. An IBM program product that is used to back up, recover, archive, and recall data sets on DASD. It is one of the non-DFP components of DFSMS.

DFSMS. DF/Storage Management Subsystem. The IBM implementation of systems managed storage. It consists of DF/DFP Version 3 or higher and four non-DFP subsystems. For IBM these are DFRACF for security, DFSORT for sorting functions, DFHSM for inactive data manager functions, and DFDSS for inactive data mover functions.

DFW. See DASD Fast Write.

Disk. The name given to the combination of platters, electronics, read-write heads, and other components in the Direct Access Storage Device architecture. Other manufacturers may use the term *disc* to mean the same thing.

DLS. Device Level Selection. The name given by IBM for two-path support on 3380 and 3390 DASD.

DLSE. Device Level Selection Enhanced. The name given by IBM for four-path support on 3380 and 3390 DASD.

DPS. Dynamic Path Selection. The name given by IBM to a feature of 3380 and 3390 devices that keeps track of the paths used by processor controllers. It is limited to devices with more than one path, so the 3380 model A04 (only one path) does not have DPS. In 3880/3380 configurations, DPS is implemented in RAM storage in the head of string (e.g., AA4). In 3990/3390 configurations, DPS is implemented in RAM storage in the 3990 storage control unit.

Dual copy. The term used with IBM 3990 model 3 control units (or equivalent) that use nonvolatile storage and keep an identical copy of one volume on a second volume on the same control unit.

ECKD. Extended count-key-data. ECKD describes usage of count-key-data channel commands but describes the nature of the channel program before it begins. The Define Extent and Locate Record CCWs are used.

ENQ. The name of the macro in MVS that calls the Enqueue Supervisor service to serialize access to a resource.

Enqueue. The name of the MVS service that serializes access to a resource. For DASD, the Enqueue service may create an I/O operation that includes a Reserve CCW to lock a particular actuator.

Environment Recording, Editing, and Printing Program (EREP). The program that formats and prints the data in the SYS1.LOGREC system data set.

Error correction code (ECC). The architecture used by IBM and other vendors to correct single bit-in-error and double bit-in-error problems.

Errors, correctable. An I/O operation that can be corrected by applying logical changes to the data already in central storage with the ECC information.

Errors, permanent. An I/O operation that was retried by the channel and control unit but the error could not be fixed. A permanent error usually results in the abnormal termination of the task asking for the I/O operation. Another term for a permanent error is a *hard error*.

Errors, temporary. A temporary error is one that is corrected by either applying ECC correction or retrying the I/O operation. Another term for a temporary error is *soft error*.

Errors, uncorrectable. An error that is uncorrectable by the storage director by using ECC correction techniques. The error may be overcome by rereading or rereading with head offset to see if the data is available on another part of the track.

ES Connection Director (ESCD). The ESCD is a hardware device that controls dynamic connectivity in the ES connection architecture. Channels and devices are connected to the ESCD so that channels and control units can communicate and channels and channels can communicate.

Fast write. A function of the 3990 Model 3 storage control unit where a write operation does not require transfer to the DASD platter before the application is free to go use the buffer for other purposes.

FBA. Fixed-block architecture. Some DASD are formatted at the factory into fixed-size blocks (512 bytes) on each track. Examples are 3310 and 3370 DASD. Very few devices in the industry are FBA. Most are formatted in count-key-data (CKD) format.

Gb. A gigabyte (1,024 Mb) or 1,073,741,824 bytes.

GRS. Global Resource Serialization. The IBM facility that intercepts ENQ requests from tasks and serializes these requests by allowing the task to continue or wait depending on the request and the state of the resource. A "resource" is just one 8-byte major name and one 44-byte minor name. Remember 44 bytes is the length of a data set name!

Hard error. A permanent I/O error that results in the application abnormally terminating because the data could not be read or written.

Head and disk assembly (HDA). The part of DASD that contains the read-write heads and platters to store data. It is the smallest replaceable part if there are problems with the physical platters or heads.

Head of string. Another name for the device that contains controller functions and the channel cables that connect to the storage control unit.

Hiperspaces. High-performance spaces are 2-gigabyte address spaces in ESA operating systems that allow reading or writing 4-Kb blocks of storage from programs. The first type of hiperspace can be accessed only by authorized programs and requires that expanded storage be installed on the Processor Complex. The second is available from nonauthorized programs and does not require expanded storage. It is accessed through data windowing services.

Home address (HA). The first field on a track. It defines the cylinder, track, and status of the track.

ICKDSF. The program name for Data Facility Device Support Facilities.

Incremental backup. A backup of a data set that was created because the inactive data manager (DFHSM or equivalent) detected that the data set changed indicator bit was turned on.

Index point. The reference point on a disk surface that indicates the start of the track. It is not a physical mark on the track, only the logical start of the records on the track. The home address (HA) must be the first record on the track after the index point.

Indexed VTOC. A DASD volume with a second volume inventory data set which contains a list of data set names and free space information.

Interactive Storage Management Facility (ISMF). The panels used with ISPF to perform storage management functions of DFSMF.

Interactive System Productivity Facility (ISPF). The TSO subsystem which provides interactive, menu-driven edit and dialog services. It is required for DFSMF and any sane use of TSO. An important, and usually required extension is PDF.

I/O. Input/output.

JCL. Job Control Language. The 80-byte card-image method to start and control batch jobs running under MVS.

Master catalog. A catalog used by one copy of MVS that points to other (user) catalogs that contain pointers to data sets on DASD and tape. Only one master catalog can be active at a time for any MVS system, and it cannot be shared with any other active MVS system.

Maximal initialization. The term used for ICKDSF initialization of a DASD actuator. Each track is checked for defects. Alternate tracks are assigned if necessary. Alternate tracks are reclaimed if possible. Each track is validated. The volume label is written and IPL text is put into place if supplied. The VTOC is created.

Medial initialization. The term used for ICKDSF initialization of a DASD actuator. Each track is validated. The volume label is written and IPL text is put into place if supplied. The VTOC is created.

Minimal initialization. The term used for ICKDSF initialization of a DASD actuator. Primary and alternate track associations are check and corrected. The volume label is written and IPL text is put into place if supplied. The VTOC is created.

Ms. Milliseconds.

MVS/DFP. The part of the IBM operating system that provides access methods and other components used by application and TSO interactive sessions.

MVS/ESA. MVS/Enterprise Systems Architecture. The IBM operating system that is an extension of MVS/XA and supports additional address spaces for data.

MVS/SP. MVS/System Program. The IBM operating system which contains all the base components such as supervisor calls, storage management, and hardware management.

MVS/XA. MVS/Extended Architecture. The IBM operating system that is an extension of MVS/SP and supports address spaces 2 gigabytes in size.

PDF. Program Development Facility. The extension to ISPF that allows extended function. Usually required.

Permanent errors. See errors, permanent.

R0. Record zero or the first record on a track after the home address.

RACF. Resource Access Control Facility. The IBM non-DFP part of DFSMS which provides security functions.

Read-write heads. The part of DASD that transfers data from the Processor Complex/control unit to the surface of the DASD platter and vice versa.

RESERVE. The name of a function or channel command word that serializes access to a single actuator by locking out other Processor Complexes from all accesses to this volume. A RELEASE CCW is issued to remove serialization.

Rotational position sensing (RPS). A function of all generations after the first that allows the channel and control unit to disconnect from the DASD actuator while the platter spins to a certain angular location on the platter.

SCDS. The Source Control Data Set contains information about the installation specifications for systems managed storage.

Service-level agreement. A written ageement between two groups at a data center. Most often the data center and end user department write down what is expected of each. Examples of the items are response times, number of jobs and resources expected, and services provided by each party.

Skip displacement. Each track has extra room in excess of the stated maximum number of bytes. If a spot is detected that cannot be used for data, a skip displacement can be assigned to skip over the error without affecting the physical block on the track.

Soft error. A temporary I/O error that is correctable by applying ECC correction or retrying the I/O operation.

Speed matching buffer. The name associated with IBM 3880 or 3990 control units which allows DASD devices to be attached to channels with dissimilar data transfer speeds. The control unit receives the record at one speed and transfers it on at a different speed.

Storage control unit (SCU). A device that connects Processor Complex channels on one side to I/O devices on the other side. IBM 3990 models 2 and 3 are examples.

Storage director. One half of a storage control unit. In both the IBM 3880 and 3990 ther are two storage directors that act as a path to devices.

String. When used with DASD, indicates the head of string (A unit) and all attached B units.

Surface analysis cylinder. The cylinder(s) reserved by the DASD to contain all the tracks with surface errors detected by the factory. Factory testing is more stringent than ICKDSF testing and these are considered the minimum areas on the platters that should never be used.

Systems managed storage. The generic name for the group of IBM and non-IBM subsystems that allow a data center to control the allocation of DASD data sets. See DFSMS for the IBM implementation.

Temporary errors. See errors, temporary.

Track. A track is the circle of data on a DASD platter that contains space for some maximum number of bytes. The data on a track is all accessible by a single read-write head positioned at one of its possible locations.

Track address. The track address is a 4-byte value that identifies the cylinder and track of a particular DASD track. It is in the format of CCHH, where CC is the cylinder and HH is the head or track address. Each 2-byte field is four hexadecimal characters long.

TSO. Time Sharing Option. An "optional" part of MVS that provides interactive timesharing from terminals attached to the MVS Processor Complex. It is required starting with MVS 4.2.

Unit control block (UCB). The MVS control block that points to a single actuator and a single DASD volume.

Uncorrectable errors. See errors, uncorrectable.

Unit. IBM sometimes refers to an orderable unit of DASD (e.g., IBM 3390 model 2) or a single actuator as in *unit control block*.

Virtual DASD. DASD that is simulated on the IBM 3850 Mass Storage Subsystem and implemented using DFHSM.

Volume. See actuator.

VTOC. Volume Table of Contents. A group of records required on each DASD volume that contains the data set names and attributes of each data set on the DASD volume.

VVDS. The VSAM volume data set. The VVDS is named SYS1.VVDS.Vssssss where *ssssss* is the volume serial number of the volume. It contains information about the VSAM data sets on this volume.

B

Super DASD

B.1. Introduction

The 1990s will be the most exciting of the data processing decades. This appendix outlines several reasons why. The architectures described in this appendix extend the definition of DASD to a new height. These architectures come from non-IBM vendors but IBM is busy developing RAID, optical devices, and very small DASD.

In the past, non-IBM manufacturers creating hardware for the System/370, System/390, or ES/9000 architecture created *plug compatible* hardware. The term *plug compatible* suggests that the data center could use the same recepticles for its hardware as if it were plugging in IBM hardware. IBM publishes specifications called *Original Equipment Manufacture Interfaces (OEMI)* that outline how electrical interfaces should be interpreted and what responses are expected by the software and hardware. Thus the name *OEM hardware*.

In the past, non-IBM manufacturers believed it was vital for their equipment to behave just like IBM hardware in order for it to sell. Usually, the hardware was described as *just like IBM, only a little bit better.* You saw one example in this book when it came to dual path access for 3380 class DASD. IBM provided internal paths to some but not all the actuators simultaneously through a particular path. Most non-IBM manufacturers claimed true dual path from the very beginning of their 3350 and 3380 competitive brands.

Some manufacturers used different techniques to achieve DASD-like results. Storage Technology Corporation (now StorageTek) and Intel created solid-state devices to provide 3380-like devices, only they implemented them with Random Access Memory (RAM) to provide very fast access times.

In all cases, the non-IBM manufacturers took special care to ensure that they followed the OEMI standards. The two architectures presented in this section also follow OEMI standards for connectivity.

> ¤ What is different about these is that they move away from IBM. The devices provide the platform for doing much more than emulation.

One example is the announcement of DASD-to-tape backup. For years (yes, even decades) we have expected to have automatic backups of DASD. Remember, we take backups for only one reason—to restore to new DASD if the old one fails. Unfortunately for our industry we take millions of backups so that we can use a very few backups to restore data. It is worth it; it just is so painful.

Watch for this and other types of innovations from all the OEM manufacturers. The success of StorageTek and Andor in breaking the OEM mold will encourage the others to start production and sales of the innovations they already have.

A word of caution is appropriate here. These are the bleeding edge of technology. As with all new architectures, you should ensure that these are right for your installation and have a plan to ensure successful implementation to solve your problems. We remember years ago when the first STC solid-state drum device appeared. We installed it in a large time-sharing network and became heroes, but not before we developed the drum-fence

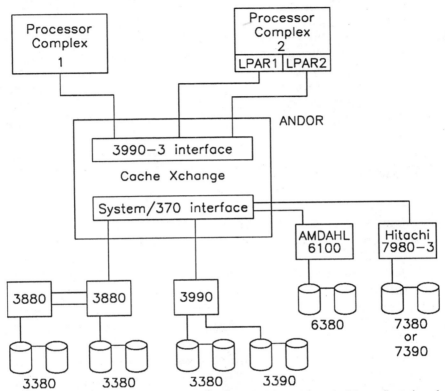

Figure B.1 CacheXchange Connectivity. This figure illustrates a possible configuration of DASD using the Andor CacheXchange to accept channel commands from Processor Complexes and provide cache services to fourth and fifth generations of DASD from any OEM vendor.

modification to make it really work. Be prepared to control your destiny!

Now let's turn to two of the super DASDs. The first, Andor, is a small box that you can place in the middle of your computer room floor to intercept and manage DASD I/O activity. It is a channel. It is a control unit. It is a solid-state caching unit. It is a RAID-1 device. It is a communications controller. You will shortly see why this is really a super DASD. It may not leap tall buildings in a single bound, but it can travel faster than the Man of Steel!

The second, Iceberg, begins as a RAID-like disk array subsystem with very large cache capabilities and data availability. It promises complete online storage management including instantaneous data backup and expansion of the robotic tape library. The success and results of these two will be played out during the 1990s. Now come with us to a future year of the Lone Array-nger.

B.2. Andor Legacy Series 690

Dr. Gene Amdahl founded Andor in 1987. The primary deliverable of Andor is a single-board System/370 compatible Processor Complex. The Processor Complex is on a single board and mounts in a standard 24-inch cabinet. The cabinet is less than 4 feet tall. Using System/370 instructions, the operating system uses a proprietary system called EPIcode. Extended Architecture (XA) and Enterprise System Architecture (ESA) are emulated with EPIcode.

The term Andor is a combination of *and gates* and *or gates* from the electrical engineering terms used in computer manufacturing. The term *legacy* comes from Dr. Amdahl's history of taking IBM specifications and creating OEM hardware.

So why are we talking about a Processor Complex in a DASD book? This Processor Complex emulates DASD and cached DASD control units.

B.2.1. Andor CacheXchange Configuration

The CacheXchange is a Processor Complex that is installed between one or more Processor Complexes and one or more control units. The original implemention supports up to 16 distinct Processor Complexes attached using bus and tag connections.

These operate at either 2.86 Mb/s (3.0 marketing megabytes per second) or 4.29 Mb/s (4.5 marketing megabytes per second).

On the back end, the CacheXchange supports up to 24 channels to attach 3880 and 3990 control units with real DASD. **It provides access to all devices from all hosts via all paths.**

In Figure B.1, Processor Complex *1* is plugged into the Andor box. On the other side are strings of 3380 DASD, 3390 DASD, Amdahl's 6380s, and Hitachi's 7380 or 7390 DASD. Any OEM DASD could be on the other side.

B.2.2. Andor Caching Capabilities

The CacheXchange provides 3990-3 cache functions for all storage control units attached to it. Cache can be configured from 64 megabytes to 2 gigabytes. The Andor cache processor can perform 32 concurrent caching operations.

In Figure B.1, the 3880 control units could be 3880 model 3 control units that do not have cache capabilities. Placing the CacheXchange in front of these noncached devices turns them into boxes that respond similarly to the latest 3990-3 cache controller with 3390 DASD attached.

> ❏   Every write to a DASD attached to the CacheXchange is treated as a DASD Fast Write.

Another difference is that the cache is backed by batteries sufficient to destage all track modifications. It has an independent nonvolatile storage (NVS) that can be configured from 4 to 32 megabytes in size.

One feature of the Andor caching algorithm is *high-priority segment caching.* Specific cached segments are identified for preferential treatment if the cache routines need to cast out segments to make room for other, most recently used, segments.

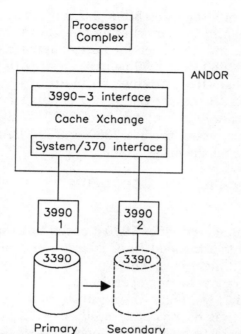

Primary   Secondary

Figure B.2 CacheXchange Dual Copy. The CacheXchange can assign dual copy or shadow disk (RAID-1) to any two DASD actuators attached to it. In this example the 3390 on the left is the primary volume and the 3390 on the right is the secondary volume. These are two completely different storage control units. This cannot be done with standard 3990-3 control units. The primary and secondary must be on the same control unit. Note the figure does not even show model 3 control units! They could be 3880-3 or 3990 models 1 or 2!

B.2.3. Andor Dual Copy

The DASD industry uses several terms for the process of making one DASD volume be an identical duplicate of another DASD volume. IBM uses the term *dual copy* when the two are attached to the 3990 model 3. *RAID-1* is a term used with arrays of small disks. Andor uses the term *disk drive shadowing*. As explained above, the reason for this is to protect the data being stored at the cost of dedicating two actuators to the data storage process.

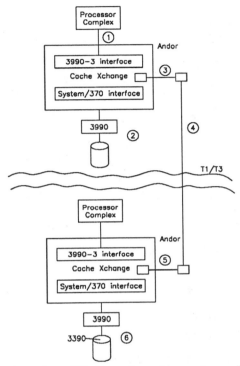

Figure B.3 Remote Dual Copy. This figure shows the remote possibilities of I/O operations in general and dual copy in particular. The Processor Complex at the top could be in one city and the dual copy volume could be in another city.

Figure B.2 shows a simple Andor installation. The actuator on the left is connected to 3990 control unit 1 and is the primary volume. The data is duplicated on the actuator on the right connected to 3990 control unit 2. The IBM 3990 only supports dual copy volumes that are on the same 3990 control unit.

B.2.4. Andor Disaster Recovery

Now we get to the reason CacheXchange was originally conceived. As data centers become more consolidated, more eggs are placed into a single basket. The larger the basket, the more golden eggs, and the more you and your company will spend on protecting the basket.

In Figure B.3, you see a picture similar to Figure B.2 except now a CacheXchange device, its Processor Complexes (that sounds wierd: a small box controlling 100–1000 MIPS data paths), and the DASD attached locally are at the top of the figure. At the bottom, maybe miles or hundreds of miles away, is another CacheXchange with more Processor Complexes (do you really need them?) and more real DASD.

The dual copy volume is miles away. This sounds like ESCON, only further away. The data flow is as follows:

1. Processor Complex at *1* issues a write CCW.

2. One copy of the data is copied to the local DASD at *2*.

3. The Andor moves the changed data to a communications device at *3*.

4. The data travels across a T1 or T3 communications line at *4*.

5. When it arrives at the remote site, at *5* another CacheXchange copies the changed data to the shadow volume.

6. The volume at *6* is now a complete shadow copy of the volume at *2*.

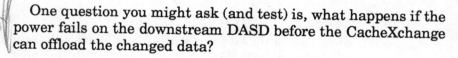

One question you might ask (and test) is, what happens if the power fails on the downstream DASD before the CacheXchange can offload the changed data?

B.2.5. Data Center Consolidation and Movement

Most of us have either moved a data center or consolidated one data center into another. With our first data center, we placed the 2314 disk packs in the back of a pickup truck and moved them to the new location ourselves. Those were the good old days!

The move required hundreds of hours of planning and a full weekend of outage to accomplish. How would you like your next move to take 30 minutes? (We have to be reasonable here.)

Back in Figure B.3, the top data center could be the old one and the bottom data center could be the new one. By duplicating DASD at the new location, you could make them all dual copy volumes until you felt comfortable with the new environment. Your test plan could include making all data available on the new system, breaking the systems apart, and running truly parallel. When everything is tested, re-create the dual copy environment until all volumes are in synchronization. Then transfer your work load to the new environment.

Of course it is not that simple, but you should see the exciting possibilities for your next data center move.

The challenge for all of us in the 1990s is to be able to manage this technology. That task will require monitoring companies to develop a new way of thinking about DASD I/Os. Timing the duration of an I/O operation from the time the Processor Complex initiates the process until the "control unit" says the operation is complete will not suffice.

B.3. Iceberg

Storage Technology Corporation (StorageTek) also has taken a different road to providing online storage. The name Iceberg sounds like this device is the tip of something very large. We are told, however, that it is named for the unheated building where it originated.

The Iceberg 9200 Disk Array Subsystem supports from 100 gigabytes of data storage with 64 megabytes of cache to 400 gigabytes of data storage with 512 megabytes of cache. Iceberg is a RAID subsystem with cache. Each data block is spread over all the disks in the subsystem.

Iceberg is targeted to store very important data. In previous environments, you could dual-copy volumes to store vital data. That approach doubles the cost to store your data. A large con-

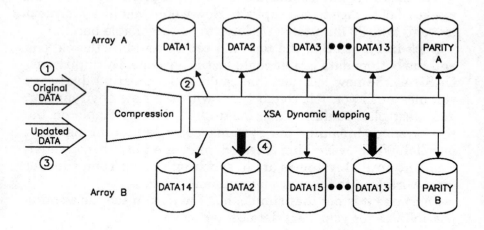

Figure B.4 Iceberg Extended Storage Architecture (XSA). This figure shows the XSA processing. Original data coming in at the left goes through compression algorithms and is mapped to several disks. Updated data goes to other disks. In all cases, a failure of one component is overcome automatically.

sideration is that data for a particular application is spread over many DASD actuators, so the only practical approach would be to dual-copy all volumes. Go ask your Vice President to double your DASD requirements to ensure data integrity. Check out your life insurance first and don't call us!

B.3.1. XSA Dynamic Mapping

Iceberg emulates the IBM 3990 control unit interface to the host with 3380 or 3390 DASD devices attached. Figure B.4 shows what happens when the operating system thinks it is writing to

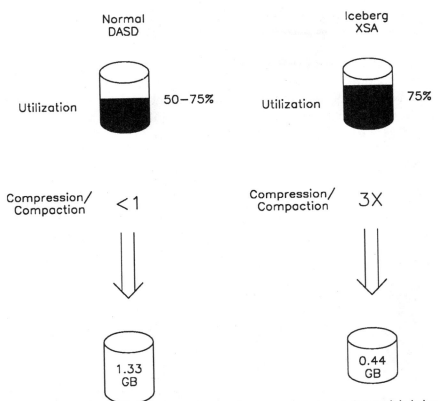

Figure B.5 Iceberg Compression. Iceberg performs compression on data as it is being imported into the subsystem and decompression when data blocks are passed to the Processor Complex on read commands.

a 3380 or 3390 actuator. The data written and read are in 3380 or 3390 track formats. The track is emulated by the XSA software. Future DASD geometries can be supported with microcode updates.

As the data comes into the device it is compressed. As it is returned to the Processor Complex on a read operation, it is decompressed.

B.3.2. Iceberg DASD Compression

Figure B.5 shows the results of the Iceberg compression. At the top a normal DASD is considered full when it is from 50% to 75% full because of the operating system's allocation routines. If a data center tries to completely fill a DASD volume, allocation failures will cause major problems. There are software routines that compress data as it is written to normal DASD for sale by OEM software vendors. They do claim up to 3:1 software compression.

Iceberg uses similar compression techniques as data is written to its hardware. The compression/decompression is done in the control unit and does not consume Processor Complex resources for the data compression.

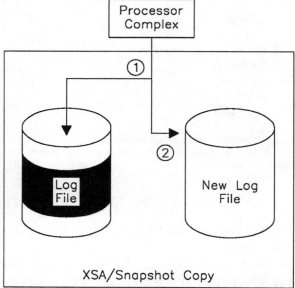

Figure B.6 Snapshot Copy. One announced feature of XSA is the ability to quickly make backups of data. In this example a log file is full and needs to be backed up. XSA can change its pointers in a matter of seconds to provide a new, empty log file with the old data in another data set. The data is not moved as with normal techniques.

Part of the space savings of Iceberg comes from the lack of gaps required on real DASD tracks. Virtually all wasted space is eliminated in Iceberg.

B.3.3. XSA/Snapshot Copy

Figure B.6 shows an announced feature of Iceberg called Snapshot Copy. Snapshot is designed to overcome a typical problem for online subsystems. If the subsystem is collecting log or transaction data, there comes a time when the data must be closed, a backup taken, and the online subsystem allowed to continue to

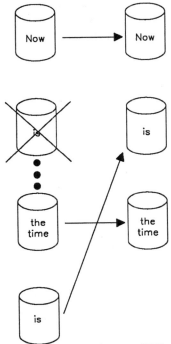

Figure B.7 Recovery Techniques. Iceberg implements RAID error-recovery techniques by not having a single point of failure. If one or two disks are damaged, the data is reconstructed automatically.

record data. Usually this is accomplished in the middle of the night or duplicate logs are used to switch from one to the other.

Since Iceberg maintains pointers to the data, it can "copy" the data by changing pointers. In a matter of seconds, the data blocks can be associated with a new name. Instant backup!

B.3.4. Recovery from Failure

Figure B.7 shows the recovery supplied by Iceberg in RAID terms. Each point of failure has a backup, including the cooling systems, power supplies, batteries, cables, cards, data paths, even the operator panel. If a disk fails, data can be reconstructed from redundant data on other disks.

The figure shows a record that contains *Now is the time*. The RAID disk that contains *is* fails. Data is reconstructed from duplicate data without the end user doing anything.

Index

X

NUMERICS